LINGERIE

LINGERING LESSONS

Sarah Veitch

This book is a work of fiction.
In real life, make sure you practise safe sex.

First published in 1995 by
Nexus
332 Ladbroke Grove
London W10 5AH

Copyright © Sarah Veitch 1995

Typeset by TW Typesetting, Plymouth, Devon
Printed and bound in Great Britain by
Cox & Wyman Ltd, Reading, Berks

ISBN 0 352 32990 4

LINGERING LESSONS

One

Made it! Leanne turned the corner of the Scottish country road and saw the stretching gilt-edged gates standing beckoningly open. Gilt-edged gates leading to a boarding-school she now jointly owned. LINGERING LESSONS, promised the sign – and she intended to linger. She had promised to live and work here with a man she'd never even met.

Not that that was going to be any hardship, Leanne mused, as she edged her scarlet Morgan into the wide paved yard and parked in the former headmistress's car space. One look at the grounds told her they'd inherited more than enough Scottish estate for two.

New location, new home, new friends, new workspace, new prospects. Only the small modelling agency she'd run for the past ten years would be the same. Mainly Men supplied male models for business magazines and clothing catalogues; it was work that she could do from this about-to-be-explored turreted abode.

Pausing to slide a smoothing palm down her chambray skirt suit, Leanne walked towards the polished oak double doors – her doors! One swung back on well-oiled hinges as her fingers pressed it, and she slipped inside. Would Adam Howard, her co-owner, be here to greet her? So far she'd just heard his voice on the answering machine.

A rewarding voice, though. Quite low, assured, compelling. She hesitated in the foyer, looking down the hall into the velvet-curtained large reception area ahead. Several yards in front of her she could see a long mahogany writing desk, a smoked glass table, four tan settees, and a wooden

1

four-legged trestle to the centre side of reception. Set on a platform, the large stool had a well-upholstered padded top that sloped down at too awkward an angle to support a human backside. Her eyes traced the thick wooden legs: it must be of antique or sentimental value. Why else would it be displayed on this steps-led dais?

As she stared, a dark-haired man in a dove-grey light-weight suit strode into the arena – it must be Adam! Leanne was about to step forward and introduce herself when she saw the girl that was following; a girl who looked about twenty to his own thirty-six. The blonde female's head was dipped low, her steps were small, her mouth turned downwards. She was dressed in a black and gold miniskirt and a vest-style golden top.

'I pay you to act as hostess to my clients – not to run off to the village and party,' said the man, as she stumbled towards the lectern.

'But Mr Howard . . .'

'The only butt I'm interested in is the one that's under your skirt!'

'I didn't mean . . .' muttered the girl, turning to put her hands on his shirted chest and looking up at him, eyes widening.

'Didn't mean to get caught? I'm sure you didn't! However, you've been found out and now you have to pay.'

He paused. 'You know what happens to girls who misbehave?'

The miscreant shivered. 'I do, sir.'

'Remind me what happens to them, Tania.'

'They . . . get spanked.'

'And how many spanks do they get for sneaking off to the village?'

'As . . .' The girl swallowed audibly. 'As many as their employer desires.'

'Exactly. Over the trestle you go!'

Leanne slunk further back into the shadows as the younger girl climbed the steps and obediently laid her belly over the punishment vehicle. Her hips were now supported so that her skirted bottom stuck out. As Leanne stared,

Adam Howard took four silken braids of rope from a wall-based hook, and carefully bound his victim's wrists and ankles.

'Just to stop you wriggling, Tania. You know that if you move about too much after you've been ordered not to, I end up having to punish you even more.'

'Yes, sir. I'll be good, sir.' Still the girl's buttocks tensed slightly as the man edged her skirt out of the way, revealing a tiny lemon crotch-thong.

'Oh sweetheart, you know you don't get to keep that on!'

'No, sir. If you untied my hands, sir, I could remove it.'

'Don't be naïve, girl. I'm more than capable of pulling down your pants.'

He looked capable of anything – of everything! Leanne licked increasingly numb dry lips as Adam bared the girl's helpless posterior, leaving the lemon scrap of cotton bunched above her immobilised feet. She should back away or show herself – not skulk around like this in the shadows. Yet part of her wanted to see the girl being . . . wanted to see what happened next.

'Such a wilful bum.' The man stroked the smooth white upturned globes. Tania wriggled, 'So disobedient.'

'I promise, sir – I'll change!'

'You said that before you went riding on my favourite steed, before you set the kitchens alight. You're always breaking promises. Always having to feel the full force of my palm on your disobedient backside.'

'Please . . . not too hard,' the girl implored.

'Yes – very hard.' He brought his hand down over one rear end cheek with moderate force. The waiting orb flinched, then relaxed again. Adam treated the twin pale globe to a similar warming, making pale-pink finger-marks appear. Leanne peered more closely at the barely marked pale skin. Maybe he was all bark and little bite. He had his head lowered, concentrating totally on the girl's posterior, so Leanne couldn't tell if his features were serene or enraged.

'Thirty light ones just to get your backside primed, then

3

I'll wallop you in earnest,' said Adam Howard. The blonde girl's head seemed to dip a little lower towards the floor.

'Whatever you say, Mr Howard.'

'Whatever you say, *sir*, if you please!'

'Yes, sir. Sorry, sir!'

'Any more errors like that and I'll have to take off my belt.'

Leanne stared at the broad grey band, and imagined it coming down on a tied waiting bottom. Judging by the way Tania had started to writhe again, her buttocks were very familiar with that particular leather strap. 'I could please you with my mouth, sir,' she begged.

'Just please me by taking your thrashing quietly.'

'I could . . .'

'Quiet *now*.'

Tania fell silent. The reception area stilled. Leanne realised that she herself was scarcely breathing. Then the large velvet-clad area was filled with the slap of hard hand on soft flesh. 'Aaah!' Tania cried.

'When you anger me, I turn warm-up spanks to medium spanks.'

The wallops which followed underlined his warning.

'Aah! Aah! Aah! Aah! Aah!'

With each slap, Tania squealed and lifted her head slightly, then let it flop down again. Her thighs tensed and untensed. Her buttocks quivered and jerked. Trembling slightly herself, Leanne watched the soft young spheres being changed from unblemished white to pastel pink to a flinching florid. How must it feel to be tied like this, robbed of your dignity; waiting for the palm or the belt to lash down?

'How many have I had, sir?' the girl gasped.

'I think it's been twenty.'

'I see, sir. Thank you, sir.'

'Only ten of the warm-ups to go.' His voice dropped a note or two. 'And what happens then, my sweetest Tania?'

Leanne saw the girl inhale sharply.

'I get a . . . get a full-force spanking on my already sore bad bum.'

4

'Good girl – you're learning. At least I'm making sure your *buttocks* are learning.'

'They'll be so obedient after this, sir.'

'They'd better be!' A gloating pause. 'Now, where were we? These warm-up spanks.' He flexed his fingers, drew his arm back, then brought his large palm into contact with the girl's helpless flesh.

'Ah! Ah! Ah!' Fuchsia-hot skin was giving way to vermilion now – Leanne could almost see it glowing. She leaned back weakly against the wall behind her as the correction went on. Why on earth wasn't this female standing up for herself, giving the bastard a run for his money? Why hadn't she told him to go screw himself when he first started telling her what to do?

Instead, Tania continued to writhe and moan as her tormentor heated her prostrate posterior. The spanks to prepare the hapless flesh gave way to harder ones that were solely designed to punish – to chastise hard and long.

Palm-prints upon palm-prints upon palm-prints. Leanne could see where Adam Howard's fingers had strayed over the backs of the girl's thighs. Saw tingling reminders of thumbstrokes leading up to a derrière that was a writhing red.

'Please . . .' Tania whimpered, as Adam caressed her buttocks and told her about the ten hard spanks that were coming to her next.

'Please what?'

'Please – mercy.'

'Are you suggesting that your employer isn't merciful?'

'No, sir, no!'

'I'm glad to hear it.' He dished out four rear-end slaps. 'I like my staff to be respectful. As you haven't been, we'll have to play the politeness game.'

'Oh God, not . . .'

'Tania – will you never learn? Now you'll have to be disciplined for protesting!' Tania swallowed and closed her jaw. Leanne also swallowed, then opened her mouth to wet her lips again. She wondered what else Tania would do that was wrong.

Adam again approached the wall ahead, and this time took something from a little door. Leanne could see it was a dildo. He flicked at the base and it began to vibrate. Tania groaned. 'Ah, dearest, I see you remember this from previous sessions.' The girl kept her head well down and her eyes closed. 'Oh well, this usually brings your voice back.' The man eased the seven-inch phallus between the female's glistening sex leaves and effortlessly slid it inside.

Jesus, she was wet! Leanne gasped as she saw how lubricated Tania was – how excited. Her own legs felt shaky, and her crotch heavy with heat. But she'd just undertaken a long drive, just inherited a former boarding-school along with a man who appeared to think he was the lord of the manor. No wonder her body wasn't working right!

'Now, we pull Vincent the Vibro out a little bit, cos Tania hasn't been good enough to deserve all of Vincent,' Adam murmured, eyes mocking.

'Please ...' Tania whimpered, trying to push back against the penile promise her employer held.

'Please what?'

'Must have ...' The toy was now halfway out of her erotically charged entrance. Leanne could see her tightly closed eyes, her silent and begging mouth, the stretch of her thighs as she tried to bear down upon the implement as Adam held it firmly in place.

'Beg for another inch,' he said.

'I beg ...'

'You can do better than that.'

'... Beg for even another eighth of an inch, sir, to fill my greedy aching hole.'

'I suppose I can give you a teeny bit more ...'

Adam fed in the vibrator a little more, and Tania became more frantic. 'Right up me. Please! I'll do whatever you want.'

'What will you do?'

'I'll ...' The vibrating pleasure was obviously making it hard for Tania to come up with suggestions. '... Make you come so good! Wear the studded collar while I'm tied like this. Have my neck fastened to the stool while I take you deep in my mouth.'

'Say what you'd be sucking specifically, Tania.'

The tormented buttocks gave another heave as she moved against the dildo. 'Your . . . your cock.'

'Good girl.' Adam fed in the vibrator almost all the way.

'Stop wriggling now. I want you to stay still as you approach your climax.'

'Yes, sir . . .' Leanne could see Tania's curvy thighs going rigid: she was almost there.

'Hold it, hold it . . .' Adam pushed the phallus in entirely, then slid his finger over the girl's clitoris. Crying out against the trestle, Tania clenched her upper legs and came.

Jesus! Would she suck him now? Would he take her from behind, still stretched over the punishment stool? Leanne stayed, as if anchored in place as the younger woman's orgasm faded from groans to mewling whimpers. Muscles slackening, Tania lay motionless, apart from the rise and fall of her chest as she breathed fast and deep.

'You're learning,' Adam said. His voice was more teasing now. He looked into her face as he untied her wrists.

'Want me to . . .' the girl whispered, hair falling over her mouth and eyes. Leanne wished she could see her facial movements.

'No. I'm finished with you now. But thanks.'

'Any time!' With obvious difficulty she stood up. 'I'd better have a shower, a change.'

'See Gerard afterwards.'

The girl's lids dipped half over her eyes, and her mouth turned downwards. 'Can't I see *you* instead?'

'I've some documents to look over, phone calls to make. But Gerard'll be in the forest around two.'

Shoulders drooping, the girl went through one of the many doors leading off from the reception area. The man took a seat behind the large mahogany desk and picked up a mobile phone.

'Gerard, I'm through with her. Can you take care of things?' He listened for a moment, then nodded. 'Be discreet.' What was his expression like now? Leanne leaned forward slightly to concentrate on his features, and he stilled, staring in her direction.

7

'Hello! I didn't hear the car.'

'I . . .' She must have parked it half an hour ago. 'It just purrs along,' she muttered lamely, stepping fully into reception.

'Does it, indeed!'

She started to walk towards him, towards the windowed part of the room. 'I'm Leanne Dell.' She drew in her stomach muscles and tilted her head slightly, gathering the poise to focus on his features. After all, it wasn't every day you saw a man spanking a grown woman after tying her over a punishment chair!

'Adam Howard,' he said, when she at last reached him. He stood up and took her hand, sure fingers sliding between hers, closing, squeezing. 'There are garages behind the school for your car.'

'Thanks, but it's survived life in central London for the last eighteen months. I'm sure it can stand the great outdoors for a few more hours!'

'Whatever. I put my Saab away in case of vandals.' The conversation seemed mundane after the chastisement she'd just seen.

'I'll find you a map of the grounds to help you get organised,' her co-owner continued. She was as organised as could be expected, Leanne thought, biting back the rejoinder. She stared at his six-foot frame as he unlocked a drawer in the bureau, noting the heavy but well-trimmed dark hair, the steadfast brown eyes and resolute lips. 'It's in here somewhere, unless Candy's . . .' Leanne glanced down as he rifled through a series of glossy photos. God, that third snap showed a woman holding her cane-striped bottom and twisting her head round to look at the camera. Had the man no *shame*?

'I'll find my own way around,' she said and took a step back, then looked at ten identical teak-effect doors. Was nothing here signposted?

'Seven of them lead to dormitories that have been converted into staff quarters,' Adam said helpfully. 'I'll show you now.'

'How come you know your way around so quickly? We only inherited the building three weeks ago!'

'Ah, but I've been here six months, just ... *overseeing* things,' Adam said evenly.

Leanne blinked twice, the pattern of events she'd imagined quickly fading at this unexpected information. 'You have? And Mamie knew?'

'Mamie insisted I run the place and arrange the conversion.'

'I thought ... assumed Lingering Lessons had been standing empty. I wasn't told.'

'What *were* you told?' Adam said, then prompted, 'I know what solicitors are like – all bogus credentialism. They dress up everything in pseudo-legal speak till it's hard to understand.'

Was he being patronising or nice? Leanne settled on the facts. 'I was told that Mamie – my second cousin – had left a former boarding-school to myself and someone called Adam Howard. The will stipulated that we both live and work in the building for a year together.' She straightened her shoulders and pursed her lips, wondering what the little smile playing around his mouth signified. 'At the end of that time each person can sell their half to the other or to a third party, but not before.'

'If you leave before then you lose everything,' Adam confirmed, nodding. I'm not going to lose *anything*, Leanne thought!

'I'd assumed we'd both be moving in this week,' she admitted. 'Maybe having a cleaner in most mornings as the place is so spacious.'

'All taken care of! I took on a housekeeper three days ago. Eleanor's from the village, recently got divorced. The village bus takes an hour to get here, so the staff all live in as part of their wages. Her rooms are along corridor three.'

'I see.' Leanne played the strap of her shoulder-bag through both hands. People were already settled here. She was being made to feel like the guest, the outsider. She scowled up at Adam Howard, but he was looking over her shoulder as if the matter were already resolved.

Leanne cleared her throat. 'Shouldn't I have had a say in all this? I mean, my solicitor said that Mamie had only left us enough money to keep the place going for the next twelve months or so. After that we have to fund everything ourselves – which presumably includes this full-time house-keeper.'

'I haven't overpaid her, if that's what you're worrying about!' Adam looked slightly surprised, even vaguely amused.

'No, it's just . . .' What if she didn't like the woman? She'd lived alone in London since leaving Rob, her husband. It would be strange sharing with someone else of the same sex.

'Paul, the gardener, has been here since Lingering Lessons was a boarding-school,' Adam added. 'His door's off to the right, there. So is Gerard's – he runs the stables. Candy's in the fifth converted dorm.'

'Candy?' She wondered where Tania fitted in.

'My personal assistant.'

Ah, she might have known! This wasn't a man to make his own tea or type up his own letters. This wasn't a man who'd known rejection, hardship, loss.

'Personal assistant to what business?' she asked lightly, determined not to be intimidated by him.

'Copywriting – for now.'

'I see – "Get Going on a Grapefruit!" ' Leanne said smiling broadly.

'No, nothing like that.'

' "Bob About in Our Bathbubble Bliss. Heighten Your Hairizons!" ' The events of the past hour had made her feel almost weightless, with an uncertainty which now trembled into mirth.

'Tomorrow I'd be happy to show you what my work is about.' Adam's voice stayed low and even, but his gaze fixed itself on her face and his lips pursed into a straight line.

'Uh. Right.'

She paused. 'You haven't said where *you're* based.'

'I've taken the former headmaster's study and living quarters in the tower block near the gymnasium.'

Leanne nodded. 'I'll take the former *headmistress*'s quarters then.' If he wanted to play lord of the manor, she'd be the equally dogmatic lady. They were co-owners, damn it – yet he'd already arranged everything!

'I'll show you to your rooms.' As if he was Lingering Lessons' sole proprietor!

'Where does . . .?' She almost asked where Tania lived, yet she wasn't supposed to know of the girl's existence yet. Leanne corrected herself. 'Who else lives at Lingering Lessons?'

'No one else.'

She tried again. 'I suppose you have a girlfriend here.'

'Sadly, no. We're so far from London that I've left all my female friends behind. I'm temporarily single.'

Maybe it was true! Though he'd had Tania bend over and bare her bum, he hadn't actually slid into her or enjoyed her hands or mouth. He'd made it clear that he employed her as a hostess, but perhaps there was a limit to what she would do for her pay.

Leanne studied him thoughtfully till he quirked one eyebrow, and she pretended to look at the wall-hung paintings of other schools and their masters. Had he failed to bully Tania into going all the way? The manner in which he'd told Gerard to be discreet – when Adam said he'd finished with the girl – had sounded ominous. And now he was either keeping her hidden or she'd disappeared . . .

'Mamie told me that you're divorced.'

'Separated,' she corrected. 'We may get back together.' She was damned if she'd let him know that the decree absolute was due any day. Christ, five minutes from now he'd have her pants down and be tanning her arse for some imagined misdemeanour! Her lower belly flipped over at the thought and her heartbeat raced. This wasn't surprising, really, given that she'd been celibate for eighteen months. Oh, she'd kissed and stroked in parked cars after champagne dates, but she hadn't invited any of them back to her flat. She'd settled for parting her own thighs when she returned home and stimulating herself.

'This way,' Adam prompted, putting a proprietary hand on her shoulder. Leanne stiffened. Men were always

11

moving women about like they were chess-pieces. She must remember to grab *his* arm sometime and frogmarch *him* around the school. She'd worked hard and long to be professional and self-sufficient. She wouldn't be treated like some helpless toy by this overbearing sod.

A corridor. A main door. 'This is where the headmistress lived.' He took a bunch of keys from a pocket in his belt and slid one into the lock.

'I'll have that now,' Leanne said, holding out her hand.

'I'll give you a copy tonight at dinner.'

'I'm usually too busy to eat dinner.'

He was an assumptive pig. He started to say something else, but she closed her ears and opened her mouth and looked up at him coldly. 'It's hardly appropriate that you can let yourself into my rooms.'

Determined not to give him a chance to argue, she pushed the door forwards and hurried in. Adam followed swiftly. Ignoring him, Leanne walked through a lounge that gave way to a study, that led on to a bedroom. Opening a door, she discovered an *en-suite* bathroom and shower. This was ideal!

'Not bad,' she murmured, refusing to show Adam how pleased she was. If he was Mr Cool, she would be Mrs Frozen-Over.

'This was just one dormitory six months ago. The builders put up wall dividers and the fittings have all been plumbed in. I helped design the layout. Mamie approved.'

'You must have been kept busy.'

'I'm always busy.' Always busy thrashing nubile young girls?

Wandering to the bedroom window, Leanne gazed out at the towers and turrets, round windows and square windows. 'Where will I find you to collect all copies of my key, Mr Howard?'

'That's my suite over there.' Following his pointing finger, Leanne gazed up across a tiny strip of the yard into a cream-walled study. She could just make out the top of a chrome and ebony desk and chair.

By looking down, he'd be able to see right into her bedroom – see everything! I'll keep the curtains closed, thought Leanne warily. Then a bolder, more prick-teasing idea began to form.

'I'm going up to my rooms to collect a book,' Adam said.

'I'll come up later,' Leanne murmured, her eyes guileless. 'I have to change.'

So far he'd embarrassed her with his lord of the manor spanking display, with his know-it-all air about their joint new home. She'd show him! She'd make him so horny for female company that he'd take off for London on heat for several days. Maybe he'd meet someone there and decide to leave the former boarding-school as soon as his year ended. She wanted to enjoy Lingering Lessons without a punishing tyrant around!

Watching with peripheral vision until he entered his room, Leanne slipped off her light chambray jacket, and reached for the waist of her white scoop-necked top, planning to lift it over her creamy full-nippled curves. Then she stopped. Adam was into spanking female *bottoms* – he'd presumably be more excited by seeing her arse than her tits. And the way the top clung to her well-toned waist would add extra attention to her bare buttocks, emphasise their perfectly rounded shape.

'Beg for it, you bastard,' she muttered, turning her back to the window. Slowly she unbuttoned, then unzipped her skirt and edged it down over her posterior. She bent to pull off her shoes, giving him a first-class view of her buttocks encased in slate-grey crotchless tights. Her pantied bottom felt tautly provocative, must look unprotected. She'd read that being spanked over nylon hurt even more than being spanked onto bare flesh!

But Adam was used to bare flesh – got aroused by it. He must have been turned on by punishing the posterior of the girl who hadn't assuaged his lust. This strip show would make him reach for himself, and want to reach for other people – people in London. People who were anywhere other than here! Keeping her backside towards him, Leanne peeled her crotchless tights away, aware of her raised cheeks as tempting target. Holding her breath, she peered quickly back through her legs – and saw that he was watching; watching and hopefully pleading for release.

She straightened to clear the silky coating from her calves, then bent again as if pushing the garments further away from her. Reached back both hands and edged down the high-legged full-sized panties, unveiling one inch of her backside at a time. She wanted him to imagine that he was the one pulling her knickers down, baring the flesh for punishment. Wanted him to picture drawing his hand back and making the taut pale globes writhe and smart.

First the topmost portion, then the full centre swell, then the curve in towards her thighs, lean and firm through weekends spent riding. Want to ride me, she taunted with her body. Want to come? For eighteen months she'd lived the life of a nun – well, almost. Within eighteen *minutes* he'd turned her into a teasing temptress who hated his grandiose guts!

At last she turned towards the window, pleased yet guilty to see his still white face, his upper-shirted shoulders. Good – she'd made him remove his jacket, coaxed him to sweat a little. Talking of which, it was time to have a shower herself.

Twenty minutes later, washed and body-lotioned and wearing maroon cotton drawstring trousers topped by a cream peasant blouse with pansies embroidered around the neckline, Leanne strolled along the corridor towards reception. She'd find the door that took her to the stairwell, climb up to Adam's room and get her keys.

Walking past prints of schoolgirls in navy shorts, she breathed in, out, in, trying to consciously slow her heartbeat. She must give no sign that she'd known he was watching her. She must show by her word, her tone of voice, by her body language that she could be – should be – jointly in control.

Four steps to his door, three ... She stopped as she heard two voices. Adam's low tone plus a female's higher pitch – both coming from his berth. 'Who makes the decisions around here?' Adam asked. Immediately the girl answered, '*You* do, Mr Howard.' Her voice was so soft that Leanne was forced to put her ear closer to the door.

Then she froze with shock and guilty surprise – someone

14

had jammed a thick document into the letter-box cut low in the door, allowing her to see into the room quite clearly. See Adam Howard seated behind his desk and a girl standing before him: a girl in a lemon cotton dress with little sprigs of speedwell printed over both skirt and bodice. She was bare-legged, but wearing taupe sandals with half-inch heels. She looked like a relic from the fifties, though her features told of some twenty-six summers, as did her caressable mass of shoulder-length brown curled hair.

'So why did you suggest that the artist should send his work here?' Adam asked. The girl held out her arms in a helpless half-shrug.

'I've known him for years. He's good, so . . .'

'Are you suggesting I'm not?'

She toed the ground. 'No, sir. I'm sorry, sir.'

'Candy, I'm going to *make* you sorry.' Adam looked her up and down, and shook his head sadly. 'Going to make you very sorry indeed.'

The girl clasped her hands behind her back, and shifted her weight from one sandal to another. 'Artists use brushes, don't they, my darling?'

'Yes, Mr Howard.'

'But a slim camel-haired brush wouldn't cause that naughty backside sufficient torment, would it, dear?'

The girl shook her head. Leanne wished she didn't have a back view, wished she could see her features. Was she angry, unsure, afraid, ashamed, annoyed?

'However, a *hairbrush* stings and glows, and that's the effect we're looking for,' Adam continued. He smiled and leaned slightly across the desk. 'Go into my bedroom and bring me the one on the dresser. The one with the smooth marbled back.'

She should knock! She should leave! And yet . . . Realising that basic human curiosity was going to make her see things through to their shameful conclusion, Leanne settled down on her knees to watch the chastisement. After all, she had to really *know* this co-owner who was fast becoming her enemy; had to learn to second-guess what he'd do next.

15

She knew now that this Candy was for it, wondered what her bared bottom would be subjected to. Had it felt the sting of the hairbrush before? Adam might use the vibrator again, the way he'd used it on Tania, until . . .

Leanne swallowed hard. Rob had used a vibrator to pleasure her breasts throughout their marriage. In turn, she'd played it round his testes, down his inner thighs. But he'd taken the sex toy with him when they split up and she'd been too busy building up her business to seek out another tremor-led thrill.

'Good girl.' Adam reached for the implement, and Leanne concentrated again on the scene before her, noting that Candy had returned with the hairbrush. 'Now bend over my desk,' Adam added. 'You can keep your dress and pants on till your arse is prepared for more.'

Did that mean for the first ten minutes or for the next ten days or so? Leanne realised with surprise and guilt that she wanted to see the girl's naked bottom. Yet she'd only ever been attracted to *males* in the sexual sense. She liked looking at other women, of course, liked talking to them. But watching them strip and take a birching on the bum was something new.

'Let's get that arse stuck out further,' said Adam crudely. '*Much* further.' By shuffling her feet outwards, the girl complied. Adam stood up and walked round the desk towards her backside, his steps measured. He stared at her rear end for a moment, then slid his right hand under her dress. 'Oh Candy, dear me – damp already. Did I give permission? You'll have to take extra strokes for these wicked libidinous thoughts.'

'Yes Mr Howard. Thank you, Mr Howard.'

Fuck you Mr Howard, Leanne thought, glaring. She half-wished it was *his* arse over the desk about to feel the hairbrush coming down. She'd lay it on hard and fast. She'd be merciless. She'd . . . she wanted to see this Candy taking it across her full expanse.

'This first walloping's for encouraging the artist without my permission. Then I'll pull up your dress and thrash you for not having sufficient faith in my design work,' Adam said.

'Yes, sir. Thank you, sir.' His employee gripped the far side of the desk with both hands and kept her skirted bottom pushed out as he decreed.

Turning to one side, Adam teased the smooth back of the hairbrush across the small buttocks under the cotton. Leanne could see that he was smiling grimly, pupils wide with lust. She pulled back lest he look in the direction of the letter-box, but his concentration was fixed on the girl's waiting hindquarters rather than on the door.

'Thank me after each stroke,' he ordered softly.

'Yes, Mr Howard.' He brought the implement whacking down, 'Ow!' Candy's body unbent, half-straightened, then she flattened it over the desk again.

'We'll have no noises other than your grateful thanks.' The girl inhaled sharply as the brush came down once more, then gasped her gratitude. 'Let's see how you're warming up,' Adam said.

He stepped back and surveyed her skirted rear. 'Edge up your dress slowly, as if you were a stripper.' Her hesitant fingers reached back and pulled the material up over her pants. They were plain and girlish – somehow Leanne had known they'd be white cotton. She fancied she could see a faint blush of heated flesh through the close-fitting briefs.

Adam moved closer again and stroked the firm pantied bottom. It wriggled at his fondling. 'Still,' he said sharply. 'Stay, still, stay.' Candy was obviously doing her best to remain immobile, but was just as obviously failing to keep her taunted bum in place. Leanne could sympathise – the caresses looked fiendishly effective, arousing yet mockingly detached.

Adam Howard's voice tone hadn't changed. Nor had his facial colour, his body language, his breathing. Leanne fancied his pupils looked dilated, but it was impossible to tell if his manhood was also distended inside the fashionably loose summer suit.

'Let's have these pants down, girl.'

Leanne winced as Candy obeyed immediately. Did she do so to avoid further punishment? If she jumped up would he restrain her, or would she meet Tania's as-yet-undiscovered fate? Leanne gave herself an internal shake. She must get a hold of her imagination. It had always been hyperactive, though Mamie had teased that it rarely turned towards daydreams that were *fun*.

Mamie! Leanne's eyes were trained on the keyhole, but her mind half-turned to thoughts of her second cousin. Could the older woman have known the copywriter was such a megalomaniac, that he'd try to rule the school in this hard-handed way? According to the solicitor, he'd done exemplary work on Mamie's Seal Sanctuary campaign, on her chain of Vegan Victuals cafeterias. Now he was doing exemplary disciplining of his second female bottom this afternoon . . .

Candy had inched down her knickers now, to reveal a small round bottom that was uniformly pink from the ministrations of the hairbrush. She twisted her head round to look at Adam, and ran the tip of her tongue over her full lips.

'Keep facing the front!'

'Yes, Mr Howard. Sorry Mr Howard.'

'What happens when you disobey me?'

'I . . . my arse gets punished more.'

Leanne leaned back awkwardly on her heels. Her mound felt heavy, enlarged, the lower lips tingling. She'd put on fresh champagne-silk micro briefs before coming here, but the gusset felt distended, drenched despite her recent shower.

Far away, across the widest part of the yard, she heard a door slam and a woman's laughter. Where were Eleanor, Gerard, Paul and whoever else *he* had on the payroll here? Did they know of this, partake in this? Had any of *them* been humiliated and soundly thrashed at Adam's hands?

'It's quite a pink bum, isn't it?'

'Yes, Mr Howard. It stings, Mr Howard!'

'Do you know how much more it's going to sting, my wilful beauty?'

'Probably masses, sir!'

At the end of each sentence Candy came close to having a slight lisp. Was arousal making speech difficult, or was she just being fawningly girlish? Leanne wanted Adam to bring the brush down hard – then was ashamed of herself. God knows, she hated domestic violence, male violence. Wanted to lock away all those weak frightened men who beat their wives in order to convince themselves that they were macho. She also detested those bullies who hit children in the guise of parenting, and she hated the drunken morons who threw insults and punches outside pubs. But this was different – cruel but consensual. Candy had agreed to this. Candy had encouraged this. Candy deserved . . . .

'. . . A very red bum,' Adam said, as if reading her thoughts. Leanne swallowed hard. Did he know she was out here, all-seeing, half-breathing? Had he set this up – and Tania's spanking – for her benefit, hoping to intimidate her and drive her away? Leanne Dell is made of stronger stuff, she thought grimly. Mamie could have told you that – and more!

'I deserve a very red bum, sir.' Candy sighed. Leanne shook her head – the words would have had to be wrung out of her! She'd have put up a fight before going over the desk, she'd have told him what she thought of him, she'd have spat. She clenched her inner thighs together as Adam again drew back the brush, and watched Candy do the same.

An inanimate object against a live, wriggling object. Inflexibility against flexibility. Hard marble against tender skin. 'This is for art's sake,' Adam mocked. 'Oh sweetheart, if your bum was a palette, the colour would be scarlet! You can't believe how hot this is going to be.'

Candy obviously *could* believe. She tensed and untensed her hands upon the desk, and her buttocks moved from side to side as Adam caressed them with the hairbrush. Awful to be teased by the very appliance that was about to tan your bared backside!

'What if I were to phone and . . .?'

'Sweetheart, you know you're incapable of usefully using your own initiative.'

'I could write to the artist, tell him it was a mistake.'

Adam fondled her bum cheeks and snorted his laughter.

'You've already made the mistake and now you're paying for it. You're going to be too sore to sit down and write *anything* for the next couple of weeks!'

Was he going to punish her more than once, then; thrash her daily? What must it be like to have your rump warmed by a palm, a brush, a cane? Leanne licked her lips. Rob had always teased her in a slow build-up to sex – but just using a dildo or his hands or a feather. Sometimes when he'd stroked her backside she'd wanted ... But you couldn't actually ask to be spanked!

Anyway, with Rob it would have been different – part of varied marital sex, an egalitarian relationship. This bastard was taking advantage of his staff. Thank God she was his co-owner, his more-than-equal, rather than someone dependent on him for food and lodgings. Beat him, best him! Leanne silently urged the docile Candy to turn round and slap his face or bite his arm.

She stared at Candy's reddened rear. She wanted to touch it. Wanted to trace the threads of glistening excitement that were leaving the girl's spread labia. As she watched, the strings stretched their way towards the carpet. If she'd been in charge, she'd have made the hot little madam wriggle some more. 'Uh. Oh. Uh,' Candy was gasping. Her sex leaves were darkening. She seemed to be trying to push her Venusian mound against the desk.

'Hold it,' Adam warned. He set down the brush and palmed her scarlet globes. She writhed and trembled. 'It's been a long time for you, hasn't it, Candy? Do you think Jon would mind?'

'No! He wants me to! He said that you could ...'

'A simple "doesn't mind" will suffice, dear.' He stroked on, on, on. 'You're much too verbal. Less talking and more thinking, if you please.'

'Yes, Mr Howard. Whatever you say, Mr Howard.' The girl scissored her thighs apart hopefully and pushed back further. Leanne could see the dark crevice that ran from buttock crease to private petals, the latter spread open like a butterfly's wings. Adam touched the tender leaves lightly. They were deep pink and distended. Candy groaned.

'I suppose I may as well service you while I'm here.' Leanne craned her neck forward at the sound of a zip going down, wondering about the size and shape of Adam Howard's erection. He was now standing immediately behind Candy, blocking out her view of the girl's impatient sex and frantic bum. What would his own arse be like? He looked as if he worked out – but not obsessively – and sounded like he was sure he could please a woman's erotic entrance and equally discerning gaze.

A dull ache settled in the centre of her chest as he pushed forward, and she realised he was keeping his trousers on. She couldn't see anything. But Candy could obviously feel everything – and how! 'Oh, oh, oh . . .' She sounded like one of those squeaky dolls Leanne had owned when she was little. 'Oh, oh, oh . . .' Leanne wanted Adam to punish the silly girl all over again.

She'd . . . Her heart shrank to the size of a walnut – someone was coming! A woman's heels were tap-tapping their way along the corridor, getting louder all the time. In a few moments, they'd come through the swing doors and into the section of the passage where she, Leanne, crouched. Adam would hear!

Scrambling backwards on her knees, Leanne got to her feet, glad that she'd worn the pumps with the slipper soles which made for silent strolling. She stepped surely and swiftly along the passageway, down the stairs and through reception, then found her room. And realised with an inner plunging dread that she didn't have the key to unlock it, and would have to . . .

Stiff-legged, she ran down the stairs, looked through the doors leading off from the main block till she found a communal powder room. Clicking the lock into place, Leanne sank into a six-foot chintz-covered *chaise longue* with matching pillows exuding lavender scent. With strangely numbed fingers, she pulled down her drawstring trousers, her pants, kicked them to the thick beige carpet. Now, now, now! she pleaded inwardly.

Holding her breath, she slid her middle digit down to her clit and teased it round and round, the familiar beloved ritual. She closed her eyes and saw Candy's crimson bottom awaiting the next searing stroke. 'Control,' Adam's voice seemed to whisper, as she pushed two fingers up herself and her pudenda pulsed its pleasure. And, as she came strongly, she silently damned the man to hell.

Two

Damn the woman! At last he'd thought he'd got everything exactly right, then she'd had to go and tease him. Had to strip and expose that rounded peach-like bottom and make him want ... Make him crave what she obviously wasn't going to deliver, but secretly *yearned* to deliver. Or had he been mistaken all those years?

Muscles hard with disappointment, with rage and with the injustice of it all, Adam pushed strongly into Candy. His shaft lengthened at her breathless 'Oh, oh, oh'. She pushed her hirsute promise back and he grimaced with pleasure as more of his manhood slicked into her. More and more.

Candy had flirted with him for years, long before her arrival here at Lingering Lessons. She had encouraged him in the wordless body-based way that the true submissive did. Mouth slightly open as if pleading for his cock and his balls, she gazed up at him. Her eyes were as wide as she wanted her thighs spread, mutely saying please.

'Please,' Candy murmured now. Adam heard footsteps clip-clopping along the corridor. It had to be the housekeeper airing the passageways. 'Maybe I should invite Eleanor in to watch you take a good hard fucking,' he said. Candy sighed. So far she'd shrunk away from the older woman's quiet inner authority. But she'd never disagree with him or put up a fight.

'Close your legs tighter, for God's sake, girl,' Adam said, thrusting lazily into his PA. 'You could take ten men in there, you're so slack and lengthy.' It was a lie, but they both got off on it.

'Yes, sir, too wide . . . must try harder. Must learn to keep my pussy muscles pulled right in.'

She shuddered with desire, and he pulled out a little. 'Ask nicely for my cock, angel.'

'Give me your cock, Mr Howard. I'd be ever so grateful.'

'*How* grateful?' He kept his shaft half out of her, denying the top of her cervix, knowing she'd arch her buttocks back towards him in order to access every inch. Not that he'd ever shafted her before – but he'd seen her watch corporal punishment videos. Had noticed the changing shades of shame and lust and surrender on her face.

'I'd take you in my arse,' Candy whispered, trying to manoeuvre herself so that his cock went deeper within her sex.

'What makes you think I *want* to ram it up your arse? I've had better offers.'

'I'd . . . lick it first, so that it was lubricated. I'd bend over your desk like this, help you guide it in.'

Adam moved his hips round and round, so that his hardness stirred her soaking sex, keeping her taunted. 'What else would you do to please me?'

'Whatever you want!'

'So if I wanted you to crawl across the room on your belly, you'd crawl for me?'

'Yes, Mr Howard!'

'You'd ask nicely for permission to suck my toes?'

'I'd beg to be allowed to do so. Yes!'

'You'd . . .' He was getting close to coming now, finding it harder to think. '. . . Strip in front of Eleanor? Drop your panties and have your backside tanned in front of Gerard and Paul?'

And Leanne, he thought savagely – he'd do his best to arrange it. It was time she saw one of the women being put through their paces by Gerard or himself. If only *she* was the one lying here, whimpering wetly and enveloping his thrusting member. Pleading for more.

'I'd lift my skirts for them. Show them my bum . . .' Candy was obviously cresting. Adam plunged his full length forward and she squealed with relief.

'What should I thrash you with as they laugh?'

'The martinet . . .' She'd admitted Jon had used one on her, the eight leather thongs licking at her full swell, her furrow, the susceptible crease where buttock curved into thigh.

'And how long should your whipping last?'

'As . . . as long as you want.'

'Perhaps an hour,' Adam mused, finding a hard fast rhythm inside her tight grip and staying there, feeling her close in on him. 'I'd wet your bottom with a sponge every ten minutes to make it burn more.' He plunged in, in, in. 'And if you moaned too much I'd take you to the shower room and tie you against the shower head. I'd whip you under the running water till your backside was begging for release.'

'Aah! Aah! Aaaah!' With a high-pitched yelp like a Pekinese, Candy let go, her quim closing in on his hot thick maleness. He could feel her sex squeezing him towards his own relief. He slid his hands forward and grasped her free hanging breasts. She wore no bra under the dress – he felt her nipples through the cotton bodice. They were erotically energised and erect.

'Like that, baby?' he muttered as she pulsed into a satiated bliss. Head slumped over the desk, Candy nodded. 'Cat got your tongue? Your boss expects proper answers, proper sentences. A little respect.'

'I loved the way you made me come, and it was more than I deserved, Mr Howard,' Candy whispered. 'Thank you, sir.'

'That's better! I think you can try quite hard when you get the right . . . *encouragement*.' Adam started to lunge firm and fast as his tension mounted. Thrust in and out, at the same time compressing her swinging tits. She was soaking down there – and was starting to bear down and wriggle. She had stayed clitorally avid and was ready to climax again.

'The martinet may not be enough to keep you on your toes.' He teased her mons some more, her sore bum hot against his belly. 'I mean, you're so assumptive, thinking this fuck is for your pleasure, when it's obviously for mine.'

'I think . . . I think I need the tawse, too.' Candy's voice was high with anticipation. 'I need to take it lots of times on my bad backside.'

'Which size of tawse?' Adam taunted.

'The two-tailed one.'

'I doubt if that would teach your little rump a strong enough lesson.'

'The three-tail tawse,' Candy whimpered, squirming against his manhood.

'You deserve the four.' His balls tightened as he pictured how it would be. 'I think the heavily waxed version for extra effect – very *concentrated*. Concentrates the mind wonderfully on the arse!'

'Uh, uh, aaaaaaaaah!' Candy cried her second release, groin muscles gripping and squeezing him.

'Mh!' Adam grunted, pushing forward, pleasure spinning from his testes to his tip. Everything felt centred on his cock, his balls, his lower belly. He closed his eyes and briefly rested his head on Candy's slender back.

'I loved that . . .' she murmured. He'd loved the sensation too – imagined it, craved it. But not with her, particularly. With . . . someone else. Still, she was a nice woman, a good woman – she didn't deserve to feel cheapened by their lovemaking. So he held her and stroked her hair for several moments after he eased himself out of her, till he felt her heartbeat wind back to a pleased and placid rhythm.

'The woman who owns Lingering Lessons with me arrived earlier today,' he said, pulling away at last and placing the used sheath carefully in the wastepaper basket. 'I have to see her now about her keys.'

'What should I . . .?'

He smiled. 'You can take time out for a shower and a rest – boss's orders! Then type up the Living Doll campaign.'

'Done!' said Candy. 'Your slogan will help them sell millions. Can I have that male doll after you've finished studying him?'

He was still smiling at the thought of Candy and a male

doll – the submissive waiting forever for spoken instruction – when he walked into reception to see Leanne sitting with her back to the punishment trestle, her neck and shoulders unnaturally stiff. Had she realised what it was for. She hadn't asked about its usage like the others did. He stopped and smiled. 'Finding your way round, Leanne? I was about to visit you in your rooms.'

'You shut the door when you left. I did the same, not realising it locked automatically. Now I'm locked out.' Her voice was flat again – as if he'd done it intentionally. He stood looking down at her moving breasts beneath the peasant blouse. God, he wanted to please every inch, wanted to make her gaze on him with fleshy hope rather than hostility. Wanted to see her groan her way to orgasm rather than glower.

He kept the smile ready but not ingratiating. 'I've been working hard on four projects. I have a lot on my mind, looming deadlines.'

'I'll bet.' Flat and dry. Though she didn't know it, he'd seen her unthawing once; she was no ice maiden. 'Keys, please.' She stood up, held out her small right palm.

He had an urge to pull her towards him by her wrists, holding her firmly by one elbow. He ached to draw back his arm and bring it forward, full force on her impudent bum. Six echoing spanks and she'd go to slap his face; he'd grab her hand and look into her eyes and tell her what he was going to do to her. See the arousal and denial and excited humility in those large grey eyes.

'Keys,' she repeated. Taking the master copy from his belt, he let it fall into her lap, watched her pocket it.

'You have a copy?' she added.

'Eleanor has one to clean your room each day.'

'I'm not helpless!' She seemed on the defensive again. He flexed his fingers. 'I'll clean it myself if you arrange for her to give me the copy back.'

'Very well.'

He stepped out of her way as she stood up to go. 'If you could clear that . . . *chairlike thing* from the dais.'

He let his smile last a long time, till she broke off contact and stared unfocusingly at the painting in reception. 'It's a punishment trestle for corporal punishment scenes.'

'Whatever.' He watched her quickly run the tip of her tongue over her lower lip. 'I want to put my business desk down here.'

Adam felt his senses slow with surprise. 'But *my* desk's here already.'

'Is that relevant?'

'I can greet clients as soon as they come in.'

'Exactly! I can welcome my own workers here.' She waved a slim ringless hand around. 'Obviously there won't be busloads of our colleagues arriving from the city, so there's more than enough space for two,' she said.

Adam leaned back against his desk. 'But I need privacy!'

'Then greet them in your rooms.'

'They aren't suitable.'

'Says who?'

He felt rage tightening his thighs, his upper arm muscles, his jawline. 'Look I'll show you. Come with me.'

Maybe she was just bored, or perhaps something in his tone told her he'd had enough, was irate at her assumptions. Whatever, she walked ahead of him towards his living quarters, walked up the stairs. He saw her firm buttocks momentarily sheathed by the drawstring trousers. Tensing and lifting, the perfect shape to be spanked.

Watch. Wait. He had to be sure. Had to *know*. Know completely. He unlocked his main door, took the mail from the letter-box and ushered her through.

Photos of twenty-year-olds dressed as schoolgirls. Most were pulling down blue shorts or lifting grey pinafore dresses as they bared their recalcitrant little bottoms. Was it too much too soon? He didn't usually invite the uninitiated into his sanctuary, but she hadn't given him much option with her confrontational ways. Was she surprised, alarmed, intrigued despite her better judgement? Adam tried to see the pictures through Leanne's darting and widening eyes.

The second set of frames showed the rattan being warningly wielded by an anonymous but obviously male hand, the shorts now lowered. The third series focused on the same bent bottoms with six pink stripes across their hemispheres. Here, a close-up showed a lower lip trembling in anticipation. There, a girl's fingers were spread out over the lines as she used both hands to cradle her punished bum. 'For Grown Up Games, Use a Jameson Cane' read the advertising line.

Adam smiled. 'One of my earlier ads. I was still new to the business.'

Her reply sounded light but mocking. 'Mm, it shows.' Did the growing urge of his groin also show as he pictured Leanne in a gymslip? He'd make her hand over her own plimsolls, would use one on that insolent little rump till it saw the error of its ways.

'As you can see, this study is too small and too out of the way to act as my reception,' he said, as she walked round the room, eyes moving to, and just as swiftly from, his posters. 'And as I occasionally work for clients who don't want sexual ads . . .'

Leanne shrugged, turning towards the door. 'So you share reception with me,' she announced. 'Is that such a hardship?'

She was being so unreasonable, so detached! He took a seat on the corner of his desk – she walked to the window – and he outlined the most recent of his ideas. 'Or we could knock a second doorway along the side, partition reception into two huge public rooms; perhaps even three.'

'Forget it!' To his surprise, she whirled round and glared at him. 'I don't want any architectural changes made to my late cousin's ideal.'

'This wasn't . . . It was the *concepts* behind the school Mamie cared about,' Adam said, watching the flush of rage rise to her cheeks and stay there. 'A school that concentrated on human relations instead of History. Not Geography or Geology, but how to enjoy the workday nine to five.'

'You think I don't know all this? I used to stay at Mamie's house! She'd come to me. Once we even went on holiday . . .' Adam stood up, and forced himself to look

29

away from the antique headmaster's cane that graced his desk. She'd read him all wrong again. Did she really think he'd patronise her? Why was she so swift to anger, to misdirected rage?

He met glare with stare. 'If I can continue. I wasn't trying to tell you which lessons Mamie wanted taught. I was going on to say that the traditionalists didn't like such a radical curriculum – that's why they took the children away.' He waved a hand round the room. 'All this thoughtfulness, this *potential* then lay idle. And now you're being just as mindlessly traditional about what *we* can do with the place!'

'Fuck you!' There was no talking to her now, no ... anything. Yet he had to engineer events to bring him nearer the completion of his plans. He took a deep breath, kept his voice even. 'Let's deal with this when we're both feeling calmer. Do you ride?'

'Horses, you mean?' She looked as though she sensed a trick.

'Uh huh.'

'Yes, I do.'

'You'll be spoilt for choice here, then! Gerard, our stableman, says he'll see you around four, and you can choose which mount you want.'

'The stables are round the back?' she enquired, pursing her lips, then reknotting the cord that held trousers round her waist.

'Mmm. Way over to the north. You can take your car if you like. The walk over the school playing-fields takes a good twenty minutes.'

'I've walked almost everywhere since childhood,' Leanne said. What was that supposed to mean? Was she suggesting he wasn't athletic? Long after she left his rooms, he found himself gripping the handle of the cane and picturing the changes it could make to her impudent rear end.

Be calm. Think. Act. He picked up the handset and made two phone calls. When he set down the receiver, he was smiling again. So she hated the punishment trestle, the photographs of these bent-over caned bottoms? Would she

30

also hate watching a bad girl being taught a lesson on her backside?

At twenty to four he stretched himself out on the recliner in the carpeted outlook room which passed as the third stable. From the outside it looked boarded up, unused. By peering through the specially created hole in the woodwork, he could espy everything in the straw-floored area in front of him. Everything – and everyone.

Gerard was *in situ*, rake in hand as he spread the clean sweet hay around the building. The area was sheltered by a high sloping roof and a rectangular opening in the front wall took the place of a door.

Groin tingling, Adam gazed through the net curtains that covered the side window. He could see Eleanor, his housekeeper, approaching the stables – but she couldn't see him. The wind tugged at her gently spiked blonde hair and the hem of her white overall as she tapped slowly forward. Her black patent shoes crunched over the pebbles, and mud from the field had splashed over her tan-nyloned calves.

Adam poured himself a cognac from the mini-bar and quickly closed the cabinet door again. From now on, he'd have to remain relatively soundless – hearing but unheard.

He knew that Gerard Kerne would have heard the housekeeper's arrival, but the man stubbornly kept his back to her till she quietly cleared her throat and began speaking.

'Mr Kerne – I'm afraid there's been a mix-up with the vegetables this week.' She looked and sounded hesitant, apprehensive.

The stable-master turned and stared. 'A mix-up? Please explain.' Gerard slid the riding whip through his hands, then back again, the long tip trailing. Eleanor stared at it, then looked away. Adam leaner closer to the spyhole in the door. She'd shown the right combination of seeing, then pretending not to. He'd chosen well.

'I . . . didn't realise I was supposed to set carrots and swedes aside for the horses.'

'Really? Mr Howard told me he'd drawn up a provisions list for you to keep things simple, clear.'

'He did, but . . . With having to prepare a suite of rooms for this Miss Dell, I forgot to keep up to date with the groceries side of things.'

Adam smiled. Suddenly the forty-two-year-old woman looked much younger than the forty-two-year-old man: much more guileless. Much more vulnerable to being talked down to.

'You *forgot*? So there hasn't been a mix-up. You've been negligent.'

'I suppose. But . . .' Eleanor ran the toe of one shoe over the back of her calves, and plaited her fingers together.

'Negligent, yet too sneaky to own up to your crimes.'

'I'd hardly call them crimes.' The hands moved out in a shrug. 'It was only some vegetables!'

'Sustenance for these hard-working horses.' Gerard pointed at the occupied stables further into the room.

He shook his head. 'Don't you *care* that they'll now go hungry?'

'Of course I care! I . . .'

'You know there are no fresh food deliveries till the end of the week.'

'Maybe I could . . .' Eleanor spread her arms out. '. . . If you told me what to do.'

'The situation is unsalvageable. They'll just have to make do with dried foods for the next three days.'

The housekeeper swallowed hard. 'I'll never do it again. I promise,' she appealed.

'You wouldn't do it again if you received a short sharp shock to your forgetful backside!'

Adam leaned forward to see his housekeeper's face. She flushed, licked her lips, looked up at the stable-master then down at the ground again.

'Bend over that bale of hay in the corner,' Gerard said evenly.

'What are you going to . . .?'

He gave her a telling flick of the whip.

There was a silence; a thinking-it-through, heavily charged type of silence. 'And if I don't do what you say?'

'I'll tell Mr Howard you didn't follow his instructions.' He looked her up and down, scrutinising her ironed and pressed white uniform. 'There are lots of women in the village who would love to play housekeeper here.'

'But I've never been whipped!'

'It's long overdue, then.' Putting a guiding hand on Eleanor's nearest upper arm, he gently pushed her towards a bale of hay in the corner. Adam peered forward and watched as the woman lowered herself down, the tension suddenly leaving her body. He looked sideways out of the window to see that Leanne was watching, too.

She'd arrived – but would she stay? From where she stood she had an unblocked view of Eleanor's back, and her backside once she bared it. And Gerard was smart enough to stand slightly to one side. Leanne could either see it all, hear it all, or she could step forward now and halt the older woman's flogging.

Adam held his breath. Then he exhaled softly as Leanne stayed her ground, watching what he was watching. 'A light cropping over that nice white housekeeper's tunic should liven your memory, my girl,' he said. It was strange to hear Eleanor spoken of as a girl – she was so efficient, so capable. Yet now, with her head and breasts out of sight at the opposite end of the hay bale, her back and bottom looked defencelessly young.

'Four strokes for negligence,' said Gerard. He pulled back the whip and brought it down over the white cotton of the woman's housecoat. With its neatly finished waist and white front buttons it looked like a dental nurse's uniform, Adam noted. But the only thing Eleanor would be nursing was her bum!

Her bottom jumped slightly as the first lash was laid on, then went limp again – her pants and uniform obviously protected it. Still she flinched a little at the next three strokes, as some of the sting obviously worked its way through.

'Have we drummed any sense into that forgetful backside?' Gerard demanded. Seconds after doling out the fourth lash, he stepped closer. Adam looked out of the side window to see that Leanne was peering forward, too. Was the man about to disrobe his hapless victim or make her undress for him all by herself?

'Let's get this pretty cover-up out of the way,' Gerard said, as he took hold of Eleanor's hem and edged it upwards.

'Please . . .' She made a half-hearted attempt to reach a hand backwards, but he swatted it away and she moved it to the front again.

'Don't be shy now, girl. You weren't so bashful when you came to see me, didn't even apologise. "Only some vegetables", you said. And me left to tell the new co-owner why she has to take a hungry stallion for a ride!'

'I didn't think . . .' muttered Eleanor's disembodied voice.

'Which is why we're teaching thoughtfulness to your arse with this riding crop. You'll be pleased to know I use this smaller switch when I'm punishing a naked backside.'

'You mean you've yet to . . .?' Eleanor pushed up from the bale and twisted back on her extended arms as he finished inching up her overall and pulling her pants down. She winced as he took the little riding crop from its overhead hook.

The larger one, with which he'd already primed her, now lay on the straw. She stared at its long thin tip then her eyes moved to the smaller stockier one he now wielded. 'Will it hurt more?' she asked whispering, pupils dark and wide and glassy.

'That's for me to know and you to find out.'

'I feel so . . .' Eleanor put her hands to her bare bum. 'If I could only wear my knickers.'

'Bad girls don't get to keep their knickers on.'

Eleanor stayed frozen in place. Gerard sighed. 'We'll have to do this a different way. Get back over that bale again. I won't whip you till you ask me to, not till you beg for it.'

'Promise?' Eleanor looked from the crop to his face, then back again.

'I swear it.' Gerard set the persuasive implement down.

The housekeeper lowered herself back over the straw. Adam could see the pink lines made by the whip on her otherwise pale chubby buttocks. Her pants and tights were bunched around her thigh tops, accentuating the swell of her naked rear. Leanne's view of that well-padded backside must be similar. But only Gerard could touch . . .

'No – not that way. Tits towards me.'

There was a heavy silence, then Eleanor pulled herself up, each movement languid.

'Now lie on your back over the bale. That's it! Spread your legs further apart.'

Eleanor obeyed, settling down on the hay and spreading her limbs out like a cross, then holding them there. The movement displayed her liquid opening inside slicked sexual leaves. 'If you want to escape further wallopings, keep your thighs this fanned out no matter what I do.' The housekeeper licked her lips, but said nothing.

Gerard knelt. And nuzzled to one side of her clit. Eleanor whimpered. Gerard paid homage to the other side, to the pink flesh above and below. Then he licked lightly at the tip. 'Uuh!' Eleanor groaned, and lifted her hips encouragingly towards the pleasure source. 'Punishment before pleasure,' Gerard said tantalisingly.

He licked on and on. Eleanor started to tense her ankles, her heels. Her face was hectic. 'Ask for the crop before the climax,' Gerard added, taking his lips away.

Eleanor opened her mouth, her eyes, half-raised her head. 'I have to . . .'

'Tell me you deserve to feel my switch across your arse; then I'll let you come, then I'll mete out the discipline.'

'But . . .' Eleanor looked at the feisty little crop and wriggled against the straw, her bottom against the hay bale.

'Lay your head back down.' She obeyed. 'Is your clit hot?' He asked, then licked it lightly. Eleanor whimpered. 'Is it hot?' he insisted. The admission seemed to be dragged from her. 'Y-e-s!' she groaned.

'You'll feel my whip for your tardiness.' He licked twice more at the delicate distended bud and it seemed to give a little twitch of its own volition. 'I'm bored with your procrastination now. I'm about to stop,' he announced.

'Christ, no!' The blonde woman scissored her legs further

apart, lifting her clit towards him. '*Please – lick it!*' she implored.

'Then ask nicely for a taste of the crop.'

'I . . .'

'Ask nicely for it on your bare arse. Plead a little. I'm getting ready to walk away.'

'Don't walk. Lick – I beg! I'll take the whipping.'

'You'll take it and be grateful?'

'Grateful. Yes, Mr Kerne, sir, yes! Take it on my uncovered striped backside. Take ten strokes, fifteen . . .'

'In fact, I think you'll be grovelling for more than that, won't you, girl?'

'Yes, sir!'

He ran his tongue around her needy nub. She raised her hips.

'Plead for a thrashing.'

'I beg for the whip, sir.'

'How hard?'

'As hard as . . . very hard indeed. So hard I can hardly bear it.'

'Oh, you'll take all I have to give.'

He licked again and again, keeping her primed, taking her nearer. 'How would you like to be positioned?' he asked, taking his tongue away and waiting for an answer.

Eleanor opened her eyes. 'Any way you . . .'

'Come on! You're not trying. My tongue's getting very tired. It needs some encouragement.'

'I . . . over the straw again?'

'I'm bored with that. Bored with you. Think I'll go and check on the horses.'

'Like a . . . on my hands and knees like a horse!' Eleanor said.

'That's better! You can be quite an inventive girl when you make the effort.' Gerard put his tongue to her tormented tip again. Eleanor moaned with relief – or renewed hunger or desire – as he tongued and nuzzled. 'Maybe I should ride around on your back,' Gerard said, between long slow licks. He raised his head. 'Use the switch at the same time to make you move faster?' he suggested.

'I need to . . .'

'I'm going to lick for as long as you sound humble. If you get ideas above your station, I'll stop for good.'

He teased his tongue over her tip. 'Need . . . need to be cropped as I crawl around,' Eleanor panted, the delicious tremors obviously worth endless debasement. Gerard trailed his tongue away as soon as her words came to a halt. 'Need my arse well warmed,' Eleanor added, and he put his lips back in place.

Teasing tongue moved on tremulous tip; lapping, circling. It had a rhythm she could rely on, if she found the right words. 'You could wear spurs . . .' Her labial leaves darkened as he licked. 'Urge me to trot round faster, harder, longer.'

'What would you have on?' Gerard murmured, momentarily taking his head away.

'I . . . Nothing.' Eleanor pushed her pudenda nearer his mouth. Her nipples were hard nubs through the cotton of her uniform. Her scissored thighs were tautening, lifting. His tongue teased away to show this obviously wasn't the right answer, for she tried again. 'I'd . . . wear a bit in my mouth. You'd hold the reins, pull my head back. I'd trot round the field like a horse being broken in and . . .' Mouth opening in an overwhelmed grimace, she let out a throaty, almost masculine cry and came and came and came.

'Hands and knees on the ground,' Gerard demanded, as the flush of her sex paled away. Adam leaned forward. He wouldn't really use the spurs, so what was he up to? Shakily Eleanor did as she was instructed, not even looking round. 'Good girl, but get that arse raised up a little – put your forearms down.'

The housekeeper let the front half of her body lean forward, and she pushed her bottom up. The earlier whip marks were now barely visible. 'As many of the crop as I saw fit, wasn't it?' Gerard murmured masterfully.

'Yes, Mr Kerne,' Eleanor sighed. Adam knew that arousal would have increased her ability to withstand pain, allowing her to take more of the crop before orgasm. Now that she'd come, her backside was vulnerably sensitive again.

Gerard was obviously aware of that, too. He knew how to put a bared female bottom through its paces. He raised the little whip and flicked it against the top of the woman's thighs and smiled as she twitched. 'Keep still, if you please, or I'll have to repeat myself. You get double each time you move away.'

Eleanor sighed, but stilled her buttocks into place. Gerard whacked at her rump again. Eleanor cried out and put both hands back over her fast-striping posterior. 'Ow!'

'What did I tell you? Take your hands away.'

Fingers still spread, she looked round tearfully. 'It's too painful!' she cried.

'Of course it's painful. This lesson has to last you a very long time.'

'But . . .' Her eyes were watchful and confused.

'Every time you go to use some food, I want you to ask yourself if some should be set aside for the horses. Every week when you make a grocery order, I want you to make sure you've catered for their needs.' He crouched down and stroked the lower curve of her bum where her fingers couldn't reach to protect herself. 'If I just *tickled* you with the crop you'd soon forget, you'd soon get complacent. This way you recall my message whenever you sit down.'

'You could finish punishing me tomorrow . . .'

'I like to punish on the same day as the crime.'

'You mean, you often take your whip to the staff here?'

'If you anger me again you'll undoubtedly find out!'

Eleanor kept her hands over her bottom cheeks, kept looking back at him, her lower lip trembling.

'Let's prove again that you do what your sex wants,' the stable-master said. He unzipped his loose brown cords and his phallus stuck out, almost up against his belly. He looked at the open entrance before him, then guided it in.

'Uuuuuuh!' the woman moaned gratefully, as he sank into her sex; then she began to gasp as he started moving. Judging by the rigour in her thighs and the flexing of her toes, Adam gathered she was almost ready to come for a second time. She'd blushed long and hard as Gerard talked her down and warmed her buttocks. She'd be shame-filled to know that both he and Leanne were watching her take what was her due.

'I'm going to fuck you till you ask for the switch,' Gerard said. 'Same game I've played already with my tongue. You should know the format.'

'Want you to keep ramming it up me!' Eleanor gasped.

'But I won't, will I, my sweet? I'll pull out, keep you on the edge for hours. I'll make you plead.'

'Beg for your cock,' Eleanor muttered as he partially withdrew.

'What will you offer for being allowed to come?'

He circled his hips, stirring her sanctum again.

'Offer . . . Couldn't you just spank me?'

'Spank you before whipping you?'

'No . . . I meant . . .'

'Mean you want a lesser punishment when you deserve much more?'

'Take a rain check?'

'The only rein check you're up for is the saddle and bridle kind!'

Eleanor shuddered with obvious disgrace and desire. Gerard kept his cock two inches inside her, holding her sides firmly so that she couldn't move backwards. 'Please . . . I need to come.'

'Need the whip,' Gerard said.

'I . . .' Her shoulders slumped. '. . . Deserve the crop against my bare arse, as often as you want to.'

'How often do you think I want to?' Gerard drove in.

'For an hour – I'd ask nicely for each stroke.'

'You'd say "pretty please sir".'

'I'd say – do – whatever you wanted, I'd take it hard and fast!'

Gerard thrust in, out, in. 'What else would you do? I can't hear you.'

'I'd neigh like a horse if you wanted, sir. Trot round and round.'

She was pushing back against his shaft, her face flushed, her eyes closed tight, her lips pursed in near-ecstasy.

'And after that,' said Gerard, 'you'd bring me the whip in your mouth.'

Eleanor cried out, belly going into an extended erotic spasm. Adam looked from the side window to see Leanne doing exactly the same thing. Her lids were lowered, cheeks pinkly damp, her mouth opening wide in a grimace of hot blind rapture. The fingers of her right hand were closed tightly on the entrance to the stables, her left palm moving to cup her quivering crotch. As he stared, she pushed her thighs together in an obvious bid to enjoy every last sweet contraction. Events were proving him right.

Three

That bastard was so wrong about everything! Leanne stumbled away from the stables, the pulsing purse between her legs still hot and heavy. Had Adam deliberately engineered her visit here, knowing that she'd see? She peered ahead through the haze of late afternoon heat, looking for his white watchful face at one of Lingering Lessons' windows. She shouldn't have given him the satisfaction of staying to watch. If only she'd confronted Gerard, asked about her horse, asked about anything. If only she'd put a stop to the housekeeper's whipping before ... before she herself had climaxed. Not that she'd liked seeing Gerard have the upper hand! But it was arousing to watch a man sliding into a swollen-sexed woman, using his skilful shaft to take her to the heights.

A *woman* could play a *man*'s body just as exquisitely. Maybe more so? Leanne thought of teasing, taunting, taming as she hurried back into the school and made for her *en suite* shower. Until now she'd only used her fingertips and tongue on the two lovers she'd enjoyed before her marriage to Rob – she'd never put birches or belts or three-fingered tawses to the test. But now she had to prove to Adam that he wasn't running the show here. And she'd already thought of a young male body she could control ...

An hour later Leanne went down to reception, hoping to find Adam at his desk. His chair was empty. Damn, she'd have to go to his quarters, face those photos of girlish caned buttocks and petulant pouts again! Concentrating on keeping her breathing even, she walked along the corridor and took the stairs to his rooms.

She hesitated, then peered through the letter-box. No Tania or Candy bent over his desk, their arses reddened. She rang the bell, heard footsteps. Then he opened the door. 'Hello! I was hoping to . . .'

'I'd like the keys to the seventh dorm, please. I've a guest due the day after tomorrow.'

'That's not possible,' Adam said.

'But there are only six of us who live in and there are seven dorms . . .'

'Dorm seven is locked.'

'I know! I want you to open it.'

'Your friend can stay in your quarters or we can put a spare bed in one of the classrooms or the recreation suite.'

She glared up at him from her disadvantaged position in the corridor. 'But I own half this place!'

'There's nothing in Mamie's will to indicate which half is yours, Miss Dell.'

She tilted her head. 'That doesn't mean . . .' He was sounding like the very lawyers he professed to disdain.

Adam stared at her, unblinking. 'Just take it on trust that dorm seven and its contents are mine,' he said.

Dorm seven *and its contents*. It wasn't just a long empty space, then! There was something in there – or *someone*? She clenched her arms to her sides. 'That's unfair!' Maybe she'd ignore his instructions. She could force the lock next time he went to the village, or climb a ladder and crawl in through the window late at night.

'Your friend can have the entire gym if she wants.'

'My friend's a *he*,' Leanne said. He wasn't to know that her relationship with Khan was professional, merely platonic. He'd been the first model to sign up with her Mainly Men modelling agency. Now he might become more . . .

Turning, she walked swiftly from Adam's door, refusing to look back and see if he was watching her. Why stoop to his level? Why give him the satisfaction of knowing she cared what he did?

Two days later, Khan limped in as Leanne was typing up contracts at her desk in reception. She saw Adam look up from his own desk, noted how his arms and shoulders stiffened, and decided not to introduce the two men.

'Khan!' She hurried towards the slender but well-muscled twenty year old and slid her arms round his neck, gazing up at him. After a second's surprised hesitation, he wrapped his arms round her waist and held on tight. 'Let's go up to my bedroom. You have to share with me.' That was for Adam's benefit. 'We'll also be sharing a bath and a shower.'

'Talking of baths, I just drove all the way down,' Khan said, then grimaced, and moved his weight to his left foot.

'I'll run you one with masses of bubbles, and wash your hair,' Leanne offered. Again she hoped Adam was listening. Soon he'd *see*!

'I felt great after you phoned! This ankle . . .' he tilted up the leg he'd been trailing ever so slightly, 'my first and last attempt at Swiss skiing! It's no trouble until I walk on it for any length of time.'

Leanne forced herself to stop measuring up the body beneath the denim shirt, saying, 'It must have ruled out most modelling.'

'Ruled out most everything! I was resigned to spending a fortnight on a friend's houseboat when you told me about the Lingering Lessons stills.'

Warm water, a hot core. Leanne lay stretched out on her bed and listened to Khan splashing about in the bath. In the past, she'd seen numerous photos of his *café au lait* chest with the slender nipples and strong black hirsute pelt. Looked at pictures of his small high buttocks inside designer trunks and wondered how it would feel to cup . . .

'I thought you were going to wash my hair?'

Her eyes stopped moving, her heartbeat almost ceased. *Do it, do it, do it!* She'd been celibate for a year and a half now. Celibate too long. Khan was alluring yet uncomplicated, with a reputation for being permanently ready for anything. And anyone? 'One shampooist coming up!' She'd always been his agent before – nothing personal. It felt strange to act so differently now.

43

Scented steam, tanned toned skin. Heavy black pubic hair and balls like hanging plums set below a flat belly. Stepping more fully into the bathroom, she knelt by the long tub and moved her facial muscles into something resembling a smile. Breathe in, breathe out. Get the explanations over with! 'Khan, I want you to know that you can stay here till your ankle's better – no strings,' Leanne announced.

She swallowed hard, searching out the calmest clearest words. 'But if you want to have more erotic fun you'll have to do exactly as I say – and I mean exactly.' She tensed her legs, ran the unyielding loofah through her hands, stared down at him. 'Even if it hurts and makes you feel small.'

He nodded twice. 'Why now?'

'I've had to get tough around here to show my so-called joint owner that I can't be controlled.'

'And we'd . . .' The rising rod of his manhood said the rest, as it broke through the bubbles.

'We'd do whatever I decided was right.'

A short sleep. Then a salad sandwich. A sweet cappuccino followed by a whisky sour. Two hours later, Khan was cleaned and clothed and lying expectantly on top of the duvet as she found work by phone for two of her other models who were still based in London. 'Time for the guided tour,' she murmured to Khan, striving to sound casual as she put the receiver down.

'Okay, but my ankle starts to hurt after five or ten minutes.'

'Some discipline will soon take your mind off it.' She reached for his hand, pulled him into a sitting then standing position, planning what she'd do to him next. 'Anyway, there are several wheelchairs in the storage room in the hall.'

Khan limping slightly, they walked down to reception. Leanne stopped at Adam's desk. He seemed to look up with difficulty. Something lifted in her chest – elation, triumph?

'Which classroom has wheelchair access?' she asked him.

'The . . . third one on the ground floor has a large ramp,' he answered. Adam ignored Khan completely.

'That'll do nicely. Perhaps you could help manoeuvre the chair once I get him inside?'

The helpless female bit – that should appeal to the bastard! 'No problem,' Adam said.

Khan looked over at Leanne. 'I'm not convinced that . . .'

'You'll do what you're told,' she snapped.

Now it was Adam's turn to look surprised. His lips parted slightly, and he stared from woman to youth, from thirty-something to twenty-something. Then they reached the storage cupboard and his attention was diverted towards angling out the chair.

'Thanks. See you.' As they reached the classroom, Leanne let the door swing back in Adam's face, then she immediately started talking to Khan very loudly. 'I've always been fair to my male models. In return I expect them to give me their best.'

'I realise . . .'

'That commitment's why Mainly Men was voted "Top Small Agency for Catalogue Clients" – and I intend to keep it that way.'

She reached for the teacher's cloak beside the board and put it on, then walked over to the writing bureau. Going into the top drawer, she took out a regulation school belt.

Khan stared at it, then sat up straighter in his chair. 'Dixon fulfilled his two-page spread in *Women Want It*, and Ali got me extra commission after he was Mr April in *Beaut Butts*.'

She flicked the belt against the nearest chair. The sound seemed to echo. Khan kept looking at the strap, cleared his throat. 'But you go on this unscheduled skiing trip and sprain your ankle. You have to pull out of the *Boys on Film* video and involve me in an expensive penalty clause.'

'I didn't mean to,' Khan murmured, eyes wide as a fawn's and leaning forward.

'I'm interested in outcome, not intention.'

'If I can make amends . . .'

'You can. Mr Howard has shown me that there's a market for punished arse – you know, nude pictures. I reckon

I'll warm yours up just to get in the swing of things, so I can decide if I want to go commercial in time.'

'You could just put rouge on my bum!' Khan suggested. His lips had slackened with mild fear, anticipation. His chest moved faster. Leanne looked down at the straining, lengthening life inside his jeans.

'I could. But I've decided the belt is what I want to use. Bend over that desk and pull your jeans down.' Say it like you mean it, she told herself, belly tremulous. Say it like Adam or Gerard would!

'And if I don't?' The youth tilted his head and gazed long-lashedly up at her.

'If you don't, I'll tell the other agencies you were difficult to work with. You'll find it hard to model ever again.'

'God, you're hard!' The boy was obviously torn between experiencing something new and fearing a loss of mach-ismo.

'And you aren't?' Leanne said provocatively, bending over the front of the wheelchair. Then she felt his pulsing promise through the denim second skin which covered his manhood.

'Jesus, yes! If you'd just grip it harder . . .'

She took her fondling fingers away. 'Maybe later. You have to taste my belt across that beautiful bottom first.'

He was hers. She'd literally had him by the cock and balls. His eyes were begging. Khan stood up and crossed to the little school desk she indicated, and lowered himself across it inch by awkward inch.

'Jeans off,' she repeated. Her eyes felt fixed on his belt as he loosened it. Then he fumblingly unbuttoned and un-zipped himself. Maybe she should have done that bit, used the opportunity to further tease his testes, giving over the moment to making him groan?

He looked back at her. 'Let them fall,' she demanded, and watched as the blue covering sagged to his calves and ankles. His Y-fronts were clingy white, smoothly outlining his firm young backside.

Light against tan. Khan's mother was Indian, his father English. The result was an assured young man who had already travelled much of the world and taken his pleasure where he would. Those immense dark eyes and that *café au lait* complexion ensured he was desired by both men and women. So far, he'd been politely deferential to Leanne as befits an employee in a hugely competitive field.

But was he obsequious enough to upset that bastard behind the door? Leanne sensed Adam was listening, watching. The old classrooms were full of drill holes and keyholes and there was a glass panel set high in the wood. He'd already heard her telling Khan what she was going to do to his luckless bottom. Now she had to follow it through.

'Four lashes over your Y-fronts, then we'll have a talk about your behaviour.' Her tummy fluttering round a core of breathless stillness, she picked up the worn school belt. She didn't believe in corporal punishment for children. But the governors before Mamie obviously had.

A waiting white-clad bottom above muscled caramel-coloured thighs. Leanne raised the strap and brought it down diagonally. Khan jumped and grunted low in his throat, then lay motionless. She tried to lay the second stroke more evenly across the centre of his buttocks, but the end of the belt just flicked higher up.

This wasn't as easy as it looked – as Adam made it look when he disciplined Tania or Candy. He must have had loads of practice; must have punished lots of wilful bums. But she had to make the copywriter realise that she was his equal. Leanne had to prove it by castigating someone of his gender as he lurked outside the door.

'I'm going to lay the third one on extra hard,' she warned. He wasn't begging like he should – he wasn't humbled. 'I mean, you've tarnished my reputation as an agent who always delivers the goods,' she continued.

'I'm sorry,' Khan said. But he didn't sound sorry, didn't sound afraid.

Maybe that was it. Tania and Candy had known that Adam could punish them hard and long, could drag them back to the punishment trestle or the desk if they tried to escape their thrashing. Gerard had had the power to hold

Eleanor over the straw bale – a power that remained un-spoken, unused, but which was nevertheless ever present – while he livened her arse.

'I'm going to tie you over the desk and then I'm going to start the four strokes again, to see if it makes you more obedient,' Leanne murmured. Khan looked round open-mouthed, and she saw the first glimmer of uncertainty in his eyes. 'Anything you want to say?'

'I . . . guess not.'

'You guess not, *Miss*.'

She waited. The young model didn't reply.

Thirty different public-school ties were displayed along the far wall. Feeling as if she was acting a part, Leanne walked over and selected four of them. It was like the first day in a new job when people pretend to be fully compet-ent, talking and performing and functioning in a state of heightened consciousness till it gradually became second nature, till it felt real.

'Put your wrists in line with the legs of the desk.'

Khan obeyed her, then Leanne wrapped both ties round and round, knotting them firmly. 'Now your ankles.' She swiftly secured them in place. The colours seemed to glow against his tan: saffron satin on hazel skin, a pretty picture. In a second she'd make his bottom equally bright.

'Take one.' She drew the belt back and brought it for-ward, aiming for the swell. It stung the underside. Khan flinched. He tensed his tethered calves, then relaxed them again. The second went higher, the third low. 'I'm not hearing "Thank you, Miss." ' She listened, waited. The fourth one tanned him closer to where she wanted it, in the fuller middle flesh.

'Let's see if that bottom's learned its lesson,' she mur-mured, trying to recall Adam's mocking words. The pressing heavy heat between her thighs intensified as she reached out her hands to expose Khan's hapless rear end, and inched his Y-fronts down.

Milky-coffee-coloured cheeks faced her, with pink strap marks near the thighs and close to his back, and one deeper dusky mark overlapping. She should have

undressed him and looked at his flesh before she warmed
it with the belt. But the main thing now was to make sure
Adam knew she was still directing the youth, still controlling the situation. The other main thing was the pulsing
pressure of her crotch.

'I haven't doled out very many, considering the money
you lost me, have I, Khan?' She stroked her middle finger
along the marks.

'No . . . no.'

'Say "No, Miss." '

He kept his head to the front. She moved to look up into
his face. 'You're not being respectful. That displeases me.
So I have to give you another four strokes on your newly
bared bum.'

It was a shapely masculine backside – a gym-worked
bum, a bum that men and woman paid money to see inside
shorts and trousers. Khan had never done nude work.
Leanne had never seen him naked before today. Now she
could discern the half-hard rod that nosed against the desk,
the slender muscled thighs, the strong black leg hair. She
reached a tentative finger forward and stroked the soft
twin sap-spheres, and he groaned.

'God, please, Leanne . . .'

'I'm your teacher now – "Miss Dell".' She picked up the
school belt and lashed it at the fullest part of his cheeks.
Khan cried out and shoved his belly forward.

'Aaah! Damn it! You . . .'

'You'll get it even harder if you don't apologise.'

There was a long pause. 'Right. I'm sorry,' Khan said.
The words sounded dragged from him.

'Add my name, boy.'

'Sorry, Miss Dell.'

'You're a disobedient pupil. A bad boy. You need to be
taught a painful lesson.' She thought of Adam peering
through the keyhole. She'd make him squirm. 'Most
grown-up boys are bad and need their lady teacher to pull
down their pants and give them red-hot bottoms,' she said,
extra-loud.

Then she raised the strap again and used it on the tender

49

crease where his buttocks ended. 'Please, Miss, I'll be better, Miss!' Khan said, through clenched teeth.

'How much better?' She used the lash to underline her words. The smooth tanned skin was pink now, and writhing. 'One last full-force stroke unless I feel you genuinely want to make amends,' Leanne told him.

His cock had gone limp. She knelt at his head and curved her arm under the desk till she found its shrunken softness; smiled and felt the power between her breasts lift and lighten as she held his manhood in her mobile right hand. 'Does he like me, Khan?' The inch-and-a-half-long slug started to harden into a purple-veined piston.

'Yes – yes, Miss Dell!'

'How much does he like me?'

'Enough to come in your hand,' whispered Khan. The big brown eyes were narrowed to slits, his mouth stretched sideways.

'But he can't come until he's tasted that last lash of the belt.'

She stood up. 'Let me know when you want the lash.' She thought of Adam who'd be shrinking inside, realising she was winning.

'Please use your hard belt on my bare bottom, Miss Dell,' Khan muttered, looking down at the wooden classroom floor. Knowing she was triumphant, had proved herself for today at least, Leanne just flicked the belt over the top of both his taut thighs.

'Look at me.' She knelt before him, put her thumb in her mouth, sucked it. Then she leisurely licked each of her fingers. 'Do you want them wrapped round your cock?' she asked.

'Yes, Miss. Yes!'

'Strokes fast or slow?'

'A hard fast rhythm!'

'I'll do it slow, then, because I'm bored. I may as well tease your pulsing young prick for a while.'

Taking a seat behind him, she slipped her arm between his legs and wrapped four wet fingers round his thickness. She slid them sluggishly up, then equally ponderously

50

down. 'Ah! Aaah!' The usually loquacious Khan seemed lost for words as she provoked him. Kept him swollen-but-not-seeded for a long, long time.

'Can't take ... Uh! Need ...' he muttered at last, then pulled against the strong ties tethering his arms and legs. His middle leg leaked and jerked further.

'You have to take it, Khan – as long as I want to give it. It was meant to be that way.'

'Yes, Miss – you're in charge, my employer! You're ... Oh God, Miss Dell, please!'

'Is this what you want?' She was murmuring mockingly now. Adam might no longer hear her. But he'd have got the message that Leanne Dell could teach a man a few tricks. Aroused by Khan's erect panting ardour, she slicked her fingers up and down just a little faster, kept him hovering and moaning, then moved her hand faster still.

A hard hot rhythm that made his foreskin dance a jig – sleek steps to heaven. Cupping her left hand beneath the boy's scrotum, she frisked his craving cock. Leanne felt the balls contract, saw his hips push forward. Almost, almost. She watched him flatten against the desk and hold his breath.

'Let it spurt, Khan!' She gave a last up and down rub and felt him let go, liquid salt squirting on to the desk as he groaned his ecstasy. 'Let it all out,' she whispered, stroking his shaft for the last time.

The last time today, at any rate. He'll be here for weeks yet, she thought. Adam might need further proof of my mastery. But for the time being ... She looked down at her breasts beneath the teacher's cloak: the nipples were probing buds outlined by the black cotton. Talking of probes ...

Khan mustn't get complacent now. She was still his superior, still running the show. She licked her palm, then slapped both his buttocks firmly. 'Just in case you were going to sleep on me, boy!' she said menacingly.

'Aah!' He sounded petulant. 'Please, Miss Dell, that hurts!'

'I know. It's meant to.' She ran a curved nail lightly along the crease above his thighs. 'Does this bit ache?' she asked, cupping his balls and squeezing ever so lightly. Leanne felt his flaccidness flicker and start to elongate as he groaned. 'Did that excite you, Khan?'

'Yes, Miss Dell.'

'But you're here to excite *me*.'

'Yes, Miss. Whatever you say, Miss!'

'Exactly – teacher knows best.'

Teacher knew she wanted to come. But not there on the wooden desk: she wanted somewhere more opulent. 'Right, boy. Let's get you to the recreation room.' She unknotted the ties and helped him to stand, then pushed him gently back into the wheelchair. 'No, just keep your pants at your feet,' she told him.

She waited for a few moments till Khan put the soft cushion from the teacher's chair under his heated bottom: moments in which Adam could get himself down to the recreation room and hide in the games recess. She'd seen round the school that morning, explored its pleasure-based potential. Now he'd see how Leanne's men serviced her after they'd been chastised!

'Right – hands on the wheels. To the rec room!' Heels clipping determinedly along the corridor, she urged the youth ahead of her to the suite that had been used for the staff's relaxation when the building was still used as a school. Suddenly Khan almost stalled the chair, and dipped his head, arms tensing. Looking up, Leanne saw Eleanor had turned the corner and was walking their way.

'Oh! Eleanor – hi!' She'd only spoken a few words to the older woman since she'd arrived at Lingering Lessons, as the housekeeper was rarely in reception. God knows what she thought of Khan in the wheelchair, jeans and Y-fronts around his feet!

'A guest for dinner, Miss Dell?'

She shook her head. 'He'll eat with me. No need to cater for him.' Leanne had taken to cooking her meals in the small kitchen that the senior pupils had used for heating snacks.

'If you want anything at any time, Miss . . .'

'Thanks Eleanor, I appreciate that,' she answered. Right now, though, she just wanted to come.

An eight-foot corner couch in restful padded green: Leanne stretched fully out on it when she reached the commodious rec room. Khan looked hopefully at the space to one side of her. 'Kneel, boy, and tell me again just how sorry you are,' she told him.

'Oh. Right!' Khan looked at his pushing-up prick, then at Leanne's turquoise summer skirt suit. Pushing her teacher's cloak to either side, she unfastened her skirt and edged it on to the floor.

Ivory silk stockings, no pants: she'd planned this well. It was to be the first orgasm for a year and a half that wasn't of her own making. 'Lick well, boy, or . . .' She fingered the teacher's belt she'd brought with her as she spread her thighs, and felt the last of her energy float away. Her head felt languid. From the moment she'd seen Khan in that close-fitting denim shirt and light blue jeans, her crotch had been begging to come and come and come.

Then she'd tied him to the desk – and the wanting had focused like a fever. She'd pulled down his pants and the heat at her pubis had laboured even more.

She closed her eyes at the exquisite warm wetness, loving the feel of his mouth against her famished mons, his tongue against her tip. 'Mmm . . . just there!' she moaned, tilting her buttocks from the couch to help him get his lips *in situ*, his mouth lapping at the sensitive, sensuous, special place.

'Ah, ah!' she squealed, almost there after ten or twelve knowing nuzzles. 'Muh . . . uh.' Everything was spiralling in her centre. Khan licked slightly to one side – was his tender tongue tiring? 'Lick harder, or I'll punish you again.' It was hard to plan, even to think. 'I'll . . . take you into the prefects' room. I'll use a slipper, make you touch your toes.' He lapped energetically above her labia, and she closed her eyes and legs, breathed fast, then faster. Going, going . . . She pushed her liquid centre against his lips and went over the top, thrusting her hips up and groaning her release.

'I think you needed that,' Khan whispered, sounding

dazed and proud. She'd needed Adam to know, to recognise her power. Yet as the sensation subsided she felt as if something was missing, there was a low dragging pull in her chest. 'I'm so hard for you,' Khan murmured, starting to move up her body.

'Not now,' she said pushing him away. She wanted a bath and a book – not a bedtime; wanted to be by herself for a while.

Swinging herself into a sitting position, she patted the seat till he sat down, and ruffled his hair. 'D'you mind if I do the me-myself-I bit in my rooms for a while, Khan? Eleanor'll be in the kitchen or the laundry. She'll fetch you a drink.'

'We couldn't just . . .?'

She fancied him, yet somehow she couldn't. 'Uh uh,' she said, shaking her head.

Warm water and a cool body gel. After her shower and cup of strong Assam tea, Leanne paced her rooms. Why not go for a ride? She'd yet to see Gerard about choosing a horse, as she had fled the stables without meeting him after he'd whipped Eleanor the other day.

Gerard was sitting on the fence beside the stables, scrutinising two foals that were trotting round. She could see him from afar as she strolled across the field paths before she got close enough to make out his sure grey eyes, lord of the manor cap and fringe of brown hair. Leanne walked faster, hugely conscious that he was watching. Then she reached that awkward distance where she was too far away to keep making eye contact, and too close to totally avoid it without looking weak. She smiled, looked down, glanced back again. Leanne was suddenly unsure how to hold her head, what to do with her hands.

'I'm Leanne Dell,' she announced. She stood in front of him at last. He stayed perched on the fence looking down at her. 'Mr Howard said you had a horse for me,' she added firmly.

'I've more horses than I know what to do with. Take your pick!'

Turning, she walked through the opening into the area where he'd tanned Eleanor's hide the other day, then walked quickly to her right and found the long row of stables. She mustn't think about the housekeeper tasting the whip!

Chestnut mares and grey stallions and piebalds nudged at her shoulders as she walked down the line of horses. She patted rough manes and smooth flanks. 'Young Candy usually takes that dappled pony there – not that she's that keen on riding.' She tried not to think about Gerard's presence behind her. 'And Adam always rides Scarab, on the end,' he added.

A black stallion – how predictable! Leanne walked up and down, gave a second pat to a large slate-grey steed. 'This beauty'll do me.'

'Kintyre? A good choice – he's spirited but biddable.' She nodded. Just like Khan!

But not like Gerard. She met his gaze, but was the first to look away. He was a good-looking man – but disconcertingly impersonal. 'Mr Howard rides often, then?' she asked.

'These past six months he's had little time, he's had to concentrate on his copywriting business. But now that the legacy's come through . . .'

'Mmm,' she agreed. Leanne looked out at the hockey fields, the obstacle course, the outdoor pool, acknowledging how lucky she and Adam were with their inheritance. 'It gives you a bit of leeway, when you own this much estate!'

She kept stroking the horse, wondering if she could find out more. 'You just arrived here?'

'Yes. Two weeks before you did. I was between jobs.'

'And Adam advertised?'

'Something like that.'

Why so secretive? she wondered.

'He told you that we only have money to pay the staff for this initial year?'

'He did.'

'Hopefully after that . . .'

Hopefully Adam would sell, and she'd buy him out and remain as mistress of Lingering Lessons. Depending on their performances, she'd keep Eleanor and Gerard on, and Paul the shy but skilful gardening boy.

'I've thought of a way to bring in some cash,' Gerard said.

'You have?' She felt her belly tighten. Don't let it be a way that involved Eleanor taking down her pants!

'I could advertise horse-riding here – put up posters about it in the village. Get Paul to bring a Land Rover's worth of people up every day.'

'There are enough villagers for that?' The bus service to the area was so poor that she'd yet to explore the countryside. He nodded. 'There are the people who run the restaurants, shops, and the supply stores. Plus the primary school across the common and the pubs. There are a lot of housewives and unemployed teenagers with time on their hands who'd love to come up here.'

'What do they do now, during their leisure hours?' Leanne wanted to build up a fuller picture.

'Most of them have to take the coach to the nearest city for a bit of fun.'

'Let's do it, then!' She started to saddle up her horse, feeling lighter. At last things were going her way!

After a slow trot that ended in a race, she walked Kintyre back to the stables. As she neared she heard two voices, with Gerard saying, 'Time you learned your lesson at my hands.'

Not again! Inhaling hard, she walked in. Gerard was leaning against the wall. Paul, the twenty-year-old gardener, was standing in front of him, staring at the straw, his head hanging.

'He's left some yew trees by the furthest fence. I've told him before they can poison a horse!'

'I have to tend this entire place single-handed! I have to . . .'

'I'll have to take my palm to your impudent young backside!'

Was submission all they thought about in this place? Admittedly the sex urge was strong, but to bare one's bottom out of doors, to kneel for the whip or the palm, was so unseemly! She wouldn't stay to watch this time. She had phone calls to make, letters to write. Watching a spanking being doled out would just be distracting. Moreover, the stable-master knew she was here.

'Give Kintyre a wipe down, Mr Kerne. See that he's watered,' Leanne commanded. Smoothing a suddenly damp palm down her jodhpurs, she walked quickly away. Her labia felt liquid again, not saturated yet, but pervaded by that knowing pleasure prickle, that signal that said please, please, please.

There was a barn ahead. She slipped inside, checking first that there wasn't a face staring down from Lingering Lessons. Adam had presumably had enough after watching her take a belt to the tethered Khan. She remembered the boy's mouth, his tender tongue making her writhe and stiffen. She pulled her jodhpurs and briefs down, leaned against the ladder which led to the hayloft and held back a groan.

Rough steps against her belly, cool air against her vulnerable buttocks. She imagined being tied to the rungs of it whilst someone with a whip stepped back . . .

She slid two digits up herself, gasped, bore down, then inserted another. She moved the mock phallus in and out; transferred the juicy threads to her clitoral hood, used two light but sure fingertips to tease round and round.

Her belt on Khan's bum, Gerard's switch on Eleanor's arse, Gerard's palm on Paul, spanking him into submission. Now she could punish. She could control, now. She could win: tease, think, rub. Leanne let out a sob of pleasure and frustration as she climaxed. At the last moment, she'd pictured herself tethered to the ladder, her backside writhing and reddening as Adam brought down the birch.

Four

One Living Doll campaign completed! Adam set down his pen and smiled at Candy as she took dictation in his rooms. 'Just type that up and put it in the post, then we've the rest of the day to do what we want.' Do what we *can*, rather, he thought. He wanted ... wanted what he couldn't yet have.

Leanne had been here for a month now, sitting across from Adam in reception. She made calls, typed letters, disappeared into various classes and dorms with the obsequious Khan. Adam lurked outside, loathing, listening, wanting to punish her and pleasure her, and knowing he had to wait. Leanne seemed to be working out how to photograph the boy to his best advantage. She was deciding which other male models to invite to Lingering Lessons and when.

Walking to the window, Adam stared out at the schoolyard, the playing-fields, the gardens with their tool-shed and orchid-filled greenhouses. *Their* land, to be loved and looked after. If only she'd ...

'All present and correct,' Candy said. She stood next to his chair. 'I'll just leave the rough copy over here, sir.' Bent obviously over the desk so that he could see the twin promise of her small buttocks, lusciously and wantonly displayed. Her pink cotton panties clung to each cheek. His groin flickered. With effort he turned his head away and tried to turn off his need.

'Time for a late breakfast!' he said out loud. Eleanor had been a gem, cooking at short notice, often at no notice. Bringing midnight suppers and mid-morning coffee from fresh-roasted beans. He pressed the button that connected him to the kitchens and said, 'If you could bring up three lightly scrambled eggs and tea and toast whenever you're available?' He'd eat in his lounge, then take Scarab for a ride.

Then, there was a knock on his door. 'Quickest cook in the country!' he joked, vaguely hearing Candy's laughter. He undid the latch, wondering, hoping. Yes, it was her! 'Good morning, Leanne!' She was wearing a lemon satin short-sleeved blouse, a close-fitting black pencil skirt with sable-shaded stockings. Simple yet stunning every time.

'I'll be doing some photo shoots in the classrooms this week, so I'd appreciate some privacy,' she announced. Adam nodded. She'd wanted quite the opposite when she was using a belt on that handsome but callow youth Khan! He spoke quickly as she turned to go. 'I didn't realise you were a photographer.'

'As I said, I run the model agency Mainly Men.'

She half-smiled and his breastbone felt lighter than it had for many days. She continued. 'I just send photo shoots to clients. You know, suggest themes and settings. If they use my models, I get the commission. They get a professional photography team in to do the rest!'

And do you punish them all? Do you come beneath their tongues? Do you . . . he didn't want to think about men sliding their cocks right up her. 'I've got some props in the biology lab, but I'll take them out if you're basing your work there. Let's go along and see if you want to photograph the place.'

He wanted to bring his lips down on hers till her body arched at the touch of his tongue, wanted to weld his hands to those supple high breasts, to squeeze until she winced a little. Fingers moving to her hair to tilt her head back, he'd slide his free palm to her bum. She'd arouse and enrage him with deft words, dismissive gestures. He'd spank . . .

'This way or that?' She hesitated as they reached two fire doors.

'To the left. The right one takes you to the prefects' quarters.'

'All sneaked cigarettes and sexy magazines, huh?'

Adam glanced at her in surprise, exulted inwardly as she looked away. So she couldn't quite maintain eye contact, then; that was fortuitous. The talk of sex – or just his presence – made her slightly shy.

'The sexy magazines shouldn't be secret,' he said.

'I guess if the teachers get embarrassed . . .'

'That's *their* problem.'

'You *would* say that – you have to make your living from sexual ads!'

'Wrong way round. I went into this line because it was a more honest living.'

'What did you do previously?'

'I was a journalist.'

He pushed open the door and they walked into the lab. He could see his living doll against the worktop in the far corner.

'There was endless corruption on the paper; pressure to exaggerate one story, hold back another. Pay-offs. Blackmail.'

'There are a lot of people who sell out.'

He leaned against the front science table – at last she was agreeing with him! 'That's why I turned to copywriting for sex-ads. There's honesty in lust and desire.'

'But some of the *images* lie.'

'Mine don't.' He pursed his lips, 'Most people can survive without the government's view of what's happening in other countries, or without the latest face cream or delicatessen dish.' He stared at her satin-sheathed breasts which were gently rising and falling. 'Fewer can live happily without the aids that bring sexual release.'

'They can use their hands!'

'Sometimes they want something more.' Much more.

'I suppose so.' He suspected she *knew* so – she just wouldn't give in.

'That's why the Living Doll meets a need.'

He watched as her eyes and mouth widened into a grin. 'A doll! Not really?'

'Really.' He indicated the flesh-coloured rubber female

at the other end of the lab. The day before, he'd propped her upright against the worktop, belly inwards. Her twin openings were clearly and compellingly displayed.

He watched the taut-skirted buttocks approach the nude oval buttocks. There was no competition. 'This isn't as good as . . .'

'Many men don't have a choice.'

He swallowed hard as she stroked the smooth beige arse, slid a finger into the forever-open vagina. 'She's quite slippery.'

'They use a special cream.'

He watched as she nervously licked her lips. 'Your sales slogan?'

' "Because You're Always Ready".' He swept his hand round the lab. 'Hence the setting. The photo's of a scientist reaching towards the doll as if he's suddenly too aroused to concentrate on his work.'

'Won't that just make people smile?'

'Sure – the concept of a sex doll always makes people smile? That's why you can buy blow-up sheep for stag nights. But they'll smile and still feel lustful. Or feel curious. Or just think "what the hell".'

'Mamie would have said that – "what the hell". She wanted to experience everything.' She looked back at him. 'Did you write sex ads for her? I didn't think . . .'

He shook his head. 'I did her "Homoeopathic Holidays" campaign, the Seal Sanctuary, that kind of project. And monthly copy for her charity on children's rights.'

'They'd have been all right here if the orthodoxy hadn't closed the place!'

He risked a comradely press to her upper arm. 'Now it's up to us to make sure that the adults here are all right.'

'Mr Howard – I wondered how many there'd be for dinner tonight?'

He turned as the new voice came from the suddenly open doorway. Damn Eleanor for breaking into the moment! Leanne had been smiling at him, nodding at him for the very first time.

'You, me, Paul, Gerard and Candy as always,' he said, fixing his eyes on hers.

'What about Miss Dell's young man?'

'I said he'll eat with me.' Leanne muttered. Eat her, more like. Adam closed his nails against his palms. So what if they were at last in tune? She still needed a good thrashing! Cooking and dining with that fawning licking youth when she could be talking and laughing with him, Adam, instead.

'What would you like? I . . .' Eleanor stayed put.

'I've filled in my menu card. I left it on my desk as usual.'

'Sorry, I must have missed it.'

'Look again.'

'There's coffee in the conservatory. It's so sunny, I thought . . .'

'Maybe later.' Eleanor was staring at him, at Leanne, at the nude beige doll.

'Miss Dell and I have work to discuss, Eleanor.' The woman nodded but stayed *in situ*. 'You can go,' he said, dismissing the housekeeper again.

'Oh . . . Right.' Slowly she backed away. Legs almost in slow motion.

'Must be her biorhythms!' he joked, when the door finally closed. 'Normally she's a hundred per cent organised.'

He smiled at Lingering Lessons' frowning co-owner. 'Shall I move the doll and all these notes and sketches from the lab so you can take your photos, then?'

She looked round. 'Mmm? The lighting's all wrong. No, I think we'll just use a classroom plus the gymnasium.' She smiled up at him, 'We're doing an Academic Attire theme, with Khan wearing the college look.'

'For whom?'

'For Conscious catalogue.'

'Yes, I know it. Their suits are first class.' He wanted to keep talking to her, keep looking at her, start touching.

'Want to help me rearrange the gym?' she asked.

'Why not?' He strode towards the lab door and held it open. Arms brushing, they walked towards the well-equipped hall. 'Isn't young Khan around to assist you?' With luck the youth had at last gone back home, gone somewhere else.

'Oh, he's down in the village, making friends with the natives. Gerard said he'd give him a lift.'

They reached the gymnasium and walked through the swing-doors, sat down next to each other on one of the low wooden benches. He turned to her. 'I didn't realise Gerard was picking up supplies today.'

'He's not.'

'Only he's never been one for village small talk.' No, more one for tanning the village girls' arses after the weekly barn dance!

'He's gone for business, not pleasure. This is the hour he collects the horse-riders every day.'

'I don't follow.' He turned on the bench to face her. He usually knew what was going on.

'The horse-rides to bring in capital. Didn't I tell you? Gerard thought it up and I agreed!'

'Agreed to rent the horses out to strangers?'

He watched as she straightened her shoulders. 'You mean *our* horses.'

'You have Kintyre. I have Scarab. The rest are jointly owned.'

'I know, but . . .'

'But you've been keeping the money, keeping this secret?'

'Not deliberately . . .'

'Hoping I'll go bankrupt and have to sell at the end of the year?'

Licking her lips now, she said, 'I didn't think . . .'

He turned to her, gaze fixed. 'No, you didn't. It's time that someone taught you a little thoughtfulness. Time I put you through your paces in this gym.'

'Yeah? You and whose army?' Her tone was slightly shrill, though her words were brave. He had to go for it!

'Sweetheart, I don't need an army. You're in the wrong. It's as simple as that.'

'If you lay a hand on me, I'll bite! I'll scratch your face, I'll kick your shins. I mean it!' She looked up at him, eyes bright, lips parted, hands tensing into human claws.

'You want a show of strength? All right. Let's both

attempt a hundred press-ups. If I fail, I no longer get to punish you. If you fail, I do.'

'And if neither of us fails?'

'We're equal.'

'If we both fail?'

'We're equal then, too.'

'No problem!'

He smiled. 'Don't you want to know what the punishment is if you're found wanting?'

'No – I won't have to experience it. I'll complete your stupid test!'

'Age before beauty,' he said, sinking down on to the polished wooden floor and getting into position. He lowered himself down, up, down, wishing she were underneath him; thought of her over his knee. He'd bare her bum and keep it squirming beneath his palm, slowly pinkening, reddening. He pressed up and down again, again, again.

'. . . One hundred!' He'd done press-ups and weight-lifting in the gym most days since coming to Lingering Lessons: just twenty minutes or so to work off stress, to help him to focus. Her own thighs were strong: he'd seen them, longed to caress them. But her arms?

'My turn!' He stared at her short-sleeved shirt with its front-fastening buttons and sheath-like pencil skirt. Watched the jet-black linen mould itself to her buttocks as she got down on her hands and knees. She straightened, flexed her wrists. 'One!' she said loudly. He could see she was putting too much energy into each push-up. 'Two! Three! Four!'

By twenty he could see her arms trembling, see the tension in her shoulders as she raised her torso up again. Each downward move was more slumped, more relieved, less control-based. Each raised movement took longer – much too long.

'Oh dear, I have a feeling I'll soon be warming my palm against your backside.'

'Fuck you!' It was a breathless mutter. As he'd known she would, she put more uplift into the next move, wasting further rations, misusing the little strength she had left. The lactic acid must be flooding her muscles by now, and that ached and burned – he'd make her arse ache in a moment. Then he'd coax her to climax after climax. He was rod-like and relentless inside his suit.

Twenty-three. Twenty-four ... At thirty, she lowered herself down and didn't get up again. He could see her palms straining against the gym floor, but her shoulders simply didn't have any momentum left.

'You agreed to this test to try to redeem yourself for cheating me. You lost. Now take your thrashing.' He stood up, looped his arms under hers and pulled her towards him. Bracing his legs, he sat back down on the bench. At last she was his to taunt, to tease, to pleasure and to punish. He breathed in the classic notes of Obsession and a faint trace of fresh perspiration, itched to bring on a heavier sexual scent.

Adam put his fingers in her hair and tugged gently forwards so that she didn't have any option but to follow. Obviously exhausted from the gymnastics, she lay muttering obscenities across his lap. 'What did you say, my dear?' he goaded.

'Fuck you!'

'You seem to spend a lot of your life wanting to fuck me. For myself, I just want to teach respect to this deceitful little bum.'

He stroked it through her skirt. 'You've been so bad.'

'It was a mistake – I meant to hand over the money!'

He caressed softer, slower. 'But you've seen me in reception every day.'

'We don't exactly talk ...'

'We don't. You glare. My palm's getting ever so angry when I think about just how often you glare at me; how often I've said good morning and just got back an abrupt little nod.'

'I ... didn't realise you did worthwhile work!'

'You didn't ask.'

'Assumed ...'

'I'm going to rid your backside of assumptions.' He

drew his hand up; she squealed and reached both her own hands back to cover it. 'Miss Dell, we agreed.'

She kept her palms immobilised in place, the fingers spread protectively over the orbs he hadn't yet toasted. 'Are you going back on your word now?'

'N . . . no.'

'Then put your hands in front.' She obeyed his command. He swiftly unknotted his tie and bound her wrists together. He had one elbow on her back, holding her firmly. She could do little more than drum her black patent heels on the floor.

'How many spanks does this bad bottom deserve for arranging the riding lessons without my permission?'

'Use your imagination!' Leanne muttered.

'Oh angel, I've a very rich imagination! In fact, I'm so resourceful that I'll just thrash you till you implore me to stop.'

'Don't hold your breath,' she said. He ran his thumb along the backs of her thighs and she wriggled. He could feel her pubis against his pulsing cock.

'So this brave bottom will take all I have to give?' He brought his palm down on her full right cheek. His body spasmed towards Eden. He knew his pleasure would peak just by spanking her, but that he'd soon be ready to come again. Then he'd play her clit and crevice till she shrieked her rapture to the rooftops. He'd bring her to ecstasy after ecstasy with his fingers, phallus, perhaps with Candy's well-taught tongue.

But first . . . He brought his hand down hard again, this time on the opposite cheek. 'I'm going to tan this bottom mercilessly. You've been haughty and conveniently forgetful. You have to learn.'

She was learning silently. He laid on four more spanks and she grunted, bucked against his maleness. Swelling with anticipation, he smacked her soft-clad bum twice more.

Hot, then hotter. She wriggled as he roasted her rear again, but still didn't plead for forgiveness. He wanted an excuse to edge her skirt up and punish her directly over her pants. Not that they would be staying on for long; she was too headstrong, too wilful. Sooner or later, she'd say or do something unreasonable and he'd bare her bottom for the very first time.

For the moment, he'd settle for greater access to her full expanse. 'Dearest, you're flattening yourself down too much. I'm going to have to put a cushion under your belly.' He set her down on the gym floor. She went forward on to her knees, her wrists still tied in front of her, and started to crawl away.

'Bad girl! I've hardly started punishing you yet. The deal was that you have to tell me when you've had enough and then ask nicely to be pardoned.'

'Sure – when hell freezes over!' She continued her clumsy crawl.

'All these clichés! I thought a model-agency owner had to be creative. Looks like I'm the enterprising one . . .'

Swiftly choosing a bolster-shaped beanbag from the thirty or so in the right-hand corner of the room, he resumed his seat and dragged her over his lap again, sliding the beanbag under her tummy. 'I could tell the others!' she muttered.

'Tell them you agreed to this contest then welshed on the deal? You've been so uppity – not eating with the rest of the staff – that they already dislike you. They'd be pleased to know that you were getting your rear end well-warmed.'

The bolster raised her bum and kept it high. He slid his right palm over first one cheek then the other; she could feel the heat of his endeavours through the cloth. 'Coming along nicely,' he said, realising that he himself was very close to coming. She'd never know.

He'd taught himself to climax without a cry. Done so years ago, sharing too few rooms with too many brothers. Everyone looking to him, the eldest, for help with school and, later, work.

'Let's start again, now that this bottom is prettily raised. Remember to let me know when you've repented.'

'In your dreams!' she grunted. And in her wet dreams; as she'd crawled, he'd seen the spreading stain across her skirt. He'd been right all along! Soon she'd spread her legs for him and their bodies would merge. Soon ...

But first he had to talk her down, smack her down, take her to her current submissive limit. 'Angel, I think you like this, really. I think it's making you hot.'

'You wish!'

'I *know*. Your pussy's wet. It's running against me.' She stopped moving. He spanked each taut-clothed buttock. She writhed again.

'I'm going to check just how sticky you are.' She whimpered as he lifted her skirt and rolled her panties down, then unclipped her stockings.

'Damn you, you bastard!' Each word was torn from her in a series of needy gasps.

'The bastard's going to stroke these little leaves apart. What's this? A liquid centre.' He circled her oiled entrance for a moment, then slid his middle finger in an inch and traced the living walls inside.

He closed his eyes for a second as his sex sac surged then emptied, bliss billowing through his trousered shaft from his scrotum. He tensed his thighs to squeeze out the last pulsing pleasure: now he could concentrate on *her*. He'd punish her, then penetrate her, thrust her slowly into orgasm. Take his second release inside her welcoming body when she'd had her fill.

'Do you like that, sweetheart?' He slid his finger further up.

'It's ... all right.' Her body bore down against his digit.

'Just all right? How about this one?' He fed in a second finger and she pushed down again and groaned.

'If I think you're lying, I'll have to spank you some more. I'll have to withdraw my fingers.'

'Don't care ...' He started to pull the pleasure source from her pubis. 'Christ, don't!' she implored.

'You want to be finger-fucked, then?'

'Want ...'

'Want another thrashing for not answering? Want me to take off my belt?' He stroked her bare bum. 'Remember, you're still across my knee, your pants at your ankles. I just have to raise my hand.'

Her glowing-hot derrière drove forward as she moved to take his fingers deeper inside her. He used both digits to thrust in and out.

'Maybe if you ask very sweetly I'll put my cock in there, to provide more friction. As it stands, I don't know that you deserve to come.'

'I've said I'm sorry about the cash!' Her voice was something new and strained, almost guttural.

'Sorry about protecting your bottom after you agreed it needed spanking? Sorry about calling me a parentless man?'

'Yes . . . yes!' When she hesitated, he withdrew his fiendish fingers a telling half-inch, felt her body tense, felt her mind give in a little. With effort, she was saying what he wanted her to say.

'Good girl.' A small gelatinous puddle had spread over the thigh of his suit. 'Angel, you're dripping all over me.' He pushed up, down, up. 'This has the rhythm of a cock without a cock's ultimate endpoint, which means it can go on for ever. If you're like this after a couple of minutes what will you be like after an hour?'

'Uh! Uuuh!' she answered. He placed one palm between her buttocks, and kept the other hand in place. She was doing most of the work now. 'I'm about to make you lick your juices from my suit with that clever little tongue of yours. And I'll thrash you with a martinet if you miss a drop.'

'Uh! Uh! Uh!' She was closer to coming now. He could feel it in her stiffening legs, in the way her hot wet channel closed on his fingers. 'I'll get Eleanor in to oversee – she knows all about cleaning, she recognises quality work.'

'Uh! Uh! Uh!' Leanne replied, mouth open, eyes shut, pussy pushing down against his deliberating digits.

'Do a good job, sweetheart, or she'll get to watch me toasting your wriggling little arse.'

'Aaaaaaaaah! Aaaaaaah! Aaaaaaah!' she shrieked. Her belly moved violently against his knees, crevice closing in as she gave three loud half-human cries, inner legs meeting again and again, arse-cheeks driving forward. Her bound wrists jerked to some inner rhythm, her toes flexed and curled.

'There, there!' He felt a rush of tenderness, wanting to take her in his arms and hold her close. But she could come again if he played the scene to its conclusion. And he could slide his whole hard length inside her and buck and plunge.

'I think you quite liked that.' He caressed her flushed nether orbs. 'But the full redness of my spanks is already fading. And I so like to see a sore crimson bottom, a nice hot swell. Otherwise I get angry. And when I'm angry, I call in the rest of the staff to inspect the wicked girl.'

'You wouldn't!' she answered desperately. At least she wasn't calling him a bastard now. Orgasm could be wonderfully persuasive.

'Is that a challenge, my dear? You know how I love our little tests.'

'No! I . . . Don't punish me any more. Don't call in the staff!'

'What will you do to put me in a good mood?'

'I'll . . .' She held her bondaged wrists helplessly in front of her, then slid from his lap on to her knees and put her tremulous mouth against his zip.

'Do you want it in your mouth?'

'No I want it inside . . .'

'Mr Howard. I was wondering . . .'

'*Eleanor* – get out!'

He jumped to his feet and automatically moved in front of Leanne as Eleanor started through the doors. The rage in his voice must have communicated itself to the housekeeper, as the door quickly swung shut again.

Adam turned to the crouching, blushing Leanne. 'Stupid bitch! She didn't see anything. You were saying?'

'I . . . nothing.'

He sank down on the bench, voice silkily soft. 'I think you wanted me inside you.'

'Just untie me. Right?' She held out her wrists. She looked close to tears. He reached out to stroke her hair. 'Don't touch me!' Leanne shrieked.

'Then how can I untie your wrists?'

'You know what I mean!'

'I do. But do you know what you *want*?' She was biting her lip, refusing to make eye contact with him.

'I want to go back to my rooms!'

'You want me inside you.'

She kept her chin dipped, and mutely shook her head.

He tried again. 'I want to enter you and pleasure you for as long as you require. I want to tease you till every last cell has had enough.'

'You just want to come! Go spend yourself in that little bimbo Candy!'

'Is that what you want?'

'Why not?'

'As you wish.' He pressed one of the eight service buttons that had once brought gym masters hurrying to the hall, but which now connected him with his assistant's quarters. 'Candy will be here in three or four minutes, as long as she was in her room.' He pulled out the knots that held Leanne's wrists in limbo. 'If you'd like to put on your pants . . .' He stared as she did, seeing the liquid satiation on her thighs, the prints of his fingers, knowing that she needed more.

'I'll go before . . .' she started, but he caught her arm.

'No – this was your idea. You'll stay and watch.'

'I don't want her to see me!'

'Then hide in that supplies cupboard.' He jerked his arm at the storage space with its slatted wooden doors.

He stared as she hurried to it and slipped inside. Her leg movements were synchronised, fast: proof that her spanking and sex glow had subsided. This scene would make her build again.

Adam smiled as his personal assistant walked in. 'Candy, I found a typing error in that letter of introduction I'm sending out. As you can imagine, that makes a very bad first impression.'

'Yes, Mr Howard. I'm sorry, Mr Howard,' Candy replied. He watched the excited blush rise to her cheeks.

'Sorry's never enough, is it?' His heart wasn't in the words. Slowly he beckoned her closer with a finger. 'We'll have to teach you some accuracy.' He pulled her over his lap. She was wearing a lacy-bodiced dress. He edged it up, vaguely registering the matching creamy petticoat. Then he pulled down the pink pants she'd displayed herself in earlier to reveal the smooth small silky bum.

But it should be Leanne across his knee! And she *had* been until – damn that Eleanor! 'A hot bottom will improve your typing,' he continued, slapping both wriggling rotundities, and feeling his groin grow hard. Adam spanked her with one hand, keeping the other on her clit, urging her to move against it. They bucked and rubbed and writhed until she came with little kitten-like squeaks.

'Do you want to please me?' he asked, then stroked her pinkened orbs. She squirmed, then slid on to her knees before him; unzipped his trousers then started to rise, obviously planning to straddle his lap.

'I think your pretty mouth will suffice.' He wanted to be inside a woman – but not just any woman. Watched as his PA hesitated, then sank down on the floor again.

Dusky-pink lipstick, a reddish-purple penis head: he stared down as his shaft was enveloped in her massaging mouth then released again, taken in and held, freed then teased. Her knowing tongue licked from root to top, kissed down, moved up towards its weeping eye, then nuzzled its ever-enlarging length.

He was slicked with her saliva. She took him deeper in, sucked harder. He thought of Leanne, watching, waiting. 'Lick faster, my angel,' he implored, flexing his right palm. 'Or else ...' Adam watched her eyes widen, her mouth close on his swollen shaft, a promissory pressure. Not long now, he thought.

He shut his eyes. These eyes had feasted on Leanne's perfect peach of a bum, his palms had spanked it. His fingers had slid in her, up her, made her come. After this, he'd pull the agency owner down on his hardness, move his hips in little circles to accentuate her pleasure, tease the tender nubs of her breasts.

Candy brushed his balls with her hair as she nuzzled the most sensitive inch of his rod, the unseeing-eyed inch. Her head bent humbly, her biddable mouth thrilled through his testes. He groaned softly as his release shot free.

'Can I do anything else for you, sir?' Candy asked, then ran a wet palm over her lips as she looked up at him.

'Just some judicious retyping, dear. But it'll wait.'

'Are you working out now?'

He looked round the gym, felt his sense of the ironic rise. 'I might be!' Adam saw her petulant pout as he cleaned himself with citrus-dampened tissues from the wall-based dispenser, then zipped himself back in.

'I've a stopwatch in that cupboard, sir, if you want your circuit training timed,' Candy offered.

'Thanks, but no thanks.'

'See you at nine tomorrow, then.'

'You won't. Remember?'

'Oh. Right. Well, in that case, have fun.'

He watched as his PA left. He'd been lucky with her: she couldn't do enough for him. Whereas Leanne . . . 'You can come out now!' he called to her. The large door opened and, flush subsiding, she stepped back into the main hall of the gym.

'Surprised you didn't just fuck your Living Doll if it's so brilliant!'

'I've never come that way.' Why would he? There'd be no point in spanking a doll. She hauled one of the larger beanbags from the corner and flopped down on it, resting on her belly.

'Doubt if anyone could!'

'They could if they were aroused already.' He'd seen the research one firm had done: 'With the help of a breast-and-buttock-stroking video and a little imagination . . .'

She snorted a half-laugh. 'Doing the sales pitch again?'

He shook his head, then an idea came to him. His groin prickled. 'Are you challenging me a second time? Looking for further spanks?'

'Screw you!' She raised her head. 'You men are so crass! We women don't need a doll to make us climax.'

'You're saying you couldn't orgasm with one?'

'With a female dummy? I'm not gay!'

73

'I suspect most of us are bi.'

She shook her head. He smiled. They might see about that side of her nature later. 'We have male dolls as well, you know,' he assured her.

'I'm still immune!' Leanne shifted her wet groin against the beanbag and smirked up at him.

'Then let's set another dare.'

Another dare he'd win. 'If you come, I get to punish you for being too sure of yourself.' And then you'll beg me to make love to you, he thought.

'Stretch, yawn! Over your knee again?'

He looked round at the rope-ladders and netball posts, spied the gym horse with its smooth, sloping back; just right for lying over. 'No, across that padded horse, bound into position, with me using a paddle on your backside.'

'Got it all thought out, haven't you?' Her eyes were cold as she spoke.

'I'm paid to think.'

'You mean *I'm* not?'

'Placing male models in mags – isn't it all a bit superficial?'

'Not when it almost destroys men and women if it's done badly!'

He sat down beside her, wondering at her rush of defensiveness, of her anger. 'Tell me more.'

'Marty my brother's five years younger than me. When he was eighteen he came third in a "Face of the Future" Competition. The prize was small, around three hundred pounds, just a local thing. But he was approached by several agencies who promised him the big time. He was so high for a while.'

'All hype, was it?' Adam had seen such businesses for himself.

'They charged for photographic portfolios, for modelling courses. He couldn't tell the genuine from the fake.'

'Yet you went into this line?' His mind tried to follow on ahead, understand Leanne's logic.

'I did, though almost by mistake! I started to help Marty

74

out – you know, did some research of my own into who was worth knowing in the business. Even found him a couple of commissions along the way.'

'And he's your top model now?'

She shook her head. 'That's the irony! He went to France with his girlfriend. I think the pressure was too much for him at that age. Maybe one day . . .'

'You miss him.' It was a statement. He could see.

'Sure. When Mum and Dad were alive they criticised, so it was nice when Marty was there for me. And now that Mamie's dead . . .'

They could have each other, if only she'd submit to him! But she needed to be led all the way like a goat on a lead.

'So, having to be independent for so long has made you headstrong?' Adam pushed the subject back towards the dare she'd made with him.

'Sorry?' she blinked, lips opening slightly.

'So headstrong you've sworn you won't climax impaled on a top-of-the-range male doll!'

'Oh that!' She gave a lopsided grin, 'Do your worst!'

'Oh sweetheart, I intend to.' Walking over to the wall, he took hold of the six-foot by six-foot bondage board he'd used for an earlier copywriting series, and lowered the wooden sheet to the floor. Strolling over to her, he took her hand and led her towards it. 'I'm going to position you so that your mind is nice and focused. All you have to think about is your crotch.'

He put his right hand behind her neck, pushed insinuatingly till she got into a crouching position on the ground, then knelt down in front of her. He took her nearest wrist and moved it towards the peg with its knotted rope.

'What are you doing?' Her voice sounded smaller than usual, languid even.

'I'm tying you spread-eagled to this board, then I'll slide the male doll underneath.' He tethered her right hand in place, and did the same to its neighbour. 'Now I'm going to lift up your skirt and pull down your pants.' He did so. Her bum was just the lightest shade of pink. It would soon go back to normal. Unless, of course, he won the dare!

'That's it, honey. You're still very wet from before when I finger-fucked you. Now you're going to get a nice hard cock instead.'

'A *rubber* cock!' she exclaimed. Her thickened voice belied the sneer of her words. She obviously wanted something to fill the ache inside her.

'Just think about it. I'll be back in a moment. Enjoy the cool air on your naked bum, he continued, then stood up, and looked down at her denuded lower half, 'After all, if I win my wager, it won't be cool for very long.'

'You wish!' He left the room. If he hadn't tied her up, she could have played with herself and brought herself to orgasm. He wanted all that pent-up need and frustration to vent itself on the stout rigid dick of the doll. After all, since she'd last come, she'd watched the foreplay-like spectacle of Candy taking a good hard spanking, seen her suck on Adam's cock.

He opened the door off reception that led to a long narrow storage space. He'd left the male doll lying on its back – but the place where it had lain was empty. He heard a noise behind him and turned: it was Eleanor.

'Sir, if you could approve the new linen order . . .'

Leanne was waiting for him. 'Not now!'

He stepped back into the reception hall as the housekeeper walked slowly away. Maybe she knew something?

'Eleanor – have you seen the male rubber doll I left here?'

She turned back. 'Young Paul took it! I saw him looking all guilty the other night.'

'Thank you.'

'Sir, if you'd just . . .'

'Forget it.' Today, the woman was being an uncharacteristic pain.

Paul was pulling weeds out of the rockery. 'I hear you've borrowed the male doll,' Adam said.

'I . . .' The boy went red, and fingered the straps of his dungarees. He rarely spoke unless spoken to.

'That's allowable – the contents of that cupboard aren't

private. Fetch it now and leave it outside the gymnasium, please.' Candy would have got off on Paul watching her half-naked body tied out, spread-eagled. Leanne might, too – given time.

Ten minutes later, Adam strolled into the gym with the doll. 'I thought you'd left me to rot!' Leanne remarked, half-joking.

'Don't you trust me?'

'I . . . guess so.' As he'd hoped, their recent talk had brought them closer. She knew a little more about his work and he'd begun to understand about Mainly Men. Not that they were exactly soul mates yet: there was still the matter of Khan sharing her rooms – and presumably her sexual repertoire. The fact that she wouldn't eat or socialise with him – her stubborn pride.

He pushed the male doll under her lower half and positioned it in place, then bound her ankles to the outermost pegs, so that she was completely scissored. 'Meet Ever Ready.'

'That's what you call him?'

'*You* can call him anything you like!' He slid a knowing thumb over her clit for a teasing second. 'You can ask him nicely to slide his eight-inch prick right up you, thick and hard.'

'Forget it!' He wound his fingers in her hair. 'Move upwards.' Then he applied a steady pressure till she did so. 'This is going to be like doing press-ups, only you just move the lower half of your body, the half that's impaled on the prick,' he pronounced.

He smiled as she lowered herself down on the phallus for the first time, and her mouth contorted a little.

'Feels nice and stiff, huh? Pretend it's mine.'

'Yeah, you wish!'

'Keep lifting your hips up and down.' He pulled at her hair when she failed to do so. 'Look at me, Leanne. Keep your eyes on me all the time.'

Half-shaking her head, she turned her sulky gaze down.

'If you don't look, I'll know you're trying to hide the fact that you're aroused, that you're losing.'

'I can take it!' She glared back at him defiantly, slightly pink marks of strain shadowing the sides of her face.

'Good girl! Down, then up, and down . . . the prick is thrusting up against your cervix. It's filling every inch of you . . .' Her pupils were dark wide pools, lips increasingly slack. 'Faster. Push! Take it hard. You know you want it.' Up and down, and up and more firmly down.

'Paul left the doll outside. Did you know?'

'Heard footsteps coming . . . going.' She was looking at him, but no longer seeing.

'I think he's ridden this hard-on too.' Up, down, up. He smiled inwardly as he saw her thighs stiffen, the see-through liquid from within spreading over the rubber balls as she rose up again. She was almost there. Any moment now, he'd make the conclusion rigorously sweeter by keeping her on the edge.

Cock deep in, half-out. Deep in. 'Gerard spanks Paul really hard. Puts him over that fence by the stables. Gives him what for if he cuts the grass in the paddock too short.' Adam moved his hands to her shoulders, pressing down so that she could barely lift her body, couldn't get that much-needed deep hard thrust.

'Paul hasn't had a lady friend for ever so long. Eleanor and Candy joke that he must be frustrated! Do you know what it's like to be frustrated, Leanne?'

'Yes . . . yes!'

'It's when your pussy's ever so hot, ever so wantful. When your mound is just begging for a big hard cock.'

'Must . . .' She tried to shrug free of his hands, but he held her firmly.

'Just circle your hips on the prick, honey. That'll keep you nice and near.'

'Have to . . .'

'Have to learn to finish your sentences? Have to get off this shaft? I could take it away if it's upsetting you.'

'Got to move down, up . . .'

'Oh, I see. Your pussy wants the cock up hard?' She'd closed her eyes. 'Look at me, Leanne. Now answer.'

She kept them shut. He slid his hands to her upper back

78

and pushed half of his body weight down, holding her motionless in place.

'Got to come! Adam, please . . .'

'Tell me your pussy wants the cock up hard.'

'My pussy wants . . .' A half-sob. '. . . Needs it.'

'Good girl. That wasn't so difficult, was it?' He returned his hands to her hair. 'Now thrust.'

Adam took his fingers away as he realised she didn't need his prompting any more. She was lost in a haze of climactic near-rapture. The prick was provoking her cervix, her G-spot, the movement pulling against her flesh to indirectly stimulate her clit.

'I hope you're not *too* excited.'

'Uh . . . uh.' She pushed faster, faster, faster.

'Because that paddle's very hard, warms the whole buttock at each stroke. I had to use it on Candy once. She lost her place during dictation. The poor girl couldn't sit down for a week!' He watched each tiny muscle contract in Leanne's face: she was going, going. 'And your bottom will be so vulnerable, strapped down over that padded horse.'

'Ah, ah, ah': the gasping half-groans that came seconds before a climax. 'If you're wicked enough to come – after you promised not to – I may even have to ask Gerard and Paul to strap you in place.' He smiled as she shoved down and down and down. 'I might be called out of the gym. If I went before Gerard . . . Well, it's imprudent to leave him alone with a switch in his hand and a girl's bared arse.'

'Aaaaaaaaaaaaaaaaaah!' The come of the century, or pretty close.

Adam hoped the gym was soundproofed. He didn't want the others to know his business before . . . well, before he was ready to tell them. 'Oh yes, sweetheart, let it out, let it go.' His own prick was painfully hard, but he'd learned how to wait: he'd had to. Learned how to take care of everyone else's needs.

He squatted down at her face level as her orgasmic flush subsided; Leanne's feathery fringe was damp with perspiration. 'Can't come by fucking a doll, huh?' he taunted.

79

She half-smiled, head to one side, eyes half-closed, feline. 'Okay, so you were right!' she admitted.

'And you were wrong. What happens now?'

'I . . .'

She still couldn't say it. *Wouldn't* say it. He'd make her say anything in time. 'You bend over the gym horse and take the paddle on your squirming bare bum until you're much less assumptive.' Whistling softly, he started to untie the bonds that held her to the punishment board.

Five

Take the paddle on your bare bum! The words sent a rush of shame through her face, a weight of hot wet tremors to her groin. She was glad that he wasn't looking at her, glad that he was removing the ropes which held her in place. He untied her second wrist. She flexed them both, lifted her body with difficulty from the wooden board, from the rubber doll with its still-hard protuberance. As he freed her ankles, she got awkwardly on to her knees. She pulled her pants up and her skirt down.

'I wouldn't bother, my dear. I'm going to paddle you on the bare. I want you to strip completely,' he ordered.

She felt her blush intensify. 'Take off my blouse? My bra?' Part of her wanted him to undress her slowly, hands sliding over each curve of smooth warm skin, renewing arousal. But she wouldn't just do as he ordered without a fight.

'You've *no* chance!' She looked up, eyes and mouth challengingly wide, then winced as more threads of wetness signalled the recent satiation between her legs, her doll-based thrusting.

'That spanking obviously wasn't enough to teach you humility,' Adam said. Leanne shivered, and put her arms round her knees, cradling them. 'That spanking' had taught her to sit more firmly on her skirt-clad rear in an effort to keep his smacking hands at bay!

'Let's get that bottom in place.' Still whistling, Adam walked over to the cupboard and took out two large thick coils of leather strap. Glancing quickly, she noticed each had a buckle at its end. What was he going to . . .? Her body stilled into uncertainty. Don't show him he's winning. Don't show him you're nervous. Don't show him you care.

'I . . . have to get back to work.' She addressed his suited back as he approached the exercise mount.

'I'll have my wager first as promised. A professional businesswoman keeps her promises.' Was he never lost for words?

'But if you tie me down over that gym horse, you could do anything!' She moved her hands almost instinctively to her recently spanked rear.

'Exactly. That's what turns you on.'

He was so bloody sure of himself. 'You wish!'

'I *know*. I'm simply waiting for you to acknowledge it. Not necessarily to me, but at least to yourself.'

'And what will happen then?'

'A lot will happen.'

'Yeah – you'll take over this place like the original despot and have me typing your letters for the rest of my life!'

She watched his cheekbones tense, lips hard as he finished fastening the straps to the front and back of the exercise appendage. Had she hit home then? Or was it her misrepresentation of the future that had enraged him so?

'One bottom required.'

She pushed her weigh down against the ground. 'Then you'll have to lift it!'

She placed her palms behind her and leaned back as he walked leisurely forward, eyes focusing on hers as he closed in.

'I weigh more than you think!'

'I'll cope.' If only he'd stop coping. If only he'd treat her with courtesy and respect.

And yet . . . Her lower belly thrilled as he ladled one arm under her knees, and used the other arm to firmly hold her lower back *in situ*. He straightened. She curved, and felt herself moving smoothly upwards. Seconds later, she was being carried towards the padded horse.

'Bastard!' She used her shod feet and ankles to kick the air, and lost even that freedom as he dumped her on the leather frame, her toes against the wooden side, arms trailing, her belly against its broad long back.

Even as she found her balance and started to rise, she felt the scrape of a strap around her waist 'What are you . . .?' His movements becoming self-evident – he was buckling the band round the gym horse then across her middle, to hold her in place.

'Now we want these lovely legs apart,' he declared. She swallowed as he bound smaller bonds round her slender ankles. He tugged on one, forcing the limb to go where he wanted it to be. Then he did the same to the other leg, till she felt her thighs being spread-eagled to the maximum, her sex hugely exposed. She twisted her head round in time to see him fastening her feet to the side-based rings.

'Wonder if this is what they mean by saddle-sore?' Adam said.

She looked to the front, then closed her eyes at his words, feeling him lift up her skirt then place it further up her back, before tearing off her crotch-soaked panties.

'Lift your shoulders up, sweetheart. We agreed that bra and top weren't staying on.'

'Fuck you! We agreed nothing!' As he moved round to face her, she muttered the words, strength increasingly fixed on the heavy languid hope of her pubic purse. She knew she needed to come.

'You *do* have a short-term memory.'

'Only when it comes to silly games!'

'Oh, I think this is real enough. I think this is very, very real.' He took hold of a handful of her hair, forcing her head to move upwards. She cast her eyelids down, refusing to acknowledge he was there. 'It's more than a game to your tender extremities, when you're tied here waiting to take the paddle on your bared backside.'

Another surge of lust. She shut her eyes.

'God, you're relentless.'

She kept them closed as he moved his free hand to her front. Felt him caress her through the satin top, sensed strong fingers against small buttons. Whimpered as the smooth material was peeled away.

83

'Won't you take off your bra yourself?'

'That'll be the day!' She looked down at the gossamer white cups with their scalloped lace edging.

'I can see your nipples straining through their casing.'

'Congratulations! You don't need an eyesight test then.'

'So be it.'

She swatted at his arm as he pushed quickly at the strap, felt the sheer soft cups give, freeing her bosom.

'In the future you'll ask me nicely to unveil these breasts, to kiss, to suck them,' he said threateningly. She swallowed. Her curves felt lost now, as if they wanted to be held and lightly squeezed and stroked, sure thumbs brushing the centres. Instead, they brushed against the cool dark leather of the gym horse.

'Now we put this second strap under your arms and buckle it up here.' Voice ordinary and light, he brought the binding up over her upper back, then tightened and secured it. 'There, now isn't that a picture! We have a pretty girl stripped to the waist, with her panties torn off and her skirt tucked all the way up.'

'I hate you!'

'For making you realise you get excited by this?' Her mind searched hollowly for further jibes or witty rejoinders. She stiffened as he walked towards the end of the exercise horse. 'Oh angel, I don't think you hate me. According to this swamped small bud you actually like me quite a lot.'

'Mmh!' She felt the half-grunt escape low in her throat as he briefly slid a finger or a tongue over her defenceless clitoris.

'Don't make a sound without permission.'

'Or what?' She was damned if she'd blindly obey, to make things easy for the man. She was mistress of her own destiny.

'Or I'll have to introduce you to that paddle for a lot longer than I intended to, to teach you control.'

She'd show him control. She'd clamp her teeth together tight. She'd take a vow of silence, stay soundless for ever. Leanne gasped despite herself as the terrible thrilling

84

sensation swept over her again. What was he teasing her labia with? It was the lightest touch, and brought the strongest sensations; brought more swollen, pressing, pulsing liquid need.

'Each sound equals one stroke of the paddle. I hope for your sake that you're not noisy!'

Keep quiet, she begged herself, her mouth pursed, fingers clenching.

'I plan to tease that soaking sex bud for a long time. Pity for you I've tied those pretty thighs so far apart!' he continued.

He'd thought of everything. She could think of nothing. Except ... He cruelly caressed the source of her passion, and she moaned.

'One warming with the paddle. I'm being merciful, not counting those earlier gasps.'

'Huh! Give yourself a medal!' She was determined to thwart him – then he rendered her helpless by playing with her disarmed clit. If only she could free her wrists or ankles, close her legs a few inches, push a hand back. If only she could escape from just one treacherous touch.

'Mm! Mmm!'

He was circling round and round. 'Three strokes.'

She wouldn't cry out again. She just wouldn't! He finger-brushed across the tip. 'Uh, uh, uh!' she yelped quietly.

'Six strokes. Fancy that – such disobedience! I'm going to lay them on now, you're being *so* ill-behaved.'

Footsteps receding. The cupboard door creaking open, then closing. Footsteps returning. Her entire focus suddenly centred on her naked defenceless rear end. He could thrash her for moments or hours, till she begged for forgiveness. He could take her bottom from its current creamy coolness to the hottest, sorest red.

'One good paddling for a bad posterior.' She felt the swish of the air around her face, sensed he was brandishing the implement in front of her. 'Look at it, Leanne. Picture how it's going to feel on your backside.' Beyond arguing, she opened her eyes, stared at the eighteen-inch-long instrument, with its broad plywood striking surface. It was a glossy varnished tan colour, and looked unused.

'An unworn paddle for a previously unpaddled bum.'

Please, she thought, her caressed clit begging for further attention, please.

'Gone all quiet on me? I'd have thought you'd be saying the sweetest things by now if you wanted to come.'

'I do want to come!'

'Then kiss the paddle and ask nicely to taste it six times,' he demanded. Beyond fighting, she put her lips to the high-gloss wood, and pressed slackly. 'And the words, dear,' he insisted. Leanne put her face down and mutely shook her head.

She sensed him move to her arse – her vulnerable arse; felt him stroke both tethered waiting buttocks. 'Are you frightened, sweetheart? You should be. This is going to sting. I'm told it throbs for a squirmingly long time. Very fetching, though – it creates a uniformly red effect with no bruising. Just like you're wearing the hottest scarlet pants.'

Get it over with! Never start! Her clit was begging: come, come, come. She tried to squirm in her bonds, found it impossible to move her craving nub against the leather.

'Save your wriggling till you've really got something to writhe about,' Adam said. He palmed her cheeks twice more. 'Pity for you that last spanking's totally subsided. This'll tan your arse more, as we're effectively starting from cold.'

She didn't feel cold! There were feverish pulsings in her groin. The tops of her breasts were torrid, tingling. Her belly was a tremulous twitch of wordless longing. Her legs
. . .

'Aaah!' She cried out as a palm-sized pain spread over one cheek. He must have used the paddle. She moaned more quietly as the oval wood warmed her other buttock. She was ready for him this time.

Don't cry out. 'You're coming on nicely, darling. Just the right shade of pink so early on in your thrashing.'

'So early on? But I've only got four more to go!'

'I know, but they're on top of their predecessors. The colour's exquisitely cumulative.' She heard his footsteps move round to her head, felt fingers in her hair forcing her to tilt her face up towards his. 'Were they sore, Leanne? If you were to show repentance, persuade me to be lenient . . .'

'Just get it over with!'

'Your wish is my command.' That even, slightly dry tone. Did nothing rile the man, did he never falter? Never feel fear or failure or uncertainty or doubt?

'I might try this on Khan,' she said, in her most taunting screw-you voice. 'His boyish bum roasts very nicely. He . . .' Leanne yelled as Adam used the paddle for the third time.

Hard wood on already-warmed soft skin. Painfulness over pinkness. She tensed, knowing the fourth paddling would follow swiftly; she had recognised during the spanking that he liked making her buttocks a uniform shade. She felt a small surge of power followed by a spreading heat: he was winning for now, but she could still beat him. With her intuition and thoughtfulness, she'd manage to understand him one day, to second-guess him and outdo him. Yet he'd never have the insight to fully know *her*.

'Two to go.' Hands in her hair again, he said, 'Won't you even beg a little bit? I think you must enjoy this thrashing.' Looking not at him but through him: need to come, need to come, need to come! 'Another two strokes, then, before we see to that little sex bud and its petals.' That little sex bud felt pulsing, pleading – huge!

Stroke five felt harder than the others as it heated her across the fullest swell of the tethered right buttock. Stroke six scorched its tender twin. She moaned quietly into the horse, then waited. Please, please, please! The words in her head, in her groin, in her belly. Aware that she would prostrate herself before him if he'd only let her come.

Something rubbed against her clit. She twitched. 'Oh, yes!'

'That's my cock, Leanne, I'd like you to beg for it inside you.'

She wanted . . . wanted him in her, up her to the hilt.

Voice hollow with wanting, deep yet thin, Leanne said, 'If you untie me, I'll spread my legs . . .'

87

'They're already spread, sweetheart; tied very far apart for fullest access.'

'I know, but . . .' Surely he wasn't going to make love to her whilst she was held captive in this way? 'If you let me go, I can use my hands, my mouth.' Be his equal, try the new tricks she'd only read about in this past celibate eighteen months or so.

'Later, perhaps. You're more than ready for now.' She held her breath as she felt his fingers part her labia.

'Adam, I want . . . but not like this.' She needed to hold him in her arms, to feel his weight on her, to grasp his buttocks and caress his hair, his skin.

'If I free you, you're to do exactly as I say,' he ordered.

She nodded into the horse. She'd do whatever her clitoris wanted. Her sex crevice ached for contact, for release. 'All right,' she agreed. Straps pulled slightly tighter as he pulled the pins free of the pinholes then released the tension. She flexed her arms and legs, suddenly unsure if they'd support her.

He seemed to understand. 'Let's get you down.' He slapped lightly at her forearms till she straightened them and moved back on to her knees. 'Sit sideways. Legs down. There, I've got you!'

She breathed in his faint cedar and citrus scent, felt herself being helped from the horse, carried across the gym, then out of it. 'Where are we going?' she asked weakly, aware of her total nakedness. 'What if someone sees?'

'I'm taking you to the former staffroom. They have this wide five-seater settee. There's champagne in the fridge there for after.' Had he planned to do this with her, or with Candy? He slid his hand more firmly under her thighs as he carried her up a stairway, and Leanne realised she no longer cared about the lovers that had gone before, or the staff who might observe them now. For the time being, she would only heed her sex – and it was silently pleading for satiation.

'Almost there,' murmured Adam, as if realising. Conceited pig! But an incredibly attractive pig with a toned lean body and knowing fingers – a man whom she could tell was going to be good in bed.

Or great. He nudged a door with his foot, carried her into a square-shaped room that would easily seat twenty. For a second, she gazed at her own naked breasts, her exposed flat belly in the oval ebony-framed mirror, then he was lowering her down, down, down towards a cushiony expanse. Her buttocks and back met the soft covering of the settee, and she relaxed into its firm but plush wide contours. She watched as Adam removed his jacket and tie before lying down beside her, propping himself up on his side to her left.

'Arch your head back.' She did, and he traced a path from behind her ear down her entire neck. *Jesus!* He seemed to have touched some secret pathway. She moaned loud and long at the vibrant tide of desire. 'Like that?' he asked. She nodded. He smiled knowingly: 'Arch again.'

'I need it in me. Please!' She tried to lift her hips, then winced as they scraped against the cushions.

'Got a sore bottom, angel? If you'd been nicer earlier . . .'

'I'm being nice now!'

'Because you want to come.'

'Don't *you*?'

'I might consider it.' She reached a hand towards his zip, but he grabbed her by the wrist and pulled her exploratory fingers away.

'I told you in the gym to do exactly as I said!'

'S . . . sorry.' She'd better not enrage him, or he'd hold out on her pleading pubis. She couldn't bear any more deprivation just yet.

'Arch again.'

She did. Another sexual surge. 'Oh Adam, *please*! I've got to . . .' She scissored open her legs.

'Put your thumb and forefinger on your right nipple. Now do the same with the left one. Oh, sweetheart, I can see that they're sensitive! Now palpate them ever so lightly till I tell you to stop.'

Leanne licked her lips, but did as he said, moved her thighs even further apart, feeling his hardness against her belly. She felt almost as helpless as she had when she was tied up in the gym. His weight was holding her down, her arms were otherwise engaged. Somehow she had to ... 'Please, put it in me. I'll do anything! Just put it in me now!'

'Ram it up you, you mean? Fuck you hard and fast and thickly? Shaft you till you've come on your back and on your belly? Come standing up, and on your hands and knees?'

'Yes!'

'I might be tired after our press-ups in the gym.'

'But I can feel you!' She chafed against his thick promise.

'I might be hard and ready because I'm thinking of someone else.'

'I ... beg. Need ...' She heard his zip go down, pushed her groin desperately upwards. Then felt something nosing at her entrance. Any second now ... He slid all the way in. She cried out; his entry was exquisite. She took her fingers from her breasts and stroked his shirted back. 'Did I *say* you could do that?'

'Sorry! Take your ... will you let me take your shirt off?' She so wanted that blissful tingling sensation of skin on skin.

'You'll feel my hand on your backside for this later.'

'As often as you want,' she lied, starting on his top buttons. He began to thrust with long slow strokes and she groaned, and lost the place.

'If you will insist on diversions.' He stopped pleasuring her to unfasten his own shirt. She lifted her lower belly and thighs, mutely pleading for more friction, for freedom from such an ongoing internal ache.

Looking down at her with what she hoped was a tender rather than a faintly amused expression, he began to move in and out of her stripped sex-soaked body. In turn, she nuzzled her nose and lips into the hirsute dark pelt of his chest. Licked both nipples, stroked the front pectoral warmth before returning her palms to his back. She could feel each set of muscles moving at will, as he found the angle that made her breath quicken, her inner voice squealing: Oh, just like that. Oh, yes!

She slid her hands quickly down to his arse, and gripped it through his summer suit trousers: two high muscular ovals. Her brain dimly sought access to the warm bare flesh, her fingers tracing the restrictive band of his belt.

'Is that what you want, Leanne?' Thrusting, thrusting, thrusting, 'Do you need to feel my belt on your buttocks?'

'I . . . no!'

'Want that thick leather to take up where the paddle left off, teaching you some manners? Making you dance a jig to its endlessly corrective lash?'

'Want to touch you!'

'Thought you said I was a bastard? A pig? Seems you aren't choosy. Seems you'll take anyone and everyone up that greedy wet hole. I mean, you and that boy-wonder Khan . . .'

Brain fogged with need, with lust, she exclaimed, 'We haven't . . .'

'Maybe I should withdraw and let *him* fuck you instead?'

'Just . . .' Hands on his trousered arse, she pulled him in. Sex-chute throbbing, cheeks flushed, mouth a pleading stiffening grimace, her hips lifted from the settee.

'I could punish you with my penis, Leanne. Keep you ever so sweetly on the edge.'

'Being good. *Anything!*' Her carnal canal was yearning, rousting. Rigour tightened each pleading muscle in her thighs.

'*How* good?'

'Taking you deep inside my throat . . .'

'Wearing a slave collar?' Leanne nodded, arching her back to take his cock deeper inside her sex chute. 'What else would you do?' he demanded.

Whatever you want, she thought. Only thrust, thrust, thrust! He was circling his hips now, cock stirring her crevice, keeping her close to coming. Think of images that will please him, make him shaft you till you come!

'You could turn the studded collar to the inside.'

'Pull it nice and tight?'

'Yes. Please, anything!'

'Clip it to a short dog lead, perhaps?'

He pushed in deliciously deeper at the words. Encouraged, she let the picture grow three-dimensional in her head. 'Dog lead, yes – make me trot around on it.'

'I'd take you for walkies.'

'In the public park so everyone could see . . .'

Immersed in her more fully now, bucking harder, her thrill-led belly rose up to meet his.

'Tether you in the dining-room, perhaps?' he suggested.

She half-sobbed with lust. 'I'd beg for scraps, for a bone!'

'Eat your food from a bowl?'

'From the ground where you'd thrown it!'

'Lick Eleanor's fingers, and Candy's, after they'd finished their meal?'

'I'd let them pat my head. I'd give a paw. I'd crawl on my belly . . .' He pushed in and out, then in again and she gave five little peaking cries, then came and came.

'It'll be nice to have a dog.' He thrust on and on. Leanne put one hand behind his head, curved the other round his waist, each cell satiated. 'Of course, I'll have to take you to training classes, teach you to fetch my paper every day,' he continued.

She gripped his hair as she felt his movements speed up, her body and brain urging him towards what she hoped was his best ever orgasm.

'And if you're ever a bad dog, I'll make you fetch your lead and bring it to me in your mouth.' He was thrusting harder, ever faster. 'Can you imagine it, Leanne, approaching me on all fours, knowing what you're in for, knowing I'm about to take that thin strip of leather to these disobedient young flanks?'

'I'd roll over with my paws in the air,' she whispered, wanting to please him. 'Then I'd crouch on my hands and knees to take my whipping long and hard.'

'How hard?'

'As hard as . . .' As she murmured her subjugation, his arms and legs went rigid and he muttered her name. She gazed up at his face, his eyes closing fast, mouth opening as if in pain, cheekbones tensing. Then he shuddered several times and relaxed against her breast.

We're incredible together, she thought. She smiled at the realisation, and stroked his head. Talk about chemistry! She wanted to lie in his arms like this until it was time for them to make love all over again. Caressing and kissing were easier than knowing what to say, how to say it, and when.

What endearments did you murmur to a man who'd been your virtual enemy up till now, a man you'd called names and clashed with every other day since your arrival? How did you act with that same person when they'd just spanked you and paddled you, then given you the orgasm of your life?

'Time for that champagne!' Adam suggested, kissing her lightly on the nose, then levering himself backwards. Leanne realised she'd have liked to hold him for longer, to watch him sleep. Now she watched as he zipped himself up, felt glad when he left his shirt off. He looked more approachable – even more desirable – that way.

She settled back against the cushions as he opened the mini-fridge and removed the bottle of Moët et Chandon. 'Have you being saving this for a special occasion, then, Adam?'

'For our first lovemaking. Yes.'

Leanne squinted suspiciously at his back. Was he being facetious? Trying to disarm her further at this most vulnerable time?

Relax. Enjoy. Mamie had always been urging Leanne to do just that: to live a little. To put workday matters aside. 'I'll drink to that!' She tried to keep her voice light, but not excited. 'Here's to pleasure,' she said.

'To pleasure.' Adam brought over the opened bottle and two wide clear glasses, and half-filled them with the sparkling liquid. 'Here's to the future,' he said. To *our* future, Leanne thought hopefully, fingering the delicate stem. If they could really become long-term lovers, life would be perfect here! Every inch of her body felt relaxed, completely satisfied. Her thoughts were happy, if half-formed, her mind – for once – lazily unclear.

Adam sat beside her lengthways on the settee: its seats

93

were so wide that both he and she could stretch their legs out.

'I told you this room would be perfect!'

'Have you . . . *been* here before?' She didn't like to think of him shafting someone else – not now, not ever. Being made love to like that had changed everything.

'Mmm? No. I just have a well-trained eye!' And a well-trained hand and a well-trained cock and . . . She shivered with a new surge of desire as she remembered. 'Are you warm enough, Leanne? I could fetch a blanket, if you like.'

'No, I'm fine.' She kissed his bare upper arm. She wanted him to stay, to hold her. Wanted to sleep in his arms.

Old-fashioned, but honest. That's what Mamie had always said. Would she be pleased to see them like this, together? Had she secretly wanted them to meet, to bond? 'Do you think Mamie wanted this when she left us the school?' Leanne mused out loud.

'I know she did! Why she even told me . . .'

'Mr Howard! You've got to come outside!' Eleanor's voice seemed to pierce through the staffroom door. 'Blast that woman! She's spent the whole day interrupting us!' Adam said irritatedly. He stared coldly at the locked oak entrance. 'Report to my study at eight this evening, Miss Peterson. Now go away!'

'But it's the horses – someone's let them escape! Gerard can't find them. He's scared the unbroken ones will cause chaos if they reach the village streets.'

'Sounds serious – I'd better go.' Adam looked at Leanne, then got quickly to his feet, his gaze distracted and restless.

Leanne reached for one of the teacher's cloaks. 'I'll come, too – I'm good with animals. I'll just dash up to my rooms and get changed.' She talked on as he buttoned his shirt. 'I'll take the Morgan to the stables. See you in ten minutes, OK?

Adam smiled as he gripped her upper arms and looked down. 'I'll make this up to you.'

'You'd better!'

He kissed her quickly on the lips.

A cool shower, then she put on a one-piece brushed-cotton leisure suit with matching tie belt in lightest taupe. The warm breeze was already drying her curves of hair as she pulled on her beige walking shoes. Still savouring the calmness that followed climax, she took the stairs to the staff garages, and liberated her scarlet Morgan for the first time since she'd arrived at Lingering Lessons.

Leanne smiled as she patted the long wide bonnet. There had been a lengthy waiting-list of buyers, but Mamie had outbid them all to buy her favourite cousin the classic car, hand-built by craftsmen. Maybe she'd take Adam into the village in her chariot one day. She edged the vehicle out into the schoolyard, then turned it towards the road that would take her closest to the stables and riding grounds.

She parked at the perimeter fence and got out of the car, walked, then ran, across the fields as she saw the others desperately spreading out across the grassland. Gerard was ticking off names on a ledger. Adam was holding a pacing, pawing white mare by the reins and gently talking her down.

'There, there my beauty.' Leanne heard Adam's voice, then Eleanor's feet. She turned from one sound to the other, to see the housekeeper squelching through the mud in her ankle boots as she raced round, breathing heavily, after two foals. A brown-haired denim-clad girl of around eighteen was leaning against the fence, toeing the sawdust. 'And don't think you'll get to keep your pants on, either!' Gerard said.

Leanne looked from one to the other. 'One of your village customers,' Adam explained, jerking his head towards the culprit. 'She sneaked back after the official lesson and opened all the doors, trying to find the horse she liked best so she could have a free ride.'

'I've said I'm sorry,' muttered the girl, casting a sideways look at them.

'You *will* be when I've time to get those jeans off,' Gerard said.

Leanne lowered her voice so that Adam alone could

hear, and winked up at him. 'I came as fast as I could, Mr Howard!'

'Right. There are eight steeds still out there. They heard some thunder and lightning about an hour ago, and they all shot through.'

They'd created some lightning of their own! Leanne put a hand on his arm. 'Surely they'll calm down if they're left to their own devices?'

'If they reach the glasshouses or the rockery . . .' Or any youngsters in the village, she realised. A horse out of control was a destructive, even deadly, force. This tore Leanne's attention away from Adam's flesh. 'Give me descriptions, names. I've got the phone in the car; I'll drive round, get back to you.' Will make you proud.

Strange shadows and television-based sounds: for hour upon hour she drove and stopped and phoned in and went on the lookout again. Led Azure, the blue-black roan to the village green and tethered him there till Paul raced down with the horsebox and took him safely home. Saw Misty and Running-Ragged in the distance and was able to tell a Land-Rover-based Adam where they were.

It grew dark. Her phone buzzed. 'Come home and get some sleep, Leanne,' Adam told her.

'Is that an order?'

'A strong suggestion! I know you won't obey me without tasting the whip.'

Desire thrilled to her groin. She shivered. 'Imagining you've got the upper hand again, dear? Hate to disappoint you, but I was already on my way.' There! Just because she'd come loud and long on his cock didn't mean he could control her. They were great in bed together – but he could forget about the whip.

'I'll go to my rooms,' she murmured into the receiver. 'No – go to mine. I'll join you eventually, when the horses are conquered.' Leanne looked at her watch: that didn't leave much time. 'Let's have breakfast in bed around midday!'

She heard him swear softly. 'Damn! Didn't I tell you? I won't be there.'

'Oh yeah?' She kept her voice casual, controlled. One night of passion hardly gave her claim to his every move and decision.

'I'm leaving at five in the morning to drive to the train station. That service'll take me to the airport, where I'm flying to London on business for a week.'

Take me too, she wanted to say. That was the trouble with new lovers – you wanted to taste them and touch them constantly, wanted them inside you for hour after hour. Wanted to slide down on their cocks as they lay in the playing-fields, wanted them to shaft you to satiation as you bent over their desk. 'Right. Have fun!' Leanne answered.

'I'm just there to arrange two advertising deals.'

'*I* must get down to some serious work of my own.'

Unfriendly words. A flat pitch. This wasn't what she wanted! They should be curled up together, caressing each other. They should . . . 'I'll tell Eleanor to leave my rooms unlocked,' he continued. 'Have a shower, some food, then get into my bed, Leanne. I'll be there as quickly as I can.'

Wet dreams. A weightless yet warm quilt. When she woke up in the morning he was gone, the faint citrus scent on the pillow a testimony to his brief presence. Had he held her as she slumbered? Surely he'd left a note?

No wake-up kiss. No loving scrawled words. Feeling slightly low, Leanne left the sanctuary of Adam's four-poster, and ran herself a bath in his quarters. Used his bergamot shower gel to refresh each over-exercised and sexually sated inch of her skin. How far had she walked last night, called the horses' names, thinking of Adam? All that after the spanking she'd experienced beforehand!

Not that she'd let him do that again – it had been so humiliating. Surely she could have pleasure without feeling that horrid hard paddle against her rear end? She could have a hot crotch without his hand heating her hindquarters. She could orgasm without being forced to push down on that dick-based doll.

Half-happy and half-unsure, Leanne wandered through

the corridors of Lingering Lessons, suddenly seeing its full sex-based potential. She and Adam could make out in those mirrored changing rooms. And what of those two large cloakrooms with their many hooks? Why, if he were to tie her wrists above her head and tease her legs apart and insert a vibrating dildo . . . She forced back the rest of the crotch-craving thought. No, she was a businesswoman – not some silly schoolgirl. When he returned from London, they'd enjoy desire without discipline.

Six

Her lover was in London, her libido was on hold – but her career was cresting. Three days after Adam left on his business trip, Leanne perched on his desk in the headmaster's study with Khan. 'Are you warm enough?' she asked the youth. Though it was summer, there was a sharp edge to the breeze wafting its way through the open windows. She looked at her favourite male model's dark bare legs.

Khan nodded. He looked good in shorts, which was just as well, for he was modelling the 'Eternal Adolescent' look. The baggy bermudas were topped by an equally loose T-shirt and matching khaki cap. Large sneakers hung, untied, from his feet as he swung them backwards and forwards. An apple sat on the desk beside him – his only prop.

'The team said they'd be here at midday!' She looked at her watch. It was almost one o'clock.

Khan laughed. 'Photographers! Probably gazing at the bottom of a pint glass in the pub. You know what they're *like*, Leanne.'

'Usually – but that fashion journalist, Sylvie, is supposed to be with them. She's totally professional. She'd have rung if their schedule changed suddenly.'

She stilled as Khan edged slightly closer. 'I can take your mind off their lateness,' he murmured in his most beguiling voice.

Leanne looked away, staring out at the glass, at the fields beyond, at her territory. Her's and Adam's. She felt the same way about her body now as well. 'It's a great offer, Khan, but . . .' But only Adam had ever made her body beg to come in such an intense and addictive way.

'You mean I'm on the shelf?' Khan sounded amused rather than upset.

'I'm sure the village girls would love to take you down and dust you daily!'

'But would they tie me over a desk and take their belt to me?' Khan queried, eyes searching hers.

'You can but ask!' Leanne looked at the walls, newly denuded of caning photos. She'd taken them down for the fashion shoot, for her own well-being. She didn't want to think about punishment – at least not until Adam came back.

'Think I'll go and see Gerard about the "Silk Looks on Steeds" shots. I told him the other day to assemble the most patient horses,' she announced.

'Ones that don't bite!' Khan called after her. 'Given that I'll be posing with the beasts for half an hour at least!'

Then a half-hour in the swimming pool for the 'Bathing Boy' set, and the same again in the wooded copse for the 'Playtime' shots. She'd spent several hours choosing the ideal locations, finding the right time of day for the most natural lighting, and ordering props.

'All set?' she asked, marching up to the stables, to Gerard. She'd left the Morgan in the garage as her limbs craved the arm-swinging briskness of a walk. She'd spent a busy few days preparing this ten-page preppy-style spread – and had a long afternoon of overseeing to get through yet. 'Just wanted to make sure our equine extras haven't done a runner again!' she joked.

'No – though that one wishes she could!' Smiling grimly, Gerard jerked his head back towards an unoccupied horse-box. The village girl who'd previously set the horses free had her arms handcuffed to a beam above her head. Her stretched immobile body was kitted out in a brown cord jacket, checked pink blouse and tan-coloured riding trews. The pull on her arms looked minimal and her legs were untethered; yet, as Leanne stared, she let out a shudder and a groan.

'Why is she . . .?' she started to whisper.

'Her pussy's had too much pleasure!' He walked slowly

over to the girl, and began to unbutton her jodhpurs. 'Come here and see.'

Averting her eyes from those of the flushed-cheeked female, Leanne watched him unzip and strip her of her trousers and jade-green panties. She stared as the soft white tummy and auburn pubic patch were revealed. Below it – with straps emanating from both sides and fastened round the girl's loins – was a small vibrating heart. 'It's a clitoral exciter,' Gerard said, smoothing the girl's wet fringe back from her forehead. 'Makes her come and come and come.'

Wonderful. Awful. 'When will you decide if . . . I mean, don't you think she's had enough?'

'It was this or a thrashing.'

'I've changed my mind,' gasped the girl, 'I'll take the birch, instead!'

'It's gone up to twelve strokes now, with you being so belated.'

Closing her eyes, she whispered, 'Christ, no.'

'Oh dear. The word "no" makes my hands start to feel very underoccupied. And you know what happens when my fingers feel restless? They put that clitoral switch on a more powerful speed.'

'God, don't!' the girl muttered, licking her lips. Leanne stared at the straw as the familiar prickling started up in her Mount of Venus. She looked back again despite herself to see Gerard's right hand fiddling with the erotic tormentor, which immediately began to emit a low vibrating buzz. 'Mr Kerne – no more! I can't bear it!' The eighteen year old pulled fruitlessly at the metal cuffs which held her wrists above her head.

'You had the choice – write a cheque for the damage, take the birch or the clitoral exciter,' Gerard said, turning away from the wriggling female. 'I'll be back in five minutes to hear what you've got to say for yourself.'

'Sir, don't! I'll take the birch on my bum! I'll ask nicely for the twelve strokes. I'll beg!'

'Want to hear her beg, Leanne?'

'I've work to do. I'll take a rain check.' Legs stiff yet

weak, Leanne followed him outside. She mustn't show that she was affected by the scene, or else Gerard would play on her weakness. She must concentrate on the modelling task in hand!

'Right, so everything's shipshape for the shoot?'

'Except her tender young charms!'

'You'll untie her when you hear our vehicles approaching.'

'Is that right? Or what will you do to me, Leanne?'

Good question! She searched for a witty rejoinder, but failed. 'Just wait and see.' The man was trying to unnerve her again. He was just like Adam. But Adam had a gentler side; had untied her before they made love, asked her if she wanted a blanket, called out her name as he climaxed, then held her tight. She kept her voice businesslike, but not abrupt: Gerard would make a daunting enemy. 'Sorry the photographer's held us up. I should be back with the team within the hour,' she said firmly.

As she approached the headmaster's study, she heard male and female voices. Good, she thought, Sylvie must be here. They could begin at last! '. . . Such pretty breasts.' She stopped – that was Khan's voice. Khan and Sylvie? She stepped closer to the half-open door.

'Don't you want me to suck them?'

'If that's what you want.' It was *Candy*'s voice!

'But is that what *you* want?' Khan murmured beseechingly, then sighed. Silence. Maybe the girl had shrugged. Maybe she'd just looked at the floor, waiting for him to unbutton her bodice. Wanting him to undo her bra strap. Hoping that he'd unzip her dress and pull down her pants. Khan had got it all wrong for once, asking this totally biddable girl to take the lead in their lovemaking. Candy needed to be told exactly what to do!

Leanne walked in and immediately gave Adam's PA her orders. 'Right Candy – see you in the swimming pool in an hour in your costume! Khan's to be photographed there. You can appear in some of the background shots.'

'Swimsuit or bikini, Miss?' Candy moved away from the male model.

Leanne thought fast. The photos were to emphasise *menswear*, so they didn't want to see too much of Candy's soft young flesh. 'A one-piece, in a dark colour, please.'

'Flip-flops or . . .?'

'No, you'll be in the water.' Khan would be out of it, posing by the springboard, the poolside tables, the water flumes.

At least he *would* be if the photographer, journalist and make-up artist put in an appearance! Candy went off to prepare, and Leanne paced up and down, looking at her watch, at the grandfather clock, at the changing patterns of afternoon sunshine. 'We might as well have lunch, Khan,' she said eventually, and phoned Eleanor, who brought up caraway-breaded honeyroast-ham sandwiches and Earl Grey tea.

Eat, drink and be miserable. By two-thirty, Leanne had had enough. Trying to keep her breathing even, she phoned the editorial number. She had to keep from sounding angry, be professional at all times. Why, a traffic tailback could have delayed the fashion team; they might even have taken the wrong countryside road, or had an accident.

'Pinner Publications.'

'*Trend* magazine, please. Editorial.' She smiled over at Khan.

'Hello? This is Leanne Dell of Mainly Men. We were expecting your team for a fashion spread around midday.'

'But you cancelled.' She listened to the surprised voice, its hesitant reply.

'No, I didn't! We've prepared all the locations, been expecting you . . .' Working for days, waiting for hours.

'Well, *someone* phoned to say you'd been flooded in a summer storm, that you'd get back to us.'

'It's been dry for weeks here!' This was useless – they were getting nowhere by trading weather reports.

Leanne tried again. 'Is Sylvie there, please?'

She was. They put her on.

'Did you take the call, Sylvie?'

'No. It came in after hours. You left it on the answering machine.'

'But I didn't – that's the point!'

There was a pause, then, 'Must be someone *pretending* to be you.'

Who'd . . .? For a moment she thought of Adam, but they were friends now, and much, much more: lust-crazed lovers.

'I don't suppose you kept the tape?'

'Sure. We keep them for a year in case there's any litigation.'

'And could you . . .?'

'Give me twenty mins, okay? I'll have to clear it with upstairs.' She phoned back after only ten minutes. 'Listening? Here we go.' Then a woman's voice – *Candy's voice* – cancelling the team's visit with her sugary lies. Why on earth . . .?

'I know who the culprit is,' Leanne told the journalist softly, her heart speeding. 'I'll deal with her now. Thanks, Sylvie.'

Deal with her buttocks, and any other soft exposed flesh that got in the way! Khan following fast behind, Leanne marched towards the indoor swimming pool, her right hand itching to roast the younger girl's interfering rear end. That was the beauty of this place – corporal punishment was permissible. She could exact a calculatedly rigorous revenge. How *dare* Candy ruin days of work, weeks of ideas! How dare she imagine she'd get away with such crass sabotage!

In a navy-blue swimsuit, almost black from being wet, Candy was crossing the pool in a long slow crawl when Leanne entered. She could see the deep cleft of the girl's bosom as she put her head to one side, eyes closed against the water's splash.

'You – get out of there now!' She exulted inwardly as the girl flinched, floundered for a second, then made for the shallow end and stood up, peering over at Leanne uncertainly. 'Come here!' she added, pointing at the tiled floor in front of her, glaring constantly.

'Please, Miss, what have I . . .?'

'Speak only when you're spoken to! Did you phone *Trend* magazine pretending to be me?'

The girl walked closer, bare feet dragging. 'Y-e-s.'

'Bend over that lowest springboard.' Leanne pointed at the long wide board, several feet of which was waist high above the tiled flooring. It was a board for children to jump from. Now it was a board for warming a female arse.

'You don't understand! I . . .'

'Silence! You're already due a bare-bum thrashing for your obstructiveness. Now I'll have to spank you over your costume first for answering back.'

Candy licked her lips, then looked up at the school's co-owner with pleading eyes. 'But my costume's wet. It'll sting so much that way!'

'It's meant to.'

'And . . .' Her gaze flickered over Khan.

'Seems you weren't nice to him earlier. He'll enjoy seeing your rump turn red. Maybe he'll help me hold you down if you get too wriggly. You aren't going to get too wriggly, are you, Candy?' asked Leanne, with great authority.

'N . . . no.'

'Good girl.' She looked at Khan. 'Take her wrists and lead her over to the board. Bend her over its side.' Khan looked from the older woman to the younger, eyes wide. '*Do* it, Khan – now! She's lost you masses of publicity.'

The youth's lips tautened. 'You're right.' He flexed his fingers. 'Want me to give her a slap or two after I've watched how you do it?'

'Only once my own palm's worn out. We have the whole afternoon ahead of us.'

Candy swallowed audibly. Smiling, Khan approached her, and grasped her forearms. Leanne watched as the male model led the unresisting girl towards her fate. Maybe Khan had seen more of Adam's work than she'd realised. He pulled the PA effortlessly over the side of the springboard till her tummy scraped against its surface, exerting a slight tautening effect on her calves and thighs.

'Keep hold of her wrists to show her she's not going anywhere.' Leanne wanted Candy to fully realise her helplessness. 'Pity that photography team aren't coming after all.' She stepped up to the girl's tense buttocks and palmed them through the wet costume, now warmed with the girl's body heat. 'Do you know how silly you look?'

'Yes, Miss Dell.'

'Know just how *hard* I'm going to spank you?'

Candy's thighs flexed, and she moved her toes. 'Very hard, Miss Dell. But I can explain, Miss Dell.'

'I'll be doling out the explanations to your sorry backside!' She stroked the waiting globes some more. 'I'll explain why I'm thrashing you, what I'm thrashing you with, how long it'll last for. I'll explain just how long you'll have to wait until you're able to sit down again on this reddened rear end.'

'Miss, I could . . .'

'There's a lot you can do with your greedy tongue and your hungry hole – I've seen you in action. But you'll save that pretty mouth for begging for mercy today.'

Leanne teased the girl's helpless swimsuited cheeks. 'Problem is, I'm not feeling merciful. And each time I think about your act of sabotage, my hand gets more and more mad.' She stroked from lower back to thigh, then up again. 'And though I may start off with my palm, my fingers may soon itch to hold a stronger chastiser. Maybe a Victorian rod or a studded strap.'

Candy shivered. 'Not the rod, Miss. That whistling sound before it strikes, the searing . . .'

'And the weals it leaves behind. Mmm. I've seen photos. Seen photos of bigger girls than you reduced to tears.'

She teased the taut flesh for the last time. 'But what am I prattling on about, when this bottom's just waiting for punishment?' Leanne met Khan's eyes for a second, his pupils wide with agitated lust. Khan might not be hugely into this, but he still wanted to see more of Candy's bottom – reddened or not – than he'd seen to date!

'Hold her firmly, now. This'll hurt more because her costume's wet.' She treated the small pert bum to a hard flat slap, then quickly followed it up with a spank to the neighbouring roundness. Leanne repeated the spanks again and again and again.

'Mm! Uh!' Candy made little breathless sounds as each blow hit home, then tensed her bum cheeks and thighs until the next one struck. Leanne drew her arm back and whacked the girl's rotund buttocks all over again.

'This is just for answering back. You'll get your real just deserts in a moment.'

'What will you . . .?'

'What do you *think* I should do?'

The PA hesitated. 'The paddle?'

'No, you've been too naughty for the paddle.'

'Or the hairbrush?'

'I've already seen you take the hairbrush on your wicked little rear.' She paused. 'Long term, they can almost feel quite nice, quite glowing. But with this act of piracy, all you deserve is pain.'

She caught Khan's quizzical gaze. It was a moment before she realised she'd virtually admitted knowing what a paddling felt like. Angry at herself and her disclosures, she aimed an especially telling slap at the girl's bent-over bum. 'No, it'll have to be the rod. I have no option. You've been so very, very dishonest and corrupt.'

She looked at Khan. 'Let go of her wrists.' She tapped Candy on the bottom. 'Stand up. Face me. Make eye contact,' she ordered, then stared into the girl's fevered face. 'Now go and fetch the thickest Victorian rod you can find and bring it straight back here and place it in my palm.'

She watched as Candy turned awkwardly towards the poolside doors. Khan touched Leanne's arm. 'Want me to follow?'

'No. She's biddable. She'll be back.'

'And if she isn't?'

'Then, my sweet, you can go to her quarters and fetch her, teach her obedience. Eleanor has a master key to every room in the school.'

'I just want to be inside her,' Khan muttered, the head of his hardness visible above the elastic of his shorts.

Leanne smiled. 'If you want to get her aroused, you have to deal with the outside.'

'You mean spank her?'

'And more. I've seen Ad . . . seen other people warming her arse, seen the way she gets wet.'

'I feel strange about hitting someone,' muttered Khan.

'It's not really hitting – not an uncontrolled, violent rage. It's more subtle, more sensual,' she assured him. Christ, she'd soon sound like Adam if she carried on like this!

'Whatever,' Khan said.

'We're going to make her little bum sorry as hell.' Leanne's belly tightened with rage at the thought. 'What she did was reprehensible.'

'I know. Who'd have thought it? Such a sweet girl, so cheerful and cute.' He followed Leanne across the tiles. 'Why do you think she did it?'

'Maybe she sees me as a threat to the future of the school.' Or as a threat to her relationship with Adam, she wondered. She wasn't sure which motive unnerved her most. She'd thought that if she was nice to people she wouldn't make enemies. She'd tried so hard to get the bosses, the models, the clients on her side. But it was the weak of mind and imagination and ego who tried to usurp you, who wanted you to fall to *their* depths.

Leanne stopped by one of the cream-coloured canvas recliners and lowered herself down, pushing the refreshment tables on either side away from her: now she'd created enough space for the girl to fit easily across her knee. She was going to taunt and flog Adam's PA till she was totally humiliated. She was going to make sure Candy never committed such an act of piracy again.

There were doors opening and closing; a slight cough. 'Get your arse over here,' Leanne said, without looking up. She saw the girl's shadow approach her. 'Right down, over my knee. Come on. Don't take all day!' she ordered, patting her fawn-trousered lap; she felt the recliner dip slightly as the girl's weight settled on her, fingers clutched round the thick inflexible rod Leanne had requested.

'Khan – take the stick from her hands so I can get her swimsuit off. There, angel, you know you don't get to keep this on whilst you taste the cane.' She tugged at a strap of the still-damp cotton.

Candy trembled, and straightened her forearms, pushing up in order to twist her head back. 'Miss Dell – please!'

'You should have thought of the consequences before you made the call.'

'I didn't . . .'

'Silence! The only sound I want to hear is this rod hitting your backside.'

The girl's voice went low. 'Sometimes with the cane, I can't bear it.'

'You *have* to bear it.'

'Even when I'm warned not to, I can't help but make little sounds.'

'For the sake of your arse, you'd better learn. I'm laying on two more for each squeak I hear from you.' Candy half-sighed, half-whimpered, and let her head flop towards the ground.

'Now, we push the second strap down this wicked arm and slide the costume all the way off to expose the disobedient little bottom.' Enjoying the girl's shamed wriggling, Leanne took her time.

Pushing the navy cotton from the hard-nippled breasts, down the slender back, over the spanked pink buttocks, Leanne left the swimsuit bunched just below the girl's paler thighs. 'Feel how it accentuates that pretty bum? Gives me a clearer target.' She looked over at Khan, who was standing a few yards away, looking awkward. 'Hand me the rod,' she said firmly.

The youth did as he was told.

'Now tie her arms behind her back with the ribbons from her hair.' She smiled to herself as the youth complied: tying the girl's arms in front of her would have been kinder and more comfortable. But today Leanne wasn't feeling kind!

'Like this?' Khan asked.

'Mmm, double knots. We can cut her free later, or just keep her tethered longer if she misbehaves.'

Candy shuddered. Leanne had seen that excited scared look before. She slid her middle finger between the girl's labia. As she'd suspected, she was soaking. 'You needn't think you'll get any relief from this,' she warned, as the PA rubbed greedily against her hand.

'No, Miss Dell.'

'What *will* you get?'

'A hot sore bottom.'

'Mm, very sore indeed.'

She touched the pinkened flesh, which was hotter than normal temperature because of the earlier spanks. 'Khan – squat by her head. See what a bad girl's face looks like as she takes her medicine.' Khan did so.

Leanne rolled the rod teasingly down the small backside. Candy quivered from shoulder to waist, toes moving rootlessly against the tiles, her ankles flexing. Her whole being seemed concentrated on her waiting twin bottom cheeks. That concentration would intensify when the rod lashed down.

Leanne drew back her arm. 'How many letters are there in "sabotage"?'

Silence whilst the girl counted. 'Eight, Miss Dell.'

'Then you shall have eight full-force strokes.'

Khan's eyes widened. Leanne suspected that Candy's eyes shut. She brought the rod down on the restless flesh, watched its immediate pink impact and jerking aftermath. She laid on a second further down the helpless buttocks, causing the girl to flinch and buck again.

'Six of the best to go, my sweet.' She drew the middle finger of her right hand along the sore ridged lines. 'I think I'll give the next two over the original ones; I so like a punished bottom to be a nice deep crimson shade. Now, ask nicely for the others.' Thrilled with power as Candy mutely shook her head, Leanne continued.

'Such a wilful girl!' She applied the third stroke higher up, at the fullest point of the swell, then aimed the fourth where the buttocks curved in to the thigh's tender crease.

'Uh! Ah!' Candy bucked at each lash, but her tied wrists and Leanne's firm hand ensured she wasn't going anywhere.

The thigh-based caning had hurt the most. Leanne had seen it in the girl's driven-forward move, heard it in the grunt that she emanated, her subsequent writhing. Loins tingling, Leanne warmed the sensitive area a fifth time, then a sixth. 'Please!' Candy squealed.

' "Please" what?'

'Please – no more strokes of the cane. I'll do *anything*.'

The words everyone said if promised punishment and pleasure enough.

'Fetch Paul,' Leanne said to Khan.

'The gardener?' Khan looked surprised.

'Mmm. He'll be most appreciative. Just think, Candy. Paul's about to see your well-disciplined backside.'

The girl swallowed. 'God no, don't! He goes into the village for a pint sometimes. He'll tell the others. They'll point, they'll laugh at me.'

'Of *course* they'll laugh. That's what this is about. Any more resistance from you and I'll bring a coachload of villagers to *watch* you take your thrashing. I'm sure Gerard would be glad to help. He always keeps a riding crop handy for recalcitrant bums.'

There was a momentary silence whilst the PA considered her options. 'All right! I'll do what Paul wants,' Candy said.

'No – you'll do what *I* want,' Leanne assured her. She traced the sensitive red lines on the bare pink flesh. 'Does it hurt, angel?'

'You know it does! You know!'

'I think your pride'll hurt even more in a moment,' she said, hearing two sets of footsteps approaching the pool.

'Found him outside the window!' Khan grinned.

Paul rubbed one boot against the next. 'I was trimming the shrubbery, Miss. It shoots up in summer.'

'And is that all that's shooting up, Paul?' Leanne stared insinuatingly at the boy's dungarees.

'I . . .' Paul looked from Candy's bared bum to Leanne's watchful face, then back again, and blushed hugely. He opened his hands in a half-finished shrug.

'Come here.' The boy took a step nearer Leanne's beckoning hand. 'As you can see, Candy's been a bad girl who's earned herself a well-warmed bottom. She has two

111

strokes to go.' The boy's eyes were fixed on the shamed protuberances. 'I've told her that if she pleases you sufficiently I won't lay on the last two lashes so hard.'

'She never looks at me. She doesn't like me,' Paul muttered. Leanne smiled to herself. Candy was speak-mainly-when-spoken-to material, and rarely said an unsolicited word.

'Doesn't she say "good morning"?' she asked, feigning surprise.

'Uh uh. Just rushes past, like I'm not good enough. Ignores me at dinner every night, and at breakfast. I mean, I do my job!'

'Of course you do – and you put in long hours,' Leanne said, stroking the even more frantically wriggling female bum beneath her palms, then playing with its lower lips, then depriving them. 'And it's about time you were rewarded. What would you like to do to this wicked girl?'

The boy licked his lips. 'You mean ... What *do* you mean?'

'Maybe you'd like her to suck you? Like to slip deep inside her pussy? Rub yourself between her tits?'

'I ...' Paul's mouth was by now a permanent gape.

'You can suggest anything. You've earned it.'

'I'd like to ...' He wrung his hands together. '... Penetrate her rear end.'

'Ram it up her arse? You'd like that, too, wouldn't you, Candy?' Leanne said, caressing the writhing rump. She held the rod before the girl's eyes.

'Yes, Miss! Want his cock up me hard, tight up my anus!'

'Right, Paul. Do you want her over another of the recliners?'

'I'd like her outside.'

The youth seemed more certain now, the slightly open mouth closing into a firm line, his hands unclenching.

'Stand up. Follow your Master of the moment,' Leanne ordered. She smiled coolly as the girl pushed her body awkwardly backwards, her tied hands and bunched thigh-based costume making movement slow. Candy went back on to her knees, then rose shakily into place. Her brow was damp, her cheeks hectic. She gazed at the ground. 'Off you go! I'll be out in a moment with my rod,' Leanne continued.

Candy looked at the cane, then quickly turned towards Paul, who marched through the doors, Candy hurrying to keep up with him.

Khan looked at Leanne. 'Will I follow; see he doesn't thrust too fast or too hard?'

'Give Paul a moment so that he sees he can control Candy without our presence. He needs to believe in himself.'

They waited. Three minutes ticked by. 'Right!' Leanne ran the rod through her fingers. 'Let's finish teaching that bad girl how to behave.'

'I think you're enjoying this!'

'Not as much as I would have enjoyed having ten pages in *Trend* magazine.' Remembering the prestige and pounds she'd lost through the girl's maliciousness, she let her hands tighten on the Victorian staff.

A low stone wall, a bent-over bum. They reached the gardens to find that Paul had already positioned Candy just as he wanted her, had removed her costume and thrown it on the lawn. 'Can I . . .?' he asked hesitantly, fingers hovering just above his zip.

'You can, but let's make it slightly easier first,' Leanne announced, as she walked over to the just-caned bottom and slapped both Candy's cheeks. 'You. Get up. Go into the school and trot to Mr Howard's rooms – the door's wedged open. Get a bottle of massage oil and a pair of ultrathin surgical gloves from the headmaster's desk.' She watched as the now-naked girl rose up from the wall, then untied her wrists for her. 'Heat the oil on the hob till it's very warm, but not so hot you can't touch it. Then bring it back here in a pretty bowl.'

'Yes, Miss Dell.' Candy gave something that would have passed as a curtsey if she had been wearing a skirt – had been wearing anything. All three of them turned to watch her nude body as she hurried shakily towards the school's main doors.

'Quite an arse!' Khan said to Paul. 'Christ, you're lucky.'

'You're telling me!' the gardener said.

Leanne smiled at him. 'Her position and what you're doing will be humiliation enough. I don't want you to hurt her further. You'll take your time edging in. You'll widen her gently. If necessary, you'll just slide up a little of the way.' She paused. 'But tell her that she looks like a cow, that she's pathetic. That she's lucky you're deigning to feed her your cock at all.'

The boy nodded, swallowed. 'She's so beautiful . . .'

'She's bad inside. She spoiled my project.'

'And you used that rod on her?'

'Spanked her, as well!'

'Won't she tell someone?'

'No. She likes it, deep down. See how wet she is? Touch her pussy lips when she gets back – she's hot as hell.'

Not that it would do her any good today – Leanne had no intention of allowing the little bitch to climax. See how *she* liked it, left hanging around to no avail for hours! 'Can I come inside her?' Paul said.

Leanne unzipped the ever-moving sweating boy, then rolled on a condom. 'Providing you wear that, you can.' She was making things easy for the youth, who was obviously inexperienced. She wanted him to have uncomplicated carnal fun.

Leanne looked at Khan. 'You might like to use these ribbons to tie her hands in front this time. They'll keep her stable.' God knows, they'd need *something* to stop her wriggling all over the place when that hot oil hit the mark!

'Here she comes,' said Paul, right hand holding his sheathed prick, the left one cupping his testes. Leanne looked at Khan, who was also hardening. Candy's small breasts stood firm and fondle-tempting as she walked.

'Hand me the oil.' If Leanne rubbed it in, the younger woman's humiliation would be complete. She'd be vanquished. 'Let's get you back over that wall; bottom up.' Eyes downcast, Candy walked towards the stone enclosure, and hestitated.

'Think yourself lucky I'm going to lubricate you first. Or do you want it in dry?'

'No, Miss Dell! I'll take the oil, Miss Dell.' Quickly, Candy bent at the waist.

Now she was reduced to a pair of waiting buttocks – which was just how Leanne liked her. 'I hope you'll hold your arsehole open for Master Paul if that's what he wants.'

'Y-e-s.' The girl half-rose up, started to put her hands back towards her opening.

'Not now! Keep your palms flat on the earth. That's it. Khan – pop over there and bind her wrists.'

Leanne smiled as the boy tethered the PA's wrists in front of her, noting how Candy's thighs tautened with excitement. 'Fetch a small pillow and put it under her belly, Khan. Otherwise she's going to push her clit against the wall until she comes.'

Khan complied. As he took the means for a solo orgasm away from the curly haired brunette, she whimpered with frustration. Leanne felt triumph and power expand in her chest.

'Right, Candy, let's get that arsehole warmed up.' Slipping on the surgical gloves, she slowly approached the girl's naked posterior. 'Oh Candy, this'll stir you up a treat.' She dipped her middle finger in the warm and lightly rose-scented oil, stopped behind the puckered opening, then set the bowl of oil on the ground. 'Ready, angel?'

Candy's shoulders stiffened in reply.

'I'll take that as a yes, then, shall I?' She moved her longest digit towards Candy's tensing bottom hole, pushed it in easily, all the way. 'Oh sweetheart, you've lots of room in here. I think you've welcomed several cocks already.' Leanne eased in a second digit, then held both of them firmly in place.

'Miss Dell, I need to . . .'

'Need Paul up you. Yes, I know. Stop talking now, or I'll have to lay on the rod again. Remember to please the boy or you'll feel my cane extra-hard.' She moved her oiled warm fingers slightly apart inside the girl then held them open, getting her ready for the head of Paul's shaft.

'All right – shove it right up her, till she feels it in her throat!' To Paul, she whispered for him to go in slow and to be careful. 'Make her beg pretty for every inch of it,' she added loudly.

Paul looked as if he might already have come inside his rubber hood. His body was trembling, eyes taking in the girl's slightly open and very well-oiled bottom entrance. 'She's ready for you, Paul. Go on. Remember how uppity she's been.'

Erection against anus. Black sheath nosing pink mouth. As Leanne and Khan watched, Paul pushed his slender hips forward, and a little of his cock disappeared inside Candy's arsehole.

'Uh!' The girl gave a surprised small grunt. The boy's shoulders unhunched an inch. He pushed in a second time. His straining shaft stayed in place.

'Circle your hips round – slowly. Now edge forward,' Leanne guided him. Watching, Leanne knew instinctively what to do. 'Now glide your hands round, caress the sides of her tits. That's it.' If the girl was aroused, she'd feel the onslaught less. Her shame was suffering enough – that and the caning. Plus the words that she was going to deliver when the punishment reached its end . . .

'Mm! Mm!' Paul groaned. He was buried halfway up the girl now, his buttocks tensing forward. 'Uh! Uh! Aaaaaaaaaah!' Unleashing one of the loudest male orgasms Leanne had ever heard, he came. Each muscle letting go of its strength, he slumped over the girl's slender back and stayed there for a moment until his shaft slipped out and lay, shrinking in its sheath, against his leg.

'Do you want to see her take the last two strokes?' Leanne asked. Pulling up his dungarees, Paul nodded. Then you can take the rest of the afternoon off.'

'Thanks, Miss Dell.' Paul looked as if he worshipped her. He was a nice young man, a hard-working young man. God knows, he deserved someone to love or at least some-one to assuage his lust.

'Candy. Bottom over my knee again. Now!' she com-manded. Khan helped the younger girl to rise, put a hand on her elbow to steer her over to the wooden garden chair

Leanne was sitting on. The PA's face was as red as her unfortunate rear. 'Looks like that little derrière's got a suntan. In a moment it's going to get tanned by my cane!' Leanne taunted. She fondled the heated cheeks. 'How many did we say you had to go, again?'

'Two, Miss Dell.'

'Pity. I'd have liked to lay on more. Of course, if you moan too loudly or wriggle too much, or otherwise displease me . . .'

'I won't Miss Dell. I'll be good!'

'Khan and Paul will be witness to that. Think of it – two grown men seeing you take your thrashing!' In answer, the girl hung her head closer to the grassy ground.

'Paul – hand me the rod.' She took the wooden staff from the boy's nerveless hand. 'Would you say she pushed her arse back to take you in, or was she wilful?'

'She made things awkward,' Paul said, licking his lips, his eyes fixed on the cane.

'Did she now? You bad, bad girl.'

'I didn't mean to.'

'It's not what we *mean* that counts. It's what we *do*.'

'I could suck him off instead! I could take his balls in my mouth! I could . . .' Candy rubbed herself against Leanne's pubis. To her chagrin, the girl shuddered and came.

'Oh dear. Oh dear, oh dear. What did I say?'

'That I wasn't to have relief,' Candy whispered.

'And what did you just do, you dirty girl?'

'I . . . I came.'

'And what happens to girls who disobey?'

'They . . . Oh please!'

'What happens?'

'They feel the cane.'

'Mmm, they certainly do.' Leanne tapped the end of the rod against the girl's expectant bum. 'The two you're due will probably be enough, so I'll just lay them on with especial severity.' Concentrating on the loss of professional standing that the girl's betrayal had brought her, she whacked the cane down low, and Candy squealed, 'Oh, that really . . .!' She flexed her bound wrists, obviously wishing she could bring her hands back to protect herself.

'It's sore, isn't it angel? And you've another equally painful one to go,' Leanne reminded her.

'I could lick your clitoris, Miss Dell . . .' Leanne felt a surge of lust at the girl's words, but she wouldn't be tempted. She had to separate punishment and pleasure. She was chastising this girl because it was warranted – not for her own sexual end. Not that she wasn't turned on: her mound felt heated, heavy. But that was merely the one good spin-off of this whole sorry affair.

'Don't be disgusting. Do I have to wallop your lewdness out of you as well?' Candy trembled on her lap, reddened arse waiting. Keen to get back to her rooms, to caress her own clit to climax, Leanne doled out the last stinging stroke. Looking at the helpless hot posterior across her knees, she could understand why Adam wanted to do this. She wanted to tease and taunt and slap.

But she had more reason than most! 'Stand up. Face me. What have you to say for yourself?'

'I'm sorry I phoned *Trend*, Miss Dell.'

'Sorry you lost me thousands?'

'Yes.'

'Abject that you lost Khan important work and tarnished my reputation?'

'I . . . didn't know.'

What *did* the girl know? That she and Adam were now lovers, presumably. That Candy's place in his heart and bed had been usurped by Leanne. She cleared her throat, wishing there was another way. 'Candy, I have no option but to fire you, and ask you to leave Lingering Lessons. I want you to vacate the school by the end of the week.'

'But Adam's my . . .'

'I've spoken to him,' Leanne lied, wishing he'd left a contact number she could use to reach him. 'And he agrees your behaviour is unconscionable, that you're no longer his PA.'

'If you'd let me explain what . . .'

Leanne was in charge here – she had to prove it! 'Go to your rooms. I've heard enough of your lies.'

She watched as Candy stumbled away, quietly weeping.

The girl had deserved that spanking, that rectum-based shaming. Surely Adam would be pleased?

Seven

A dressage whip, a multi-speed pleasurer, and a braided cat: the gifts in their padded boxes inside his briefcase, Adam let himself into Lingering Lessons and began to climb the many stairs to his rooms. Had it really only been a week since he'd left his beloved school, its fresh green acres? He'd expected Leanne to phone him at least once.

He'd called *her*, but Eleanor had explained she was out-doors with Khan and Candy. Hopefully it was work rather than play. He didn't want to think of her and the youth – her and anyone, in fact. He wanted to use the silk ribbons he'd brought home to spread-eagle her fast to his four-poster bed. Then he'd nuzzle each nipple ever so gently till she arched her back and whimpered without permission. He'd lightly whip her inner thighs till she pleaded with him to enter her, to thrust until she came.

Sleep. A shower. Refreshed by both, he phoned Eleanor and had her bring up two buttered croissants and a glass of Chablis.

'It's brunch, really. I had an early breakfast on the train!'

'Shall I tell the others you're back?'

'No need.' An hour from now he planned to be with Leanne, pushed deep up her fillable furrow – pinning her wrists, berating her buttocks, satisfying her sex.

Food. Wine. Now they'd make their music. Groin tightening in anticipation, Adam walked smartly to the former headmistress's rooms. She must be there or in the grounds, for she was notable by her absence in reception. Any moment now he'd pull her into his arms.

He knocked, waited, then knocked again. Walked to the nearest intercom and buzzed the kitchens. 'Eleanor. Have you seen Miss Dell? I have to discuss the quarterly budget.' Discuss be damned! He listened to the housekeeper talk, and filtered out the trivia. 'On the mountain wall? Ah, I see!'

The people before Mamie had believed that tired boys were trouble-free boys. They'd believed in exercise. As such, they'd turned the huge outdoor bell-tower into a climbing arena, complete with rockface and ropes. The floor was padded, giving the children access to height without horror, to an arduous climb without arctic cold.

Silently Adam let himself into the stretching hall. Leanne was halfway up the nearest face, her small feet and hands finding purchase in the created crevices. A rope round her middle was linked to a pulley. She'd be jerked into mid-air – well away from the rock surface – if she fell.

Sure proud buttocks, lithe limbs: he admired the view even as he wished to strip it of its covering. He could bend her over that step machine and . . .

And she was coming down. When she reached the safety of the floor, still facing the wall, she threw her arms in the air as if in silent victory. 'Leanne Dell conquers the ramparts!' he said.

She spun round, hand on her heart, mouth opening in shock and surprise. 'Oh, you!' She ran lightly over to him and slid her arms round his neck. He breathed in Obsession. 'I was just working off some energy – it's been a frustrating week,' she explained.

'Good!' He brought his lips down on hers.

'I meant work-wise,' she smiled, when he at last pulled away. 'I'd set up this *Trend* ten-pager . . .'

'Forget work for now.'

He moved his hands to the sides of her breasts and caressed them. 'I'm about to give you a spanking, cos you didn't phone.'

Her eyes went down, lips parting, breath quickening. 'I didn't have your number!'

His fingers tightened. She must be playing hard to get again. 'I left a note.'

121

'You must have hidden it well. I thought *I'd* been forgotten!'

'Quite the reverse – I've brought you some gifts.' He reached for his briefcase, brought the springy fibreglass whip out, put it in her right palm and curled her fingers round the handle. 'Looks like I'll have to use it only a few moments from now.' He gazed down at her. 'Can you imagine how this'll feel on your bare bottom?' He kissed her nose.

'You wish!'

He brought the dildo out, running his thumb over the thick round tip as he maintained eye contact. 'It's a new shafting type, Leanne; it expands with your body, inch by pulsing inch.'

He switched it on, and watched as she let go of the whip, fingers moving towards the source of satiation, 'I'm going to put three cushions under your belly, then slide this in.'

She licked her lips, pinkness spreading across her cheeks. 'You'd be making yourself redundant!' she teased.

'Uh uh. I'll hold your hands above your head so that you can't control your pleasure. I'll tie your legs.'

Her bosom moved faster. She swallowed twice. 'You should save these ordeals for Candy. Believe it or not, I've had to give her the sack!'

The sack! He stopped moving, stopped talking – just stared at her. What was she saying? He'd started to think they'd got their priorities right. Candy was part of the plan, knew the pitfalls and the pleasures involved in his long-term project. She understood!

He switched off the dildo, let it fall to the padded floor. 'You don't have the right to . . .'

'When she jeopardises my career, I do.' Leanne tilted her head back, hands going to her hips, then to her sides.

'But she's in *my* employ.'

'She's a traitor under my roof!'

'A traitor?' Now she sounded like some melodramatic actress in a fifties movie: he'd expected more of her. 'She's completely reliable. I've known the girl for years!' He paused, searching for the right words, the right image.

'You only have to raise your voice to Candy and she jumps through hoops.'

'Well, she raised her voice enough to pretend to be me on a magazine's answerphone! She cancelled my project; cost Khan and me thousands of pounds.'

Khan. So that beautiful boy-bimbo was still around. Adam felt his jaw tighten with irritation. The boy's sprained ankle was taking an unconscionable time to heal. 'But what would her motivation be?'

'Jealousy.'

That made no sense: Candy would have all she wanted when Jon returned from overseas. The girl was passive, patient, lived on peace and pleasure-led punishment. 'She's not the type.'

They were inches from each other now. He noticed she'd taken up a legs-braced warring stance. With effort, he relaxed his own hands and arms. 'Didn't you talk to her?'

'A little. She admitted she did it as soon as I asked!'

'But did you find out *why*?'

'She . . . not exactly. Isn't it obvious?' Her mouth pursed into a firm line. 'Khan and I spent days getting things right!'

She was looking beyond him now, words racing out in confusion and fury and hurt. 'The team was due. The locations were set. We waited and waited. She ruined everything, the jilted little bitch!'

'Jilted? You mean Jon's . . .?' He saw the stillness in her face, the realisation. She thought that *he*'d ditched Candy, that that was why the girl had made the call. But their relationship hadn't been like that, it wasn't covetous. Leanne had no right to assume.

The streak of hardness, of destructiveness that lurks in most of the human race, took hold in him. 'What makes you think I've finished with her? I've brought her back a reformative cane and a Lochgelly tawse.'

Her lips parted slightly. 'You mean you'll . . .'

'Take them to her arse? Yes, if it's warranted. But I'll hear the full story first.'

'Fuck you, then!' She turned quickly to go, but he grabbed hold of her arm.

'Oh no, you don't! Let's sort this out right now, before it becomes a bigger issue. Press that amber button. It'll connect you to Candy's rooms.'

'Not for much longer, it won't,' Leanne muttered, pressing the button then holding her finger on it. She sounded brittle and cold as she spoke into the intercom. 'Mr Howard and I want to see you in the climbing tower now.'

He stared at her as she idly played the ascension ropes through her hands, admiring her high curved bottom in the jet-black cycling shorts. She was wearing a matching cropped top that left her lightly tanned midriff tantalisingly bare. He wanted to encircle her waist, to kiss her long and hard, to move his hands down to cup her shapely buttocks, pulling her close until her sex was pressed to his.

Low heels on linoleum. As he searched for a word or deed to plug the chasm between them, a breathless Candy appeared. She'd obviously been washing her hair or showering. Small droplets of water clung to the shoulders of her white lace dress. Her ivory-coloured sandals showed her pink-painted toenails. The morning warmth had already dried the fringe and tendrils round the sides of her makeup-free face.

'I'm glad you're back,' she said shyly. He noticed she didn't look at Leanne – but that wasn't unusual. He pulled over a bench, indicated to the school's co-owner to sit down, then sat down next to her; a stiffly formal team. 'I've come back to dissension.' Taking Candy's hands in his, he pulled her close till she was squatting at his feet.

'Miss Dell tells me you made a phone call pretending to be her.'

'Y-e-s.'

'Why did you do that?' He watched her lashes cover her eyes. Then silence. 'Candy – answer! You know it'll be worse if you disobey.'

'I . . . I can't tell.'

'You mean you won't.' Adam gave a helpless, half-finished shrug. The girl's eyes were beseeching now, but he couldn't show weakness. 'You know what will happen if you enrage your landlord and boss.'

'Yes, Mr Howard.'

He looked over at Leanne, who snorted through her nose and mouth. 'See – she didn't tell you either!'

'I'm sure she will, given time.' Letting go of the agitated girl's hands, he smoothed her hair with his palm, staring down at her. 'Her aching clit will make confession short and sweet.'

He watched as Candy licked her lips, head dipping towards the floor as if it held the answers. This simply wasn't like her. He knew her so well! Knew what made her come – and what made her want to. Now he'd have to put her to a pleasurably painful test, when he'd rather be chastening then cherishing Leanne.

Damn Candy, with her subterfuge! 'We'll have to teach you obedience, sweetheart,' he said. He pressed the buzzer that connected him to Paul's bleeper. A few moments later, the boy's 'Yes, Mr Howard?' drifted down the intercom.

'There's a large board with a circuit box and a phallic-shaped butt plug in the third hall cupboard. Bring it to the climbing tower, please.'

'Not the vibrating . . .?' Candy whispered. He looked at her, surprised, then remembered they'd seen it used in the *College Head Gives Correction* video. The female student in the story had wriggled, begged.

'The very same. It made her awfully good. Do you remember? She apologised so sweetly for playing pranks on the teacher after her bottom was fucked hard.'

'But I've already . . .' Candy looked at Leanne, who shook her head. The younger girl then put her hands over her pants.

There was a timid knock. 'Come in, Paul!' Even at the age of five, Adam had never been as hesitant and awkward as this youth was at twenty. 'Just set it down there, in the middle of the floor.' He watched as the boy lowered the platform, straightened, eyes flickering towards the crouching girl.

'You can go,' Adam said, dismissing the young man. Paul obviously liked to look.

'See you at dinner,' he added, as Paul took a step

backwards. The gardener cast a swift glance at all three of them, nodded, and left. 'A candidate for an assertiveness training class, I feel!' Adam joked.

'Maybe *you* just need one in humility,' Leanne said. Walking to the centre of the board, he ignored her comment. He'd discipline her later. For now he had to find out what his PA's lies were all about.

'Right, angel. The butt plug's ready for you. He watched her move slowly forward, eyes fixed on the flesh-coloured protuberance. Fixed to a broad base on the board, it looked like the first three inches of a stiff thick cock. 'Suck it till it's nice and wet, while I get the ointment to make your bottom slippery.' He felt his shaft jerk into life as she got down on her knees and took the mock penis in her mouth. He wanted a thick lubricant that would sensitise Candy's entire anus. There would be moisturiser, to help assuage rope burns on one of the shelves.

Scanning their contents, Adam located a tub of scentless cold cream. It would soon be warmed and spreadable! He walked back towards the board, aware of the kneeling girl but all the time staring at Leanne. Was she excited or annoyed? One could read either expression in her lightly flushed cheeks, her unwavering eyes, her set mouth and slightly forward closed body language. He pushed her to react.

'Candy – get over Leanne's knee. She's going to make you very greasy.' He took several large strides towards the model-agency owner, and handed her the tub of cream. 'Lubricate her arse-hole. Work the cream in all the way. She's in for a long session.' He tensed for her refusal, then relaxed as she took the vessel and unscrewed the top.

With one last wide-eyed glance at him, the PA went over the older woman's lap. He turned away as Leanne pulled Candy's white lace dress back. If he watched this scene in detail, his cock would grow achingly erect. Forcing his mind back to the punishment he was to inflict, he crouched down by the board, located the circuit box, and put the switch on to its first gentle speed. There were six settings, but he doubted if he'd have to use all of them. Candy creamed too easily. After her second or third orgasm, she'd be ready to tell.

'Come here.' He glanced over as she slid from Leanne's knees, her dress again covering her bottom. The school's co-owner had taken the PA's knickers off, and they lay in an ivory ball at her feet.

'Position yourself over the love plug. It's going deep up your arse to teach you some manners.' He made his voice cold and crude. Inside, he just felt irked, slightly angry. By now he should be inside Leanne! 'That's it,' he encouraged. The girl gasped as the plug slid up all the way. He realised he should check in case she was just pretending to be impaled on it. 'Lift your dress up for a second, angel. Good – nice and tight.'

A beige cock up a pink bum-hole. Candy let her dress float down again as Adam started to bring the straps around her thighs, tightening them to hold her legs fast to the bondage board. He buckled them both, then fetched a slender six-foot pole from the cupboard's climbing props, fed it down the back of her bodice and bound it there. Next, he tied her hands together, and pulled them up before tethering them to the pole high above her head.

Now Candy was merely a sensitive bottom entrance impaled on a butt of pulsing pleasure. 'Think of the girl you saw taking this on video, Candy,' he said softly. 'Remember how her whimpers went on and on?'

'She couldn't bear . . . She begged for mercy.'

'She didn't earn it.'

'She . . . Mr Howard, please! How long?'

'Till you tell us why you lied about Leanne's work, or until I decide you need a red-hot bottom.'

'It's already . . .' Candy gave a peripheral glance at Leanne again.

'I mean with my belt.'

'Want to start pleading yet?' he added mockingly.

Candy's lips settled into a pout. She looked straight ahead, her nipples pushing through the lace – like twin dark bullets. 'As you wish.'

He walked over to Leanne and took a seat. The agency owner snorted. 'I'd do more than shove a plug up her!'

'I'm sure you would.' He studied her face. 'But less is more. You want to *persuade* your victims, not break them. A subtle vibrating intensity soon builds up.'

They sat in silence, listening to the low unwavering hum. Candy's breasts were fattening, elongating. For five whole minutes she sat squirming in her bondage, helplessly impaled on the resonating anal plug. Then Adam watched her entire body tense, and she let out a guttural groan of pleasure. Her fingers tightened in rapture against the pole that held her wrists in place.

'Orgasm one,' he said quietly. 'With the plug centred in her base, it builds to an all-over climax. If I was feeling really ruthless I'd bind little vibrating hearts on her nipples as well.'

'Gerard has ...' Leanne broke off, and wrinkled her nose as if annoyed at herself.

'I'm sure you'll tell me everything later.' He looked at her coolly, appraisingly. 'When I've taken that fibreglass crop to your arse!'

'I'll be talking to my lawyers, if you don't get her out of my life!'

'We'll find out what she has to say, *then* I'll decide her future.'

'I've already decided I don't want her in my school!'

'Or in my bed?'

'I ... fuck who you like! If the best you can do is that little liar ...' Leanne's voice sounded rough and cynical. Did it just show further signs of spirit, or was it proof that she cared?

'Keep watching. She's starting to build again,' Adam said. God, if it was Leanne's butt clamped to that plug, she'd be telling a different story. Her arousal and peak had been so strong the week before, that he'd thought she was going to pass out. And I'd bring you round, and punish you again, then please you, he thought savagely.

He forced his attention back to the matter in hand. Well, to the plug in Candy's bum. It was Candy's arms now straining against their bondage as Leanne looked on. 'You can't escape, baby,' he said reasonably. 'I've got your arms and legs tied in place.'

'Mm. Uh!' Candy obviously didn't want to come again as quickly or as severely. She needed to reach a plateau, then rest.

Punishment through pleasure. Adam watched as her body spasmed into orgasm for a second time, mouth opening like a little animal. Her calves flexed on the ungiving board even as the back of her head moved frantically against the pole. 'Did you like that? Did my sweet little baby like that? Does she want to tell her nasty boss anything before he makes her come again?'

Candy stared mutinously at her lap, her swollen breasts still shuddering. A trickle of saliva ran down her chin.

'More resistance? That's bad. That's very bad.' He moved to the circuit box and put his hand to the second switch. 'I'm going to have to increase the power.'

'Oh don't! I can't stand . . . So hot already . . .'

'Angel, you ain't felt nothing yet.'

He upped the speed limit on the thick creamed plug. The humming noise deepened, quickened. 'More vibrations per second working their way round those anal nerve endings, sweetheart. Exciting your bottom, your labia, working their way to your clit.'

Candy moaned low in her throat. 'She'll submit soon,' he murmured, sitting back beside Leanne who was staring at the action.

'What if she doesn't?'

'She'll feel my belt.'

'I don't know if that'll . . .' Again, Leanne seemed to think better of her words. What was she up to? In his absence, she'd become difficult and querulous again.

She needed to come. He needed to come. This scene should be their foreplay! Instead, the only person climaxing was a damp-browed, open-mouthed Candy, whose writhing torso told its own tremulous tale. By keeping the rush of blood to her crotch at its peak, each orgasm was faster and more powerful than its predecessor. Too much, too soon.

'Oh please! Oh no!' Candy squealed.

He loved those flickering lids, that teeth-clenched tensing

129

mouth before the shrieked abandon. 'Are you excited again, baby? Does the butt plug make you come? If you don't tell all after this I'll put the phallus on a higher speed. I'm told it's almost unbearable. Pleasure that's close to the most exquisite pain.'

'Aaaaaaaaaah!' Candy cried out into the tower, her cries echoing round the rockface and through the rope ladders. The portion of her dress that clung to her crotch was dark with sex-slicked shame. Immediately her shudderings stopped, Adam approached the board and squatted by her shoulder. 'Why did you ruin Leanne's work, Candy?'

'I can't say!'

'So be it.' He flicked the switch up another notch: he wouldn't be bested. He'd teach her humility if he had to stay there for hours more. He sat down beside Leanne again, staring at the erotic action.

'How long will you . . .?' she asked him.

'Till she's completely servile, of course.'

'What if she never admits to anything?'

'Then I'll have fun trying to make her obey.'

He looked at the agency owner's huge dark pupils and parted lips. Damn her, she was excited. If only she'd admit it – then admit that being tied down over the love plug would arouse her too. 'That could be you down there, if you fail to phone me again.'

'Planning to go away every week, are you?' Not if he came back to civil wars like this!

He had a life-plan to undertake, had a limited amount of time in which to set events in motion. Arguments like this were detracting from his energy, his time. 'Last chance, Candy,' he said. 'How hot does your labia have to get? Such a distended dripping clitoris! And that poor stretched bum-hole, just begging for release.'

He watched Candy's obvious inner fight, her eyes searching the room for mental distraction. Saw how she tried to rub her wrists against the pole to create a diverting pain. But her body knew what was happening; knew that each sentient cell was becoming excited, felt the rush of heat to her tingling tender mound.

'I could keep you like this all day, Candy. That plug up your butt, just ruthlessly resonating.'

'Can't . . . Please . . . Need to . . .'

'There are three more speeds to go. On the last speed the cock elongates by half an inch at a time, until it totally fills you, till you can't take any more of it.'

Near-rapture was obviously racing through her clit again. She moved her head restlessly against the wooden staff. 'You're so held open, so filled, so defenceless,' he murmured. 'Don't you want to beg for release?'

'Mh! Uh!' Little sounds came from within Candy; they were beyond control, beyond reason. Each noise and gesture governed by her growing ecstasy; ecstasy that her body didn't quite want yet, had already overdosed on.

'Oh baby, you can't bear it,' Adam whispered softly as she stiffened and came. Her cries were strangely hollow now, something wild and sweat-slicked and frantic, every sensation centred in her crotch.

'Tell,' he said, putting his hands on her shoulders. They shook with exhaustion. 'Just say it, Candy. I won't be angry if you tell the truth.'

'Please have mercy. I can't tell you!' She stared at the board.

He flicked the plug's power off, then stood up abruptly, 'In that case I'm going to tan your arse till you do.'

He walked to the buzzer, then spoke into the intercom. 'Eleanor – sorry to bother you for a second time. Yes, we're still in the mountain tower. Bring me my international directory and my mobile phone.'

'What are you planning?' Leanne murmured. He turned to her, and saw how flushed and watchful she looked.

'I'm going to phone her fiancé abroad.'

Candy's eyes widened. 'Can I speak to him? Please!'

'Only if that's what *he* wants. I don't think you've earned it. In fact, all you've earned yourself so far is a very sore bum.'

Silence. He looked from the woman at his side to the woman at his feet, and wanted them to change places. Wanted to make Leanne ache and plead for his cock. But first he had to sort out the mess he'd found, end the anarchy; return peace and purpose to the many rooms of Lingering Lessons.

Footsteps, then Eleanor's low courteous cough. Adam had been abrupt with the woman when she'd interrupted him and Leanne in the biology lab. He smiled at her appreciatively now.

'Thanks, Eleanor. It's nice to see *someone* in this household knows what they're doing.' He looked tellingly at Candy and Leanne.

'Will there be anything else, sir?'

'No. You can go. See you at dinner.' Going by the current climate, she'd be the only one there.

An African office isn't the easiest place to reach from a Scottish school. After much crackling and several introductions in different languages, Adam got through to Jon. 'It's me. Candy's usurped a project of Leanne's. She needs serious discipline. I wondered which implement would aid her correction the most?'

He stared at his PA as he spoke. He and Jon went back years; they had met when Adam had interviewed the man for a feature on corporal punishment. It was their friendship – their shared tastes, their knowledge of each other – that allowed him to speak like this now.

'The heavy strop, huh? The double-thickness one that's made of leather? I reckon that'll stop her getting up to further tricks.' He indicated to Leanne to untie the girl from the board. 'Candy, go and get it from my cupboard. You know the one – it's got a wooden handle. Fetch it now!' Candy nodded, backing away slowly. 'And for every moment you dally, you'll get an extra lash.'

'Other than that . . .?' He continued his call. 'She's a first-class assistant!' He listened to his friend, then looked meaningfully at Leanne. 'Not as quickly as I'd have liked.' Then he asked Jon a few catch-up questions about his safari expeditions. 'Right, she's back, looking very sorry for herself. Ten from you, you say? Consider them doled out!'

He hung up, smiling, then let the smile go and looked his PA up and down. 'Leanne, tie her wrists above her head to the rope-ladder wall. That's right, so that she's facing the rock surface. No, just leave her feet unbound.' He studied the scene. 'She can keep her dress on for the first ten strokes – they're from her fiancé. Thereafter, pin that skirt up and I'll give her a long hard session on her bare arse.'

Eyelashes flickering downwards, the younger woman walked with small slow steps to the wall. Leanne hurried to overtake her, reached out and grabbed the heavy strop. Candy stared at it, then held her arms up to receive the bindings. He was surprised how quickly Lingering Lessons co-owner bound his trembling PA in place. 'I think you've been practising, sweetheart!' he mocked.

Leanne gave a twitch of her mouth, a half-shrug. 'It was my project she ruined. Want me to give her the first ten?'

'No. That's my job. You can watch, be warned.' When he took the strop from her hand, she stuck her tongue out at him. 'You're building up to a taste of this as well.' He flicked its thickness through the air. She took a hasty step back, then sat on the board, choosing the end away from the anal plug. She was now facing Candy's bottom. Adam turned so that he faced the same way.

'Ten strokes, then you get a chance to confess. If you don't, we lift the skirt of your dress up.' Candy's toes moved against the padded surface. Her buttocks seemed to tense beneath the dress.

'One.' He laid it on from above, following it up with a second from the right side, a third from the left, a fourth coming in underhand with especial severity.

'Aah! Aah!' Candy twisted her bottom from side to side and made a little yelping sound at each stroke. Five. Six. He was going to make her arse the deepest red. He felt stony, focused. She'd lied and cheated, deserved everything she was about to get.

He laid the seventh stroke on high, the eighth one low. The girl was twisting, gasping, groaning now, but her bound wrists ensured she had no means of escape, that each lash hit the target. 'You should have thought of this before you made that phone call, before you refused to tell me the truth.' He doled out the ninth lash and she whimpered. Pitilessly, he added the tenth in the same sensitive place.

He walked up to Candy and took her flushed hot face in both hands. 'This is where it really gets sore, sweetheart. You'd better tell me. Otherwise that pretty dress gets lifted up.'

'I ... can't!' As if the effort of moving fully was too great, Candy shook her head about half an inch each way. She tensed her cheekbones, closed her eyes tightly.

'Leanne – perhaps you'd like to bare this disobedient little lady's bum?'

'Maybe she's had enough.'

He looked at the model-agency owner in surprise. Earlier she'd urged him on to greater punishment, had thought the anal plug wasn't sufficiently severe. 'She'll have had enough when she tells all, when she obeys.'

'Well, we could give her a day or two to reconsider,' Leanne said, looking suddenly intense and watchful.

'One should punish soon after the crime, make clear the connection,' he explained wearily, then lifted up the dress himself.

He stopped, and looked more closely. 'Angel, who did this to you?' Thin red lines had been brought back into sharp relief by the general rush of heat to the girl's buttocks. Overlapped by the thicker marks of the strop, they'd obviously been made by a novice with a cane.

'Leanne did.' For a moment he thought he'd imagined Candy's reply. He looked at the school's co-owner, who was reddening slightly.

'Well, she usurped my project,' Leanne muttered. 'You were away!'

'Fair enough. But why didn't you tell me?'

'You ... um ... didn't ask.'

'Don't be ridiculous!' He wanted to shake her for the evasive way she'd dealt with this. 'You've just watched her being chastised a second time for the same act.'

'She still hasn't told!'

'That's not the point. To hold out on us this long, she

134

obviously has good reason.' He untied the girl's wrists, and took her in his arms. 'All right, Candy, let's get you comfortable again.' He moved back to the bench, holding her on his lap in a sitting-up position. She immediately hid her flushed face in his shoulder, arms round his neck.

'One for the family album,' Leanne muttered.

'What else did you do?'

'I . . . Does it matter? I still don't want her here. She's a menace.'

'Candy? What else did Leanne do to you?'

The younger girl kept her head against his jacket. 'Made Paul sod . . . put it up my arse.'

'Christ, Leanne, that's twice in a week she's been . . . *I* monitor what I do. You've been completely thoughtless!'

'You reckon? I thought about it a lot!'

'She has to know you can be kind. Otherwise, she just gets frightened.' He looked at the school's co-owner steadily.

'Fine by me!'

Leanne was on the defensive again. She needed sorting out. She needed to learn humility. His cock hardened as he thought of a plan. 'What you've done is assault. I mean, Candy and I have our little games, but you merely abused her. You realise there's nothing to stop her from going to the police?'

'Yeah. Right!'

He took his PA by her upper arms and held her out till she looked at him. 'Candy, you heard all that?'

Lashes still covering her eyes, she nodded then whispered, 'Yes.'

'Good.' He picked up the mobile phone. 'The local code plus 356 will get you through to the station. Just tell them what Leanne did, how she coerced you with Paul's help.'

Candy took the unit and stared at it sadly. 'Khan was there too!'

'Three against one?' He stared at Leanne. 'You could go down for that.' She'd go down on him before he was through with her! Or . . . 'Perhaps you'd like to show Candy how truly repentant you are, make amends?'

135

'I don't believe she'll charge me with assault!' Leanne muttered. Adam raised his eyes at Candy, who pressed a number on the phone, then another.

'Even if they believe Candy agreed to take the cane, the police'll still know you get off on thrashing younger women,' he said. He paused and stared at her frozen face, his eyes fixed and watchful. 'They'll know you encouraged Paul to commit buggery on the girl.'

'I . . . All right.' Still sitting on the board, she toed the anal plug with one foot, not really seeing it. 'I'm sorry. Okay?'

'It's a start, but it's not enough.' Adam stroked his PA's silky head. 'Candy fears the lash as much as you. It hurts as much. It makes her cringe and tremble.' He stared at Leanne. 'But she takes it every time because she knows how sweet the aftermath is. The agony then the ecstasy.'

Leanne seemed to be having difficulty knowing what to do with her hands. He watched as she laced her fingers together, then let them drop by her sides, before crossing them over her bosom. 'I'm telling you that the poor mite took the strop ten times with only her dress for protection. I think she deserves a little relief.'

Leanne nodded, as if to herself, then her mouth dropped open. 'You can't expect me to . . .'

'It's that or the police.'

'I've never touched another woman!'

'Until last week you hadn't had your arse paddled either. But you survived.'

'It's not the same thing! I mean, I'm not bisexual.'

'You don't have to be. This isn't for your pleasure. It's for Candy's.' He looked at Leanne's moving breasts and fast-breathing tummy. 'You owe her an exquisite come.'

'How am I supposed to give that?'

'You have a tongue in your head.'

'Me and . . . you must be joking!'

'We're not.'

He, Candy and the police against Leanne. She wouldn't want the world to know she'd caned the younger woman. She was still too caught up in lying to herself and to them about what got her sexually excited and why and when.

'Phone the authorities, Candy. Let the men see the marks on your bottom.'

'For Christ's sake! All right – you've won. I'll do it! Let's get it over with.'

'Don't rush the girl. She likes it to last a long, long time.' He wanted to spend an age just watching, taking in the view of Leanne kneeling and nuzzling on the ground.

'Ready, angel?' He pushed Candy gently from his lap, kept his arms on hers and eased her into a standing position. 'How exactly will we place you? I think you're too tired to keep standing up, and that bum's too sore for you to sit down.'

He buzzed for the gardener, and smiled when he arrived. 'There's a square-shaped pouffe in the staffroom, Paul. If you could bring it to us we'd be most appreciative.'

'If he stays to watch, I'm out of here!' Leanne muttered, as the boy went to fetch the padded square.

'No, we're not being as cruel to you as you were to Candy – it'll just be the three of us.'

'*You* don't have to stay!'

'Sweetheart, don't be naïve. I'm the one who's running the show.'

'No change there, then. Been back a few hours and already you're telling us all what to do!'

'Only because you got it so wrong in my absence.'

'Surprised you didn't leave an instruction sheet.'

'That mightn't have been such a bad idea, my dear.'

Issuing instructions had been his life. As the eldest of six brothers, he'd organised the daily family agenda. Had sent each sibling off to their various sports clubs on time. He'd fixed them up with a space in the house to do their homework. Dad had gone out, Mum had turned on her TV, and he'd taken charge.

Now he'd always take charge. If it wasn't actually in his genes, it permeated his nature. Without his strength, his focus, the eight of them would never have survived. He stared at the two women before him. Now he'd ensure that the nucleus of Lingering Lessons also lived on, became self-financing. And he couldn't do that if his authority and actions were undermined – by Leanne.

He glared at her compelling curves in the cycle shorts and close-cropped top as Paul brought back the pouffe. 'Good man. Now take the platform back to the cupboard. We're finished with it for today.' He hoped Leanne heard the inference, hoped her sphincter tightened with tension. He'd ease that oiled plug up her unused anus yet!

Its multi-speed phallus sticking out like a real one, Paul dragged the board across the mountain tower then eased it from the room. There was a silence. He watched Leanne staring at the padded square the boy had left behind. 'Fetch two large cushions from the cupboard, Leanne, and lay them next to the pouffe.'

'What are . . .?'

'Just do it, then you'll see.'

Back unnaturally straight, arms swinging by her sides, Leanne marched over to the shelves, knelt down at their foot, which was recessed. She came out holding two velour-covered cushions about four feet wide.

'Put one there.' He indicated an area on the padded floor. Leanne obeyed him. 'Candy put your back on it. Leanne put the second cushion under her head.' He watched as the agency owner complied. 'Now, Candy, put your feet on top of the pouffe. That's it, legs spread apart as far as you're able. See how that keeps your poor sore bottom off the ground?'

Leanne was standing at the girl's head, moving her weight from foot to foot. 'Leanne, you should be at her tail!' He ordered, watching the woman's limbs tightening. 'No, Candy, don't move. Leanne crawl in at the side and come up between her legs, then kneel there. Good girl. Now, dip your head forward. Mmm, that's it!'

He dragged his bench closer, bringing it three feet from her face, from his PA's lower lips which were slicked from her earlier orgasms.

Leanne stared at the pink petals, then turned to face him. 'I can't!'

'Think of when you made Rob come with your mouth.'

She stilled into watchfulness as he used her husband's name. 'How did you know about . . .?'

138

'Just concentrate on the question.'

'I . . . felt powerful, I guess.'

'You liked making him tremble, hearing him groan, feeling him expand beneath your tongue, seeing him quiver?'

She remained like a statue for a moment, then she nodded. 'Yes.'

'Teasing Candy's no different. Her clit will grow bigger. She'll whimper for your tongue.' He stroked his right hand down the thick soft waves of her hair five times, six times, seven. 'Trust me. Do as I say.'

'No one will know?' Her eyes flickered round the rock-faced room.

'Candy won't tell. As for Paul and Eleanor, they're busy.'

'And you?'

'Scout's honour.'

'You were *never* in the Scouts?' she laughed. She was right. He'd never needed anyone to organise him, had always been the organiser. He didn't intend to change that now.

He moved her face gently in his hands till it was in line with the other girl's opened thighs. 'Start moving your mouth around the outside of her clitoris,' he demanded.

'Oh Christ, do I really have to do this?' came the high-pitched breathless plea from Leanne.

He pushed her nose closer to Candy's hooded nub, watched her grimace then lower her head the rest of the way, lips moving into a pouting shape. 'There, that wasn't so difficult. But keep it slow.' He felt his shaft twitch as she closed her mouth on the younger girl's mons, then brought the tip of her tongue out again.

'That's better. Do it until I tell you to stop.' Mouth against mound, tracing round and round her clit, arousing each pleasure-led pathway. He stared at Candy, noting the small movements in her cheeks, the sharp breath-based movements of her bosom. 'Now lick just above her clitoris, the way she likes it best,' he told Leanne.

He could see the outlines of Leanne's nipples through the cropped top, the dampening skin above her décolletage. 'Can you feel how close to coming Candy is?' he asked.

139

She gave a half-nod, her tongue continuing to perform its delicate task. The younger girl's breathing quickened, and she whimpered. 'She needs it, Leanne. Just keep tonguing her right there.' Candy's fingers were flexing on the cushions as if trying to extend their length, toes moving to some frantic inner Eden. As Adam stared, she exposed her throat by tipping her head.

'Hold that rhythm, Leanne. Feel her wriggling against your lips. You can keep her there for an hour if you want to.' He remembered the project was to humiliate the school's co-owner. 'But fulfil your ultimate objective. We'll both have to spank you soundly if you fail.' He smiled at them. 'I wonder what else we'll have to do if you can't make Candy come?' Leanne ignored his words, kept tonguing, tonguing, tonguing. 'Have Paul parade you round the garden in a slave collar, perhaps?'

Small light licks above her darkening drenched labia: he saw Leanne's tongue hasten at his threat. 'Candy might have some ideas of her own, don't you think?' He allowed a pause for the idea to sink in. 'We could tie you up, pull down your pants, hand her a judicial birch that's been soaked in water. I think she'd soon get to work.'

'Mmm. Mmm.' The younger girl's thighs were tensing, mons pushing down.

'Keep the place, Leanne, or I'll have to thrash you,' he warned.

Saliva slicked sensation.

'Ah! Ah! Ah!' Candy cried out.

'She's going. Hold it sweetheart. Keep the rhythm. Lick! Lick hard!'

Candy's lower torso pushed against Leanne's face, her thighs against the other woman's hair. A momentary tensing quiet, then, 'Aaaaaaaaaaaaaaaaah!'

'Tongue till the contractions ease.' He could see he didn't really have to say the words; Leanne was intent on lapping out the last of the girl's rapture. Was she enjoying the control aspect or just determined to get it over with?

'All right, take your head away. You've made amends.' He had to remind her that the act had been to put her in her place, to teach her to be humble. Leanne sat slowly back on her heels and wiped her mouth. 'Thank Candy nicely for letting you lick her pussy,' Adam told her.

'I . . . Oh fuck off!'

'*Say it*. Otherwise she may show the villagers what you did.' He smiled as the image built. 'You might have a queue of bad boys from the village ringing your doorbell wanting their bare bums warmed.'

'But I thought . . .'

'That we wouldn't tell the police if you licked? We won't, as promised. But there are other people in the vicinity who'd love to know who put these cane marks on Candy's arse.'

'You bastard!'

He stared at her steadily. 'Say it.'

Eyes fixed on the floor, Leanne mumbled, 'Thanks, Candy, for . . . for letting me lick out your pussy.' The younger girl was slumped back against the cushions in a post-orgasmic state.

He wanted to come. He wanted the mouth that had just pleasured a pussy to please his prick. 'Did that excite you, Leanne?'

'Yeah, sure.' Rolling her eyes upwards to underline her sarcastic grating tone, she continued, 'I've converted to Sappho!'

'Didn't you heat up just a little bit?'

He pushed Candy's legs gently from the pouffe, took hold of Leanne, and started to edge down her cycling shorts.

'What the hell are you doing?'

'Just checking for wetness.'

'But she's . . .' Leanne started, eyes darting Candy's way.

'She can watch you writhing under my fingers.'

'You wish!'

Leanne put her hands on his chest. 'Get her out of here, then we'll . . .'

'I want her to stay.' He was testing her. How badly did she want to preserve a little dignity? Would she trade it for the climax of her life?

'I'm going to shaft you till you've come three times,' he whispered, guiding her right hand to his prick, which was thick and ready.

Leanne looked wildly at the prone but wakeful Candy. 'Give it to your little bimbo instead!'

'Is that what you want?'

He had a feeling they'd been here before.

'I don't care!'

'So be it. Candy, lie on your tummy over the cushions, sweetheart. Lift up your dress.'

'You mean you'll . . .?'

'Fuck her? I thought you just told me to.'

He watched Leanne scrabble backwards. 'Go on, then!' she said.

'Sure you won't stay to watch?' He stared at each departing curve as she marched across the room. God, he wanted her! His balls, his cock, his very essence ached.

The door slammed shut. He'd pushed her too far, too soon, taken her beyond her current limit. If he'd just carried her from the room after she'd licked the other girl's clit . . .

'Mr Howard?' His assistant's voice brought him back. She was lying on her tummy. He looked at her scourged sore buttocks, her slicked dark sex.

He wanted to be inside Leanne! To shaft this other woman felt like a betrayal. Yet his prick was pulsing its urgent requirement for release. 'Turn over on your back, love. That's it. Unbutton your dress. Now hold those pretty breasts together.' He groaned quietly as he unzipped his shaft, and slid it between her tits.

He thrust up and down, pretending he was inside Leanne's wet core, her pulse of pleasure, ramming in and upwards, filling every inch. He'd hold her legs above her head, watching his cock disappear inside her, seeing the shame and pleasure vying for supremacy in her pouting mouth.

He stared down at Candy, who gazed at his cock in her cleavage. He knew that she was willing him to reach his rapture, a reward for the times he'd made her come.

Veined dark phallic flesh in light-tanned tit flesh. He moved faster; hard against soft.

He'd have to punish Leanne for leaving the room, have to strip off her cycling shorts. Would double one of the ropes and use it to lash the sensitive twin orbs of her naked posterior. He'd fasten her lengthways over the bench, put a pillow beneath her tummy, take both buttocks from pink to deepest crimson, make her squeal. Oh God, said the inner voice in his head, his balls. Oh yes! Almost, almost, almost. He moaned as his sensation shot free, squirting over Candy's throat, then running down towards her unfastened dress.

Adam laid his head on his PA's breast, and closed his eyes for a moment. He felt her shift slightly beneath him, touch his hair. His testes felt empty, his cock untensed, his head still replaying the pleasure. A much needed moment, but nothing like Leanne . . .

'Time one of us got some work done around here!' Feeling the strength return to his limbs, he stood and then helped the smiling girl up and kissed her lightly. 'Go and have a shower and a sleep, all right, angel? Start on the "Femlust" project when you're through.'

'Yes, Mr Howard. Consider it done, Mr Howard.' Candy pulled up the bodice of her dress, then put her knickers in her pocket before walking carefully away.

His own thoughts returning to the events that had just passed, Adam followed more slowly. He was pleased that Leanne had punished his PA for a genuine misdemeanour, felt reassured that she was beginning to appreciate the cane's persuasive power. But he was angry that she'd tried to sack the girl – his girl – enraged that she hadn't yet recognised who was ultimately in charge.

Eight

Good, they were arguing again, had reached a state of crisis! Eleanor stepped back into the shadows as Leanne rushed out of the main tower room. For a moment she'd thought the model agency owner would let Adam make love to her in front of Candy. After all, she, Eleanor, would give herself gladly to the man. So what if it involved an audience? It wasn't every day a woman found a lover so sexually adept.

Not that she'd been with Adam yet – but she'd watched him pleasure Leanne and Candy. She had seen their grateful loins arch towards ecstasy, heard their ravenous whimpers and moans.

But Eleanor was still waiting for her moment. She'd no sooner been interviewed and taken on by Adam at Lingering Lessons than Leanne with her classic car and equally classic looks had arrived. Leanne with her softly curled auburn hair, large thoughtful eyes and tailored wardrobes. A woman with credit card statements from all over Britain, an address book with contacts throughout the world. At first Eleanor had thought she had no chance any more, that the agency owner would conquer Adam Howard's libido. But now she was fighting back.

She stared at herself in one of the corridor's glass-panelled doors as she pushed it open. Adam must have noticed the weight she'd lost and the tone she'd gained since working for him. He'd smiled at her so appreciatively when she'd brought him the mobile phone and directory. The hours spent at the hi-tech hotel gym in the next town had obviously paid off.

Leanne had rushed out of the tower – now she would obviously need a friend and a confidant. Eleanor finger-combed her recently feather-cut soft blonde hair. She wanted to become both the woman's peer and her substitute parent. She'd heard Leanne tell Khan that her mother and father were dead. They'd obviously set her up well before their early demise – she had everything: the education, the business, the self-belief. It wasn't fair.

'Miss Dell?' She knocked lightly on the woman's door. There was the length of pause one expects when someone is tidying themselves or the room, creating order. Then the door opened part-way.

'Eleanor. Hi!' No hint of surprise. Leanne probably thinks I'm here to offer her new bed linen. Probably sees me as a sexless drudge, she thought. She returned the smile, and quickly scanned Leanne's features for proof of her recent run-in with Adam. There was no trace of any tears.

'I wondered if I could talk to you? I'm divorced, as you probably know, and I've got a bit of a problem. It's ... well, delicate, so I can't involve Paul or Mr Howard.'

'Of course! Come in.' The younger woman swept a welcoming hand into the room. 'Excuse the chaos. Just push some of these fashion spreads out of the way.'

Glossy paper, glossier guys. Eleanor forced her eyes away from their muscled promise, took a seat, then looked up at her employer. 'I've been meaning to get to know you better for ages,' Leanne added, taking a chair opposite. 'It's ridiculous, just saying hello in the corridor most days when we both live in the same place!'

Your loss for not joining us at dinner, Eleanor fought back the remark. 'I hope I wasn't disturbing you.'

'No, I was just planning my next business move.'

Move back to England. Leave this school! Eleanor kept her face slightly nervous but pleasant. Declined an offer of liqueurs, coffee, tea. Leanne leaned forward, widening her eyes, her features saying *tell me*. She'd never tell the truth ...

'So, Eleanor, what can I help you with? I promise this won't go any further.'

'It's Mr Kerne. He and I have been . . . *walking out*.'
Only nine years or so separated her in age from Leanne,
but she was determined to use terms that made her sound
much older. The model-agency owner mustn't see her as a
rival, a threat.

'Go on.'

'We . . . well it's lovely having a male friend at my age.
After my husband lost interest I felt so unloved, so un-
wanted.'

'Mm,' Leanne nodded. 'I can remember. My own
divorce will be through any day.'

But you didn't have three teenage children, no job, no
skills. Weren't born to a hard rural life where marriage is
till-death-us-do-part, and too bad if it damn near kills you,
Eleanor thought. 'You'll understand, then, the need for . . .
companionship.'

Leanne nodded warily. Eleanor lowered her voice.
'Problem is, he has unnatural needs.' She saw the agency
owner stiffen.

'What exactly . . .?' Leanne started to ask.

'He likes to take a riding crop to my backside!' Eleanor
watched the woman's blush rise.

'And you don't enjoy . . . I mean, you'd rather he didn't
do that?'

'I hate it,' Eleanor lied.

There was a short pause. Leanne licked her lips. 'Have
you told him?'

'I . . . hinted. In my day we didn't talk about such things.'

'If it's not what you want, you must let him know immediately.'

Easy for you to say! 'What if he leaves me?'

'It's his loss.'

'If you were in my shoes?'

'I wouldn't do anything I didn't want to do.'

Nod thoughtfully. Bite your lip. Seem grateful, weak. 'I
wish I had your strength, your certainty!' Had a silver
spoon, an inheritance of a school and its grounds. Leanne
had all that: the class, the cash, the confidence. But she
lacked Eleanor's hard-won patience, her subterfuge.

146

'I suppose you'll have to get used to life without male company here.'

Leanne shrugged. 'I have Khan.'

'He's your boyfriend?'

'No. He works for me.'

'I meant someone special.'

'Oh? Oh, well ... my work keeps me busy. One day maybe, when I've more time.'

Liar. Whore. She'd made time for Adam Howard all right, letting him paddle her bum in the gym, shaft her sex in the staffroom. She'd have spent even longer in his arms, his bed, if Eleanor hadn't paid that teenage girl to create a diversion by setting the horses free. God, she'd enjoyed hiding in the stable, seeing that little bitch wriggle against the clitoral exciter Gerard had strapped to her for hour after hour.

'Well, I hope this has helped.' Leanne stood up. Did that mean their *tête à tête* was over?

'I'll tell Gerard he can't whip me any more. Can I come and tell you what he says?'

'Erm, sure!' Leanne stretched out a hand and patted the other woman's arm. 'I ... admire your courage. It can't have been easy for you coming here with such personal things.'

A congenial smile. 'It wasn't, but – with your running a business and all – I feel you're someone I can look up to. And Gerard's tastes have been preying on my mind.'

Three bye-for-nows, two waves. She smirked to herself as she reached the end of the corridor and started down towards reception. She'd made contact! She'd gained the younger woman's trust. Leanne saw her as Gerard's now, as a slightly unsure and rather weak divorcée, not as Adam Howard's future wife.

Time for a strength-giving and flesh-firming swim! Eleanor took her bikini from her room, then traipsed lightly to the poolside. Sometimes, when the water was empty, she swum nude. She made for the rows of changing cubicles, then stopped, noting the sleek tanned shape beneath the surface. Adam was in the water, at the deep end.

She could dive in! Or stay out and pretend she hadn't seen him. Hesitating for a second, she turned towards the nearest cubicle, stepped just inside it, leaving the door ajar. She turned to face the far wall, a casual bather, giving her employer a complete view of her rear end.

Now she'd take off her housekeeper's dress! Holding in her stomach and tensing her ribs, she reached up and pulled the white cotton from her arms, her head, and let it fall to the tiles. Slid her hands back to unhook her open-mesh-effect bra with the scalloped edge. She had slender shoulders, a tanned back that sloped down into fecund haunches. He'd see ...

After freeing her breasts, Eleanor pulled down her pants, slowly unveiling the sun-kissed curves beneath the triangular scrap of satin. Finally nude, she turned round to show Adam – and saw Khan.

He was standing in the middle of the pool and gazing openly at her. He stepped back as she caught his eye, and turned away, swimming for the shallow end. Damn! It was a case of mistaken identity. Under the water, he and Adam were similarly dark-haired and tall. Eleanor took a step nearer the younger man. The striptease had aroused her. She might as well make use of the beautiful-bodied Khan.

Smiling, she slid into the pool, used the breast-stroke to swim up to him, cool water on heated nipples. 'Sorry about that! I thought I was on my own here,' she said casually.

'I . . . shouldn't have looked.'

'Oh, looking's not a crime! In fact, it's nice to be admired. Since my husband walked out . . . Well, you know.'

'We all need to be appreciated,' Khan said. Eleanor's eyes caressed his *café au lait* chest, then moved slowly downwards.

'Mmm,' she murmured, 'we do.' Her mind raced ahead, trying to find a way that would make him want to drag her over his knee, to spank her bottom till she came.

'Not that Adam would like his staff being naked together like this.'

Khan grimaced. 'You reckon?'

She looked through the water to find that his cock had

grown hard. 'Uh uh. He likes to run a tight ship. You know – order, discipline.'

'Oh. Right.'

'I could tell him you were spying on me!' she teased, brushing a hand down his front. He gasped and his erection thickened further.

'Why would you do that?' Khan asked.

'To see if he threw you out.'

'Don't you want me to stay?' Khan's strong hands encircled her waist. She felt delicate, desirable.

'I might.'

She nibbled his left earlobe, then whispered, 'So what are you going to do to make sure I don't tell?'

Khan's eyes searched hers. 'I've never been one for puzzles.'

Drag me over your lap and roast your palm against my buttocks. Make me wet! she thought.

She waited. Khan nuzzled her throat; he fondled her bottom, stroked the crevice. Her body flickered into action. She wanted something rougher, wilder, more out of control – but she didn't dare ask. She'd just finished telling Leanne that she hated Gerard's whippings. If Khan told the agency owner that Eleanor actually *wanted* to be spanked . . .

'I'll lead the way!' she announced, then wrapped her fingers round his cock, and started to move towards the pool steps, the throbbing youth breathing hard as she tugged him. She could at least get into a position where she could fantasise.

Ten heavy-duty rubber rings were stacked up near the provisions cupboard. Eleanor lowered herself over them; Khan moved on top of her back. 'This feels precarious!' he said. Exactly. And my master's told me he'll use his birch on my bottom if I topple the lot.

Her rubber perch swaying; getting wet, wet, wetter. Slave, I'm warning you. Her Master shafting her in her head as Khan's cock started to thrust in and out. 'Imagine if Adam comes in!' he moaned, his hands on her tits, squeezing, stroking. Or Paul or Gerard or Leanne.

Gerard would have her over his lap in a second, his belt

on her buttocks, hard and often. Christ, he wouldn't half leather her for a stunt like this! Since that day when she'd got the grocery order wrong, he'd thrashed her for over-salting the dinner, for saddling a horse wrong. For singeing his shirt collar, for being late . . .

Gerard had a way of looking at her that made her feel small yet incredibly sexual. He'd use his hand to heat her hindquarters and would somehow oil every interior inch. 'Yes, yes! Do it hard, go in deep,' she moaned to the bucking Khan, sensation speeding. 'Ram it up me to the hilt!'

Cheap words. Big plans. With him on her side, she'd be even closer to winning. Fuck me, baby! she thought. Her master making her undress before him, ordering her to kiss the cane: twenty strokes for being slow and another twenty if you let these rings topple over. The rings swayed as Khan pushed in especially hard, and she came.

'God, yes!' Khan strained forward, then collapsed against her back. Eleanor gasped the last of her own spent need, then opened her eyes and stared at the tiles. Okay, so he wasn't her type, but he could be useful, malleable. 'We must do this more often,' she said.

Afterwards, she stared at her much-fingered breasts and belly in the mirror, seeing what Khan had both seen and fervently fondled. This was the body of a real woman, who'd had to fight for every favour – not some had-it-easy-with-a-doting-Daddy bitch. She ran her palms over each stretch of skin, fondling it into frisson after frisson, enjoying her unblemished and increasingly emphatic hollows and curves. Eleanor looked deep into her own clear-blue eyes. *She* could pose for Adam's adverts, share his bed and do his bidding. She and he would have everything together if she could drive Leanne out before the end of the year.

Nine

'For Mr Howard?' Leanne fingered the long slim package the postman had just handed her. 'I can go and get him.' She wanted an excuse to talk to Adam; she had only seen him in passing since she'd fled from the mountain room three days before.

'It's recorded delivery, Miss, not registered. Your signature will do fine.'

Mild disappointment creating a dragging feeling in her gut, Leanne took the pen and book from the driver and signed for receipt of the parcel. 'I'll see he gets it immediately,' she murmured, an idea forming. She'd walk to his rooms now and hopefully be asked to stay.

But first she'd try to work out what was in the parcel! Pulse speeding at the minor deceit, she fingered the object thoroughly through its wrapper. It was phallic-shaped, with two ridges like a cross at the end. It felt like a hard anal dildo, the ends stopping the impaler being thrust all the way inside the tight recess.

Probably some product for Adam to write about – or maybe for personal consumption? She'd quite like to see him on all fours, taking it up the arse. She'd make him plead for less or more, give him a nerve-endings test of his own medicine, turn him into a whimpering bundle of arousal just begging for release. Damn the man for making her think about him, hunger for him. Damn him all the more for not seeking her out since she'd fled.

Alerted by a movement, she looked out of the corridor window to see Paul bent over one of the white garden tables, his jeans round his ankles. Khan's cock was clothed in an extra-thick anal condom. He was rimming it around Paul's welcoming exposed rectal hole; a well-lubricated hole that looked as it had been soundly finger fucked.

She stared at the bottle of ecstasy oil on the trimmed lawn – it was half-empty. Then she looked down at the glistening contours of Paul's bum, and felt her labia quicken and pulse. The boy would be feeling the take me – take me – take me tension experienced as the dominant partner kept his lover waiting, just before ramming all the way in.

Do it! Do it! She pressed her thighs together as Khan pushed into the gardener inch by inch, began shafting. Pinch his nipples, use your free hand to take his balls to the limit, make him squeal and jerk.

She wanted the sound show as well as the peep-show, so she edged the window open three inches and could just discern both boys' rasping breathing through the still summer air. Khan's small milky-coffee-coloured bum was thrusting forward towards the gardener's paler bottom. Paul's cock was up hard against his own stomach, half-covered by Khan's fondling right hand.

The watcher and the watched: she could be the spectator any day. But the spectacle? Maybe if she was really aroused before Adam brought the audience in ... Rock-hard flesh in a yielding rectum, stoked new nerve endings. Paul cried out, thigh muscles tensing, and white liquid jerked in spasms from his cock.

'Uh!' The boy's wrigglings were too much for Khan, who strained into the crevice and the condom one last time, then stood, panting, cupping his own balls, his shoulders sagging. After a moment he put his fingers to his phallus and carefully withdrew.

Leanne stared hollowly down at the scene. Have sheath, will enjoy sexual travel. Khan would take anyone in any position: if only she could be as quick to take her pleasure, as free! But she wanted one special sexual man – had had him, had loved it. She would be irrational and emotionally bereft if she let him, Adam, get away.

Hurrying to the former headmaster's study, she planned

what she'd say to the enigma, formed flirtations round the parcel. If you're looking for an orifice to slide this in – something like that. Sexual, unsubtle, a teased wet tunnel showing it needed release, seeking rapture. And he'd switch the damn thing on, rub its buzz down her front, and then . . .

'Ah!' The swish of a belt, a cry of pain. Jesus, was he still thrashing Candy? Leanne stopped outside his door. Damn, the letter-box was closed. She could knock with his parcel, she could open the door, she could come back later. She stood, listening to the girl take another lash.

'Please, Master, I'll be punctual next time. The drive took hours!' That wasn't the PA's soft voice. A cold grip took hold of Leanne's stomach, and stayed there; he was teaching obedience to someone else's bottom. And as chastisement was foreplay for Adam, that meant . . .

'Oh God, don't pull down my pants. So sore already!' A whimper, then a pause. Leanne sank to her knees and edged the letter-box open, wedged it in place with her slip-on shoe. She saw a girl in her twenties leaning over an armchair; her knickers were at her knees, her dress hitched up.

Focusing more intently, she took in the luckless pink arse which was facing sideways to the door. The girl's head was hanging over the chair arm. As Leanne stared, Adam walked from his back rooms into his front room. He held a heavy black rubber oval which tapered to a handle in his hand.

'Sit up. Look at this.' He held the implement out to the girl, who trembled as she scrambled back to survey it. 'It's called a ferule. I use it on a bad girl when she's over my knee.'

'Do you use it for long, sir?' The girl's eyes were glassy, wide. She was breathing quickly through her open mouth.

'Until she's so hot and sore I know she can no longer bear it. *Then* I give her five more.'

He settled himself on the second armless chair and patted his lap. 'Come on sweetheart. Don't keep me waiting.'

'My roadmap was old! The school's so tucked away!'

The girl put her fingers over her already punished bottom and stayed in place.

'It's not my fault that you're so disorganised you miss an appointment.'

'I know, but . . .'

He moved the ferule from side to side, a warning gesture. 'I still have to vent my annoyance by taking it out on your arse.'

'The belt was so sore!'

'It was over your dress and your pants. That was just a warm-up.'

'Such a thin dress, Master.'

'You'll be sent home without it if you don't get that backside over my knee right now!'

At the threat, the girl pushed herself back from the chair she was kneeling on, and slowly approached the suited Adam. Leanne watched on, feeling cheated, dazed. She'd come here to give herself to him, take his cock deep inside her. Was she really so easy to replace?

'Good girl. Lay yourself down. Kiss the ferule.' The stranger did so. Adam adjusted his position so that her bum was hoisted further in the air. He looked down at it for a moment, then reached for a cushion, raising her haunches further by sliding it beneath her wriggling tummy. 'Now I can really get to work.'

'Oh!' The girl gasped loudly as the black rubber further warmed her helpless cheeks.

'I'm told it throbs when you've had a sufficient number.'

'It . . .' She broke off as he doled out the second lash. '. . . It throbs now!'

'Then think how much hotter it'll be by the time I've finished with you.' Leanne watched him fondling the girl's bare bottom. 'You'll never be late for a business meeting again.'

She, Leanne, was always on time, always organised. She was prettier than this other woman. She had more spirit, more charm! How could he? She'd tried so hard to be the best – in bed and out of it. Rob, her ex-husband, had never once complained on the sexual front. Quite the reverse!

After his promotion, he'd syphoned most of his energy into his work. She'd still had some left over. She'd used her mouth, her hands, her imagination to take his mind off stocks and shares; offered bare breasts to distract him from a bullish market; dressed in ivory stockings and white crotch thongs to shift his attention from negative equity.

'Aah!' There came a third squeal from Adam's anonymous female friend, his willing victim. If she and Adam had been alone for long enough, if he'd got her excited, then she Leanne might have agreed to a session like this.

But she hadn't based her philosophy on might-have-beens; that was for losers, for people who labelled themselves in terms of who'd done what to them, and who'd never moved on. She'd put the indifference of her parents and the legacy of their negativity far behind her. She was leading a positive life!

A life without this man? Their lovemaking had made them seem so right together. Christ, she'd even started having the type of thoughts you had at lovestruck sixteen! Little flash forwards in which she saw them as an item in ten years' time, celebrating their togetherness. Still thoughtful, sexual, appreciative – if just a little smug.

No smugness now. She stared as Adam teased the bottom of the unknown girl, running the smooth black rubber over its heated contours. 'You can take twenty more with this, or opt for a little test to redeem yourself instead.' There was a long pause. 'Decide now, or you'll get both! I hate indecisiveness.'

'I'll . . .' The girl licked her lips. 'Can you tell me what the test is, please?'

'No. I can only tell you that I'll make the punishment fit the crime if you warrant further chastisement. Who knows, sweetheart? Your exam results may come as a pleasant surprise!'

A clitoral exciter? A vibrating anal dildo? A male doll? Leanne went through the various options in her head. She felt rooted to the spot, hurt yet curious. If he was intent on teaching this rival a lesson, then she wanted him to take

155

the girl to the heights! Or to the depths. Wanted to see her quiver and plead for a climax, crawl for each pleasure. Wanted to ... Christ, where were they off to next?

She scrambled back as Adam said, 'Smooth your dress down and walk to the athletics stadium. Just follow the signs.'

'And you'll ...?'

'I'll be there in a few minutes to give you extra instructions. Meanwhile, just take one of the poles out of the equipment shed you'll find there. Have a can of sports drink if you like.'

The athletics stadium! Leanne took off along the corridor, jumped the stairs two at a time and rushed through reception. It was just as well she'd been keeping agile. She would have to put the various huts and outhouses between herself and the other girl if she was to avoid being seen. She had to know just how far he'd go with this fawning female; find out if she was going to be around for days or weeks.

A small green Polo in the car park: the girl wasn't exactly in the upper income tax bracket, then! Having thought the thought, Leanne immediately felt ashamed of herself. She herself had been born into a tiny flat with a shared toilet. Mamie had been the successful one in the family, the ambitious one. She'd seen some creativity in Leanne and nurtured it ...

Concentrate on today, tomorrow! She ran faster, climbed quickly over a boundary fence. The stadium was empty, each bench clearly delineated in the sunlight. The long equipment outhouse was unlocked.

Leanne slipped inside, opened the window until she heard the sparrows chirping. Good, she'd be able to hear the terrible twosome as Adam put the stranger through her test. She looked around, gaze probing for a protected place. If she hid behind these diagonally propped trampolines, the girl wouldn't see her. She edged her slender body in the gap behind the furthest one, and held her breath.

There was silence, bar the birds. At last, she heard footsteps on the gravel pathway. Then more light flooded the building as the door opened again. 'Poles,' muttered a female voice – *the* female. She'd presumably known Adam in London, but why come here now?

Metal on concrete sounded, and that of the pole being dragged forward. Another crack – presumably the can of juice being opened. Then the door closed slowly, and Leanne crept from her hiding-place. Cautiously, she moved forward so that her line of vision extended a little way, and peered out of the lace-covered window. Good, she could see the girl scuffing her sandals against the grass as she walked round the now horizontal pole.

Fair hair in a back-length pony-tail. She's always hated that look on anyone over six years old, and now loathed it doubly. A faded chambray dress, well-curved bare calves. No socks, and presumably she'd left off her knickers, hoping that the breeze would cool her well-warmed bum.

The girl stopped, looked over, then hung her head. Adam appeared in his lightest grey summer suit and a lavender shirt with a breast pocket. Did he have some fiendish device in there to make her clitoris crave to come? 'All right! Let's set up this exam. I started to punish you for your slowness, your poor timekeeping. Now you're going to prove to me that in future you'll move fast.'

He indicated the extended sandpit many yards ahead. 'You take your run up to that, then pole-vault. I'll mark the area. First I'll mark the place you have to reach as a female novice, and the one I have to reach as a male.'

'Then what happens?' The girl sounded young and unsure.

'You make six jumps.' Leanne heard the slight smile enter Adam's voice. 'For each time you fail to meet the required length, you take five spanks with the ferule. Each time *I* fail, I'll knock ten spanks off your total. Sounds fair?'

'Yes, Master. Thank you, Master.' Christ, the girl was such a wimp! Leanne tensed her cheekbones in disgust, to show an unseeing world she was appalled by this behaviour. She watched as Adam placed a blue marker on the sand, then a red marker some several feet nearer to the sandpit's onset. His and hers.

He strolled casually back. 'I've given you an advantage, as you see. Off you go, then.'

The girl bent at the waist and picked up the pole, then glanced at him for approval. She ran awkwardly and slowly at first, and then faster, holding the metal diagonally. Stopped, launched herself briefly into the air, came down, swayed then steadied. She was several inches away from the red plastic marker.

Slowly she returned to Adam. 'Five strokes with my thick rubbery friend.' He took a tiny notebook from his pocket and wrote the number down.

'I'm sorry, Master.'

'You will be, when you're over my knee with your arse turning scarlet. Now try again.' As Leanne watched, almost forgetting to breathe, her rival again raced towards the sandpit and again failed to meet the required mark.

Five, ten, fifteen ... 'Shall I remind you how sore it's going to be?' Adam told her. He sat down on the low wall and pulled her over his knee, lifting up her dress to expose her buttocks. The girl quivered over his lap as he stroked her rear cheeks. 'Imagine how it'll throb after thirty more strokes. How you'll whimper!'

'I'll try ever so hard ...'

He set her down, and she stood up again, cheeks flushed, eyes frantic. She made the jump, stopping inches short of the mark. Again she ran, till she'd made all six attempts at the pole-vault; made them and failed.

Thirty throbbing tastes of the ferule on her naked posterior, unless ... Leanne realised that she wanted Adam to win, wanted to see her rival humbled, punished. Succeed, succeed, succeed, succeed, succeed! As if picking up her plea, he made jump after jump with ease, poise, agility. Squatting on the grass, the unpunctual watchful girl bit her lip.

Breathing quickly, he walked up and stood before her. 'As I've just shown, you can do it if you try.'

'I was ...'

'You weren't really trying. I see this in business, in relationships throughout Britain. I won't tolerate it here.'

158

'I know! If you'll give me . . .'

'A second chance? I might – after you've taken your thrashing. You need to learn discipline. You have to obey.'

'Yes, Master,' muttered the girl, her eyes fixed on the grass, her hands plucking again and again at its plushness.

'Now all I have to do is get comfortable before I use this implement on your tardy backside.'

He looked towards the outhouse window. Leanne shrank back, retreated further and more quickly as he walked towards the building. Damn! She edged behind the layers of trampolines, shut her eyes as she heard the door's warning creak. A pause, then she heard something being pulled across the floor, looked through the metal frame to see him dragging one of the trampolines out of the doorway. Thank God there had been four to hide behind!

Leanne moved back to the window. Adam had set down the low bouncing table in the centre of the grass. As Leanne watched he sat down on the edge of it, his feet touching the ground, his eyes staring at the failed pole-vaulter. 'I'm waiting,' he said menacingly. With a shudder, the girl walked over to him and lowered herself over his lap.

'Thirty, we said.' He edged her dress up and tucked its hem under her arms so that he had full access to her naked bottom. 'Oh sweetheart, this is going to hurt so bad.' He picked up the ferula and lined it up with her left buttock cheek, six inches above it, then brought it down with an audible whack.

The girl jerked, but stayed in place. Leanne silently urged Adam to lay on a second stroke. As the female stopped moving, he warmed her right orb with the same degree of strength.

I shouldn't want this, but I do, Leanne thought, in the way that sometimes you want the escaped prisoner in the film to get away because you like him. She wanted Adam to thrash this girl because it excited all of them in some primitive unethical way.

A third stroke. Then a fourth. The helpless bottom was quivering now, tensing before the lash fell. Leanne's right hand strayed to the front of her button-through skirt. Then stopped – she was still holding Adam's parcel. And she had a feeling she knew exactly what it contained!

With suddenly clumsy fingers she pulled off the sticky tape – she would replace it carefully later – and pulled out a non-doctor vibrator with variable speeds. Please let it include a battery, she thought. She switched it on to the lowest frequency, aware that if she could hear every sound outside the hut, that they could hear loud buzzing. She felt its satisfying quiet promise between her fingertips.

Pleasure through her panties. She partially unbuttoned her skirt, slid the dildo in, putting it vertically outside her knickers. She closed her eyes as the prickles spread through her, then forced herself to open them again. She wanted to see ... Leanne saw a reddening arse wriggling under a black rubber bat. 'How many to go now, sweetheart? I hope you've been counting.'

'I've had ten strokes on the bare, Master. Oh, please!'

Please dole out the rest, and make her beg. Show her who's Master. Hold her down and raise the bat and ... Leanne moaned as rapture drew near. She kept the devilishly efficient dildo in place, kept her eyes fixed on the punished bottom, watched the humiliated whimpering slave. For those were the terms in which the girl presumably saw herself, as she called Adam her Master. Called and pleaded and trembled across his knee.

'Lash eleven coming up,' said Adam. 'Which buttock should I land it on? Isn't it kind of me to give you the option?'

'Yes, Master.' The girl sounded doubtful.

'So, tell me.'

'The ... the left.'

The rubber came down and she squealed.

'Now thank me nicely for giving you what you asked for.'

A long sigh. 'Thank you, Master.'

'Such bland phrases! You can do better than that.'

He teased the ferula across her naked cheeks. 'Problem is, when I hear such little respect it makes my right arm enraged and it strikes down harder. Sometimes I see a naughty bottom in front of me and just don't want to stop teaching it who's boss. I just spank and spank till the person it belongs to begs real pretty. They end up with such a hot backside, whereas if they'd just been obsequious from the start . . .'

A momentary silence. 'Thank you for . . . for warming my wicked arse, for teaching me manners,' muttered the girl, writhing with embarrassment. 'I deserve to feel the ferule on my bum till I do what I'm told.' Adam laid on another stroke and the girl whimpered. Leanne moaned behind clenched teeth, doubled forward and came. Waves of delight rippled through her clit, her lower belly, her sexual crevice. Tension peaked, then faded from her nipples, her thighs.

Leanne straightened up to see that the girl was coming too, her fingers flexing against the trampoline's give, her toes contracting. She was moving against Adam's lap, presumably rubbing herself against the hard promise of his cock. 'You'll take extra for this,' he warned. 'You weren't given permission.'

'So hot . . .'

'You're hot, are you?' He seemed to contemplate her arse for a humiliatingly long time. 'I've something that will put paid to that warmth you're complaining about. Then we'll finish toasting that wicked posterior and hear your words of gratitude for a while.'

Leanne leaned forward as Adam dumped the girl on the ground, and shrank back as he approached the outhouse once again. Drat it! She got behind the remaining trampolines, held in her stomach, fought against the urge to close her eyes.

She was a woman – not an ostrich! She couldn't bury her head or her heart; she knew exactly what was happening. Adam had brought down some girlfriend from London after Leanne refused to make love to him in front of Candy's watchful gaze. Now he was getting by, making do, surviving. Using the girl the same way she, Leanne, had used Khan.

So much for not playing games, for being honest! She'd always prized truthfulness in both others and herself. But now? She wanted Adam in her arms, but she didn't want to beg. She wanted a one-to-one commitment. Then again, she didn't want to appear overly possessive, the jealous type.

Someone else was giving him what she'd refused. Someone inferior! Leanne stared at Adam's suited torso as he turned his back on her and reached for a length of hose. Coiling it into a manageable whirl, he walked out again into the sunshine. After a moment's hesitation, Leanne vacated her hiding-place.

She resumed her window view. The reddened arse was now out of sight – the girl had smoothed her dress down. She was standing, cupping her hands over her clothed bottom, her crossed legs falling to hide the wet stain that had spread from her crotch.

'You like being wet, don't you, sweetheart?'

'Y-e-s.' The girl faced him, but seemed to centre her gaze at his chest.

'Even told your Master you needed a cool down.'

The girl nodded, looking miserably at the hose.

'Some nice cold water, then we'll mark that pretty bum again, give you permission for a second climax.'

'Couldn't I just . . .?'

'Speaking without permission? No.' There was a pause, whilst he connected the hose to the outdoor water tap, then he looked her up and down. 'Put your hands on your head, my wilful beauty. Stretch those elbows out at the side, feet parted. Keep them there.'

The girl obeyed. The first jet of water hit her breasts, flattening the chambray to her taut high curves, hardening the nipples. The second made the garment cling to her gently tapering waist. 'Aaaah!' she cried out, bringing her hands in front of her as if to ward off the water.

'That's bad,' Adam murmured, 'that's very bad indeed.'

'No! Please! I didn't mean . . .' The girl put her palms back on top of her head and looked at him pleadingly.

'I gave you an order. You defied me. You have to learn.'

162

He picked up the ferule and walked up to her. 'Bend over. Further still. Grasp your ankles at the front. That's better! Now keep holding them till I tell you to let go.'

Lift up her skirt, Leanne urged from her vantage point behind the curtain's lace. Adam walked around the girl twice, obviously enjoying her trembling limbs and hot flushed features. Then he stopped and edged her dress up, setting it over her back.

Rosy red bottom cheeks and a slicked wet furrow. Lingering Lessons' co-owner stared at the stranger's badge of pleasure and pain. Unbidden, her fingers strayed to her own swollen sex. If she stayed and watched she could come again – the vibrator made it so simple. An exciting spectacle before her, an arousing resonance below.

One whack of the ferula landed on the girl's dark buttock divide. Leanne watched the pinkness spread across the twin orbs. Both raised cheeks quivered. 'Now we'll cool that bottom before we warm it again,' Adam murmured, picking up the hose.

'I could please you so much . . .' The girl started. She sank to her knees, and reached for his zip. Push her away! Ignore her! As Leanne watched, dry-mouthed, Adam stroked the girl's fair hair.

Damn him – she was out of here! Refusing to wait around to see some cosy sex scene, Leanne slipped from the outhouse and edged round its side until she put the building between her and the busy twosome. Clutching the vibrator and the wrapping-paper it had arrived in, she hurried across the fields towards the school.

Forget what you've witnessed! Just shower and eat and work. Maybe he'll explain later. Perhaps he thinks you don't want him to touch you any more after that stupid mountain-room scene.

She reached the school's small back door, and hurried inside, not wanting to go through the front way which led to reception. Eleanor might be there, leaving some message for herself or for Adam. Paul might pop in to find out which corner of the grounds his bosses wanted landscaped or relaid. And she didn't want to see anyone; she wanted to sit quietly and muse on what to do next with the handsome co-owner. She wanted to work out a strategy that would maintain her dignity, yet win his love.

'Ah! I was hoping to find you!'

As she tiptoed up the stairs to her corridor, Eleanor suddenly loomed above her. Leanne felt ridiculously caught out, guilty, and said, 'Oh. I was just . . . Hi!'

The older woman smiled. 'I was wondering if you'd seen Mr Howard? Candy says he's had some important long-distance phone calls.'

So it looked like the servile PA was staying around.

'He's over by the athletics stadium.' She thought through the scenario she'd just witnessed, realised how she'd felt when the woman saw her with Khan that time she'd belted his bottom. 'Best not to disturb him, though. He's with a friend.'

'Female friend?' Eleanor's eyes seemed to grow bigger at the prospect. 'I saw a strange car in the car park.'

'Probably hers.'

'So,' the older woman leaned forward on the stair, 'what's she like?'

'Um, hair in a pony-tail. In her twenties.'

Eleanor nodded. 'Probably his wife.'

'His *wife*!' Leanne heard the hollow note in her voice, and quickly tried to bring the tone down a level. Eleanor didn't know she and Adam had been intimate. 'I didn't realise he was a married man.'

'They all are,' Eleanor said vaguely. She was still blocking Leanne's path.

'Well, I must shower and change.' She realised she looked dusty and damp, blankly post-orgasmic. 'I . . . went out for a run through the grounds.'

'You certainly look after yourself.'

'Well, if you exercise, you need less sleep. And with the business . . .'

'Going well, is it?' Eleanor asked.

It had been going spectacularly, until Candy intervened!

'Getting there.' She wondered how much the older woman understood about being self-employed, an unsalaried person. Some people thought you just put in an hour or two when you felt like it, whilst others appreciated the sustained effort required.

'Great to work your own hours, I bet.'

'It is! But they end up being longer hours. I mean, you don't get sick pay or holiday pay when you work for yourself.'

'Being here's like a holiday,' the housekeeper said.

'In a way.' She smiled at the older woman. 'I love it here, too.'

Or would if Adam loved me, or would make love to me. 'But moving here obviously involved quite a lot of upheaval and expense.'

'Still, you've got that pool, these grounds, all these rooms for your background shots!' Eleanor reminded her.

'Oh, I know. I've been really lucky.'

At times like this she'd rather have Mamie to talk to, though, rather than this legacy where she was so alone.

'*And* your phone's always ringing.'

'Some of it's just models looking for jobs rather than people putting any work my way.' She realised belatedly that Eleanor's rooms were on a different floor, as was the kitchen. 'I didn't realise you'd be able to hear my calls.'

'Mmm? We've a mini-switchboard off the utility room. A light goes on to indicate which of the staff quarters is being contacted.'

'Right, the wonders of technology – which reminds me about that wonderful electric shower I'm about to have!' Brain coming up with that parting sentence, Leanne slipped quickly past the housekeeper and completed the journey to her rooms.

Tepid water on warm labia. She rinsed the slippery proof of her climax away, worked tangerine-scented gel through her hair, under her arms, beneath her breast curves. Then she finished the cleansing ritual with a cooler aftermath.

It was too hot to get dressed. Naked, Leanne walked into her bedroom, flopped down on the bed on her belly and reached for a fashion mag. Christ, that boy was pulse-racing! Strong dark chest hair leading down to a flat hard belly. Large dark come-get-me eyes, a slightly superior cant to the mouth.

Reasons to be cheerful, part one. Men like this were still around – and she was technically available. Reasons to be cheerful, part two: she still had Adam's recorded delivery vibrator, could use it post-haste to register her own desires.

The few videos she'd seen on the subject showed women wanking on their backs with their legs scissored apart, but most times she preferred to tremble on her tummy. Stretching out her right arm until it reached the buzzable dildo, Leanne edged it under her front until it was centred beneath her pubic bone, mound keeping it in place. Rob had held her vibrator like this, making her squirm and pant till she almost sobbed her orgasm. Then he'd slid his cock inside her as the last pulsatings faded and brought her to her pinnacle again.

No Rob now. No Adam – at least not today. Christ, she wanted male hands on her tits, her arse, her pubes, wanted it fast and frantic. Who could she . . .? Gerard would oblige. She thought of his hard eyes and his even harder whip hand: she'd be satiated, but vanquished. And when she'd given her all – when she'd wept and begged and promised everything and delivered most of it – there would be no after-orgasm kisses or gentle hugs.

Gerard was Adam without finesse, Adam without emotion. Gerard was Eleanor's, anyway – if not exclusively. The housekeeper thought he was her special beau, but he'd thrashed Candy and the village girl who'd freed the horses. She'd even seen him reprimanding Paul.

Paul! Leanne delayed switching on the vibrator, as if some lustful lover was about to walk in to take her to the heights, then back again. For all his shyness, Paul seemed to be enjoying a varied sexual life. The youth had been cropped by Gerard, sucked by Candy, buggered by Khan, each encounter leading to a climax. Plus she'd seen the boy taking oral simulators and vibro penis rings and pulsators from the cupboards, so he obviously had fun by himself.

The kind of fun that Adam promoted in his work. She stared into the pillow as the undoubted truth took hold.

She hated the man's ability to forget her existence; his capacity to punish someone new, then pleasure them. But she had to admit at last that his copywriting work was worthwhile.

Here Paul had access to a small group of people who were prepared to take their thrills freely and joyfully. But in the city he'd have been just another frustrated young man, frustrated until Adam's erotic ads let him enter a world of love plugs and self-comforters. The copywriter even promoted a lightweight birch with a special handle which allowed you to flagellate yourself!

That heated glow without the preparatory shame – and no man around to see you take it. No one to whisper, 'Plead just a little sweetheart . . . let's hear you beg.' She switched on the dildo, shifted till she had it just below her clit. We have countdown. Leanne pictured Adam approaching with the paddle, herself tied like a spread-eagled offering over the bed . . .

'Fuck you!' she would say.

'You know you get extra punishment for that.'

'Fuck you in triplicate!'

Eyes daring, hips tensing, the wooden oval coming down on her. And again. And again. And . . .

'Tell me when you're ready to lick my feet.'

Never, Never, Never, she would think.

'Oh angel, you know you want to get that pretty tongue out, really, to crawl across the floor.'

'You wish!'

'You always do it in the end.'

Only to reach orgasm. No because . . .

Thrashing hard, then harder, then even harder still; her body bucking and writhing. 'Master, please, anything!' Christ, how had that slavish word got in?

'Anything? If you can be more specific.' Skimming the paddle across her exposed sore rear, Adam would give her a wooden warning.

'I beg to wriggle across the carpet on my belly, take your toes in my mouth.'

* * *

Rapture! She cried out into the pillow as her buttocks convulsed, soft pussy pushing against the vibrating hardness. Leanne thrust it inside her to fill the sudden hollow as the contractions throbbed to an end. Playing with herself always brought on intense joy, took away the physical and mental tension. But afterwards she sometimes wished there was a man available to take her in his arms.

Still. Letting the dildo roll further down the duvet, she thanked God for Parcel Post and for her own supply of Sellotape. In a few moments she'd have a quick wash then rewrap the sex toy. She'd tiptoe along the corridor and just leave it in Adam's letter-box as if it had just arrived. Until she came to terms with the knowledge that he might have a wife – came to understand her own increasingly subservient fantasies – it was best that she kept out of his way.

Ten

So, she liked to spy, did she? Adam stared at the foot in the slip-on shoe poking from beneath the stack of dusty trampolines. Then he picked up the hose and carried it from the outhouse, towards the waiting girl. He'd give Leanne something to watch, to think about. Though the video only called for a long CP session, Beth-Marie's teasing eyes and 'What can I do for you now, sirs?' had shown she lusted to go all the way.

He'd settle for halfway – her mouth or fingers. Adam had refrained from making love to another woman since blissfully entering Leanne. A connection of mind, soul, body – it sounded hackneyed, but had felt so real.

He joined the hose to the outdoor water tap, looked Beth-Marie up and down till her gaze faltered. He'd meant to go and talk to Leanne after she'd fled the mountain tower several days before. But work and house queries – his, if not hers – had intervened to keep them separate, and each time he'd knocked on her door she'd either been out or hadn't answered. Nor had Khan.

Short of breaking down her door, what could he do? She was rarely at her desk in reception these days, and, since she'd pretended she hadn't received the note he left before going to London, he refused to leave another one. Eleanor had hinted that Leanne and Khan were working at hands-on fashion shoots – Khan's hands on Leanne's breasts and bottom, no doubt – in the school's many rooms.

Now she was hiding in the equipment area, presumably to peek at himself and the amateur actress as they rehearsed their equally amateurish film!

Real punishments, real sounds. That was what the discerning video-watcher wanted. Not perfect model bottoms with blusher added to create that spanked look, but normal curvy bums that had been warmed by a leather belt. And genuine sound effects – a drawn-in breath, a surprised half-cry, the moans of chastisement for climax, plus the sobs of correction laid on to lead to a spectacular cresting come.

Beth-Marie would soon come a second time. He turned the water jet on, saw it thin and tauten the material round her breasts, and her belly. Automatically he gave the orders and watched them being obeyed. The tiny tape-recorder in his breast pocket would pick up most of the sounds. He'd have them amplified. If the machine was found wanting he'd talk to the experts, make the video another way.

An outdoor setting wasn't ideal for sound – but it was perfect for scenery. At a later date he'd install the cameras, record each writhing session, each orgasmic high. Male viewers would love her taut-thighed rush forward with the pole-vaulting, the way her bottom jiggled as – dress flying out behind her – she launched herself into the air. Would adore this hose's jet as it exposed each crevice, soaking every inch of her sweat-slicked skin.

See how other women want me, Leanne, he thought, as Beth-Marie unzipped his trousers and scooped his semi-hardness out, immediately rendering it rigid. Her admiration wasn't a surprise to him: he'd always done well with the female sex. He looked good, was intelligent, aware. He knew what he wanted. Problem was, he didn't always want *them*.

Leanne, Leanne! He closed his eyes as warm lips wetted his shaft, tuned in to his imagination. Suck me or else you'll suffer, feel my belt. A frantic moving mouth saying, 'Please Master, mercy.' That depends on how much pleasure you give.

Beth-Marie was giving more than enough for now. His legs tensed as his balls tautened. This wouldn't take long. The spanking he'd doled out had stirred him. He'd swelled further as she tasted the ferula across both bottom cheeks.

Take it in deeper. Do it now. He looked down, watching his responsive rod disappear inside her lips, and stared at her kneeling posture, her shadowed eyes. 'Come on, sweetheart. You can do better.' Words to wetten her, phrases that would make her orgasm spontaneously or sneak off to enjoy a clitoral self-caress.

'We might make you do this on the video to a whole line of people,' he announced. His fingers sought the most sensitive inches of her neck and stroked them till she groaned against his manhood. 'Make you work for your money. Imagine, angel, being forced to lick a dozen sets of balls.'

Her nipples were outlined projectiles now. They were peaking, pulsing. 'Put your palms on your tits, baby.' Beth-Marie quivered as she tongued the underside of his shaft with especial friction, giving some harder licks. 'Oooh, yes, I think you like that. Now squeeze.'

Her own thumb-pads rimmed her breasts. The head of his cock was in her mouth. Her wet dress was flattened to her well-warmed bum – a heightening picture. His hips moved forward, straining of their own accord. Then the exquisiteness flooded through him, upper body tensing for a moment, his fingers tightening in her hair as the exquisite throb pulsed through.

Beth-Marie took her hands from her nipples and wound them round his thighs. Slowly she edged her head back, and gently freed him. 'Was that what you meant by "meals and refreshments will be provided"?' she asked shakily, before wiping her mouth.

'Something like that.' He edged his shrinking manhood back inside his close-fitting black briefs and rezipped his trousers. Did corporal punishment enthusiasts want to see oral sex as a culmination to the chastisement, or did they want the entire hour and a half devoted to punishment scenes? He could phone round some of his contemporaries and ask; watch some more of the current videos, perhaps arrange to have a loose-leaf survey distributed through *Correction* magazine.

'Do these guys need attention?' Beth-Marie nuzzled curiously at his balls, which obligingly tingled.

171

'If they do, they'll have to wait for my work to finish.' When she continued to tease the tender tissue Adam added a firmer 'That's it for today.'

He took her hands in his and helped her upright till she was facing him. She cast a sly sideways glance at the ferule. He ignored the hint. 'You know I go back tomorrow, Adam, don't you?' She put both palms on his shirted chest.

'You can stay on for an extra couple of days if you like – think of it as a free holiday. That is, if that camp bed in the classroom doesn't keep you awake.'

'The décor's in a class of its own! There's a cane and teacher's cloak to my right, a tawse on the left wall hook.'

'It stops guests getting complacent!' If Leanne heard this she'd quiz him again on why the girls couldn't sleep in the seventh dorm.

Talking of girls . . . He looked at his watch. 'Nikki and Nani should have finished their naps by now. They're doing the next sound bite.'

'You'll let me know if I've passed?'

'You've passed! We need three actresses. In a few weeks I'll have had more serious talks with the recording people, get some harder distribution figures, then we'll do this for real.'

'Why can't we do it fully now?'

'The voice tapes I sell will help pay my production costs, will give me an idea of who wants to buy the video. It's best to test the commercial waters first.'

Sensible to the last. He'd heard other entrepreneurs talk of what they were doing, and when; watched their big plans merge into bigger loans and really big issues like repossession. Adam had learned enough from them to know he had to start small.

Start small, then expand to meet future costs. With the right team at his command, the right woman . . . He smiled gently as Beth-Marie stood on tiptoe to kiss him on the lips. If he'd met her when he was eighteen, he'd probably have married her. He'd have been so desperately grateful to find someone who shared his sexual tastes. He'd craved a partner throughout those early years when his body convulsed at the thought of a woman being pulled over a man's knee and held there. Sensation had thrilled through each cell as he pictured her being scorned and spanked. Not that the scorn was real – deep down, men like him adored their women. It was as if each moment of their sexual life together was emphasised, enhanced.

Adam sighed, remembering how perfect he and Leanne had been. Beth-Marie kissed him again. 'Have a shower and get Eleanor to cook you a meal, Beth-Marie,' he told her.

There were more and more women nowadays who liked the same things as him. He wanted a sexually submissive mate he could stay with for life. Someone compatible with that part of him that was controlling. A woman who'd blush and quiver but ultimately climax again and again under the knowing stern strokes of his hands.

He watched the amateur actress walk slowly away aross the fields. She was an experienced masochist, she knew he wasn't a monster. If only the outside world could even begin to understand! He wanted what made *him* feel good, made *her* feel good. It shouldn't matter what the dance was. What counted was the whole glorious spectacle, not the individual unusual steps. But no, the papers had to use their censoring words and vicious phrases: 'kinky . . . perverted . . . deviant . . . disgusting . . . sick'.

Their lack of openness was what was sick, their hypocrisy. Which of their staff hadn't at some time given a playful love-bite, a teasing buttock slap? Who hadn't held their partner's wrists above their head, taken them to a pleading nirvana by switching on and off the vibrator? Adam just went a little further than that.

His choice, his rooms, his willing partners, his honestly expressed inclinations. The ones who really got into trouble were the ones who forced their sexuality underground. The gay men who married women. The bondage lover who never shared his fantasies with a loving partner. The leather fetishist who settled for silk.

Briefly weary, Adam unclamped the hose, coiled it tight and walked back to the outhouse. He looked with

173

peripheral vision towards the trampolines; no shoes peeking out! Presumably Leanne had left her hiding-place to peer through the window lace – she might now be crouching behind the spare tennis nets, the netball stands. He glanced round before hooking the hose back in place, looking for a hem, a human shadow, an inch of shoulder . . . hoping to tease her out, and to talk.

But she'd gone. He felt a sudden hollowness in his head, a dragging at his breastbone. Damn that woman for being so unpredictable, so torn between being giving and remote! She was friend then foe. Lover then rejector. Picking up the ferula, he started to march towards Lingering Lessons. He was going to sort this out with her now!

Sort *her* out. The black rubber punisher rubbed gently against his leg as he walked. It had made Beth-Marie's bottom so pinkly pretty that he ached to use it on Leanne. He had a genuine reason for punishing her – she'd been spying on him. Such a sneaky little girl, so wilful. You should be ashamed.

Words of warning in his head, the means to chastise her in his hand, he felt strong and sure as he took the stairs to her corridor. He knocked on the main door of her quarters.

'Who is it?'

Damn, he'd lost the power of surprise! 'It's Adam Howard.'

'I'm too busy to talk right now.'

'It'll only take a moment.'

'Yeah? I thought you were otherwise engaged.'

If she'd stayed around she'd have seen him dismiss Beth-Marie, heard they weren't an item. She had to learn to trust him. He wouldn't apologise for taking some comfort whilst she kept away from his bed. He wouldn't cajole through the door like some worried father. 'Gerard noticed some loose tiling on the extension roof. I just wanted your authorisation for the repair bill. I can phone a firm in the village later today.'

'You do that.' Her voice floated back, flatly hostile. God, he wanted to make her squeal, teach her some manners! With a last look of loathing at the closed door, Adam walked away.

The girls awaited him. Even buying this rehearsal time hadn't been cheap: Nikki and Nani were much sought after. Punishment magazines could increase their circulations threefold with a front cover showing the identical submissive Chinese-Malaysian twins. Adam had seen them on TV in an Amsterdam hotel: visually stunning, but ultimately too acquiescent for him.

He'd recoup his expenses today by taking stills of the naked sore-bummed subs. He would make several sets, each with its own theme, freeze-framed moments that would whet his clients' appetite for the forthcoming video. They could see the girls under the riding crop, their red lines, and imagine hearing them gasp and squeal.

Fetching his camera and tripod, he set them up in what had been the school's girls' changing rooms, and trained them on the communal shower area. This section of the video was to be called 'Wet, Wet, Wet'. It would feature sequences similar to the one he was about to photograph, and would include a hose scene after the pole-vault. Wet bums felt each welt especially hard.

He buzzed the kitchens. 'Eleanor, the girls are in my rooms. Can you show them the way to the showers?' He laughed. 'No, strictly business!' Did he have *two* girlfriends indeed! The housekeeper wasn't a fool: she probably had a fair idea what was going on. He'd told her at the interview that his work was sexually explicit. He just hadn't confirmed his specific tastes.

Hell, Gerard had shown her what they were about – and she'd come back for more, and kept coming. Six women from the village had applied for the live-in position. He and Leanne were lucky to have found one of a similar bent.

Now to bend Nikki over – and Nani. He turned to face the sound of their footsteps. '. . . Still finding new parts of the building after almost four months here,' Eleanor was saying, with a hint of pride in her voice. All three of them ambled through the changing room doors into the outer cloakroom.

175

Standing in the drained footbath section that led on to the showers, Adam smiled. 'Did you have a nice rest? That train takes an age. One day we'll have an airport!' One day he'd see that this place was given due prominence on the map. But to do that he needed fame, money, support staff. And sexual magnets like these yellow-skinned, black-haired girls.

'We have energy now!' Apart from a slight ellipticalness, one would have thought English was their native language. Not that the script Adam had drawn up called for a large vocabulary. Just the very real sounds of gasps and groans, of palm on thighs, of persuader on backside.

Talking of which . . . He handed them each a towel. 'Get them wet and roll them up when I tell you to. Nikki – it's a straightforward scene. You playfully push your sister in the shower and she slips on the soap and hurts her bottom. She decides to get her own back by tanning yours!' He paused. 'These are the stills, remember, so you'll have to exaggerate the facial movements which show your anger. I'll tell you when to freeze in place.'

Okay, so it wouldn't win the Cannes Palme d'Or award – but it would be a climactic prize for many. And it would bring in much-needed cash. Eight months from now, he and Leanne would be financially on their own, Mamie's golden year ended. They'd need enough money to pay staff, repairs, heating and telephone bills.

When a roof the size of Lingering Lessons' leaked . . . He snapped the shutter as the girls turned on the water and soaped each other. He needed much more contingency money. These still photographs would just bring him a living wage. In the next few months, he'd have to turn his business plan into an earning actuality. He'd need girls like these two, plus Candy. And he wanted Leanne.

The twins had a superficial understanding of the power play at work. He watched as Nikki held up her arms and Nani tied them to the shower head with the ribbons from her long black tresses. They knew about ropes and welts and orders. With Leanne, it was a more instinctive en-thralling thing. She tuned into every gesture, every

dominant nuance of his speech. He could see the compli-
mentary submission – or the fight against it – in the
flickering of her eyes, the sudden dip of her head.

'Tell her what a bad girl she's been. Don't worry about
the words – we're just checking the sound tone.' He
switched on the recorder. Words through water might
prove difficult, he decided; in which case they could dub
them on at a later date.

'I'll slap her clitoris! She really doesn't like that. It makes
her wriggle!' Nani murmured, looking at the tied and waiting Nikki. Her back and bottom were towards the camera,
each sallow buttock as yet untouched.

These were merely throwaway words and glances and
phrases. The woman he wanted to share his life with
wouldn't look, sound or be like this. Nikki and Nani invited punishment at every turn in a way that was blind,
unthinking, mainly visual, whereas Leanne Dell side stepped and sparred all the way. She would make him slough
off each layer of disdain with his fingers, palms, his tongue,
till she slid into subservience for a little while, an incom-
plete surrender. Thereafter she'd quickly reassemble her
dignity, rebuild . . .

Talking of building, he had to put together the founda-
tion of the mail-order goods, had to make the voice tapes
and photographs. He looked at the twins, who were dancing beneath the mobile sprays of water. They didn't seem
submissive now. But other punishment people had told
him that a sharp look and a sharper whip hand soon
brought pert bottoms and petulant personalities into line.

Setting the appropriate speeds on his camera, he walked
up to the jets. 'Right, girls! Nani – flick the wet towel
against her thighs. Good. Now harder, faster. Nikki, you
just respond as your body wants to. Uh-huh.'

Nikki adopted a pushing-in stance as she instinctively
strove to avoid the wet hot lash, wrists holding her helpless. 'Concentrate on the centre of her arse now – ten or
twelve strokes in quick succession as if you're really mad,'
he told Nani. He stepped closer and closer. Colour, texture
and release: he'd capture them all, make them available to

men throughout the world as an aid to the imagination, as a prelude to pleasure, taken either with others or alone.

Pleasure. Such a weak word to describe sensation, satiation, bliss – the way he'd felt with Leanne, the way he wanted to feel with her for ever. 'Use it more at an angle, Nani. That's it, as if you want to mark every inch of that pretty arse.'

'I mark her mound!' The mischievous twin flicked the towel between her sister's legs. Nikki let out a howl and kicked back with her right leg, flexed foot crashing into Nani. Too late: Adam tried to sidestep the latter girl's flailing arms.

'You fool!' He saw the tripod and camera being knocked sideways, turned as they hit the ground, a corner of black plastic case bouncing along the tiling.

'Sir, I didn't mean . . .' Nani stuttered.

'But you did.'

'I could take your mind off . . .' She reached for his zip. He slapped her hand away, genuinely angry. He could live without delays like this.

Taking hold of the naked girl by the wrist, and leaving her sister tied to the workings of the gentle shower, he marched her out to the changing rooms, sat down on one of the low benches, still holding her before him by the arm. 'I'm going to spank your wet bum really hard for tormenting poor Nikki. Then I'm going to teach you restraint and decorum in my rooms.'

He pulled her slender sallow body over his knee. 'Do you know what I keep in my rooms, Nani? The cutest little French ticklers and clit stimulators – they make a dirty girl get so wet, and plead so pretty.' The Oriental shivered with fear and anticipation, her small oval buttocks displaying a sheen from the recent shower.

'I haven't thrashed a yellow arse before. I wonder if it gets as red as a white one does? I'll enjoy finding out.' He flexed his right hand, then brought it down with medium force, preparing the flesh. He spanked with the same rhythm for the next five minutes till her bottom was wriggling, till he knew she was ready to take much more.

Not mentally ready, of course. He'd spoken to enough submissives to know that the nervousness never left them. Though they fantasised about being held down, thrashed, the trepidation they felt during a real chastisement didn't ever go away. No, their buttocks shrank from the lash every time, their minds seeking words and phrases that would redeem them. As Nani was doing now.

'I'm about to start your proper spanking. Go fetch your sister and bring her out to watch.'

'Sir, no! She likes to make fun of me.'

His study of humans had shown him that identical twins were often rivals, far from close emotionally. 'She'll be in good company, then. I'm going to make fun of you, too.'

'Please, sir . . .'

'To the showers. Now.'

He helped her slide from his lap, watched her walk stiff-leggedly through the footbath. She must be aroused already: this relatively mild warm-up spanking wouldn't have caused her to move differently due to pain.

Murmuring voices, a shriek, a laugh, then the twins came into the changing area – Nikki taking the lead, eyes wide with pleasure, Nani keeping three or four feet behind. 'Hurry up, Nani. I hate a girl who dawdles. My palm wants to slap down,' Adam said impatiently.

'I pulled her into the shower with me and made her bum wet again because it stings more,' said Nikki proudly, looking sideways at her twin.

'Did I ask you to do anything?' he asked disapprovingly.

'No, but . . .'

'No. Exactly. We'll let Nani punish you for your presumptiousness after this.'

He looked harder at the sulky girl. 'Sit on your arse while you still can and watch your sister being put through her paces.' He ordered Nani over his lap, then turned his attention to her pinkened wet bare bottom again.

He was going to slap it till it turned red. He toasted her right buttock, then her left, repeated the chastisement. Adam brought his flat hand down on her curvy bum several times. '. . . Replace the camera! Won't charge for my time!' Nani kept yelping. Ignoring her attempts to remedy matters, Adam gave her the spanking of her life.

When he stopped, Nani was sobbing quietly. Her buttocks continued to move. Her toes wriggled, and trembled. 'I may not be finished with your backside yet,' he said, stroking the tender flesh, realising just how angry Leanne's refusal to open her door had made him. 'But I'll help you take your mind off your thrashing for a little while.'

'Thank you, sir.' Nani wrapped her right hand gratefully around his calf and squeezed lightly. He wondered if she'd thank him when she saw what he had in mind.

Pleasure that was almost a punishment in itself – a drawn-out denial of sexual satiation. His mood lightened as he realised he could incorporate such scenes into his video at a later date.

'Right, angel, it's down to the correction chamber for you,' he announced. He'd been turning part of his suite into a special room used solely for chastisement. Nani would be the first to taste its exquisitely refined restraints. Would Leanne be second? Or third? He'd been sure from the moment he saw her ... He hadn't envisaged their union taking as long to fully crystallise as this.

Hands over her bottom so that he presumably couldn't get in some extra slaps, Nani walked before him from the changing rooms, her twin sister following. At the first landing, with its branch of corridors and doors, she turned to stare at him. She saw the coldness in his eyes and looked away.

Stepping in front of her, he marched smartly to his suite, opened the main door, and ushered the girls inside. They'd looked at the photos of caned arses in his study, had rested in his bed after the journey. But they hadn't been in his punishment room till now.

Taking a key from his belt, he undid the lock and watched them stroll into the inner sanctum. He shut the door and leaned against it. 'This is where girls who've been naughty learn to behave,' he told them.

But he'd promised Nani ecstasy for now. 'Move your feet further apart. Make it quick!' He spent several moments looking through his deep cupboard after making the order, giving the Oriental girl time to reflect on what he was about to do. His goal achieved, he took one of the smaller spreaders from its place on the third persuader-packed shelf.

A spreader was simply two ankle cuffs with a strong metal bar in between. This kept the legs at a certain distance from each other, allowing the conqueror access to the other's sex and buttock crevice. 'Stand still, or I'll really give you something to wriggle about!'

He buckled the cuffs securely. 'Good girl. Now let's tie your hands.'

'Oh, please. I hate . . . I promise not to touch my punished bottom.'

'It's not your bottom I intend to concentrate on, angel.' At least, not yet.

Again he strolled slowly back to the cupboard. Anticipation was all! He scooped up the wrist suspension cuffs, black leather lined with softest sheepskin. She could writhe and chafe, but the bindings would never hurt her, but would just hold her in place.

'This'll keep your fingers away from your pussy.' He bound the cuffs around her wrists and hooked them to the chains that hung from the beams beneath the ceiling. Her arms were now pulled tight above her head, her legs apart and held by the spreader. He could do whatever he liked!

And he liked to tease a very wet clit. Smiling grimly, he went to the shelving for a final time and picked up a feather. Nani groaned low in her throat when she saw it. She obviously knew what was coming next.

'You're a clumsy girl when there's a camera around, aren't you?'

A sniff. A nod. 'Yes, sir. But I can change!'

'You're going to change to a feather-light touch in future.' He held up the plumage, smiled grimly. 'This will show you how.' How he loved his work, was good at it – no, great at it! If only the pussy he was teasing belonged to Leanne . . .

Slowly he slid his right hand between Nani's labia,

181

opening them slightly. He took the wet excitement he found there, and moved it up and round until her entire sex was swamped with desire, open and ready. Standing before her, he put the tip of the feather above her clitoral hood and stroked it down.

'I'm going to tempt that little bud like this for a long time. I don't want you to cry out. And that's an order.' He played the light quill over her sex again and the helpless Oriental closed her eyes. 'How does that feel, sweetheart? Does it make you want to come? Make you desperate?' The tethered Nani pursed her lips together. He'd make her assent.

'Just some nice strokes on the tip for a little while.' He taunted the tender tissue twenty-five times, watching the film of perspiration form between her breasts, and on her forehead.

'Nikki, I think your sister's pretty arse-hole isn't getting nearly enough attention. In fact, it's feeling quite left out.'

Nani moaned. 'Don't let her . . .'

Adam nodded towards the cupboard. 'Bring over a slightly larger feather than this one, and play it down the sensitive crease in her backside,' he commanded.

The second naked girl obeyed. He kept up his own teasing task as he watched her use the feather on her stretched-up and leg-spread sister. Now Nani was being offered exquisite sensations from both sides. Not *too* exquisite, though – the touch was too light and varied to ensure a reliable rhythm. He watched as she pulled on her cuffed wrists to try to push her clitoris closer to the sensuous source.

'Don't be greedy, sweetheart. Remember Mr Howard knows best.' He handed Nikki the smaller feather, and accepted the larger one. 'Now you tease her pussy while I concentrate on her arse-hole for a while.' He walked slowly round, cock hardening slightly when he saw her hot pink bum and equally well-warmed thigh tops. Christ, that had been some spanking he'd given! Small wonder her pleasure bud was pleading for release.

Make her wait and wait and wait. The ultimate relief

would be all the sweeter. He used the lightest strands of the feather to tease from top to bottom, even as Nikki provoked the quivering nub of her sister's sex. Nani was making small grunting sounds deep in her throat, her spreader-held legs taut with sexual tension. 'Please,' she begged. 'Oh, please, Mr Howard. I really can't take much more.'

'You'll wait as long as I want.' He glanced at his watch, and decided it was time to give her some pleasure. 'Nikki. I think it's time you made your sister climax.' The girl he was addressing grimaced, and she ran the feather over her twin's pussy lips again. 'Did you hear me?'

'Y-e-s.'

'There's a thick black strap-on dildo on the fourth shelf. Put it on.'

He walked round to face the tethered girl. 'Let's get those wrists unfastened – but don't touch your clit or bum.' He unbuckled the cuffs, then undid the spreader. 'Flex your ankles while you can, sweet. We're about to stake you out on my four-poster bed.'

'I like your bed. I like you.' Nani's right hand fluttered in the direction of his crotch, her dark eyes watchful, as she spoke.

'I'm glad to hear it. You're going to like what your sister does as well.'

'She's bad to me cos I'm prettier than her!'

'In that case you'll have to coax extra-nicely to try to get her on your side.'

'One dildo.' Nikki came back, the corners of her mouth turned down.

'Let's get it buckled.' He spanned his fingers round her waist to belt the contraption on, and felt a surge of sex drive. Both girls had such smooth sallow skin.

And jet-black pubic hair. He stared at both wiry triangles as they sat on their haunches on the bed. The thick black phallus protruded from Nikki's lower torso. 'We'll need you on your back this time, Nani. *Now!*'

Looking downwards, Nani got into place atop the duvet, held her arms out so he could tie them with soft rope to the bed's pillars. He stroked her exposed breasts till she moaned quietly and lifted her hips. 'Time to tie your feet. We want your legs apart as far as possible.' He bound the rope round her left ankle, and secured it to a post, then did the same with the right, making the knots firm but not painful. Now she was spread-eagled in the shape of a cross, her labia wet and open and ready for what came next.

'Place the dildo at her entrance, Nikki. Slide it in about an inch.' He watched Nani's mouth open in a relieved pout as penetration began. 'Now stay there for a moment.' As he stared, Nani tried to raise her hungry hips from the bed.

'Relax sweetheart.' He stroked her hair. 'I'll decide how much dildo you deserve, when you get it.' He smiled coolly. 'If at all.'

'*You* fuck me!' Nani muttered. Six months ago he would have done. Now, fool that he was, he was being faithful to Leanne, to her sexual memory. He looked down at Nani's slender dark-nippled body.

'I've got better things to do.'

He faced Nikki, who was still crouched over her sister's thighs, the dildo's tip inside the hidden hole, hardness inside wetness. 'Right, Nikki, give her another inch,' he commanded. Adam watched the face of the bound girl on the bed, noting the tiny muscles round her mouth, her cheeks that said *more, too much, just there*, in a silent language. 'Now start rotating your hips.'

Nani moaned as the six-inch thickness stirred her inner core. She gazed up at her tormentors with glassy eyes. Her loins moved up, down, up as best they could, given her tethered position. Her spanked bottom rubbing against the bed must have been feeling sore. He could put scenes like this into the video. His pulse quickened. Some day he'd do this for real to his spoilt Leanne!

'Now lie across her and thrust in and out.' Nikki, on top, obeyed. The girl underneath gasped at the change of rhythm. Then her inner excitement adjusted to the tempo and she started to twitch once more. 'Keep still, Nani,' Adam reminded her. He crouched by the girl's head, wound his fingers through her hair. 'Remember how much my palm hurt your backside. You don't want to feel my strap on top of it.'

'No, sir. I won't move!'

Nikki thrust and thrust and thrust. Her nipples were brown bullets. Her fringe fell forward into her eyes. Her lips and cheeks had darkened. He looked at her sister, and saw the same eroticised effects.

Nani arched her back the little she could, a base wild movement. 'Oh dear, I'll have to thrash you now. I told you to obey,' he murmured.

'Please . . .'

He wasn't really going to punish her again – but she didn't know that. Her clit would get more and more excited as he told her what he was going to do.

'I have some bondage gear in my cupboard. I'll add an item to your body each time you wriggle. You're already getting a collar with a strap that links your arms to your neck with wrist restraints.' Nani closed her eyes; and her mouth. Her tummy trembled just a little. 'You're really not trying, are you, sweetheart? Now, I'll have to use the blindfold as well.'

He kept his hands in her hair, watched the dildo-bearing Nikki thrust and thrust. 'Can you imagine: your eyes covered, your hands bound high up your back, that little bottom exposed to me and to my stiffened birch, the thick correctional one?'

'Mm . . . aaaaaaaaaah!' Nani wailed, and came and came.

'Pull gently out of her pussy . . . gently, I said!' Christ, those sisters really didn't like each other. 'Nikki, go and wash the dildo and put it back on the shelf.' He started to untie Nani. 'Have a quick shower *en suite* then get back here. I'm sure you want your revenge.'

He smiled as Nani walked shakily away and Nikki came hurrying back minus the dildo. This was the first time he'd relaxed since that phenomenal foreplay in the gym with Leanne and their ensuing passion. So what if he was taking a couple of hours out of his working time? He'd sent Paul down to the village to buy or borrow a decent camera. Until the boy returned, there was nothing much to do.

Except see that Nikki got her just deserts. She'd shafted her sister carelessly, and needed to be taught a lesson. She perched on the bed and smiled at him innocently, asking, 'What do we do now?'

He smiled back, walked to the cupboard, and brought out two wrist-to-thigh cuffs.

'Are you going to thrash her again? You said you would! Can I help? I can use a rattan!'

'No.' He looked into her eyes as he added the next sentence. 'These are for you.'

'But I fucked her like you asked!'

'You did it unsubtly. Now I'll show you what it's like to be ill-treated.'

He noted the girl's excited yet fearful eyes.

'She's the one who broke your camera.'

'Only because you kicked her very hard.'

Nikki started down at the bed. 'Don't let her . . .'

Her twin came back. Adam took hold of both girl's wrists. 'Now the three of us are going to . . .' He realised the twins were staring over his shoulder, and turned round. '*Leanne!*'

'I . . . knocked, but you didn't reply.' Her cheeks were hectic. 'The door was slightly open. Eleanor told me to tell you that dinner will be delayed by an hour.' Why send a messenger? Why hadn't the housekeeper just phoned, or come herself?

'Right. Thanks.' Belatedly, he let go of the girls. 'This is Nikki and Nani. We're rehearsing a video.'

'I'm sure you are,' Leanne said.

Her voice was heavy with censure, with hurt. 'I was doing the stills, but the camera got broken. Paul's gone down to the village to buy a replacement. You can check.'

'Well, my project awaits . . .'

He looked at her honey-coloured shirt-dress and knew that he loved her.

'Please. Stay.'

'Not my scene.' She let the door to his punishment room gently shut. You coward, liar! He sensed rather than heard her hurrying through his other rooms and temporarily out

186

of his life once more. Why couldn't she admit her real desires? She could get turned on by peeping at scenes like this in the stables, the athletics stadium. She had been soaking, frantic, for friction after he used his palm and his paddle on her.

'Nikki – stand over in the corner so that you're facing it. Move forward three feet. Put your hands by your sides.' His enthusiasm had waned for this now, but he couldn't show his employees any weakness. He glared at the girl till she sulkily did as she was told.

'You like that lady?' she asked.

'She's the school's co-owner.' He walked over to her and bent to fasten the thigh cuffs in place. They were six inches wide, made of heavy leather, black and thick.

He buckled slimmer black bonds to her wrists. Then he used the chrome-ring shackles from each to clip the cuffs together so that Nikki's wrists were chained to her thighs by two chunky metal rings. The strong bands were to make sure she couldn't move her arms more than an inch from her sides, and to remind her of her helpless captive state.

'Nani – fetch the shoe-sole paddle. Your twin used her feet to give you a kick, so that hard leather punisher seems fiendishly appropriate.' He watched as the girl brought the implement back. 'Now, Nikki – bend over from the waist.' The movement gave Nani complete access to her sister's bottom. 'Right – line that paddle up with her arse.'

Black leather on a yellow bum: when this video got made it would be highly erotic. He'd bloody well make Leanne sit down and watch it with him for the full hour and a half!

Now *there* was a thought. He grabbed hold of Nani's arm. 'Let's get you both through to my headmaster's study.' Leanne could see into that, she could then see he wasn't having intercourse with either twin. They'd watch together from her quarters, matched voyeurs enjoying real action foreplay. He'd run his hand over and over her pantied bottom as they saw Nikki's bare one being thrashed.

'No strikes at her back or below the thigh, but don't spare that arse.'

Leaving Nani to see to Nikki, he marched to Leanne's rooms. Knocked once, twice, three times. 'It's me.' He sensed she was in. 'You're going to taste my whip for your refusal to answer!' He paused, listened. 'At least go to the window and see the rehearsals being made!'

Small sounds in the inner sanctum. He could break down her door and haul her to his rooms – haul her over his knee, more like, and spank her into submission. But, much as he craved it, that would just be common assault. He walked away, his cock hard, his mind harder. Deep down she had to want to be, and live, like this, too.

Eleven

She wouldn't give him the satisfaction of looking! Leanne lay on her belly staring at her notebook, then nibbled the top of her pen. She wouldn't, shouldn't. And yet . . . Drawn by a need to know, by the shadowy curiosity that makes us stare at a road-accident victim, she sat up on top of her duvet and peered through the window at Adam's headmaster's room.

One of the Oriental girls had her back – and her bum – to the glass, her arms pinned close to her sides by some black and chrome restraints, her feet held by the metal bar known as a spreader. As she watched, a girl of the same height and looks pulled back a shoe-sole-tipped implement and whacked it against the side of the other female's helpless backside. The punished girl shuddered, but stayed obediently in place. Or did the spreader stop all movement? Would . . .?

This was an Adam-scrawled script, staged for her benefit. Yet still the unbidden prickles surged through her loins. Wallop her hard, bend her over, hold her, some inner voice urged. Her true voice? 'Warm that arse again and again and again!' she muttered to herself.

Yellow flesh being punished to a pink glow. Leanne slid her own fingers inside her honey-coloured shirt-dress. It was too hot for panties. Too hot, now, to watch this without bringing herself the craved-for relief. Round thumb-pad on long wet labial leaves, stroking down, down, down, the well-worn route to satiation. Foreplay was the bare-bottomed scene before her, and each watched wallop brought her nearer to coming.

Getting closer, closer. She found it harder to stand now, but even harder to walk away, thighs and calves going rigid. Her breath was something vaguely familiar, throat aching, hot and dry. Paddle on arse. Arse taking paddle. Leanne sensed the unheard moan as the Chinese-Malaysian girl thrust her torso forward, trying but failing to evade a single searing stroke.

This works for me, excites me, she thought. When she'd climaxed where she stood, when the other two girls looked like they'd similarly found relief, she flopped back down on the mattress, sure that Adam would soon be back, knowing she didn't want him to see her like this. She had to think the situation through and come to terms with it. I thrill to people being talked down, bent over, having their arses roasted. I want to see them writhing and coming under the cane.

Enough! She opened her eyes wide and let them flood with the primrose-yellow promise of the room, forced them to focus on normality. Adam had liberated something in her, or maybe she'd just freed some suppression by herself. Not that it made sex any clearer. She didn't know if she was dominant or submissive, or a confused, shifting mixture. She wanted to watch others being spanked and scolded, whilst a smaller more furtive voice said: Imagine if it was you being stripped naked and held.

Leanne stared down at the tooth-grazed lid of her pen. She had to forget about her changing sexual tastes, and find some fashion-theme ideas instead. Had to secure a salary for her male models rather than think about girlish well-flogged bums!

Buttocks. That made her think of a 'Short Cuts' theme, with men in cut-down denims. No, it had all been done before. How about 'Pack Those Trunks' – fun vacation pics of men in swimming gear? It might appeal to the weekly mags, but the monthlies would find it too pedestrian, too banal.

Shorts, trunks, bums . . . Got it, she thought, and smiled at the ceiling. Adam's posturing had just paid dividends! This concept might win her agency the *Be Seen* journal's fashion spread. That meant nationwide exposure, formidable fees.

Think. Plan! It would involve employing a couple of female models as well as her usual male ones. But she'd got to know lots of girls in the trade who were always on the lookout for new contracts, for work much less lucrative than this.

If she secured it, that is. And she would, she would! Offloading the sudden surge of concepts from her head to the paper, she stretched out on the bed and reached for her mobile phone and address cards. She'd do all her work from her rooms rather than sit at her desk in reception today. She wasn't ready to face Adam with his wife – or whoever. Nor did she want to see him up close with those cutely cruel Oriental beauties, or have any part in his video rehearsal games.

Other women. Other games. God, why were the great-in-bed-and-intelligent-with-it ones usually hitched or in some way committed? Why couldn't they at least be *honest* about their marital state?

Time for work, not play. Flicking through her address file, she located a number. Took a deep breath, then another, then made the call. Got through to the publisher's operator. '*Be Seen* magazine, please.' They rarely asked who you were if you sounded professional. A moment later she was buzzed through to the appropriate extension. This was it! 'Can I speak to Gilly Skanes, the Fashion sub-editor, please?' With a magazine this prestigious, she daren't go quite to the top!

There was the usual on-hold music, something electronic and new. She phrased her intro in her head, then rephrased it. 'Ms Skanes? I run Mainly Men, the model agency. My name's Leanne Dell.' She paused. When she'd worked from her flat, she'd just met her models at the location grounds, and taken basic photos. Sent them to the editors and waited for them to arrange the final shots, and for the commissions to come in. Then she got paid for supplying the models, and paid them from her extravagant fee.

It was different now that she was operating from a rural

Scottish boarding-school – more special but less convenient. Staying upbeat and optimistic, she outlined the
situation to the woman, told of Lingering Lessons' vast
sensual scope. 'And I've worked out a way where I can still
supply you with the complete package if you're interested,
and not waste staff time,' she continued.

'Tell!' The woman sounded open to suggestions.

'I'll take the rudimentary photos and fax them to you on
day one of my models' work. If you like the underlying
concepts, you can commission by return and despatch a
photography team to Lingering Lessons. I'll book my boys
– and a couple of girls – for the week.'

'We'll probably just need them for a couple of days.'

'I'll keep it flexible. When you're finished I can use them
for other things.'

Yeah, like provoking Adam into endless jealousy, she
thought. She forced back the thought: she was no longer
into power posturing, she was moving towards sexual honesty. Leanne smiled into the receiver as the woman said
that she'd talk to her editor, that the project sounded just
right for *Be Seen*. Later that morning, the magazine
phoned to say they'd love to see the introductory photos.
Grinning, Leanne put down the receiver, then picked it up
again.

'Jason? Leanne Dell here. I was wondering if you could
come to the school for a week. Mmm, we're going places!'
Four similar calls later, she put down the receiver, then
buzzed Eleanor on the kitchen line. 'I'd be really appreciative if you could organise five camper beds in the
classrooms. We're having guests!' She listened for a moment. 'No, I'm much too busy to have fun. This is strictly
business!' She wrote down two more fashion ideas as her
own words infiltrated her brain.

'Strictly Business'. That would be the title of her erotic-
yet-amusing fashion theme. She'd need some special furni-
ture, made a note to contact a film production props
company or freelance carpenter within the hour. Short
term, this was going to cost her, but she'd more than recoup her money when the magazine paid. And think of the

192

kudos a *Be Seen* commission would bring! The exposure would take her several steps closer to being one of *the* agencies, the ones the best models yearned to work for. The ones that supplied beauties for the Italian catwalk year after year.

And that was what she wanted, wasn't it? Leanne rolled on to her back and flattened her hands behind her head, surprised that the idea didn't make her pulse increase or her imagination quicken. Once, the mere thought of such success would have made her feel warm and especially alive. Now? Maybe the move to this vast place, and the on–off affair with Adam, plus Candy's betrayal, had all tired her. Maybe she needed a rest.

Not now, but later. She'd set up this major work, then talk to Adam about the women in his life, their place in his affections. She'd breathe deep, stay cool and focused. If he still wanted her, he'd have to let go of the others, perhaps travel to Barra or Uist with her on vacation for a week. They'd go for long walks along the coast, eat salmon salads, drink malt whisky. They'd simply *be*.

For the moment, *she* had to be the organised efficient one! She pulled on her hessian-weave slip-on shoes. She'd walk round the school now, deciding which of her models would go where and what they'd be doing. She'd think of quarter-bared bums and half-formed wrist restraints. Would look for texture, colour, light.

Five days later, Leanne contemplated Simon's silky brown hair, his heavy tweed suit, the way the sunlight shone against the buckle of his briefcase. 'This'll be for their November issue so we'd better shut out that sun a little bit.' She nodded to Khan, who hastily limped across the room to close the blind, his bad ankle still paining him. Small wonder, when he'd been horse-riding and hill-walking, and dancing at the village ceilidhs. The youth just wouldn't stay still!

Simon looked like a younger Charles Dance – a country gentleman. For this shot he had to look slightly less proper though. With Leanne's input, *Be Seen* was about to surge towards the risqué: a bad-boys and naughty-grown-girls routine.

'Right, arms through the holes!' she continued, winking at the youth, keeping the atmosphere determinedly light and playful. This wasn't one of Adam's heavy punishment sessions. She just wanted a hint . . .

. . . Of restraint, of domination. Enough to make the most jaded male buyer look twice at the photo and hence the clothes. This picture was to be called 'The Stock Market'. It featured Simon in a traditional wooden stocks, his suit trousers unbuttoned and pulled down just an inch or so to show designer underpants clinging to his taut high rear end.

Christ, it would be so easy to pull his trousers and his underpants all the way down! With his arms enclosed in the stocks, he was completely at her mercy. She could stroke and squeeze his exposed buttocks whilst he squirmed for hour after hour. Could break off to have meals, come back, taking his cock into her knowing mouth and fingers. Making him get hard, then harder; hearing him plead.

'Ready when you are, Miss Dell!' Simon murmured, running his tongue along his lower lip. 'These trousers itch!'

'Stop complaining, or I'll really give you something to cry about!' Her words were teasing. She wondered if Adam would see any of this. It wasn't quite six yet: he might still be sleeping. It was all too easy to picture his thick black hair on the smooth white pillows of his bed.

'Khan – open these middle slats so that the sun shines on the buckle of Jason's case.' *Be Seen* would list the stockist of both briefs, briefcase and suit in the actual fashion spread. They'd sent all the garments to Lingering Lessons by express delivery a few days earlier. 'Okay, Jason, just gaze towards the window.' She clicked the camera. 'Now take that bundle of fivers from Khan and smile down at it.'

Monopoly money: guaranteed to make the reader smile. The cash had already been used in their 'Money for Nothing' photo in the same set, in which red-haired model Pauline spread the notes over the waistband of Jason's silk boxer shorts whilst he lay atop a work station with his hands behind his head.

Now for the 'Pretty in Place' fashion statements! Ushering Shona, Jason, Simon, Pauline and Bernie to the executive boardroom, Leanne gave them a few moments to change into the requisite costumes. Then she started to arrange their smoothly pampered languorous limbs.

'Shona – stand up and lean forward about ninety degrees across the desk. No, keep holding the file, as if you're about to hand it to Simon.' She watched, nodded, then walked behind the girl and took six snaps of her navy-blue pinafore mini-dress riding up to show a hint of white satin knickers, thigh-length woollen socks. 'Great!' Leanne took a deep breath. 'Now, Bernie, just pull down her pants a little bit and lay the ruler against her flesh. Keep smiling. We're going to caption this one "Executive Stress".'

They moved from the boardroom to the bedroom. Gerard's room had a king-sized brass-headboarded bed. He'd kindly lent them his suite to use for the location. Guiding the others to his opulent quarters, Leanne got prepared. 'Pauline, sit up on the pillows. Have the book open on your lap, cover-side up so that we can see it's a passionate read. Khan – drape that raw silk scarf lightly over her wrists. Simon, lie down next to her and take hold of the ends. Look thoughtful.' She captured the hint of bondage on film. *Be Seen* would love it! Not since their 'School's Out For Ever' spread, which featured women in their twenties posing as gymslip mums, would they have aroused such controversy. They'd get numerous column inches in the press.

Submission with a just-joking smile, punishment with a pun: it was perfect. Many people quipped about being masochists whilst deep down it turned them on. This gave them the opportunity to look openly at the situation without feeling threatened or going underground.

Who would you do it with? Where? For some, these would be previously unasked questions. What would it feel like, taste like? Would you groan loudly or just whimper? Cry out? The many questions as a new partner held you with his weight or her weight and pinned you to the duvet. Heartbeat speeding, mind musing: what if he or she took it further than this? How would I react if they held my hands above my head, tied my legs apart and teased my sex parts? Spanked my bum?

She had to concentrate on her work, stop getting wet! Leanne forced new words through her brain. 'Khan – tie that wrist bind in the loosest bow. Mm, keep it subtle.' She smiled at the twenty-year-old female model, 'Okay? At least that tunic's nice and light for the season. Poor Simon in his winter suit!'

Then it was time for long leather boots à la dominatrix, guaranteed to beat the snow and the subservient. Picking them up, Leanne walked with the others to the stables, and looked at her watch. 'We'll just do this set, then we'll stop for a tea break.' She fingered the damp tendrils at the back of her neck. This was tiring work – but the sooner they completed and faxed the stills, the sooner she'd get the go-ahead and get her (and their) money; get to talk to Adam, maybe get away from all of this for a week or so! Much as she loved the school, she hated the stress between herself and its co-owner. She hated the fact that Candy was still around.

Leanne had made sure that the little bitch couldn't sabotage her plans; she'd told the sub-editor to phone her back if anyone pretending to be her cancelled. 'Mm, a rival has been causing problems,' she'd murmured, happy to let the woman think it was a competing firm rather than an individual girl.

A safely secured cheque was vital now – they had so many stills to dress up for, so many poses to set, so many settings to secure, that this project had to reap dividends. Cautiously she took eight or ten shots of each clothes-perfect pose. A developer in the village had a darkroom in his cottage. He'd promised to process the film without delay.

'Okay, Pauline – hold the riding crop in both hands and look down at it thoughtfully. Jason, you kneel at her feet and start to pull off one of her boots.' She winked at Gerard, who obviously thought that the *girl* should be the one to kneel, to take the crop across her hindquarters. 'If you can just bring the roan and the stallion a couple of feet closer, Mr Kerne. That's it!'

Erotic but ambiguous. The man might be about to receive thanks for removing the boots or a whipping for some unseen misdemeanour. The woman might be a kindly rider of mares, or merciless rider of men. Leanne reloaded, reshot, as models changed into cord jackets, velvet jodhpurs and calfskin boots behind the stables. Khan limped from the trunk of clothes to the men, in his role of substitute wardrobe mistress. They all broke off briefly when Eleanor brought them a tray with two pots of Earl Grey tea.

Then it was back to work. 'Hand your teacups to Khan! Follow me to the teacher's study. It's time to shoot the "Homework" theme!' She unpacked the props. 'Bernie – suck that diamond-set pen as if it was a clitoris. Shona – set down that filofax and stretch your arms up above your head to show the embroidery on those breast pockets. Higher . . . Just there!' They took photo after photo before moving Pauline and Jason on to the cavernous four-piece bathroom, both dressed in monogrammed towelling robes from Paris fashion houses: his and hers.

What would he do to her, and she to him? These shots had to hint at what might happen when the photographer went away, leaving easily bared and already-aroused male and female bodies.

'Sit on the side of the bath, your sides just brushing,' Leanne suggested, licking her lips as she fastened on their gold-link ankle chains. Once she'd have refused to fasten such slave-like restraints to her models. Now she had to concentrate on not climaxing at what came next!

'Jason – pick up that report and look at it intently. No, hold it down a bit so that we can see the neckline of your robe, a hint of thick chest hair. Pauline – bring your hand forward and playfully slap his bottom as if you're chastising him for working too hard. Just frown a bit more in concentration. Jason – look slightly surprised.' She gazed, secured the shot, looked at the pages of instructions she'd written for herself. 'Now let's . . .'

197

Walk. Think. Pose. Do it all again, And a third time. At last she looked at her notes. 'We're finished for the day!' She gave a mock curtsey at their cheer. 'You know where the changing-room showers are. There's the games room off level two if you want chess, cards, snooker or videos. Relax. Have fun.' She grinned tiredly at them all. 'There's a salad lunch in the dining-room. Eleanor serves dinner at seven.' A pause. 'I'm off to the village to get these films processed. After that, you'll probably find me in my rooms.'

Pats, hugs. They'd all worked well, all wanted to be seen in *Be Seen*. Leanne walked to the garage and liberated the Morgan. Smiling like a lunatic, she drove to the film processor's cottage. Everything had to be just right!

It was – it was flawless. An hour later, she gazed down at the numerous stills, some of which were still gently drying. She could fax that one and that one – and those three! As for the stables shots, the sun had picked up the matt surface of the calfskin coat, contrasted it with the shiny chestnut dapples of the horse, the high-gloss riding boots. *Be Seen* readers would want to be seen in these clothes! 'Real classy, aren't they?' the retired chemist murmured, gazing down at the photos.

'Real classy,' Leanne agreed.

Now to show the editor such class! When the colours had fixed properly she slotted the pictures into a plastic wallet, and carried them to her car, driving back to the school in the early-afternoon sunshine. She hurried to reception, to the desk where they kept the fax machine. Adam was taking a call at his desk.

'Mm, I have it before me now, Josh – a pre-programmable vibrator. Means the woman can tie herself up after she slips it inside her, pretend it's a man varying his speed.'

'Visitor in your room, Leanne!' Shona shouted down the stairs.

'Who?' Their remote Scottish location didn't exactly allow for drop-in sessions.

'Can't remember the name. Something about a catalogue.'

Damn! Leanne looked at Adam.

'Want me to fax these through for you?' he asked, covering the mouthpiece with his hand.

'No, you're busy . . .'

'Josh is about to check some sales figures, wants me to hold.'

So he did have a thoughtful side! She nodded. 'The details are all there,' she told him. Picking up the photos that she wasn't going to fax, she hurried towards the stairs.

A man of around five foot six with thin strands of too-long hair was sitting on her bed. 'I've come at a bad time, haven't I? You look exhausted,' he said.

'No, it's just . . . Can I ask who you are? I wasn't expecting anyone today!'

'I phoned to speak to Leanne Dell about an hour ago. The woman who answered told me to come round immediately. Surprised *me* too!'

Leanne hauled out a seat, sat down three feet from him. 'I've got some models working here – one of them must have picked up the extension.' She'd chide them for it later. 'I take it you're local, as you got here so fast?'

'Mm, I'm a manufacturing rep.' He named a factory in the next village. 'I was wondering if Mainly Men could appear throughout our new overalls and boiler-suits brochure?'

Leanne laughed lightly. 'Sounds like familiar territory! We've done dental coats and tunics before.' That had been in the early days when she was trying to find work for her brother and his colleagues: before she and Adam had inherited the boarding-school.

Picking up her pad, she made notes of fees and potential costs, spin-offs, repeat commissions. At last she murmured, 'Yes, we'd be delighted to do business with you.' Just because she was riding high – well, starting to – she wouldn't forget her roots, the kind of people who had helped her. She would never forget that she was dispensable even though she was good.

Catalogues like this provided bread-and-butter money rather than caviar. But she hadn't lost sight of the fact that she'd have to work full-out at the end of the twelve-month period, when she and Adam had to start meeting their *own* accommodation expenses. Lingering Lessons was a wonderful legacy, but keeping it heated and landscaped and in good repair required commitment and hard work.

If only she didn't feel so flat at the thought of yet more poses and photo-calls! Roll on that holiday, she thought. 'No, I can send my models to your preferred venue,' she told her visitor.

They talked appointment dates and wardrobe fitting and booking fees; at last she finished the meeting. 'No, really,' said the rep, 'I'll find my own way out.' Anxious for confirmation of her fax, she buzzed Adam in reception. But he was still engaged! She went downstairs, where he was laughing on the phone. She looked at him, then at the fax machine. He followed her gaze and put his thumb up, then broke off his talk briefly to say, 'Leanne – it's done!'

Now all she could do was wait. The magazine had said they'd get a decision to her by close of business. It was three-thirty. She'd been organising the models since first light that morning. Putting a 'Do Not Disturb' sign on her door, Leanne stretched out on the *chaise longue* and floated down into much-needed blankness. Waking twenty minutes later, she cleaned her teeth, drank some mineral water and ran lightly downstairs.

'Sorry – not what we're looking for'. She stared, frozen, at the faxed sheet. She'd been so sure that her ideas and presentation were infallible, that the job was hers.

Run to your room. Lock the door. Hide! The part of her that would always be a little girl gave the protective orders. But, given her responsibility to the others, how far could she flee? Within the hour she'd have to tell the models, pay their expenses out of her own pocket. But first, she had to try to understand.

Maybe bondage themes were still too risqué. Or maybe clubland fetish gear had ensured they were overexposed. She'd got the formula wrong somewhere, she'd obviously miscalculated what was needed. Had the equestrian detail been too much? She could get rid of the whip, have the male riding a gym horse for a more humorous or surreal look.

Ask and ye shall receive. She'd never believed in glib statements, but . . . She picked up the mobile, put it down, picked it up again. The call was going to be awkward, unexpected, but if she stayed clear and contrite then surely they wouldn't mind.

The publisher's name, the magazine's name, the sub-editor's name: she went through the list of connections again. A few hours ago she'd been so happy doing this, so forward-looking! Now she felt rejected, almost direction-less.

'Gilly? Leanne Dell of Mainly Men. I got your fax. I'm sorry the project didn't appeal to you. I apologise if this inconveniences you further, but I wonder if you could possible explain your decision to me, for future reference?'

A sigh. 'It's just that we're fashion leaders, not followers. Themes like yours have been done to death.'

'Was it the wrist-based scarves? They were more for fun!' Damn, she'd promised herself she wouldn't beg and she sounded like she was begging. She listened. 'I don't under-stand. I *did* use your clothes. The package sent express delivery? Mm, tweed suits and bathrobes and boxers and filofaxes.'

She felt her heartbeat speed. 'Look, I know this sounds stupid, but can you fax me back a couple of the images I faxed you? I got someone else to send them in. I'm begin-ning to wonder . . .' She watched as the grainy pictures materialised before her eyes.

A woman at the seaside in a black one-piece, her stocky stiff back to the camera. A man with his beige trousers rolled up to his knees, squinting at the sun. She stared down at page after page of ordinary-looking adults in or-dinary beachwear doing ordinary beach things. 'Gilly, these weren't the ones I sent!'

Weren't the ones I *wanted* sent. There was a difference: the kind of difference that changed your approach to other people, to life. She'd know that Adam was not immune to the charms of other females, but she'd trusted him not to ruin her business, trusted him to do what was right. He'd sat there, laughing in reception, giving her the thumbs up. She'd been so trusting. He and Candy must have been a team all along!

'I still have other copies of my photos here. Can I fax them over now? The colours aren't as good as the ones that have gone missing.' She listened. 'Yes, I think I know who's behind it. The police? I suppose you're right.' She fetched the envelope from her rooms and faxed Gilly the images.

Leanne waited in reception till the phone rang, and the answer was yes. 'We're pleased to give you the work.' In editor-speak that meant 'we want it, need it, love it'. Superlatives weren't British magazines' style.

The arrangements made, she put down the receiver, and made for her quarters. She wouldn't tell the authorities about Adam's sabotage. He could still tell about her caning Candy, say how she'd stripped before her window in order to arouse him in the early days. And how she'd come while he made her ride a doll, cried out again and again with Adam's own cock inside her. He might even have videoed her rapture. She'd look less like a wronged businesswoman than a woman scorned.

I never want to see him again. The realisation sank from her brain to her heart. Both felt leaden. She'd been so credulous, so hopeful, so ridiculously wrong! How could she stay on now? It was a fight she no longer cared to win. He could have his bloody boarding-school! She'd go back to London, start again.

Do something different, maybe retrain. She had some savings, plus stocks and shares that Mamie had left her. Assuming the models went ahead with her bondage theme, she'd soon have the *Be Seen* commission cheque. She could book a hotel room till she rented a flat. Maybe she could take a photography diploma, sell studio portraits. She'd always been quite good. At least, better than Adam, with his amateurish holiday snaps.

It would have been risible if it wasn't so bloody tragic. Christ, she'd left the package by the machine for him, put her future in his sabotaging hands! If she hadn't, he'd doubtless have got Candy to make another call pretending to be Leanne or one of the models. If she'd stayed at Lingering Lessons, she'd have had to spend the rest of her life watching her back.

Back; time to go back to the city. She'd leave tomorrow night after phoning essential business contacts and friends to tell them where she was heading. That would save them phoning her here and getting Adam, giving him the opportunity to gloat.

Keep it upbeat, light. She'd hint to the models that she had to leave on business, that they must just do what the photography team told them to. It wasn't such a lie. Her business could be anywhere now – she might go to France, spend some time with her brother, Marty, winding down.

Leanne splashed cold water on her face, poured herself a *crème brûlée* liqueur and sipped the sweet spirited sustenance. She knocked on the window to Khan, who was down in the grounds teaching the others to boxercise, then composed herself for his knock and ushered him in.

'Adam tried to ruin this fashion contract.' Her most important ever fashion contract. 'He faxed his holiday snaps over to the magazine,' she told him.

'He wouldn't.' The youth's lips parted in surprise.

'I asked him to fax my rough photos, but he substituted his own. The fashion editor confirmed it.'

'Are you sure it wasn't Candy?'

'Same difference! Let's face it, he's the one who insisted she stay on here after I gave her the sack.'

'You should talk to . . .'

'I'm sick of talking.'

'Give him a chance to . . .'

'I'm going to *act*.'

She ruffled the boy's glossy black hair. 'I'll leave tomorrow after I've sorted everything out. Don't tell anyone, okay? I've had enough scenes to last me a lifetime.'

'Where will you go?'

'Mm? London for a night or two. I'll make some decisions, then go to France for a break.'

'I'll come with you.'

203

'Khan – I need some time alone to think.' She smiled at him. 'Driving solo is therapeutic. However, I'm happy to give you the money for the train.' She squeezed his hand. 'But you'll get more work if you stay. Gilly liked my fashion themes when she saw the brief. I'm sure she'll love the final product! The *Be Seen* photo team will be here before I leave.'

'Guess I can't freeload for ever, huh?'

'Not even you!' He was so nice, so full of helpfulness and humour. If only she could fall in love with someone uncomplicated like him.

There was only one other person she ought to tell. Steeling herself to withhold any slanderous detail, Leanne walked slowly down to the kitchens. Eleanor had been kind to her, so she shouldn't just abandon her more needy friend. At the same time, the woman had a sharp eye and tended to gossip. Leanne would have to be circumspect. After all, Adam was Eleanor's joint employer, and she'd presumably continue working for the man for some considerable time.

'Only me!' She popped her head round the kitchen and smiled. The older woman was turning radishes into salad roses. 'These are brilliant! Wish I could do that.'

'Why bother, when you can pay *me* to do it?' Eleanor said, with a knowing laugh.

'I . . . won't be paying anyone for much longer. I'm leaving tomorrow.' In fact, as soon as she'd greeted the *Be Seen* team.

'But I thought you were happy here!'

Apart from one special night – now soured by what had followed – happiness at Lingering Lessons had always just evaded her. She'd hovered on the brink of ecstasy, but something she'd called pride or fear had stopped her going over the edge for more than a moment. Now she wondered if her instincts had been warning her against Adam Howard's treachery.

'Changes at work!' she said. That wasn't a lie.

'This place too out of the way for you?' Eleanor asked her.

'Well, for some of my clients. To them, London's the only city that exists!'

'I'll miss our chats.'

'Eleanor – thanks. I only wish we'd got to know each other sooner.' She touched the housekeeper's arm.

A sisterly moment, then, 'What time do you leave?' from Eleanor.

'Tomorrow, after some magazine fashion team arrives – probably in the evening.' She saw the shadows on the older woman's face, 'Don't worry! I've always enjoyed through-the-night driving. I'll be fine.'

'Mr Howard'll want to have a farewell dinner in your honour.'

She forced herself to keep making eye contact. 'At the risk of sounding secretive, Eleanor, I don't want him to know. I hate farewells, and . . . Well, I may even be back if my business priorities alter.' Only in my dreams, she thought.

'It won't be the same without you.'

But few things stayed the same, or ought to. Life was about change, about transition. Look at her – in a few strange weeks Leanne had changed her thinking, her lust-ful bent. *He*'d started to make her into what *he* wanted and needed. Now the non-sexual side of his quest for power was forcing her to flee.

Twelve

'Right you – these pants are coming down!' Khan walked without knocking into Candy's room and grabbed her upper arm, holding it tightly.

'But what have . . .?'

'You've ruined Adam and Leanne's love for each other, that's what!' He'd watched his employer slowly admit her feelings for Lingering Lessons' copywriting co-owner, had seen her emotions reflected back in the man's watchful eyes.

Leanne and Adam were *meant* to be together. They had the same style of intellect and ethics, the same approach to life. Lighthearted though he, Khan, was about his own affairs and flirtations, he refused to let anyone else destroy something meaningful and good.

'Where are we going?' Candy mumbled, as he marched her towards the door.

'Going to a place where I can thrash you till you tell me what's been happening.'

'I . . .' Her cheeks were flushed, lips parted. 'I don't know what you mean!'

'Maybe a sore bum will awaken your understanding.' He decided to get some of Adam's implements from the cupboard in the hall. It wasn't really his scene, but he had to make her realise he was serious; make her tell the truth.

Keeping a firm hand on her elbow, he walked her to the reception hall. Khan took out leather restraints for her arms, her legs, her feet, then a coil of rope to help him be creative. Adding a devilish-looking sex toy and particularly merciless cane to the bag around his waist, he ordered, 'Take your clothes off here.'

'Someone might see!'

'Exactly.' He used one finger to tilt her chin till her face lifted to his, and saw the dread and sexual excitement flicker and expand.

'But I was punished for . . .', she played with the pleats of her dress, '. . . for making that phone call.'

'I'd have thrashed you till you told the truth.'

The girl gazed up at him, eyes dark and wide. 'I didn't think you were into . . .'

'I'm not. I'm doing this for my friends.' He smiled. 'It means I don't climax and then feel relaxed and forgive you. Means I can use that cane on your helpless little bum for a very long time.'

He was good at this. He could be great at this! He'd always been confident where sex was concerned – any kind of sex in any situation. Since arriving here, he'd seen and heard enough male dominance to know the actions, the words, the empowering emotionless tone. But could he actually . . .? He played the cane through his fingers. Yes, thinking of Leanne's drawn white face, imagining her driving away from her lover and her inheritance, would give him the impetus to bring down the stick on Candy's wilful backside.

'Dress off.' He watched as she pulled the lacy folds from her belly and breasts, and let her dress fall sadly to the ground. 'Now your bra and panties.' Khan stared as her pouting pink nipples and recently trimmed pubic patch came into view. 'And your sandals. I have some special shoes in mind.' He glanced down at the glossy restraints by his feet. Candy shuddered, then obediently kicked her low heels away.

Naked, she stood staring at the ground.

'Look at me,' he demanded, then fastened a thick leather cuff round her waist as she did so, taking hold of the smaller wrist cuffs that were attached to the part above her bottom. 'Put your arms back.' She obeyed him and he fastened on the two black cuffs.

Her arms were now shackled behind her back, crossed over, and effectively bound to the waistband. It was time to similarly restrain her suntanned feet.

'Step into those.'

Candy looked down at the chained-together stilettos, then slid one foot cautiously into the right one. Holding on to his arm to keep her balance, she angled her foot into the left. 'I can't walk!'

'Yes you can. You just have to take very small steps.' He'd seen such a punishment walk performed on one of Adam's videos. Kneeling for a moment, he bound two small leather straps over the tops of both shoes so that she couldn't kick them aside.

'You're going to teeter before me to the boundary fence.' Her eyes went wide. 'But that means any passing villager can see me!'

'Mmm, doesn't it just!' he teased.

She looked around wildly. 'And if I don't do what you say?'

He picked up the cane and flicked it across her naked rear, stinging the full swell in a casual warning. 'You don't have much choice.'

'Ouch!' Candy tried to flinch away, and almost toppled on the long slender heels.

'Take it slowly, silly.' He put his fingers on her upper arms, and turned her manually towards the door.

'Walking in these will take ages!' Candy complained, her lips pressed petulantly.

'It will give us masses of time for a very truthful chat.' He slid his palm over her buttocks and repeated the gesture. 'A very *painful* chat, if you don't come up with some answers.'

'I can't!'

'You can and you will.'

He held open the door, watched her shuffle out into the sun. The hobble-chain ensured that each step was small and careful. 'Start walking towards the fields on the south side. If you tell me what I want to know, I'll be kind enough to open the gates.' If he didn't, she'd have a devil of a job getting over each fence with her arms locked behind her and her ankles effectively chained.

He got into step at her rear. 'Tell me why you made the

initial phone call pretending to be Leanne.' Khan watched the girl's shoulder-blades pull back slightly as if she'd taken a deep breath. When she kept walking forward, he brought the cane sideways across the natural crease where her twin orbs sloped into her leg tops. Candy gasped, then took four faster steps forward, and had to jerk her body smartly upwards to avoid a fall.

'Let's try again.' Another swish of the cane. Another red mark on previously creamy flesh. Another girlish exclamation. 'At this rate you're going to have the hottest arse in Christendom before we reach the boundary gates,' he joked.

'Don't care!' He saw the fear and excitement and determination in her eyes as he swivelled her round to face him. Maybe he could capitalise on that excitement? There was a convenient fence coming up.

'Candy – get your belly against that wood,' he ordered. When she hesitated, he lifted her up ten inches so that her shackled heels were on the second bar, then bent her over, over, over. Now her bare bottom was cruelly and fully exposed.

'Not the cane,' she moaned.

'Oh, you'll get the cane again after this until your backside's obedient. But first I'm going to teach you compliance with this.'

Unzipping his jeans, he scooped his hardness out and nudged it between her thighs, guided by the wetness. Used his middle fingers to open her further, then poised himself to enter her. 'I'm going to fuck you good and hard, but I'm not going to let you come. Not until you tell me why you've betrayed Leanne twice this summer.'

'I did not! I only betrayed her once!'

'Once, then.' He wasn't convinced she hadn't been behind this second act, but even finding out why she'd made the phone call would explain her basic motivation. 'Prepare to have an aroused hot pussy,' he murmured, sliding in.

It was like entering a grip of molten syrup. His balls surged at the pleasure. He felt his manhood swell; stood with his feet on the ground and his hands on her waist and his cock deep inside her; watched himself start to rock lazily in and out.

'Why were you such a wicked girl?' he asked, moving in, out, in.

'I didn't want to!'

'Just like you no longer want to feel the cane on your helpless rear end?'

'Hate the cane! Hate the bright red marks!'

'I know. I've watched you with Adam. You like the all-over heat of the belt or the paddle. You're going to take much more of the rattan, though. Unless . . .'

He slid his arms between the slats of the fence till he found her pendulous breasts – soft spheres of sensitivity – and pumped them gently like udders as he shafted her sex. 'No climax, Candy. Just the hottest squirming bum. Just strangers watching. Or sexual relief and an end to your correction if you tell.'

Silence. He thrust in up to the hilt, then pulled almost fully out again, rewarded when she gasped and tried to push her pudenda back against him. 'Hold it. Don't be greedy. You know you're not allowed to come,' he reminded her. With her arms bound up her back, she couldn't touch her clit. The stiletto chains meant she couldn't walk away. Her bent stance over the fence ensured she couldn't even straighten. He had her where he wanted her – and she wanted to go all the way.

Her breathing started to speed up. She flexed her calves. He pulled mercilessly out, vaulted over the fence so that he faced her. 'Look, Candy – you're not getting any of it!' He chafed gently at his cock and squirted its light warm liquid over her hanging breasts.

'Need to come!'

'No, angel. We're going to let you cool down again.' He had a few hours till Leanne left: time to extract a full confession. He licked his middle finger and traced the inside of Candy's mouth, ran it tantalisingly over her full lips.

'Please . . .'

'Please tell me why you sabotaged Leanne's work.'

210

'Anything but that. *Anything!*'

He looked at his half-hard member. 'In a few moments this'll be ready to take you almost to the brink again.'

He stayed in front of her, stroking the sides of her breasts, till his shaft regained its proud upwards slant against his belly. Shielding it with one hand, he climbed sideways over the fence till he faced Candy's rear, then located the entrance to her quim. 'Oh you're absolutely dripping!' He thrust powerfully in.

He could pleasure her for twenty minutes or more, now that he'd orgasmed. She looked like she'd last about three. Was whimpering, squirming against the fence, trying to push her lightly caned globes back against him. 'Tell, Candy, tell!'

'Can't!'

'There's a large tree stump in that corner there. I could tie you over it. You'd be so near to the ground that I'd have lots of space to bring the rattan down. If you think your bum's sore *now* ...' He gazed at her pink-laced rotund buttocks as he bucked in and out. She was seasoned at this. She could take much more. She'd have to. 'I haven't really started yet, you know,' he taunted.

Candy groaned low in her throat. She still didn't say the words he wanted to hear. He'd have to vary his approach. It wasn't working. Maybe an unexpected kindness would do the trick.

'Answer yes or no to one question. If you do, I'll let you come before I continue your thrashing.' He felt her stiffen hopefully against him. 'Were you working alone on this?'

A breathless pause, an indrawn breath; he stopped his thrusting. Then a very reluctant 'No'.

'Good girl. Were you ...?'

'You promised!'

'I did.' He quickened his thrusts until the head of his cock was brushing the tip of her cervix. Slid his right hand round to cup her pussy, stroked her nipples with his left. Felt her hot walls closing in on him, tighter, tighter. Knew that she was about to climax even before she ground her arse into his belly and called his name.

'Did you say Khan or cane?' he teased, as her postorgasmic contractions ceased. Carefully he withdrew and threw away the sheath, which was lightly streaked with pre-come fluid. He hadn't let himself climax, he wanted to hold back so that he could sexually torment her further. Assuming he had to, of course.

Silence. 'Let's finish our little stroll. Such a lot of pussy juice running down your legs! If any of the villagers see, they'll know what you've been up to.' In truth, the local people had no incentive to walk the lengthy countryside journey to the school's boundary wall.

But Candy didn't know that! She'd spent most of her time in Adam's study or taking dictation in reception or sunbathing in the patio area. She hadn't explored the outlying village like Khan.

What made a good worker want to ruin another good worker's life? 'You like Adam, don't you?' he asked, lifting her from the fence again and turning her in the direction of the boundaries.

'I love him.'

'You love ...'

'Like a brother,' she added hastily.

'You don't have sex with your brother,' he said, aiming a warning slap across the crease between her buttocks. 'Don't lie like that.'

'I meant I'm not *in* love with him. I love my fiancé, Jon. He's coming back to marry me.'

'I've heard. So why not wait to be pleasured by *him*?'

'He's been away for months. Said I didn't have to go without stimulation. He and Adam ... Their relationship goes back a long way.'

'And Jon knows of your affairs?'

'He ... sort of lent me to Adam. I've worked for Adam before, and always fancied him. Jon knows that. It's been ideal!'

'And what about me?' He turned her in the direction of the boundary wall.

'Jon doesn't know about you.'

'So you're being wicked.' He picked up the cane and

212

walked more closely behind her, tapping it against his leg. Candy shuddered.

'What happens to girls who are wicked?'

'They . . . get very hot backsides.'

'Mm, they do.' He used the slender stick on her hind-quarters again, the streak of heat forcing her to move forward on her manacled shoes.

'Right, so you're not jealous of Leanne's relationship with Adam.'

'I wasn't even sure if they were having one!'

'They are.' Or would be, if he had his way. Both of them had obviously taken risks in order to become self-employed and self-financing. They deserved fulfilment, should enjoy more than just work, work, work.

'I'm not jealous,' Candy confirmed, shuffling slowly around a sapling.

'Envious of her career, then?'

'No, I've . . .' She blushed. 'I've always preferred taking orders. Never wanted to run the show myself.'

That gave him another cue. He put one arm to her bound wrists, held her in place whilst he stroked her exposed small hindquarters. 'Who's running the show now, Candy?'

She trembled with sexual desire and subservience. 'You are, sir.'

'That's right. And what do I want to know?'

'Who spoiled Leanne's project.'

Aha! She was starting to trip herself up. 'So you know of one project that was spoiled.'

'The shots of you and me in the pool. I said so, didn't I!'

'You phoned the magazine and cancelled the shoot.'

She nodded. 'You know all that! Leanne heard my voice on the answering machine.'

'Who made you do it? You said there was one other person involved. Who was it?' The girl tried to move forward again. He aimed the cane high up her cheeks, making a clear line where the elastic would be if she wore full-size panties – not that she'd be protecting her bottom in them for a very long time!

213

There was a dry stone dyke looming up ahead, its rough stones piled expertly one above the other. 'We're about to bend you over this, you bad girl, and give your bum the fucking of its life.' He put a firm hand on her shoulders, bent her over the wall till gravity took her upper body the rest of the way forward. Khan licked his fingers, using one of them to rim its wettened way round the entrance to her arse.

'If you want full satisfaction, just tell me the perpetrator's name,' he taunted. He stared at her resolute bum, then caressed the tiny buttock crease hairs till she shuddered. 'It's so sensitive, isn't it Candy? The slightest touch makes you want to come.' He teased his middle digit in a little way, then edged it out. 'Do you know what I've got for your bottom? An anal longfinger, that's what.'

He ran a pitiless finger down the exposed crease again. 'Have you seen one of those before? It goes all the way in, then it vibrates ever so gently till the thrills spread right through you.' He put the slim plastic probe at her entrance. 'And do you know what we do after that?' He caressed her dividing crack. 'That's right – we take it out. You see, only girls who squeal get to come, and you've been wickedly silent. Too quiet to enjoy release.'

The girl stiffened, but was forced to stay in place over the dyke, her bound-back wrists and shackled feet rendering her helpless. Khan contemplated her expectant bare bottom, then edged the anal pleasurer in.

Candy grunted with tortured bliss. Khan switched on the thicker base and she grunted a second time, bottom muscles clenching and unclenching. 'Like that, do you, angel? Want more?' He'd give her just enough to get really worked up, but not enough to stimulate her writhing body to orgasm. At least, not yet.

'No climax for you till you tell,' he repeated, moving the dildo in and out. Candy started to make little breath-whimper noises deep in her throat. Her nether regions tensed, increasingly frantic. 'I mean it,' he warned. 'I can keep you here for hours, on the edge.'

'Need to . . .'

'No, you want to.' He pulled the source of pleasure out,

palmed her buttocks. 'Candy, for your clits sake, get it over with.'

'I didn't even confess to Leanne!'

'I'm not the same as Leanne. I'm a detached outsider.'

'I haven't told anyone yet!'

He squeezed her nether cheeks. 'Tell *me* and I'll make sure you don't get the sack. That's a promise.'

'I don't care about that!'

'Right, sweetheart, let's excite that poor bottom again.' She whimpered as he switched the longfinger on. 'Keep it in this time, please. I was so close to coming!'

'Give the name of the saboteur and you can come a dozen times.'

'Not that!'

'*Only* that.' He had to hold firm on this. He played the probe inside her dark recess for a second time.

'Mh! Uh! Ah!' Within two minutes Candy was sounding like a bitch in heat, the slight sweat on her back testimony to her excitement.

'Oh dear, don't tell me I'm going to have to pull this out again?'

'No! Anything! Except . . .'

'You're being so wilful. And when a girl's this difficult, her pussy and bottom have to live without any kind of release.'

He pulled the hard promise from her stimulated canal, pulled gently at her lower lips till she tried to move against his fingers. 'Keep still now, Candy. You have to learn to pass the frustration test.'

'How long?'

'I've got all day.' Providing Leanne didn't leave early. 'As long as I can see by the moon, I can keep you wriggling against this dildo all night.'

She was breathing fast, her inner thighs and vulva dripping wet, every fibre of her body screaming that she needed it. She'd get it – and he'd get the truth out of her – yet. He played casually with her nipples as her body slowly calmed down, kept her without penetration for three minutes, four minutes, five.

'Mm, what have we here?' he murmured at last. 'A vibrating longfinger. I wonder where that goes?' Candy tensed up with lustful anticipation as he ran it over her back. 'Well, what do you know?' He slowly moved it down to her bottom. 'It fits in this hot wet space.'

He pushed it back up her waiting hole, its low hum disappearing high inside her, kept hold of the thickened root and moved it up and down a little way. 'Apparently, there are lots of nerve endings in the arse, Candy. Did you know? Can you feel them? Sensation that starts there can spread . . .'

It was obviously spreading to her quim, her clit, her lower belly. She was wriggling, breathing like a long-distance runner. He should pull out. Thought about it just as she squealed, a long high exclamation of rapture that sent the grey doves flying from the trees in search of greater safety. A squeal that startled Khan.

'Damn you, you weren't supposed to . . . You'll have to be corrected for this, should have told me you were nearing completion.'

'Just came on . . . couldn't help.' Moisture stood out like dew on her naked back.

'Like I won't be able to help toasting my palm across that sex-crazed little posterior!' He half-lifted her from the dyke, led her over to a tree stump and sat himself down. He patted his lap insinuatingly, then waited. Licking her lips and blushing slightly, she bent her legs and he helped her lower herself over his knee.

Her bound-back arms meant that she couldn't hold herself in place. He made sure her head was turned slightly to one side on an unscratchy area of the grass, then gave his attention to her recalcitrant bottom. Khan spanked one pink cheek then the other again and again. 'You quite enjoy this bit, don't you, dear?' She wriggled some more with shame. 'Hope you're not getting excited again, cos this time you're not going to get to come for ages. Maybe not today.'

Once a woman got really hot, she could come and come and come. He'd seen it twice before with his own girlfriends when circumstances triggered a particularly long-held fantasy. Once a woman had reached that mindset, she would climax hard and fast. 'Was it a rival firm put you up to this?' Four stinging spanks brought forth no answer. 'Oh Candy, deep down you must want that bottom warmed very thoroughly. You've left me no option but to tie you to a tree.'

She rose to standing position with him slowly. She seemed dazed, opened her mouth as if to speak, then closed it again. 'I think you're getting closer to confessing.' She licked her lips as he steered her towards the highly appropriate copper birch. He studied her back-bound hands and shackled feet, and decided they already held her nicely in place – very nicely. All he needed to do was tether her to the trunk in some way.

Thoughtfully he unwound the soft rope from his bag, wondering if at any stage he'd need to use the nipple clamps, the handcuffs. Khan brought the binding under her bound arms before crossing the rope over her back and bringing it to the front of the tree. He pulled on the slack till the bindings were bearably tight. He'd read in one of Adam's books that many submissives loved to be securely bound, rendered totally helpless. Some even got off on it, without the need for chastisement. And an achingly aroused woman was more likely to tell him what he wanted to know.

In an ideal world he'd have fastened a mirror to a further tree so that she could see his movements, anticipate each whack for several seconds. For now, his mocking warnings would have to do. 'I'm picking up the cane. Mm, that round bottom makes an excellent target. Do you know it can't escape by even a quarter of an inch? It's just waiting for it nicely. Looks like its silently begging for this.'

He tapped the rattan against the backs of her naked thighs and Candy tensed the appropriate muscles, then relaxed them. The second she did so, he laid on one stroke of the cane.

'Who sabotaged Leanne?'

No answer. A second stroke went diagonally by mistake.

The cane was hard to control if you weren't used to it. Not that it really mattered. He wasn't there to make her arse uniformly pretty. He was there to make her tell!

Leanne would love him for it. But then, Leanne loved everyone, was generous with her knowledge, her time, her money. Someone must have really hated her to spoil her work plans – someone who'd used Candy as a tool.

'Does this person have something on you? Something you've done wrong? Some sexy pictures you had taken?'

A shoulder shrug. 'I don't care about me!'

But she cared about *someone*. He thought of all the greatest true stories he knew, inspired by either love or hate. Candy wasn't a hater. So she'd done this for love.

'This person has something on Jon?' he asked. Candy's bound arms tensed. Aha, he had her there! He thought fast. 'Jon's done something wrong and some rival of Leanne's has found out, has made you make that wicked phone call.' He looked at her naked silent beauty. 'Candy – we can call the police and stop whoever it is who's blackmailing you and Jon.'

'Not the police! You don't understand!' He watched as she writhed against the tree, knew she needed some human comfort. Stepping closer, he pressed the full length of his body against hers.

'Then make me understand.' A pause. 'If you do, I won't tell whoever it is that *you* told me.'

A gulping sob. 'She'll know!'

So it was a woman – but then, there were more women than men running small model agencies. 'Candy, she doesn't have to find out you're the one that told me. At least, not till she's arrested.'

'But she can still hurt Jon!'

'How?'

'She has relatives in Africa, says they'll plant weapons and political papers in his hut, as if he's planning a coup of some description. They'll tip off the authorities. He'll be jailed over there. She has prison friends . . .'

'Who does?'

Another sob. 'Oh Khan, I could lose him! And I've loved him so long.'

'This woman. Is she sophisticated, London-based?'

'No.'

'Has she shown you any proof of these criminal friends?'

'Uh-uh.'

'So it's all just verbal.'

The naked shoulders relaxed a little. 'But she *could* be telling the truth!'

'Then let's warn Jon to be extra-vigilant, to tell his employers about what may happen. That way he can protect himself in advance.'

'I thought about that. But she said if I phoned she would have him killed!'

'Candy – the woman isn't omnipotent! She can't know what you're saying on the telephone line.'

'She does!'

'You're telling me she has access to your calls? Does she work for the company?'

A shake of the head.

'Has she planted a bug in your room?'

'Uh-uh.'

'Then you've nothing to worry about. Unless . . .' He stepped to the side of the tree and pulled Candy's head back till she made eye contact with him. 'Unless she's already based at the school and can listen in!'

Khan saw in her eyes that he'd found the truth. 'It's Eleanor, then.'

Candy gave a reluctant nod. 'She made me do it!'

'Forced you to cancel the first project?'

'Yes.'

'And the faxed photos?'

'I don't know anything about them!'

She had no reason to lie now. Somehow Eleanor had to be behind that, too. If she'd sabotaged two projects, God knows what else she'd do. The woman was an unknown quantity; an enemy on the doorstep that Leanne and Adam knew nothing about.

What if she found out that Adam was going to try and stop Leanne from leaving, as he surely would do if word got back to him? Would she resort to force, in order to keep them apart? Or were there things Eleanor could say which would make the agency owner leave Lingering Lessons instantly without ever confronting her lover, actions she could employ that would devastate the guileless Leanne?

'Candy, we've got to get back to the school – and quickly!' Stopping only to untie and unmanacle her, Khan started to race towards the school.

Thirteen

As the girl submitted to the suspension cuffs, Adam's testes tightened. Pull her arms up, spread her legs wide, whip her hard! he thought. This video was unusually articulate, arousing. It would be easy to write a page of copy on it, for one of the punishment magazines.

The brunette miscreant on the screen was about to be punished. Adam gazed longingly at the image as her Master finished binding her so that she stood, helpless, stretched in a virtual cross. She wore a black leather peephole bra and micro-style matching panties. He leaned closer as her superiors peeled the latter garment from her curves.

The pants were now just below her thighs, accentuating her suntanned buttocks. Her Master walked over to her and she smiled in her bonds and kissed his proferred hand. Why didn't she tell him what she thought of him, spit? If this was Leanne being chained in place, she would have slapped and cursed before the chains went round, given him a sweet sexual struggle. Adam would have had to work hard to make her so aroused that she'd be ready to submit.

Ah, Leanne! He thought almost hourly about the woman. If only she wasn't so down on Candy. His PA had been great, had worked long hours, longer weeks for very little money. She had put up with his finger-fucking and vibrator-based sex after Jon had told him he could go all the way with her.

But he couldn't, after he'd made love to Leanne. It would be the equivalent of shaking hands with strangers wearing your idol's worn glove. He wanted to be true to her sexual memory; true to it until they came together again. He'd give her a couple more days to get used to the idea of Candy's continued presence. Try once more to get his PA to explain.

He adjusted his suit trousers which suddenly felt uncomfortably tight. Christ, that girl on the video had a bottom worth whipping! He had identical bondage equipment downstairs; he could maybe talk Leanne into viewing this with him. After that . . .?

At least she'd seemed happier the other day, when she asked him to fax those photos. Pity Eleanor had been so quick off the mark that he hadn't got a look at the things. But he'd had to get that document for Josh, and she'd had some pages of her own to put through the machine, so he'd given her the go-ahead. She'd looked pleased to help.

If only all the women in his life were as easy to please as her! Leanne could be so changeable, so quick to take offence. Why couldn't she have an easygoing side to her like Tania, Beth-Marie and his various other video-making beauties? Why couldn't she admit, just for once, that the belt made more than just her bottom ache? Not that he wanted her to be totally malleable. He just wanted . . . he wanted her here, in his arms!

And on his cock. God, he was hard, really wanting; wanting to be inside someone, inside Leanne. The girl on the screen was now being moved to a wooden beam that ran from one wall to the other, and was being tied over it. Holes specially cut into the wood left her sex lips and clitoris free; free to be taunted and teased by a series of Masters as they strolled almost casually past.

Clack, clack! It took him a moment to realise that there really was someone using the brass knocker on his door, that they weren't just sounds on the video. Could it be Leanne? He deliberately left the tape running. 'Come in!'

'I'm in a reviewing mode,' he murmured, turning his head to see Eleanor. She was wearing a black velvet choker and a waist-slashed midnight-blue dress. On her right arm she wore a studded wristwatch. His brain drank in the effective images, and his balls sang. 'I could do what she does,' she murmured, staring at the girl on the video, and walking across the room towards him in bare feet. He caught the glimpse of an ankle chain, gold links with a padlock. She sat down, and her now-slender thigh brushed his.

Fourteen

'You've got to come now!'

Leanne jumped and let go of the crinkle-fabric skirt she was packing as Khan burst through the door.

'Khan, I've decided. I'm going.' She picked the maroon garment up and slotted it into the spare space in her suitcase.

'But you don't have to! I've spoken to Candy. She's explained!'

'Explained what, exactly?' She listened as her favourite male model told of Eleanor's threats, of Eleanor's plans, of Eleanor's subterfuge. By the time the boy had finished, he was almost breathless. 'I reckon she must want Adam for herself!' she muttered.

'Sounds like it.' She looked at her case, then pushed it away, new warmth spreading through her. 'Do you think he still wants me?'

'I know he loves you,' Khan said.

'He's told you?' That didn't sound like Adam!

'Another man can tell.'

'Khan – you're the *best* man!' She gave his arm a loving squeeze – a platonic squeeze.

'Does that mean I'll be getting a pay rise?'

Leanne hesitated. He relied on her: she'd have to tell him of her latest plan. But that could wait till later. Suddenly all she wanted to do was to hold Adam, to kiss him full on the lips. She'd graze her teeth over his nipples, his flat firm belly, slide her tongue down his muscular frame . . .

'Is he in his rooms?' she asked.

'I guess so.'

'I'll go now.'

'I'll come with you.'

'Khan – two's company, if you know what I mean!'

'I won't stay if he's there on his own. But if she's ... I mean, I don't want you bumping into Eleanor. Let's face it, we don't know what she might do.'

Leanne stared at him. It was hard to have an enemy, especially this virulent an enemy, and particularly someone who'd smiled at her and shared her secrets, said they prized her as a friend. 'You actually think she'd hurt me?'

'She's hurt your business, and your love life. Why take chances?' Why indeed? The only chances she'd take now were in Adam's arms.

And in his bed, and on his floor and ... She had a feeling that over time they'd take things further and further. Not *things*, she corrected herself as she walked towards her front door: it was time to stop hiding behind vague words. They'd take her sexual *desires* to the heights.

'So Candy doesn't wish me any ill,' she said, as they hurried along the corridor and down the stairs.

'God, no.' Khan shook his head to emphasise his words. 'She's devoted to Adam. If you let her, she'll be devoted to you, too.'

'If only she'd told the truth!'

'She thought she was doing what was best, protecting Jon from Eleanor's evil. He's going to come here and live with her after his work in Africa is over, seemingly.'

Better and better! She'd feel happier with Jon's hand rather than Adam's spanking young Candy's cheeks. A few moments from now, Eleanor would also cease to be a rival. Surely even Adam would insist that she left the school?

They reached Adam's door. Leanne listened. She heard his voice and Eleanor's, and another two voices she didn't recognise. Khan lifted his arm to knock. 'Wait!' Leanne grabbed it. 'Let's find out what they're up to!' Find out if he was going to be unfaithful to her, if he *was* really involved in Eleanor's sabotage plans after all.

'I wish we could see!' Khan muttered.

'We can, if he's left the study door ajar.' Faintly embarrassed at her practised hand, she wedged the letter-box open with her straw-weave sandal, and angled herself till she could peer through the study into the living area. They saw Eleanor and Adam watching a video of a brown-haired girl in her twenties having her clitoris teased.

Good – that explained the strangers' voices. Bad – he was sitting horribly close to the clingily dressed housekeeper. Why had he invited Eleanor here? He was too far away for Leanne to see if Adam was hard inside his trousers. How dare he look so relaxed and in control in his linen suit!

'They should have buckled her down tighter,' Eleanor was murmuring. 'See how she can pull just a fraction of an inch away? Her Master should have made her feel her pussy is totally constrained, for him to do what he wants to her.'

'Some men like to see the woman writhe a little,' Adam said mildly, eyes fixed on the screen, hands folded. 'I think the general concept excites.'

'Excites *you*?' came Eleanor's husky murmured question.

'I told you – this is work. I'm not here to get excited.'

Leanne stared as the older woman put her stroking fingers over Adam's crotch. 'Oh, but I think you *are*,' Eleanor said.

'What have you come to see me about?' Leanne let out her breath as Adam pushed the housekeeper's probing hand away.

'Mmm? Oh, there's a window in the utility room which needs replacing. Paul broke it playing football.'

'I'll see to it.'

The woman sidled closer. 'No, I can do that.'

The girl on the video was being ordered not to come. A moment after the instruction was made, her face and buttocks convulsed into ecstatic spasms. A close-up of her pubis showed the strings of her pleasure. 'She's for it now,' said Eleanor with obvious satisfaction, one hand straying towards her own cleavage-showing breasts. She glanced slyly at Adam. 'What would you do if she was your girl and she disobeyed?'

'Thrash her, then repeat the test more quickly.'

Leanne felt the rush of blood to her lower belly; she couldn't look at Khan.

'Want to try it out?' As they stared, Eleanor propelled herself over Adam's knee, and lay there expectantly.

'No,' he said.

Silence. Christ, Eleanor must have felt such a fool! Leanne felt almost sorry for the woman, even as another part of her rejoiced that Adam wasn't interested in her flaunting.

'Do you think I'm being forward?' Eleanor whispered, twisting her head back. Her eyes were still full of desire and expectation. Leanne realised that the housekeeper was misreading all the signs.

'I think you're a little overwrought, that you should go now and we'll resume our normal relationship tomorrow.'

'I'll have made you so happy by tomorrow night!'

'Miss Peterson, you'll make me happy by removing your weight from my knee.'

'Sir, you don't understand – I've been naughty. I've burnt the dinner and forgotten to restock the wine cellar. I deserve to have my bottom whipped!' As Leanne and Khan watched, she pulled down her ivory silk cami-knickers to reveal a well-exercised firm bottom which bore some faint pink stripes, presumably from Gerard's riding crop. 'I've been so wicked, Mr Howard, so very bad!'

'I'm sure you have. I'll have to ask Mr Kerne to take his birch to you.' Leanne swallowed. Adam was trying to let Eleanor down gently.

'He's not in charge, Mr Howard. You are, sir.' Eleanor wriggled her rear and pushed it closer to his face. Adam had his hands on either side of the settee, no part of his body voluntarily touching her. His lips were set, his eyes focusing somewhere ahead of him in pity or in rage.

'Isn't it a pretty bottom, sir? It colours up so good.'

'I'm sure it does, but I only have sex with the woman I love.'

Eleanor twisted her head back, cheeks reddening with surprise or fury or humiliation. 'I could make you love me!'

'I love Leanne.'

'But she . . . she wants that Khan to move in with her. She asked me to replace her double bed with a king-sized one. Made it clear they don't intend to get much sleep!'

Leanne gasped at the outright lie.

'Want to go in now?' Khan muttered.

'No – let's see what happens next.' She half-wanted Adam to thrash the scheming liar, make her repent.

'I've yet to make a commitment to Miss Dell, so she's technically free to see other people, including Khan.' His mouth set further, Adam continued, 'I still want you to take your backside away.'

Instead the woman sat up, pressing her breasts into his chest. 'She tried to drive you mad with desire in the early days, you know. She told me she hoped you'd go back to London to see former girlfriends!'

'She was just threatened at the prospect of a partnership.'

'Well, I'm ready for one any day!'

As Leanne and Khan watched, they saw that his focus seemed to go beyond the woman on his lap, who was now undoing his top buttons. 'I've loved her for so long.'

Eleanor undid the third buttonhole. 'But she's only been here such a short time.'

'Oh, I knew she was the one for me long before that.'

'The mystery deepens!' Khan murmured, turning to Leanne and winking.

She shrugged. 'I've no idea what he means!' Leanne watched as the male model's grin turned into a grimace and he swayed for a second, then toppled sideways into the door. His elbow caught the wood, and bounced off it, quickly followed by his knee. She grabbed hold of him. 'Quick, run! He'll have heard us . . .'

The door flew open. 'Get in here, Leanne!' Adam said.

Hand on her mouth, she stared at him. 'And you too, Khan,' he said.

'We've something to tell you,' Khan muttered, holding his betraying ankle. 'It's about Eleanor.' All three of them sidled into the suite of rooms.

228

'Did I hear my name?' Eleanor stood up. Her mouth was lifted in a stiff smile. Her face was flushed. She kept smoothing down her dress over her stomach. Leanne wondered if her panties were covering her arse or stuffed behind one of the cushions.

'You bullied Candy into sabotaging Leanne's photo shoot,' Khan said.

'Nonsense! I've never . . .'

'And you somehow got hold of those faxed photos and replaced them.'

Adam looked up. 'Yes, Eleanor faxed some work of Leanne's.'

Leanne stared straight into the older woman's eyes, though her words were aimed at Adam Howard. 'She sent in some holiday snaps instead and lost me the *Be Seen* commission; at least initially.'

Adam walked up to his housekeeper: 'Is this true?'

'I . . . Who said? Prove it!'

'This isn't *Crown Court*. You're being dismissed from your job, not being sent to prison.' He looked her up and down, face immobile. 'But you owe us an explanation at the very least.'

'I'm out of here!' Eleanor said, making for the door. Leanne took a deep breath, then stepped in front of her.

'Eleanor – what did I ever do to you? I thought we had the beginnings of a friendship. I don't understand.'

She watched as the other woman looked at her in a sudden fury. 'No, you probably don't! You think that as long as you look good, then everyone will like you. We can't all afford Armani jackets, you know!'

What on earth was the woman talking about? Still, it was useless to fight rage with rage. She wanted answers. 'Eleanor, I don't own an Armani.'

'But you've got classy clothes!'

'A few pieces. In my line of work, I have to look smart. After all, I'm asking others to pay for glamour.'

'Exactly! People like you make me sick. You have it all!'

Temporarily at a loss, Leanne looked at Khan, who had sunk into a seat and was rubbing his weak ankle. Then she turned to Adam, who was standing three feet away from them, looking all too ready to intervene. Leanne gave him a half-smile, something lifting inside her chest as he returned it warmly. A few moments from now . . .

But first she had to discover why the housekeeper hated her so much. 'You say I have it all, Eleanor – but is it wrong to aspire to having good clothes and a car? Some contingency capital?'

'Course not! It's just people like you, born with a silver spoon.'

God, she'd been misread! 'I grew up in a two-roomed flat with a toilet shared with three other families. One labourer's wage packet between four of us. Beans on toast or just plain toast for tea.'

'But you sound so . . .'

'I won a scholarship to a private school. Did extra homework throughout primary in order to get my grades up. I didn't have a good start in life, but I made damn sure I carved myself a good future, because I didn't want to live the life my parents did. Didn't want their negativity, their endless complaints.

'They must have encouraged you, though.'

'Yeah – encouraged me to leave and get a job! They had no time for education.'

The older woman's eyes weren't quite so good at maintaining contact now. 'I thought everyone wanted their children to get on in life?'

'Some don't. It increases the parents' own sense of inadequacy.'

'I guess I never thought of it that way.'

Eleanor was looking at her differently now. Her eyes showed the first glimmers of understanding. Their upbringings might even have been similar, Leanne thought sadly. They'd simply followed different paths. 'With you being in modelling, I thought you'd had an easy start.'

'I got into it to stop my brother being exploited after he was placed in a modelling competition.'

'I didn't realise.'

'You never asked.'

'Eleanor – we have to let you go in the circumstances,' Adam said. God, this was awkward! Leanne looked at the flushed features of the woman as she nodded, then looked sadly at the ground. 'But we can give you a reference for your housekeeping. We won't mention this episode unless we're asked about your honesty.'

'I feel so stupid!'

Leanne pursed her lips together. 'I've been jealous myself, envied other people. I know what it is to want.'

Offer comfort, Leanne thought. She touched the older woman's upper arm. 'You can stay on for a few days till you get new accommodation sorted.'

'No, I'll take a taxi to the village now. There's a live in post at The Jacksonville up for grabs. Saw the card in their reception window. I'll get Gerard to pack and send on my things.'

Leanne nodded. This probably wasn't the right time, and yet she might not see the woman again. 'There are some first-class managerial positions at big city hotels for organisers like you.'

'We'll see.' Still obviously humiliated at her own actions, Eleanor managed a twisted grin. 'Thanks for taking this so well.'

'Life's too short to hold a grudge. Hell, we all have our bad days!' The woman's behaviour had actually been worse than bad, but the important thing was that she wouldn't do it again.

'Bye, then,' Eleanor said. The door opened, then swung shut.

Leanne turned towards Adam, a new smile starting. 'Khan – you're free to go now,' Adam said.

'Oh. Right.' Leanne felt her heartbeat start to increase as the youth left the room, leaving her with her one-time-only lover.

'Now I have to punish you for eavesdropping,' Adam said.

Fifteen

Was he serious? She'd thought he'd want to make love right away, thrust deep inside her. 'Khan persuaded me to . . .'

'I may arrange to have him dealt with yet.' He paused. 'Eleanor tells me the boy is moving in with you?'

'She's lying!'

'Then there's no one else?'

'No one.' She stepped closer, intending to wrap her arms round his neck. Once she'd kissed and held and stroked him, she'd feel bolder, better. Leanne felt the area behind her breasts hollow out with disappointment as he stepped away. 'So I alone am responsible for checking your behaviour, Leanne.'

'You wish! I'm very self-reliant.' And slightly scared, she thought.

'Does that give you the right to jam your shoe in my letter-box and peer through my door?'

'No, but . . .'

'No. Exactly. Which means I'll have to take that self-same shoe to your prying little arse.'

'You wouldn't dare!' She licked her lips as he retrieved the straw-effect size-four from the door flap and played it through his fingers.

'Wouldn't I just?' he teased.

She forced herself to meet his gaze, felt the soft circles round her nipples swelling, tingling. 'I bet I can make you ask nicely to feel the shoe sole,' he said.

'You're on!'

'Good. Come and sit over here.' He settled back on the

232

long settee and patted the cushions. Legs surprisingly drained of energy, Leanne crossed the room towards him and sat down.

'Let's start with an apologetic kiss.'

'Nice to hear you apologising!' she joked, lifting her mouth to his, closed lips to closed lips.

'Horny?' he whispered, as her touch turned into something firmer and she inserted the tip of her tongue.

'Might be.' Leanne pulled away. She'd be damned if he'd goad her into gasping for more, begging for his attentions. She was determined not to give in too easily, and forced her features into a nonchalant blank.

'So the lady isn't sure?' He ran a knowing finger down the side of her neck to the collar of her blouse, traced it across her throat to the soft Obsession-scented skin above her cleavage.

'Might just be bored,' she murmured, rubbing the tip of her nose against his.

'Then we'll have to work at changing that, won't we, Leanne? Can you think of a way?'

Wordless with desire, she shook her head. Smiling lazily, he put his back against the settee arm and pulled her on to his lap so that her legs were scissored to either side of him. 'Hot in here, isn't it?' he asked quietly, slowly unfastening the buttons of her short-sleeved white blouse and stroking, assessing every inch of her skin as it was bared. 'Mmm? I'm just warm,' she countered as he pulled the garment from her unresisting body and threw it to the floor.

'I think this bit will get quite scorching.' She closed her eyes as he slid his thumb inside her bra to her left nipple, slipped the other over her right nipple, then moved to the sensitive puckered flesh around each. Looking into her eyes as he touched, he teased her areolae into tremors. 'In fact, this bit's so toasty that we'll have to strip your brassière away.'

'Sure you can cope?' she asked, half-sarcastic, as a throaty challenge.

'Watch me.' She didn't want to watch. Instead, she bit playfully at his ears as he undid the hooks, exposing the curves beneath the covering. He tasted faintly of citrus shower gel and salt.

'Such pretty bared breasts.'

She half-laughed, half-snorted. 'Give the man a round of applause for his efforts!'

'Oh, there's a lot I can do . . .'

There was. She knew there was. Her eyelids moved beseechingly down as the pads of his thumbs again returned to the nerve endings around her nipples and reawakened them. Other lovers had suckled there with vulnerable bent heads and she'd felt maternal towards them. But Adam was more formidable, all man.

'Yes, very hot indeed,' he said, tracing his digits round her flesh. 'But as you tell me you're just warm, we'll have to heat you further. How do you think we'll do that?'

'Use your imagination!' She nuzzled into his shoulder, hiding her face, feeling the familiar pricklings start at the top of her labia, the beginnings of a soon-strengthening pubic pulse.

'Oh angel, I'm imaginative, some say fiendishly creative . . .' Tilting her face back till her eyes met his, he settled her weight more comfortably in his lap before returning his thumbs to their waiting targets. He stroked round and round and round and round and round.

'Adam . . . Please . . .'

'Please what?'

All she could think about was the heavy swelling warmth of the tips of her bosoms, the equally demanding swelling between her legs, still imprisoned in her brushed-denim divided skirt. It hid her fast-wettening crotch. Damn him – she wouldn't ask to feel the sandal against her backside! She moved her head quickly down to lick his nipples, determined to arouse him into making love to her rather than making a target of her arse.

'Cat got your tongue?' No, the bastard had got her pussy, long before he'd even touched it. The middle of her breasts, if teased gently enough, sent thrust-it-in-me signals between her legs. 'Saying nothing,' she muttered, the words half-slurred with desire as she pushed her groin against his and felt the hard clothed push of his erection. 'Got anything for me?' she added, into his shoulder, rubbing her sex lips insinuatingly against his swollen shaft.

'Mmm, a straw-weave shoe.'

Bugger it! She'd laid herself wide open for that. A heavy pull was taking energy from her brain, her eyes, her vocal cords. Her shoes were made of light flexible material. Maybe a thrashing with the sole wouldn't be so bad . . .

'Right, use the fucking shoe, then!'

'You're about to get extra strokes for unnecessary swearing.'

'Oh, sorry. Didn't realise we were still at school!' She realised her error as soon as she said the words.

Adam looked mockingly back: 'My dear, we're very much at school, or hadn't you noticed?'

'I mean, you're not the teacher!'

'Well, I'm having to teach you not to spy on others and not to swear.'

He half-smiled. It was a controlled smile, a knowing easy smile. She knew he loved it when a woman writhed under his belt or paddle. 'So, you want to feel your own shoe on your bottom, do you? In that case we'll have this divided skirt pulled down.'

'Will we now?' He put three tenderising fingers to the shorts-like garment and rubbed very lightly through it to her labia. Inhaling hard, Leanne knelt up on the settee and quickly obeyed.

Now she was wearing just her pants. He was still fully dressed, and she felt vulnerable, slightly silly. Her mons ached; for a cock inside or for fingers or a mouth outside; for some kind of release. 'Sweetheart, you can't keep those on.' Well, she could, but she didn't want to! She knew what she wanted – his cock inside her – and she wanted it now.

She held him round the waist as he pulled down her pants, exposing her full firm bottom. He cupped the rounded cheeks for a moment and her body stilled. She slid one pleading hand down his groin, touched the thickness, held fast. 'Want you inside me.'

'Now tell me what you *deserve*.'

'I deserve . . .' He touched her clit again and she leaned heavily against him on the settee as her body flooded with longing.

'Deserve the shoe on my backside,' he prompted. 'Say it now.' Adam stroked her glistening sex lips three more times till she groaned out loud, 'Say it, Leanne. There'll be no more touching, no more pleasure, until you do.'

'Deserve the shoe on my backside,' she muttered, staring at the cushions.

'Come on. You can say it more loudly than that!'

He teased. She told. 'Good girl. Now go and fetch your footwear and bring it over to me.' He'd left it on top of the drinks cabinet. The journey seemed to take a long time. She was hugely aware of her already-bared buttocks and the rest of her naked form.

Reach for the mahogany top. Pick up the sandal. Try not to think about where – and how often – it's going to be whacked. Turn. Start walking back.

'Stand there. Hand me the shoe. See, that wasn't so difficult!' he said. The submissive walk was one of the most embarrassing she'd ever made in her life. 'They teach dogs to fetch slippers. Do you think you've been a bitch to me, Leanne?'

'Takes one to know one.' Spank me quickly – get it over with. Then let me come! she said inwardly.

'That's a rather glib answer for a bright girl. I expected more from you.'

'Maybe the company just doesn't inspire!'

'I can inspire bare bums until they behave. Do you want to see? I think you do, really. I suspect you're quite curious to find out how that shoe will feel on your wicked backside.'

'I could just use my imagination!'

'But then you wouldn't get to come. And I think you want me to make love to you.' God, she wanted him. She wanted him a lot.

Silence. Her pelvis ached with unmet need. She'd stared at the carpet so long that it was starting to shift beneath her gaze, the red and black flecks of wool shimmering, merging.

236

'Get over my knee, Leanne, and I'll use your sole on you, exactly as you asked.' This wasn't really what she craved, of course. She just needed to come with his manhood pounding inside her. This punishment was simply a means to an end . . .

Staring somewhere ahead, she got on to the settee on her knees, pushed her upper body forward till she was lying across his lap. Her arms felt redundant. After a moment's hesitation she buried her face in her overlapping hands.

'Right, let's warm this bum; its owner was spying. Let's toast it with her shoe,' he announced.

She felt him slide the canvas sole across her waiting bottom, taking it from one side to the other, then moving it down to repeat the gesture. Each time the shoe touched part of her helpless derrière, she felt a new rush of lust. 'Wriggling already? You must be having guilty thoughts, anticipating this thrashing, thinking about how much it's going to sting,' he goaded.

Shoes didn't sting – they produced more of an all-over heated throb. Leanne fought back the words. If she was rude, she'd get extra. And he'd realise that she'd flicked through some of his punishment magazines in the hall cupboard, in which submissive girls revealed what made their bums react.

'Ready, steady . . .' Christ, he didn't half like prolonging the build-up. She felt him stroke each tensing cheek with his sure hands, then he softly whispered, 'Go!'

And he flicked the sole against the crease above her thighs.

Leanne immediately felt a wide band of heated sensation. This isn't so bad, she thought, relaxing, then winced a little as he repeated the smack further up. 'Ouch!'

'Don't speak without permission.'

' "Ouch" is an exclamation – that's not speaking!'

'You're not doing linguistics. You're learning to do what you're told.'

'You wish!'

'That's another five whacks for disobedience.'

'But that's not . . .' She closed her mouth as he doled out

all five on top of each other across the centre of her bum. 'Aaaaaaah!' she shrieked. She winced at the focused band of fire.

'Any more talking and I'll really give you something to moan about.' She quivered, but kept quiet, rubbing her swollen pouch against his suited legs.

'How much longer?' she muttered a moment later. How much longer till you take me in your arms, slide inside me? How much longer till my body convulses with rapturous release?

'How much longer do you *think*?'

'Five more strokes?'

'For spying? For using Khan to make me jealous? For trying to tease me into leaving Lingering Lessons all those months ago?'

Oh, oh! She chafed her crotch against his jutting hardness. 'But I thought I was just getting thrashed for forcing open your letter-box with my shoe.'

'At the onset you were. Problem is, when I have such a badly behaved bottom beneath my hands, I can't control myself. I just have to punish it for all the other odious things its owner has done, too!'

'We'll be here all night then,' Leanne muttered sarcastically. She'd be damned if she'd show him she was cowed.

'A long session – exactly!'

'But I have to . . .' She stretched back her right hand and curled it desperately round the stiff promise of Adam's cock.

'Naughty! You haven't earned that yet. Though we could negotiate.'

Anything. Everything. Only fuck me. 'Please . . .'

'How about this? You ask me nicely for a fuck. I give it to you, then we continue your chastisement. You get walloped with your own shoe till your bum is the colour of that cushion on the chair.' Leanne squinted through a haze of desire at the dralon circle.

'Right! Whatever.'

'Let's hear it, then.'

He took his strong hands from her back, and she eased

herself up till she was sitting astride his legs. Her flushed face buried itself against his shoulders, her labia feeling equally flushed and frantic. 'I want . . .'

'An hour's worth of nipple strokes?'

God, she only needed a few thrusts of his cock or teases of his hand and she'd come like a wild thing.

'Please, no!'

He laughed. 'I'm listening!' Adam put his fingers to her tits and renewed each light caress till she couldn't bear it.

'I need to . . . need to come.'

He continued his relentlessly arousing caresses. ' "Need" is a very strong word, Leanne.'

Her lips were open now, eyes almost shut, her areolae mutely begging. She put her hand to his zip, but he pulled it away. 'Want to,' she muttered. She licked his neck, slid her arms under his crisp white shirt and up his back.

His thumbs continued their unbearably pleasing paths.

'*Where* do you want to, Leanne? Come on, don't be shy.'

She needed space to stretch out in, room to thrash about. 'On your bed, the four poster . . .' she groaned.

'What way do you want it?' The same way as he probably did – but she wouldn't say.

She half-shrugged, a last-ditch stand. 'Whatever you like.'

'Whatever I like.' He repeated the words thoughtfully, his thumbs continuing to touch-taunt her tits into rapture. 'Mm, that's a difficult question. I'll think about that for an hour whilst I play with these.' The bastard! She loved him. She hated him.

'I can't take it . . .'

'If you knew what you wanted, it would help.'

Leanne moaned. Another wave of hot thick longing rushed from her lower belly to her labia. 'On my hands and knees on the bed,' she muttered into his shirt.

'Ah, you mean monkey-fucked?' He took her arms from round his waist and held them in front of her. 'In that case, we'd better take the monkey to its lair.'

His large right hand in the small of her back, they walked through the lounge to the bedroom. Leanne's clitoris urged her to walk faster but the swollen purse between her legs made movement slow. The warm air brushed at her naked bust and waist. Clear strings of supplication leaked slowly from her sex leaves. Adam bumped against her as she stopped to open the bedroom door and she felt the taut full promise beneath his suit.

'You'd better go in first – shut the curtains,' she murmured. When he wasn't playing with her pleasure-dome, it was easy to be the one giving the orders.

'Could leave them open. Maybe Paul or Gerard would like to see me fucking you.'

She felt a slight resurgence of her power at the thought of the many men who wanted her. 'Maybe you'd rather Gerard fucked me instead?'

'Oh dear. That wasn't wise. That really wasn't wise.' Shaking his head, Adam walked into the room and whisked the calico covering over the window. Leanne's fingers strayed to her clitoris. If she could only give herself that first orgasm, she'd be able to hold out until Adam gave her a second and hopefully a third. She needed relief this very moment and he was obviously going to make her wait for a pitilessly long time . . .

'Hands at your sides,' he said, coming back, and sliding his arms around her waist to march her into the room.

'I got bored waiting.'

'Oh sweetheart, you've been so bad today. You'll have to wait a lot longer yet.' She turned to face him, her lips meeting his, five or six soft sweet kisses; kisses she hoped would tempt him into letting her pleasure swiftly peak.

'Is this you trying to make amends?' he asked. Was it only fifteen minutes ago that she'd sworn at him and refused to apologise? When they were simply looking at each other it was easy to be petulant. But when his fingers brushed her clit and then moved callously away . . .

'Monkey-fucking, I think you said?' she reminded him, starting to unbutton his shirt, but he stayed her hand.

'No love, it's *your* clothes that have to stay off – you're the hot one.' She gazed at his suited body, then looked down at herself. She studied her round firm breasts, her tapering waist and flat suntanned tummy, and refused to look in the mirror at her presumably pinkened rear end.

'Let's get you on to the bed.' The satin quilt felt plush beneath her palms, the aquamarine mosaic that adorned it seemed to be glowing. A slight breeze ruffled the closed curtains and accentuated the warm bareness of her bum.

'Hands and knees,' Adam ordered. She wished she could hear his zip lowering. She needed him desperately.

'Might not feel like it now,' she muttered, trying to take control of the situation again.

Briefly he slid his palms over her scolded buttocks. 'Might not feel like this?' he asked. As she got into doggy position, he reached through her thighs and found her enlarged libido button, saying 'I think this needs it.'

'Ah! Ah! Ah! At each measured preen, Leanne cried out, moving urgently against his digits. The bastard was right.

'The test is not to move.' She straightened her limbs and held her breath, inwardly begging for attention. By looking between her tautened arms, she could see her tits hanging down. She stared at her udders, softly pendulous, her trembling tummy. Gazed at the hirsute curve between her legs, Adam's immobile right hand.

'I'll touch you here for a while.' His middle finger settled on the wetness around her clit. She whimpered and moved against it. 'No, I refuse to let you come if you don't stay still for me. Let's start again.'

'Going to . . . got to . . .,' she said through panted breaths.

He took his hand away. 'Ask for it nicely.'

'Please . . .' The fingers returned to entice but kept her waiting. 'Please fuck me,' she added gutturally.

'There! That wasn't such a difficult task.'

She heard his zip going down, then he slid his cock in and kept it there. She gasped with gratitude, felt the cold metal fastener pressing against her arse till he pushed his opened suit trousers down to his knees.

'Want more?' he asked, starting to shaft her harder. He felt urgent, deep, distended, his engorged head filling her craving cavern as she clutched the pillow and breathed fast. She could feel the fronts of his thighs rubbing against the backs of hers as he thrust into her like a dog riding a hot bitch, his arms gripping her waist and occasionally reaching up to hold her tits as if they were reins.

'Yes! Yes!' Harder. Faster. She couldn't think, couldn't see. Everything felt centred on her soaking sex.

'Just like warm oil,' Adam murmured, thrusting strongly. 'So squirming, wet.' She could smell her own scorched salt scent, could feel perspiration running down the sides of her neck and down her back.

'That test we were doing. You weren't meant to move . . .' He slid one hand round the front of her left thigh to her clit and kept three digits pressed there. She rubbed hungrily against it. 'You have to keep in place,' he told her.

'Or what?' came the half-gasped challenge from Leanne.

'Or I'll stop touching.'

She wanted . . . wanted something more. 'What else will you do?' Enraging him, daring him, she half-wanted the threat of future punishment.

'I'll pull out and just make you suck me instead.' Christ no – her sex had felt hollow from the time he started arousing her helpless areolae. She needed to keep him inside.

'I'll . . . try not to move without permission.'

'Can't make it too easy – I'll have to lick my hand.' The sensation of wet digits on an already broiling wet clit was exquisite.

Leanne groaned as she tried to obey his orders. 'Stay, stay.' Thrusting in and pulling back, then plunging in harder, the outsides of his cock excited the insides of her passage, his fingers touching her ecstasy button.

Almost, almost. Little animal noises formed in her throat, louder squelching ones sounded between her thighs. His and her breathing quickened. 'Have . . . Have to . . .' He slipped his middle finger down her clit and drove his shaft in especially hard against her cervix and she came.

'Oh yes, baby. Let it out, baby,' Adam muttered, increasing his speed. Leanne's weakened arms bent and she went forward on her elbows, arse raising further as her head went down. 'Christ, that's brilliant!' Adam muttered in his close-to-climaxing voice, still shafting strongly.

'Do it harder,' she said.

He was building now. She could feel the rhythm of his thrust changing to small and fast, his hips hardly moving back, his cock going forward, forward, forward. 'Uh,' he went, balls banging against the backs of her thighs with their craving cargo. 'Uh, uh, uh!' He strained against her bottom, against her back. She could feel the tremors of pleasure coursing through his legs, his concave belly. Hear the almost otherworldly rapture in his wordless voice.

When his sighs had subsided, she lowered herself on to her tummy and stretched a hand back to ruffle his hair. 'God,' he muttered, 'I wish I could stay inside you.' She closed her thighs over him and squeezed till he whimpered. 'Damn! I'm about to slip out ...' He gave a little cry of loss as his shrinking shaft left the warmth of her sex.

'We can put it back in later,' he assured her.

'Later?'

She rolled over onto her side and went into his arms as he added, 'I haven't finished with you yet.'

Leanne felt as if most of the water in her body had turned into steam and filtered away. 'Any chance of a mineral water?'

'Nice to know I'm not spending the rest of my life with an alcoholic, dear!' The rest of his life? She couldn't let him see how pleased she was; he had a large enough ego. He kissed her nose. 'There's some Perrier in the fridge.'

'Where's the ...?' She looked round the large square bedroom.

'Mmm? It's hidden inside the cupboard that supports the CD player. It was a present from Mamie,' he explained.

'She used to give great gifts, didn't she? Gave me the car!'

'The Morgan? It suits you – a classic. Like your perfume and your clothes.'

'About that water ...' She looked at him, and realised he intended her to fetch the drink herself. 'Back in a moment!'

'Hang on – I'll join you. I want you to see something. A reminder of your very first day.'

243

Leanne sat up in bed, and started to get out, feeling slightly self-conscious. She didn't want to sit around naked under his watchful gaze! After a moment's thought, she hurried round the suite of rooms, gathering up her blouse and divided skirt. Quickly, she shrugged into them. He could keep the underwear as a souvenir!

Though she hoped there'd be lots of other sexually satiating times. So far, they'd misunderstood the lot, had stayed away from each other's arms and beds and conversations. Now she wanted them to be lovers and co-workers, even friends. Leanne sat down in the overstuffed chair with a glass of lime-flavoured fizzy water as Adam shrugged on a midnight-blue dressing-gown before switching on the TV and slotting a video into the machine.

'I've watched this one before, but I only noticed this voyeur the other day.' On the screen, Tania appeared in reception, was talked down and bent over the punishment stool. The camera was obviously unoperated, trained on just one part of the vast hall. Its gaze showed the second half of the arena, the dais, various portraits, and the doorway leading into the school.

'See there?' Adam pointed to a slightly more elongated shadow in the corner of the foyer. Leanne nodded. Damn, had he known all along that she'd been watching? 'Why didn't you introduce yourself?'

'I didn't . . . wasn't sure what was happening; if it was a game or not.'

Still wasn't, for that matter. Just after that, poor Tania had disappeared, never to be mentioned again.

'We were making a punishment video, Leanne.'

She tightened her tummy. 'Who's the girl?' Please make this right. *Please* don't say she's an ex-wife or special girlfriend.

'Friend of Gerard's from London. I don't think you ever met her. She went back to the city that very day,' he explained.

'I thought you'd . . .' What? Kidnapped her as a sexual slave? There were some things she could never say. 'I . . . why didn't you let her stay in the seventh dormitory?' In the locked dormitory, the one he'd always been so determined to protect.

'No one stays there. It's . . . It's all I have left of Mamie. Her sculptures, her library of first edition novels, her Victorian dolls.'

So the rod-hard lover hid a softer side! New knowledge tingled through her breasts. 'Why didn't you tell me?'

'I'll *show* you later this evening, if you like! Technically, half of these things are yours. I was determined that you wouldn't sell them.'

'I wouldn't sell Mamie's prized possessions for anything!'

'I know that now.'

She looked over at him as he sat on the settee. In a moment, she'd find an excuse to go and sit beside him. Not that she should need an excuse – but he could still be a daunting and changeable man.

'We really just saw the superficial side of each other at first,' she said in a quiet voice.

'In a way. But in another . . . Well, I felt as if I knew you the first time I saw you.' His eyes raked hers.

She stiffened, sensing a secret. 'I heard you tell Eleanor that you'd seen me before.'

Adam seemed to be focusing intently on her face, as if memorising her features. 'It was at Mamie's party – in her mews house, about three years ago. You were there with . . .', he seemed to have difficulty with the name, 'with Rob.'

'I didn't see you.'

She'd have remembered if she had. He wasn't someone you walked past without tingling at least a little.

'I didn't want you to. Well, that's not true. I did at first!' He walked to the fridge, poured himself a white wine, then sat down again on the settee. 'You were with him and another couple. The other man said something authoritative to you and you looked up, then cast your eyes down a certain way and changed the subject. A moment later, I saw you in the hallway kissing Rob. Your eyes were closed, cheeks flushed. I could see your nipples. I knew then that

245

you . . . *complimented* me, even if you didn't know it.' He must have known that she'd come by being spanked.

'And you just left?'

'I told Mamie you were the most enticing woman I'd ever seen. I wanted her to arrange for us to meet, but she said that the time wasn't quite right, but that luck might be moving in my direction.' Mamie had known that Leanne was increasingly unhappy at Rob's long working week.

'So I waited,' said Adam.

'A celibate lonely life?' she teased.

'Oh, there were girlfriends, of course, but I kept them casual. I travelled to your part of the city a few times and just wandered around, hoping to see you there. I thought the connection between us had been severed when Mamie died, especially when she left instructions that I was to stay away from the funeral and the will-reading. Then my solicitor told me she'd jointly left us Lingering Lessons, and I understood.'

'The ultimate blind date on my part!' God, it was great to be talking like this. 'But why didn't you tell me you wanted me when I first arrived here?'

'Then you might have entered into a relationship because you were flattered, or bored, or just generally sexually curious. I needed to know that you got off on being chastised.'

A telling pause. 'The jury's still out on that!' She laughed. How could he say these things when she was sitting across from him under bright lights, with no shoulder or armpit to hide under?

'Oh, the jury knows what's right,' he assured her.

'But you could have had Candy, or those Oriental twins you had round the other day!'

'They have the subservience without the spirit.'

'I've got the spirit all right!'

'You do. It gives me something to tame.'

'You hope,' she muttered, looking awkwardly away.

'Talking of which, we still haven't finished punishing that backside for spying and swearing.'

Leanne stuck out her tongue as far as it would go. 'Fuck you!'

'Your bum must recognise it needs a further thrashing.' The earlier wallops with the sandal sole had faded to the faintest glow. How could he tell? She played her fingers over a small wine mark on the chair arm. 'Come over here and take your punishment, then,' he told her.

'That'll be right!'

'I'll add on five minutes' worth for every moment you procrastinate.' He patted his dressing-gowned lap.

'Hope you can count to a thousand!' Easy to be brave over here, whilst still sitting on her bottom.

'To infinity, if that's what your rear end requires.' She tried to push her backside down more firmly against the chair as he leaned forward, and wished she'd put her pants back on under her divided skirt.

'Do I have to come and get you?'

'Do what you like!'

'Once your bare bottom is under my palm, I intend to.' A pause, then, 'Oh dear, such intransigence! This is going to hurt a lot.' He seemed to cross the space of carpet very quickly. She looked up at him with I-dare-you in her eyes, caught her breath at the determination in his, feeling suddenly nerveless. He took hold of her right hand and pulled her smoothly up.

Best get it over with. Staring at the carpet a few inches ahead of her, Leanne let herself be led from her chair towards the settee. Her legs moved woodenly. Her heart felt stilled. She could hardly breathe, as he slowly sat down, holding her in front of him.

'Good girl. Over my knee,' he said. When she hesitated some more, he used her wrists to pull her over, over, over. His limbs felt rigid. Her face sank into the worn leather of the couch.

'Let's get that bottom higher in the air.' Leanne whimpered and closed her eyes as he slid a cushion under her belly. This was awful! 'If only you hadn't used such nasty words to me and stalled so long,' he continued.

She had to rally. 'Bet you've heard worse!'

'Oh, much worse – but the culprit's always had her

247

bottom roasted. Few of them have made the same mistake a second time.'

She swallowed hard. 'Can't I make full restitution?'

'Your buttocks are about to.'

'I meant I could apologise . . .' She twisted her head back pleadingly.

He picked up the shoe. 'I'll give you a choice – forty whacks with this or a hand spanking until your bum's as hot as I can make it.'

It wasn't much of a choice. 'Couldn't I just . . .'

'You're wasting my time.' The sole had already turned her bottom a warm pink, so it would take relatively few hand spanks to redden it even further. Would that sting less than forty with the canvas sole?

She was still trying to put off the deed. God knows, she'd never been spanked as a child. It was wrong to hit kids. Even her thoughtless parents had known that. But she was a thirty-three-year-old woman and he was a man of thirty-six, and she'd taunted him and sworn at him and peeked into his rooms. 'Before you, I'd never been spanked,' she stammered, as he ran his palms over her squirming rear.

As she mused, she felt his strong sure hands on the soft waistband of her skirt, waiting for him to pull it down inch by merciless inch, exposing her bottom for the second time that evening. Leanne swallowed hard as she felt the material being smoothed back into place. 'Quite a warm bum, for such a cold girl,' said her tormentor. 'But I've put it back where I found it. As you're being more polite, for now I'll let you keep your skirt on.'

Leanne closed her eyes as he continued to instruct. 'I'll spank this arse till it feels like it's learned its lesson.' She wondered if she should thank him. Then the first slap ricocheted down, and she decided just to damn him to hell.

'Ouch – that hurt!'

'It wasn't exactly meant to tickle.' He repeated the spank, this time on her helpless twin cheek, and Leanne cried out. 'Can you imagine another twenty like this? Thirty? Or maybe I'll make it forty.' He stroked her waiting hindquarters as the punishment picture sank in.

'Isn't there anything I can do?' Leanne muttered, wriggling at his touch. Her facial and buttock cheeks felt doused with heat, her labia distended.

'You can accept your discipline with good grace and thank me nicely when I'm bored with correcting your arse.'

He slapped her left globe then her right through the light brushed denim, her cheeks jiggling with each double spank.

Leanne hid her face and dug her fingertips into the soft leather. 'How many am I due?' she gasped, driving her body forward against his knees in a vain bid to avoid the full heat of each palm. 'Have I many to go?' she prompted. She hadn't known a hand could be this hateful.

'Too many to count,' her co-owner said.

He toasted her backside with another ten or twelve full-force spanks. Leanne cried out, and twisted her head back. 'I can't bear it!'

'We'll have less talking and movement, or I'll have to bare it for you, then get in the rest of the staff.' He caressed her hot sore globes through her skirt. 'I'm told it hurts even more with all your friends watching,' he goaded.

The humiliation ... Anything but that. 'I'll be quiet!' Leanne closed her eyes and her mouth and put her face obediently back into the settee.

Spank flared out over spank. All she could think about was her helpless posterior. 'I'll do what you want!' she promised through clenched teeth.

'I just want you to keep silent.'

'Aaah! Ouch!'

'Or I'll take down your skirt and give you what-for all over again!'

'But ...'

She felt him shake his head. 'What did I just tell you? I'm tired of your disobedience. I've had enough.'

He stopped slapping her arse. For a moment Leanne wondered if her ordeal was over. 'What did I say would happen if you were noisy?' That he'd pull her skirt down. She shrugged.

'You mean you weren't listening?' Not answering was making things worse.

'No! I . . . Please Mr Howard, I *was* listening.'

'What did I tell you?'

'That I had to be quiet or you'd . . .'

'I'd punish your bare backside.'

Leanne thought she was going to cry. 'But it's already so sore!'

'It's about to get a great deal sorer.'

Was 'sorer' grammatical? This didn't seem like the time to find out. 'How about if I . . .?' she started to suggest.

'Do what you're told? Keep quiet? That would save your bottom future sessions. For now, this skirt will have to come off.'

He stroked her captive bum through the concealment of the cloth. 'I can feel the heat, my dear. It's warming up nicely.' Leanne whimpered as his fingers traced the line where bum met thigh.

'Pull your skirt down for me, that's a good girl.' She felt another surge of shame at the thought of this further debasement.

'And if I don't?'

'Then I'll have to do it for you, and that won't bode well for your backside.'

She'd have to do what he bid. She didn't want to anger him any more. His wrath was buttock-based! Trying not to think about how her posterior must look, Leanne edged the elasticated waistband down over her cheeks. 'Keep going. I need the whole expanse quite bare.' She denuded the central swell of her posterior, then the part that sloped into her legs, shoved the garment down to knee level. Leanne looked back at each finger-marked red oval, at the pink marks over the tops of her thighs.

'It hurts, doesn't it?' the man said, caressing the heated globes. Leanne writhed at his touch, then felt the renewed rush of pudenda-based pleasure.

'Yes, sir.'

'Say "Thank you for teaching me, sir." ' Blushing, she muttered the words.

'That's no good. That isn't servile enough. A bum that's

been properly spanked is properly servile. I'm going to have to teach this one to show respect.'

Hard palm met soft cheeks. Leanne grunted and pushed forward, but the cushion beneath her belly ensured her bum was a suitable raised target. The bastard had his elbow over her back, holding her down firmly. She couldn't escape.

'Can't I . . .?'

'We've been through all this before. It earns you extra.' Extra heat. Extra humiliation. Extra pain.

At last he doled out the last arse-heating slap. Whimpering, she let herself slide down his body till she came to kneel between his legs. She wrapped her arms round his waist, kissed his stomach. Nuzzled the thick length of desire through his suit trousers then eased down his zip.

Edging his manhood out, she licked the pearl of lust from its head, then tongued over the smooth purpleness. Leanne felt his hands under her arms. 'Stand up. Bend over that table with your hands gripping the other side of it. I'm going to make you come again,' he told her.

She was halfway there already! The table felt glossily smooth against her breasts, and stuck to her lust-smeared lower midriff. She felt him parting her legs wide, then even wider, until she was totally exposed, and cried out with relief as he slid all the way into her seeking sex. Yes, yes, yes, yes, do it! she urged, arching her bottom back to take him in further. His cock was pounding into her, his belly slapping against her spanked bum, fingers on her nipples. 'I'm looking down at your red arse as I fuck you,' he said coolly as she flushed hotly and came.

Leanne felt him thrust on, on, on, feeling and hearing the signs of his increasing rapture. God, she loved the way he moved inside her, the way he held her tits, the way he breathed. 'Love it like this . . . need it,' she muttered, beyond shame. She heard him let out a hot-breathed half-human cry and felt him push into her as if he were merging every last eighth of an inch.

'Jesus!' he cried, 'Leanne. *Leanne!*'

It was wonderful to hear him call her name, to feel him

inside her, his arms gripping round her waist even as his cock slipped out against her thigh back. 'Let's go back to bed and rest,' she murmured, then lay there in the four-poster, too happy and excited to sleep.

'We must thank Khan for recognising Eleanor was the saboteur,' she said, after a few minutes.

'Mmm, it must have been her who stole my letter to you when I left for London on that business trip.'

'It said nice things, did it?'

'It said if you didn't behave, you'd be whipped!'

She licked his neck, and paused for a mouth-to-mouth kiss.

'You'll be rewarding Khan with extra Mainly Men assignments?' he asked.

'Well, someone will! I'm handing the agency over to my brother. He's about to return from France.'

'You're not leaving?' He sat up straighter in bed. 'I may have to take you captive!'

'No, I plan to be here for a very long time.'

She paused. 'But I've come as far as I want to with this work. In the past two weeks I've realised that it no longer inspires me. And Marty's grown up a lot. He's returning to London a wiser man.'

'As for this wise woman?' He took her nearest earlobe between his teeth and skimmed it for a moment, sending tremors downwards. 'What will you do instead?'

'Well, I'll still have a large financial stake in the agency, which'll allow me to freelance for a while. I thought I'd hire a photography coach, work at going professional.'

Adam looked at her more closely. 'Would you become the staff photographer for my new corporal punishment magazine?'

'So *that*'s that you've been planning all these weeks!' She thought of bared bums and canes. Swallowed quickly. Would she get too embarrassed, identifying with the punished girls? But then she could give as good as she got – Khan's bum proved it! And she'd taken similar photos for that fashion spread in *Be Seen* . . .

'Sure, if your fees are right!' she joked. Leanne lifted his fingers to her lips and bit teasingly at each, then sucked the thumb and stared up at him.

'With the money from the stills and videos, plus the magazine sales coming in, I should be able to pay a decent rate.'

'It'll give me a chance to show how another female views such carnal correction. Just as long as you don't expect me to pose!'

She saw his hardening stare, and shut her eyes. Christ, she felt turned on by the image of being humiliated before the lens, although it was something she didn't actually want to do just yet.

'I'd make you set up the camera in advance, take photos of yourself being thrashed by Gerard, whilst Paul watched.' A pause. 'Gerard and I have been friends for years – and confidants. We often talk of the punished bad girls' bottoms we've seen!'

Ignore that one. He was trying to disquiet her again. She reached for a change of subject. 'Paul's been lucky to find this place.' Then she vaguely realised she was talking too much. 'He's so shy . . . If it wasn't for Gerard making him taste the whip, he probably wouldn't have a sex life.' Leanne stilled as she realised the potential in what she'd just said.

Organisation. Sex. CP. The time, the place, the under-standing. 'Adam – why don't we open this as a sort of playschool for submissive adults?'

'With me offering strict tuition, you mean?'

Her mind fast-forwarded. 'Mm. You, Gerard and I could teach the lessons. The grown-up pupils would pay charges in the form of an enrolment fee.'

Adam was sitting up straighter against the headboard, staring at her. She thought ahead, and continued. 'We'd give them tests – and cane them if they failed.'

'Should bring in quite a bit.'

'A lot! And we could get Candy to make up adult-sized school uniforms. Charge training fees to put them through their paces in the athletics field and in the gym.'

'I'd be headmaster, of course,' Adam said. She could

253

hear the excitement in his voice, even if he hadn't yet con-
gratulated her on her idea.

'And I'd be headmistress, with equal rights.'

He turned and took her by the shoulders, gazing deep
into her eyes. 'The headmaster is in charge at most schools.
Sometimes he has to discipline his deputy.'

'He can but fantasise!'

'Oh, he can do more than that.' He took her nearest
nipple in his thumb and forefinger and pressed it gently.
'He can tease a hungry clitoris and bare a womanly bum,
and flog . . .'

'Flog?' she whispered, licking her lips.

'Mmm. Headmasters use a tawse on their charges, but a
birch on their girlfriends.'

'Girlfriends?'

'Unless one special girlfriend tries extra-hard to please
with her fingers and her tongue.'

'What if she fails to please?' Leanne whispered, putting
her hands behind her back and closing her legs hard, to
deny him access. Smiling, Adam reached for the belt that
hung warningly above his bed. 'In that case,' he murmured
– and his eyes were full of love and a hard sure knowledge
– 'I have to teach her bum a lesson that lingers for a very
long time . . .'

NEW BOOKS

Coming up from Nexus and Black Lace

Lingering Lessons by Sarah Veitch
April 1995   Price: £4.99   ISBN: 0 352 32990 4
Leanne has just inherited an old boarding school, but she has to share it with the mysterious Adam Howard. Only one thing is certain about her new partner: he is a true devotee of corporal punishment. The last thing Leanne expects is to be drawn into his sordid yet exciting world, but the temptation proves irresistible.

The Awakening of Lydia by Philippa Masters
April 1995   Price: £4.99   ISBN: 0 352 33002 3
As the daughter of a district commissioner during the Boer War, Lydia has plenty of opportunity for excitement – and plenty of sex-starved men to pleasure her. But their skills are nothing compared to the voracious sexual appetites of the local tribesmen, who waste no time in taking the stunning sixteen-year-old captive.

Sherrie by Evelyn Culber
May 1995   Price: £4.99   ISBN: 0 352 32996 3
Chairman of an important but ailing company, Sir James is having trouble relaxing. But in Sherrie, seductive hostess on his business flight, he has found someone who might be able to help. After one of her eye-opening spanking stories and a little practical demonstration, money worries are the last thing on Sir James's mind.

House of Angels by Yvonne Strickland
May 1995   Price: £4.99   ISBN: 0 352 32995 5
In a sumptuous villa in the south of France, Sonia runs a very exclusive service. With her troupe of gorgeous and highly skilled girls, and rooms fitted out to cater for every taste, she fulfils sexual fantasies. Sonia finds herself in need of a new recruit, and the beautiful Karen seems ideal – providing she can shed a few of her inhibitions.

Crimson Buccaneer by Cleo Cordell
April 1995   Price: £4.99   ISBN: 0 352 32987 4
Cheated out of her inheritance, Carlotta Mendoza wants revenge; and with her exquisite looks and feminine wiles, there is no shortage of men willing to offer her help. She takes to the seas with a rugged buccaneer and begins systematically boarding, robbing and sexually humiliating her enemies.

La Basquaise by Angel Strand
April 1995   Price: £4.99   ISBN: 0 352 32988 2
Oruela is a modern young woman of 1920s Biarritz who seeks to join the bohemian set. Her lover, Jean, is helping her to achieve her social aspirations. But an unfortunate accident involving her father brings her under suspicion, and a sinister game of sexual blackmail throws her life into turmoil . . .

The Devil Inside by Portia da Costa
May 1995   Price: £4.99   ISBN: 0 352 32993 9
Psychic sexual intuition is a very special gift. Those who possess it can perceive other people's sexual fantasies – and are usually keen to indulge them. But as Alexa Lavelle discovers, it is a power that needs help to master. Fortunately, the doctors at her exclusive medical practice are more than willing to offer their services.

The Lure of Satyria by Cheryl Mildenhall
May 1995   Price: £4.99   ISBN: 0 352 32994 7
Welcome to Satyria: a land of debauchery and excess, where few men bother with courtship and fewer maidens deserve it. But even here, none is so bold as Princess Hedra, whose quest for sexual gratification takes her beyond the confines of her castle and deep into the wild, enchanted forest . . .

NEXUS BACKLIST

All books are priced £4.99 unless another price is given. If a date is supplied, the book in question will not be available until that month in 1995.

CONTEMPORARY EROTICA

THE ACADEMY	Arabella Knight	
CONDUCT UNBECOMING	Arabella Knight	Jul
CONTOURS OF DARKNESS	Marco Vassi	
THE DEVIL'S ADVOCATE	Anonymous	
DIFFERENT STROKES	Sarah Veitch	Aug
THE DOMINO TATTOO	Cyrian Amberlake	
THE DOMINO ENIGMA	Cyrian Amberlake	
THE DOMINO QUEEN	Cyrian Amberlake	
ELAINE	Stephen Ferris	
EMMA'S SECRET WORLD	Hilary James	
EMMA ENSLAVED	Hilary James	
EMMA'S SECRET DIARIES	Hilary James	
FALLEN ANGELS	Kendal Grahame	
THE FANTASIES OF JOSEPHINE SCOTT	Josephine Scott	
THE GENTLE DEGENERATES	Marco Vassi	
HEART OF DESIRE	Maria del Rey	
HELEN – A MODERN ODALISQUE	Larry Stern	
HIS MISTRESS'S VOICE	G. C. Scott	
HOUSE OF ANGELS	Yvonne Strickland	May
THE HOUSE OF MALDONA	Yolanda Celbridge	
THE IMAGE	Jean de Berg	Jul
THE INSTITUTE	Maria del Rey	
SISTERHOOD OF THE INSTITUTE	Maria del Rey	

BLUE ANGEL SECRETS	Margarete von Falkensee	
CONFESSIONS OF AN ENGLISH MAID	Anonymous	
PLAISIR D'AMOUR	Anne-Marie Villefranche	
FOLIES D'AMOUR	Anne-Marie Villefranche	
JOIE D'AMOUR	Anne-Marie Villefranche	
MYSTERE D'AMOUR	Anne-Marie Villefranche	
SECRETS D'AMOUR	Anne-Marie Villefranche	
SOUVENIR D'AMOUR	Anne-Marie Villefranche	

SAMPLERS & COLLECTIONS

EROTICON 1	ed. J-P Spencer	
EROTICON 2	ed. J-P Spencer	
EROTICON 3	ed. J-P Spencer	
EROTICON 4	ed. J-P Spencer	
NEW EROTICA 1	ed. Esme Ombreux	
NEW EROTICA 2	ed. Esme Ombreux	
THE FIESTA LETTERS	ed. Chris Lloyd	£4.50

NON-FICTION

HOW TO DRIVE YOUR MAN WILD IN BED	Graham Masterton
HOW TO DRIVE YOUR WOMAN WILD IN BED	Graham Masterton
LETTERS TO LINZI	Linzi Drew
LINZI DREW'S PLEASURE GUIDE	Linzi Drew

Please send me the books I have ticked above.

Name . . . .

Address . . . .

. . . .

. . . .

. . . . Post code . . . .

Send to: **Cash Sales, Nexus Books, 332 Ladbroke Grove, London W10 5AH**.

Please enclose a cheque or postal order, made payable to **Nexus Books**, to the value of the books you have ordered plus postage and packing costs as follows:

UK and BFPO – £1.00 for the first book, 50p for each subsequent book.

Overseas (including Republic of Ireland) – £2.00 for the first book, £1.00 for the second book, and 50p for each subsequent book.

If you would prefer to pay by VISA or ACCESS/MASTER-CARD, please write your card number and expiry date here:

. . . .

Please allow up to 28 days for delivery.

Signature . . . .